Semper Fi

WITH A SIDE OF

Donuts or Bacon

D1565886

CLAIR LEARNER

Copyright © 2022 Clair Learner
All rights reserved
First Edition

NEWMAN SPRINGS PUBLISHING
320 Broad Street
Red Bank, NJ 07701

First originally published by Newman Springs Publishing 2022

This is a work of fiction. Much of the content is based on the author's personal experiences, although many of the incidents have been created for literary interest. The training, as described throughout the book, was that in effect for new Marine officers in the late 1980s. Any errors in nomenclature or usage are the author's alone. With the exception of public figures, any resemblance to persons living or dead is purely coincidental. The ghost may be fictional.

Neither the United States Marine Corps nor any other component of the Department of Defense has approved, endorsed, or authorized this product book.

ISBN 978-1-63881-666-9 (Paperback)
ISBN 978-1-63881-667-6 (Digital)

Printed in the United States of America

With love to Al who jogged my memory, helped me over the rough spots, and watched this book evolve. And to Sandy, who left us before it was finished.

CHAPTER 1

Introductions

O N A platform atop a sixty-foot-rappelling tower, I moved with my fellow SPCs (staff platoon commanders) to an approximately four-by-four-foot hole with padded edges. Two ropes, tied to heavy steel-anchor points affixed to the platform, disappeared down the middle. Once we had all gathered around this mystery feature, our instructor welcomed us to the hellhole. My head conjured up all kinds of images—fire, cavorting demons, lava, other generally hot and unpleasant stuff—but my fellow SPCs murmured their understanding and anticipation. I, however, had no idea what was in store for us. Despite the thirty-five-degree temperature and cutting wind, I could feel sweat start to trickle down my back, dreading what would happen next.

As we gathered around the hole to wherever, we watched one of the instructors rig the ropes to his Swiss seat. He allowed himself maybe twelve feet of slack in the ropes, stepped over to the hole, yelled downward that he was on rappel (receiving an answering, "Staff Sergeant Murray on belay"), and sat on the edge of the abyss with his legs dangling. Then he calmly slid off. Into nothingness. Standing about a foot from the edge of the hole, all I could see was the bottoms of his boots as his rope played out, caught, and jerked him upside down. Then his head appeared as he made his way to the ground guided by the staff sergeant on belay.

I knew what "on rappel" meant. It meant bouncing down a very solid wall, tethered to a rope. The only similarity the hellhole had to rappelling was a rope. Two of them, in fact. I knew the hellhole was supposed to simulate free fall roping from a helicopter (which I hadn't planned on doing a lot of). I knew it looked scary but was perfectly safe (if you executed it as directed).

The rational part of me understood all of the above, but I was still scared shitless. You see, I'm terrified of heights. I get woozy when I even consider climbing three feet up a ladder, let alone voluntarily jumping through a hole cut into the deck of a sixty-foot tower.

I knew I only *had* to do it once.

So I volunteered to go down next.

Heights. Hellholes. Helicopters. You're probably wondering how I got myself into this predicament. Well, it all started with the Idiot.

*****

My name is Abigail "Abe" Drinker Rush, and I was born and raised near Philadelphia, Pennsylvania. Though thirty, I'm currently *not* married, committed, or otherwise romantically attached to a man, woman, or therapy animal.

I'm the eldest of three children, having two younger male siblings: John Kaiser VI (JK), almost twenty-eight; and Timothy Winthrop (Tad), age twenty-five. My family is pretty much a gag-gle of homebodies, so my brothers have settled in the Philadelphia area. I thought that's where I'd spend my life too, but that totally got derailed when I married a Marine captain and got to live in romantic places like Camp Lejeune, North Carolina, and Okinawa, Japan.

I, however, currently reside in Virginia, stationed at Quantico, the "Crossroads of the Corps," or as some refer to it, "The Crossroads of the Crotch." Just sayin'.

Like my siblings, I attended public school and went to an Ivy League college. Unlike my brothers though, I didn't immediately go on to an MBA or law degree. Instead, I joined a small consulting firm located in downtown Ardmore, Pennsylvania, while I figured out what I wanted to do when I grew up.

I met my ex-husband, Tom Maxwell, at a mixer hosted by my company. The purpose of the gathering was to schmooze with other local businesses, and we had invited the local Department of Defense recruiting station comprised of representatives from the Army, Marine Corps, Navy, and Air Force. Tom was a Marine first lieutenant and attended the mixer as that service's delegate. In dress blues and tennis shoes (to use a Marine Corps metaphor), he was such an exotic creature that was so obviously out of its element, I took pity on him and struck up a conversation. In retrospect, he wasn't so much exotic as odd, and his discomfort was due not to shyness but the fact that he was too dense to carry on a conversation in *any* social setting. What I initially took as naivete (and continued to convince myself so for the next two years) was really just plain stupidity.

By our second year of marriage, I had woken up to smell the offal and realized I had just lied to myself.

My usually understanding father had been opposed to the marriage, not because Tom was "not like us, dear" (my mother's mantra) but because he wasn't what my father thought a man (and husband) should be. He sensed a lack of purpose and backbone in my fiancé at the time and considered our marriage unevenly yoked oxen, suspecting that Tom had no drive and would hold me back from where and what I could be. Dad didn't care if my husband were a plumber or a pirate. He just expected me and my younger brothers—but more especially me—to find a partner who was truly a partner, not a millstone.

Even as we started the processional down the aisle to my waiting groom, Dad was trying to persuade me that I didn't need to go through with the ceremony or the marriage. Uncharacteristically he even offered me money and stock options not to go through with the union.

Of course, being in love with the idea of being in love, I refused and embarked on what would be the biggest mistake of my life.

Considering where it eventually led, however, it was probably the pivotal event of my life rather than an out-and-out mistake.

I quit my job at the consulting firm when Tom got transferred to Norfolk, Virginia, and waited for him every night—and most weekends— to come home and at least make leaving my job worthwhile. I never considered he might be having an affair as he was too challenged to be duplicitous and too transparent to lie about it. It slowly dawned on me that he couldn't manage his time, either personal or professional, though he consistently attributed his mismanagement to the mercurial nature of the needs of the Marine Corps.

I wanted to understand what was so challenging about his job that he couldn't have a home life. I figured if I got inside the organization, I could navigate my marriage with a better understanding. So ever one to take the bull by the horns, while Tom (now dubbed "The Idiot") was on a short training deployment, I went to an OSO (Marine Officer Selection Officer) and processed the paperwork to attend OCS (Officer Candidate School). The Idiot was furious but too late to the party to intervene. Even had he considered doing so, I had set my course and was moving forward to execute it.

I was commissioned, attended TBS (The Basic School) and requested—and was assigned—motor transport as my MOS (Military Operational Specialty). I joined the Idiot, who was now at Camp Lejeune, and I gave it my best shot, but it just didn't work.

When I told the Idiot I wanted a separation and then divorce, I saw another side of him. Bitter and hurt, he did everything he could to make the dissolution of our marriage as difficult for me as he could. In retrospect, I realize his challenges with pending punitive charges for alleged falsified travel claims (that is, he was inflating his travel expenses on temporary duty paperwork in order to pocket a profit) was working on him, but I had no knowledge of that angle when I initiated proceedings. All I knew was I just wanted to walk away. Idiot, on the other hand, wanted not only to stand in my way but destroy my personal and professional reputation in the process.

Sherman and his scorched earth, marching through Georgia, were nothing compared to the Idiot on a rampage.

The battle with Idiot waged for more than a year during which time I was transferred to Quantico to attend Amphibious Warfare School. I was due orders upon graduation in May. Since the divorce was at last final, I arranged to have my household goods packed up and stored as I executed a year's unaccompanied orders to Okinawa. As we divided up the possessions of seven years of our marriage, the Idiot had to leave his mark there, too. He seemed to have an uncanny sense of what would most emotionally damage me. Records I had acquired in college, pictures of places he had never been, and bits of family furniture that had significance for me because of the memories associated with them. He even made a case for acquiring my college diploma since it had "sentimental value" for him. Not. I was so desperate to disentangle myself from the mess we called a marriage, however, that I had quasiagreed to relinquishing several items that I had truly wanted. (Mind you, *quasiagreed* to. A Rush *always* keeps a rational brain cell when confronted with emotional—possibly hysterical—situations, especially when they might impact money.)

When Idiot insisted that he had a claim to my bridal china, sterling, crystal, and linens (all heirloom, all passed down from generations of Rushes and Drinkers), I finally came to my senses, fought back and managed to salvage most of my pre-Idiot possessions. I didn't wish him well on what he did get. I hoped he choked on them.

Okinawa had been my escape from the disappointment of my failed marriage. My new duty station at Quantico, Virginia, was going to be a sans-Idiot beginning, and I was looking forward to it.

*****

My experiences in Quantico are the underpinning of this entire book. I'm not crazy. Well, no crazier than your typical Marine. And yeah, yeah, I know there are a lot of people out there who're convinced that Marines, by virtue of service or by wanting to *be* in this branch of the service, are nuts.

And please note, for those of you still living in the Dark Ages, there really *are* female Marines. They don't spend their days making and fetching coffee. They actually know how to handle firearms, set up ambushes, and nowadays even pilot aircraft and serve as infantry officers. If you're reading this book and expecting to be titillated with *Women Marines Gone Wild*—sexy escapades in camo and crotchless skivvies—don't go any further. It ain't here.

CHAPTER 2

A Change of Plan

"CAPTAIN RUSH, XO wants to see you ASAP."

I looked up from my desk for the past year (and which I was happily cleaning out) and noted the battalion S-1A standing at the door to my office. I had spent the past year in Okinawa, at Camp Kinser, in the southern part of the island.

"Hey, Staff Sergeant," I responded. "Is he mad? Do I need to wear a flak jacket?" I expected at least a smile, maybe a small chuckle in response to my question. There was none.

"No idea, ma'am. The XO'll have to tell you what this is about. I'm just the messenger."

Staff Sergeant Atkins looked noticeably uncomfortable. Not at my attempt at levity, but he likely knew why the XO had summoned me, and I could only assume it wasn't good. The XO hadn't sent the S-1 himself—a captain, just like me, and a good friend who would have given me a heads-up—but had instead dispatched the stoic S-1A. Staff Sergeant Atkins was discreet, never gossiped, and was the soul of propriety. All good characteristics for the battalion's legal chief, but something that didn't work to my advantage if I wanted to get some insight into why I was being summoned. I would just have to wait.

Message delivered, the Staff Sergeant disappeared down the passageway toward the admin office. I strained to hear if there were any loud colorful obscenities coming from that direction. When he was really pissed off (or really happy, which was seldom), XO had a tendency to bellow. There was only silence—not exactly a good thing where the XO was concerned—so I prepared to face my executioner by shrugging into my utility jacket. It was even hotter and muggier than usual, for an Okinawa summer since the air-conditioning was on the fritz (again), and I had shucked my utility jacket while I packed boxes. Since the XO was a stickler for proper military attire (really, anything properly military), I donned the jacket—immediately noticing the change in airflow—broke a sweat, and headed to whatever fate awaited me.

My current assignment was S-4 (Logistics Officer) at Third Maintenance Battalion, headquartered at Camp Kinser, Okinawa, but with various components sprinkled throughout the island. Our battalion, at two-thousand-plus Marines, was pretty large for a combat-service support organization since we provided maintenance for all ground equipment in Okinawa, and also supported the Corps' MPS (Maritime Prepositioned Shipping) ships when they pulled into the port of Naha. As the S-4, I was responsible for supporting *our* support to the Fleet Marine Forces. Because our unit was geographically dispersed, I traveled a lot, up and down the island, in a HMMWV (High Mobility Multi-Purpose Wheeled Vehicle) driven by my unendingly lame-joke-cracking logistics chief. It was a really cool job. Nothing at all like the life as a consultant I had left behind as a civilian. Boots and utes instead of pantyhose and a business suit. Unabashedly jovial SNCO (staff non-commissioned officer) companion versus politically correct rod-up-their-butt fellow consultants. Yeah, I had lucked out.

A summons to the XO's office this close to my departure date didn't bode well, however, and despite the heat, I shivered at what might be waiting for me.

I pictured the XO with an executioner's hood and ax, or maybe a hangman's noose, and wondered how he could chew tobacco and spit with a mask on. Oh, bad Abe! How can you joke at a time like this? Whatever you do, don't laugh. If he smells levity or blood, you're toast.

I found Major Manheim, the XO, at his desk, *his* utility jacket draped over the back of his chair, and I immediately regretted having put mine on before I responded to his summons. The office was like a sweatbox, but I sensed that his red face was not due to the temperature. I gazed longingly at the fan trained at his desk and hoped against hope he'd put it on oscillate if I had to remain here more than a minute.

Stopping in front of his desk at a modified parade rest, I didn't have long to wait. XO always got to the point quickly and not too gracefully.

"Have a seat, Abe. I need to talk to you." He glanced at a piece of paper on the desk in front of him. "I thought you were going to MCRDAC," he barked. No greeting. No "how ya doin'?" And no fan turned to oscillate.

I sat down, but I wasn't comfortable. I smelled trouble.

"I am, sir. Got my orders. With proceed, travel, and leave, I should report in there mid-September." I had finished a master's degree in acquisition before transferring to Okinawa last year and was looking forward to using my education and motor transport background at the Corps' acquisition command to work development and production of its entire truck fleet.

"Nope. Change of plan." Major Manheim spat some of his chew into a plastic cup, got even redder (if that was possible), and squinted across his desk at me.

Still no move to redirect the fan.

"Ah, come on, sir. Where am I going? Shit's Creek? The brig? You do know that whole thing at Christmas where we nominated you to be the baby Jesus in the living nativity was just a joke, right?" Nobody got my jokes. I was the Marine Corps' Rodney Dangerfield.

My lame response didn't even get a chuckle from him. Uh-oh. *This was bad. This was very bad.*

"Abe, we got a mod to your orders yesterday afternoon. If you doubt me, take a look." He pushed a piece of paper across his desk for my inspection. I reluctantly took it and confirmed my Social Security number, MOS, and name. According to this loathsome notice, I was still going to Quantico but not to MCRDAC. I was being diverted to TBS. Or "Asshole Factory" as so many of my fellow officers referred to it.

"There has to be some mistake, sir. Do I *look* like a picture-book Marine? Do I *act* like a role model? They don't send people like me to TBS to train impressionable second lieutenants, sir. They send people like me to places where I get stuff done and can't ruffle feathers."

This really didn't make sense. The Marine Corps carefully screens officers to instruct at its schools, whether Officer Candidate or Top Level. MOS proficiency, knowledge of Marine Corps policy, and first-class PFT (physical fitness test) score were initial qualifiers. Depending on the school, there would be other requirements. More importantly, the Corps-assigned officers that looked and acted like recruiting posters. True, I was neither fat nor ignorant. I ran a first-class PFT, and I knew my job. I could converse in words that had more than two syllables. Thanks to my grandmother, a venerable Philadelphia Main Line matron, I knew which fork to use at the table and how to participate in (or manage) a social discussion in polite society. But that's as far as the similarity to officer instructor criteria went.

"Nope. I delayed telling you about the mod until I had a chance to talk to the XO at TBS, Lieutenant Colonel Kowalski. Time difference kind of complicates things, but I wanted to verify with him before breaking the news to you."

I could feel the blood roaring in my head and my face start to flame. The XO must have noticed. Heck, we must have looked like scarlet-faced bookends by this point.

He reached over and turned the fan to oscillate.

"The Corps has to be pretty desperate if they have to divert someone like *me* to TBS." I didn't check the bitterness in the tone of my voice but, just to be sure I couldn't be construed as being disrespectful, added, "Sir." The XO and I got along well, which was surprising since he was all spit and polish and I was...not. If there were anyone with whom I could be myself, it was him (within reason of course). And despite the delay in delivering the news to me, I appreciated his reaching out to my redesignated command for clarification. He'd made sure to get it straight.

"I know it sucks, but this particular needs of the Corps trumps the acquisition job, Abe. TBS only runs two companies a year that have a woman's platoon. Since they need two female captains, one assigned to a company and one on deck, HQMC maintains two female captains on staff. Unfortunately one of those captains just resigned, and the other is pregnant, which was also just announced. For the past two weeks, all the noncombat company-grade monitors have been searching for two replacements. Obviously there are certain criteria for assignment, and you make all of them. You're the first choice, they're still beating the bushes for the second. To further complicate it, a company that will have a woman's platoon starts in just five weeks. The company staff reports two weeks before that to get settled, schooled, and prepped for lieutenants reporting aboard."

Sensing my next questions or protest, Major Manheim held up his hand before I could respond.

"A year and a half ago, you were screened to be the First Lady's military aide. You were even one of the final three candidates, correct?"

"Yes, sir." My response was truculent. He was right. A year and a half ago, my then-monitor had informed me of this "honor," and I had been pretty vocal about my aversion to the assignment. Nothing personal against the First Lady, but there were two reasons for my resistance. First, I was going through a very painful and difficult divorce, and I just wanted to focus my attention on getting through it. The job and the First Lady deserved nothing less than 150 percent, and at that time, I knew I wasn't up to giving that. Second, I suspected most of my monitor's motivation for screening me was to leverage my education and social background. It would have been a coup for him to assign a Philadelphia "socialite" (as he called me, which was *not* the case) to the highly visible billet.

Fortunately for me, but not my monitor, my boss at the time had contacted my monitor's boss at the time, and the two field-grade officers had agreed this was not a smart, let alone compassionate, move. Certainly I didn't want to be considered because of my background, but both senior officers realized this was just not the thing to do to somebody going through a really bloody divorce. They had intervened, my then-monitor's plan was shut down, and six months later, I got my requested orders to Okinawa. Okinawa was my escape from the Idiot.

True, I had a new monitor, and like the other company-grade monitors, she had a knee-jerk critical fill; the screening was in my HQMC record jacket, and I was in transit to Quantico anyway. I just wished she had had the courtesy to give me a heads-up first.

Fate had spared me once. It was time to pay the piper.

"I'm sorry, Abe. I know how much you were looking forward to MCRDAC, but note that the orders for TBS are only for a year. Lieutenant Colonel Kowalski says you will do two companies, back-to-back, one lieutenant and one warrant officer, and then you'll proceed to MCRDAC." Having delivered his unwelcome message, the XO sat back in his chair as his magenta face transitioned to only slightly red. "You won't be able to take a full thirty days of leave, but you'll have a couple of weeks to set up quarters and take delivery of your household goods. You've already had your ditty move picked up, right? As I recall, you were kind of late getting that one done." Ooh, that was a jab. Snarky, XO. Diversionary tactics.

Yeah, he was right. Duty obligations had caused me to delay the pickup, and I was already behind the power curve. Ditty moves were intended to get your uniforms and various essential items (like all the great stuff you picked up on trips to Hong Kong [personally financed] and South Korea [for duty]) shipped back and awaiting you upon your return. I was going to have to mail back uniforms or pick some up in Quantico if my TBS duties required more than utilities.

Sometimes my stupidity rivaled the Idiot's.

"Yes, sir. I arranged for the stored goods to be delivered as soon as I hit the States. I guess I'll have less time to set up the house before I start company staff workup. The ditty move won't be there until a week or so after the larger storage shipment, so I'll have to have someone at the house to accept that delivery. I suppose company

workup will be hectic, so I probably won't be able to accept the shipment myself."

One of the friends I had in mind to manage the delivery was an
old classmate from my time at TBS. Since he was a lawyer, he went
through the course as a first lieutenant, was already a major to my
captain, and assigned to the HQMC legal office in Arlington. He
lived further north than Quantico, but I was already contemplating
how much beer it was going to cost me to lure him down to Stafford
(where my house was) to accept the shipment.

"We'll talk again before you fly on Thursday, Abe. In the
meantime, if you have any questions, feel free to contact Lieutenant
Colonel Kowalski directly. Here's his contacts. You can come into the
office and use your desk phone."

As I stood up, Manheim handed me a piece of paper with both
DSN (Defense Switched Network) and commercial numbers scribbled on it. Wow, a lowly captain authorized to contact a lieutenant
colonel. DIRLAUTH. Of course, I would contact him directly. *Not.*

"I know it's not what you expected, and I can't say it will be
a good experience since I've never done a tour at TBS, but hey! It's
second lieutenants. They do some stupid stuff. If nothing else, you're
for sure in for some shits and giggles."

I offered my farewell and headed back to my office to finish
packing. The XO answered with a dismissive wave as he reached over
to redirect his fan.

As I passed the S-3 (Operations) office, I heard Major (select)
Ciserio, the S-3 himself, yelling at my back.

"Hey, Rush. Come in here. I want to talk to you."

Yuck. The last person I wanted to see right now was Gabe
Ciserio. He was, in my humble opinion, a total douchebag, but that
was an observation I wisely kept to myself. True, he looked like a
recruiting poster—just as wide and about the same depth as cardboard movie art. Almost everything that came out of his mouth was
asinine drivel, and I was always astounded to think he had been commissioned, let alone selected, to field-grade officer. Oh, and he and
the Idiot had been best buds back at Camp Lejeune, before the Idiot

got caught "allegedly" falsifying travel claims and given the choice of resignation or prosecution. Hint: Idiot chose resignation.

I had already initiated the legal separation process, and Idiot had already moved out of our Stafford house (the house my father had helped us buy with a hefty deposit, and for which I made the mortgage payments) when the word got out about the alleged falsification claims. I honestly had no idea that the Idiot was under investigation. Douchebag immediately came to Idiot's defense and started rumors that if the charges were true (and it was obviously untrue, according to Douchebag), it was because Idiot was desperate to put himself at risk in order to maintain my lavish lifestyle. Oh, and I was sleeping around, probably even with farm animals. Hmm, and here I thought I had been at home, alone, wallpapering and working in the backyard or in class at Base, working toward my master's.

With the divorce final, I headed, with relief, to Okinawa, only to have the Douchebag report to the same unit three months later. His reputation as a rumormonger preceded him, and Major Manheim offered to sit on him for me once the first spurious gossip reached his ears. Although I appreciated the offer, I declined. I fight my own battles and refuse to go into a battle of wits with the unarmed. All I had to do was wait, and he'd step on it with no help from me. He did. Over and over and over again.

"If you need to talk business, come to my office. I have to finish packing. If you just want to BS, don't bother. I don't have time," I replied, stepping back into my office.

"You are so screwed." I heard directly behind me. He had actually followed me to the door of my office. "And I am a superior officer. You come when I tell you to."

I glanced up from the box I was already stuffing with miscellaneous military manuals. "You're not a superior anything. You're not even senior. The other term for a major select is *captain*, and we're the same rank. So bite me." Of course, my part of the conversation was quietly offered. Douchebag's had been (and would continue to be) loud. He was so easy to manipulate.

"You are screwed, screwed, screwed," he taunted, practically dancing in delight. "You're walking into Grunt Land at TBS. Those infantry types are going to eat your lunch. They'll have you crying and whining for your mama by the end of your first day. Boo-hoo. Good riddance, bitch."

"You kiss your wife with that mouth, Ciserio? Or is it your dog?" I didn't have time to say anything further, as I heard Captain Chuck Myer (the S-1) just outside my door.

"Gabe," he barked. "CO wants to see you. Now."

Douchebag flashed me one more baleful look, composed his features, and sauntered toward the CO's office, ignoring Chuck, who remained behind.

He winked, offered me a nod, and disappeared. I really didn't know if the CO summons was real or Chuck's invention to keep the situation from getting out of hand. Had Douchebag continued on his tirade, it would have been loud and inappropriate. I knew that. Chuck knew that. Unfortunately Ciserio didn't.

But with my departure, he would be somebody else's problem.

*****

On Thursday, I bid a fond farewell to the XO and Chuck (I was going to miss them) and boarded my freedom bird back to the States. I had no idea what lay ahead. I just knew it was time to take the next steps in my personal and professional lives. Had I known what awaited me in Quantico, I might have considered requesting an extension to remain in Okinawa.

CHAPTER 3

More Than One Challenge

WAS BACK in the States, but the transition was frenzied. As I had anticipated, the TBS class I was to join, Delta Company, staff workup was frantic, with days starting at 0600 and ending whenever.

My stored household goods had been delivered while I was on my too-short leave, and I had pretty much set up my town house so it was livable. The ditty shipment from Okinawa had arrived today, but thankfully, my lawyer buddy, Kelly Bach, was able to oversee its delivery.

That evening, before I could fit my key into the front-door lock, it swung open, and I looked up at Kelly standing in the door-way, proffering a Diet Coke in one hand and sporting a broad smile on his kind-of goofy face.

"Well, well, well, it's about time you got home, Abe," he taunted.

I grabbed the Diet Coke, just about drained it in one gulp, and grunted. It had been a very long day, and the lieutenants hadn't even reported in yet.

"No 'Hi, honey, I'm home'? I cooked dinner and everything, and here it is, 1930. The roast is ruined. And so much for my souf-flé." Kelly was so much not a 1960s-sitcom mom, but he had the perky jargon down pat. All he needed was a ruffled apron and heels.

Now *that* would have been a sight. A well-over-six-foot-tall muscular hunky Marine dressed like June Cleaver.

I smelled something edible but didn't think it was roast beef. More like overheated pizza. But at least he was offering food. Though the kitchen was at the back of the town house, the first floor (except for the powder and dining rooms) was one contiguous space. Since the kitchen was connected to the living room, food smells—good or bad—had a tendency to greet you as you came in the front door.

"I'm really sorry I couldn't get home earlier, Kelly. It's been nuts. I think snoozing through that hey-diddle-diddle-up-the-middle infantry stuff we got when we went through TBS is coming back to haunt me. And I'm still beating myself up on the O-course." To illustrate my latter inadequacy, I pulled back the sleeve of my T-shirt and held up my right arm, black and blue from the armpit to the elbow. When I had gone through TBS, women had run a downsized version of the men's O-course. Now women tackled the same course as the men, just with small ramps to accommodate the difference in height at some obstacles.

Kelly pulled me into my small foyer and offered an empathetic bear hug as I dropped my helmet bag on the floor. There was nothing romantic or sexual in Kelly's gesture. He was just a hugger, and I had seen him offer the same comfort to guys. Well, not to a lot of guys. Most seemed to prefer back or butt smacks to establish connection. I understood the back thing, but the butt thing? Women just didn't do that.

As we made our way back to the kitchen, I noted the three large (about four-feet high) cardboard boxes positioned in the living room. They were intact and appeared unopened, so Kelly had been a gentleman and not broken into them to check out my skivvies.

It was Tuesday. Lieutenants reported in throughout the weekend with duty to start the next Monday. Work wouldn't get any easier, so I'd turn my attention to unpacking the shipment sometime.

Noticing my sidelong glance at the boxes, Kelly cleared his throat and offered, "If you want me to come back Friday night or Saturday, I can help you unpack. Maybe go out for dinner afterward? Not a date. Friends. And you buy as payback?"

I noted a hint of hope in Kelly's voice and didn't want to hurt him. He had been my friend for almost six years, and I didn't want anything more than his friendship right now. We had met at TBS but reconnected at Camp Lejeune when one of my troops was court-martialed, and Kelly had been assigned as his defense counsel. Kelly was crazy smart and a crackerjack lawyer. I'd not been surprised when my Marine was found not guilty. At 6'5" and sturdily built, Kelly was physically intimidating, though probably the gentlest person I knew. We talked books and music; he liked biographies and Mozart, while I preferred post-WWII Southern writers and Beethoven. He collected Waterford Crystal while I appreciated good blue-and-white crockery. And most importantly, he had stuck by me during the ugly divorce. He listened to me during my crying jags and kept me from becoming a raging drunk when I tried to drown my fear and disappointment and anger in alcohol.

I sensed Kelly wanted more, but I wasn't going there just yet. Despite almost two years since my divorce, I was still raw from its effects on me, personally and professionally. You can't swear off dealing with men, however, when you're in the Marine Corps where the male population far exceeds that of women. I had no problem serving as a Marine officer. I just wasn't looking to get involved with anyone, civilian or military, just yet.

"Thanks, Kelly, but we have lieutenants starting to roll in on Saturday. SPCs are expected to be in the area between 0800–1600 Saturday and Sunday in case the Training Officer has any challenges getting them settled. I'd welcome you stopping by either or both days, though. I could use the company, and maybe we could head over to the O-course, and you could help me with technique."

Kelly was taller than me by ten inches and had pretty good upper-body strength (as did I), but the O-course wasn't so much about muscling through the obstacles. It was largely how you approached the obstacle and managed it. The inside of my right arm was black and blue totally due to my lack of technique. Maybe Kelly could provide a different perspective.

If he was disappointed, he didn't show it. "Sure," he replied. "There *is* hope! I know a master sergeant who can teach anybody how to assault the course. He lives down here in Stafford. I'll see if he can start working with you this week, but maybe the three of us can work the course on Saturday afternoon." He made a sniffing movement, nose to the air like a bird dog making scent. "I smell… desperation." Well, like duh, Kelly. "From the mess on your arm, I take it your biggest challenge is managing the up-and-over bar?"

The up-and-over was the second obstacle, eight feet off the ground. There was a small ramp, only about four inches high for the women (and vertically challenged men) to use, though I couldn't imagine any red-blooded-male second lieutenant utilizing the ramp, no matter what his height. For women, though, with an average disparity in height of eight to ten inches from their male counterparts, it was indeed necessary. The description of mastering the obstacle runs something like this: "The runner has to go over the top of the bar either by executing a kip or by a technique referred to as a 'college-boy roll.' Executing this technique requires the participant to do a pull-up and then hook one armpit over the bar. He/she must then hook the opposite leg over the bar and, in one motion, kick down with the free leg while rolling over the bar."

Yeah right. To date, I had been launching myself at the bar, right arm up and then curled around the bar, and desperately trying to sling my left leg over it to roll over and down.

"If the Master Sergeant can meet this week, that would be even better so I can start practicing, but I don't want to take up too much of his time. You, on the other hand, would probably just be picking your nose and drinking beer this weekend, so you can keep me company on the course," I responded.

"I'll get you his contacts, and you can work out schedules and figure out payback for his time. I think he drinks Mountain Dew. He's a Baptist," Kelly offered. A common Marine medium of payment was beer, so I appreciated Kelly's volunteering the alternative. "Go take a quick shower. You're ripe. I'll be able to enjoy my dinner more if I'm not sitting across the table from a compost heap. I'll get dinner on the table."

As I headed upstairs to shower and change, I wondered, again, why I hadn't met Kelly before I met the Idiot. True, Kelly had been in law school then, and I was still a consultant, but it just didn't seem right that he came into my life too late. Whoa, Abe. This is your bud. Don't ruin it by thinking *what if* and leading him on.

When I returned to the kitchen, smelling noticeably better (even to my nose), Kelly had already pulled a large pizza out of the oven. It looked a little dry, but that was my fault. He had also thought to get Chinese takeout in order to honor our new tradition of "Sino-Italian pig out."

As I grabbed pizza and ladled Three Treasures onto my plate, I looked back into the living room. "Delivery was scheduled for between 1000–1300. Did they get here on time, or did you get excuses why they were late?" Military movers were infamous for being either infuriatingly late or unexpectedly early.

"Believe it or not, they got here at 1330, so it wasn't too bad," Kelly managed around a mouthful of moo goo gai pan. "Total time they were here was about a half hour since there were only those three boxes, and I had to get the paperwork straight in case you have a claim. One rattled, so I had them open that one up. No breakage. And relax, I had them tape it right back up so you wouldn't think I was sniffing through your skivvies." It's like he had read my mind. Go figure. "I noticed something peculiar, though, and it's not because I've been drinking. I popped my first one when you came up the driveway." Kelly stopped and looked embarrassed.

"Well, what?"

"You know I'm pretty grounded and common sense, right? And I'm a lawyer. I deal in facts. I'm not—"

I cut him off. "What?" *Holy crap. Get to the point!*

"When I left to pick up the pizza and Chinese, the middle box was aligned with the other two right in front of the fireplace." He stopped and looked at me.

I flung my hands in the air. "What?" I snapped again. I was bone-tired, my brain was full, and this wasn't like Kelly. He was a talker, always chatty, even loquacious. I, on the other hand, was a listener. I had seen him in action in a courtroom—well spoken, respectful, and disarmingly charming. I'd watched him lure spurious witnesses, representing either defense or prosecution, like flies into his spider's web of "nice." And then he'd attack. Politely of course, but Kelly was not shy, and truly had the gift of gab. The uneasiness I was seeing right now had me impatient, but even more, uneasy.

"Abe, it had moved. All were lined up in a pretty straight line. The right corner of the box had shifted out by four inches. Here, let me show you." Kelly pulled back his chair and headed over to the fireplace where the boxes sat and pointed out the middle box which, indeed, was canted out of what had probably been a straight line.

"Was this the one you had them open?

"No, the one to the right of it."

"That explains it. They must have moved it when they opened the other box," I reasoned. "Everything's still sealed up. I appreciate the heads up, though. Maybe I have some big-ass mice or, worse, a snake."

I absolutely loathed snakes, not in a girly way. I had seen what habu snakes could do to a pet or even a human, and copperheads were a big deal in Virginia. I tolerated, even encouraged, black snakes, but I didn't want one taking up residence in my house. The thought that one might have slithered in while this or the larger shipment had been delivered made me cringe. If it were the latter, that meant I might have had a roommate for at least a week.

Kelly relaxed a bit but pressed on. "Agreed. But if you have mice or a snake, they have to be pretty big. Do we want to have a look around the house just in case?"

I agreed, not because I was in the mood to search my house at 2100 when I had been up since 0400, but the thought of a snake taking a nap in or under my bed was unsettling, to say the least.

An hour later, after searching anything and everything that would provide a snug hidey-hole for a snake or cache of mice, we had found nothing and called it quits.

Kelly propped the tire iron he had removed from his car (and which he had carried while we searched) against the front door and headed back to the kitchen to help me clear up before he departed. I had retrieved a baseball bat from my guest room to carry during our safari and staged it at the bottom of the steps to take back upstairs. I resolved to pick up another bat or even a spade to keep downstairs.

My first instinct had been to stage a 9mm (pistol) on each floor, just in case. I almost immediately discarded that option, though, as I didn't think blowing holes through my floors and walls as I stalked a real (or imagined) pest was one of my better ideas. It certainly wouldn't endear me to my neighbors.

"Thanks for the help today, both the shipment and the search," I said to Kelly as I handed him his tire iron and opened the front door. "I really owe you big-time. And not just dinner or beer. One of the other SPC's father-in-law has season tickets to the Redskins, and he offered me a couple for a weekend that they're doing a family thing and can't use them. Would you be interested?"

I knew Kelly disdained the Redskins and anything associated with the team to the point of referring to them as the "Foreskins." Understandable, since he was from Wisconsin and a staunch Green Bay fan, but prime seats at a football game were prime seats at a football game, right? I'd just make sure it wasn't a Redskins-Packers game if he accepted. If that were the case, he'd be mightily embarrassed if he had to sit in Washington seats to watch his beloved Packers play.

"You don't owe me anything, but I'll take you up on the tickets. I could use a laugh, and I have a buddy that I owe a favor to, so yeah." Was I disappointed he didn't set my sharing the tickets with him as a condition of acceptance? Well, not really.

"Okay. I'll talk to him tomorrow and get back with you. And I appreciate the Master Sergeant's contacts. See you Saturday?"

"Good to go. We can firm things up on Friday. I'll have boots and utes for the O-course, but I'll come down in civvies and change at TBS." The O-course was navigated in T-shirt, combat boots, and utility trousers—one of the few times a Marine, in uniform, was outdoors with no soft cover (hat).

I gave Kelly a hug, shut the door behind him, and locked the knob and dead bolt. Though I was beat, I considered opening and emptying one of the boxes before I headed to bed but quickly abandoned the idea. I'd get to them sometime.

*****

Thursday afternoon, I met Master Sergeant Bennett at the O-course, relieved to see that he wasn't much taller than me, and though he was built like a weight lifter, I knew he faced the same vertical challenges in navigating the obstacles. Both of us were already stripped down to T-shirts, trousers, and boots, so there were no salutes. We shook hands and introduced ourselves and then headed over to the obstacles.

"Do you have any problem negotiating the rope, ma'am?" The last obstacle on the course was a twenty-foot rope.

"No, Top."

"Would you mind demonstrating your technique, please?"

Maybe he didn't understand that the rope wasn't my problem, just the second damn obstacle. However, I walked to one of the ropes, hauled myself up, wrapped my right leg around the rope, and shinnied to the top. After slapping the horizontal support that held the rope, I hand over handed to the ground. Master Sergeant just grunted as he led us back to the beginning of the course. Side by side, we faced the up-and-over, the second obstacle (the first one was a low vault, no problem). The up-and-over had tasted my blood. It fed off my frustration. Was it my imagination, or did I hear diabolical laughter wafting around it?

"Let me see your right arm, ma'am." Wow. He wasn't wasting any time getting down to business. I pulled back the sleeve of my T-shirt and held up my arm so he could see the solid purple bruise running from my armpit downward.

"Ouch, worse than I thought." He cringed. Well, that really inspired me. "Ma'am, the O-course does require a certain level of upper-body development. You have that, but the course is 75 percent technique and 25 percent strength. Most women struggle with the rope. You have the technique for that down pat. Now it's just applying technique to the up-and-over, and once you master that, you won't look like an eggplant."

Ha ha, Top. Easy for you to promise. But I'll listen.

Two hours later, after some really colorful expletives on both of our parts, I was making it over the up-and-over and flying over the low jumps. The combination, log wall, medium rollover log, and vault logs continued to be a challenge but would just require time to master and establish a rhythm. Even the double-pull-over bar was achievable by leveraging the technique I had learned from the up-and-over. Obviously I knew how to manage the rope, but when I tried to tackle it at the end of my workout, my by-then-noodle arms were on strike, and I only climbed a couple of feet before I dropped to the ground.

Noting my dragging feet and zombie arms, the Top called a halt to the festivities. "Was I right, Captain? Piece of cake, once you break the code." He was, indeed, correct, and I wasn't going to begrudge him satisfaction with his, and my, success. I nodded and smiled.

Message delivered, he said his goodbyes, promised to be at the course at 1300 on Saturday, and headed to his pickup truck.

"Top?" I yelled.

He stopped and about-faced. "Yes, ma'am?"

"Where'd you learn to instruct like that?"

He cracked a broad shit-eating smile. "I'm the S-3 training SNCO here at TBS, ma'am. It's my job, but I don't usually get officer requests for help. Makes me feel good to be of assistance, though. By your leave, Captain." With that, he climbed into his truck and rattled down the gravel road back to the main drag.

Well, I had at least somebody in my corner here in Grunt Land.

CHAPTER 4

Captains, Conspiracy, and Baseball Bats

THAT NIGHT, I slept the best I had in two weeks. Maybe it was sheer exhaustion, or maybe it was relief that I didn't have to battle the up-and-over anymore. Whatever the reason, I was completely asleep, maybe snoring a little and certainly drooling, when something startled me awake. I wasn't sure if it was a sound from the park that abutted my end unit, or the other side, but the older lady that lived next to me was always suspiciously quiet. I suspected she'd see me come home (whenever), then would walk around with a glass pressed to our shared wall, hoping to hear rapturous moans or sharable gossip. I hated to disappoint her, so some nights, I just did some rhythmic thumping on the upstairs wall for five or ten minutes, all the while groaning and (mutedly) shrieking various men's names. I'm sure by this time, I was the notorious harlot of Hampton Court (our street) to our neighbors.

My exploits of the previous evening were likely related to the other biddies by 1000 the next morning over coffee and Danish.

Whatever had wakened me didn't repeat itself, but I got up anyway and went to stand at the top of the stairs, straining my ears and eyes for a sound or movement. Nothing. As I turned away and headed back to bed (planning a side trip to my bathroom since I was already up), I heard the faintest furtive sound downstairs. *Ah, geez.* I stepped back into my bedroom, donned my slippers (Just in case the noise was a huge snake. I didn't want him brushing over or around my bare feet.), grabbed the baseball bat that I had leaned behind the door, and headed back to the top of the stairs. Again, silence. I knew I wouldn't go back to sleep unless I investigated, so I waited another minute to ensure my eyes were adjusted to the dark and crept down the stairs. So, Nancy Drew, what are you going to do if it is a somebody and not a something? I'd think about that later (My standard mantra when confronted with something I didn't want to immediately resolve. Maybe not the best practice with a potential burglar in my house, though.).

At the base of the stairs, I glanced first to my left and assessed the dining room. Nothing obvious, even when I bent over to peer under the table and chairs. So I slowly passed through that space and headed toward the threshold to the kitchen. There, I paused and scrutinized floor, cabinets, and countertops and noted nothing more out of place than the wrapped stick of butter I had inadvertently left out on the cutting board. Or *did* I leave that out? Had the snake decided he wanted a midnight snack, opened the fridge with his long snaky tongue, and rooted through its contents until he found something to his liking? Did snakes eat butter? Maybe it was a human intruder that I had disturbed as he started to assemble a ham and cheese sandwich? No, not ham and cheese. People usually preferred mayo or mustard for that combination. Maybe toast or—

I settled on the explanation that I had just left out the butter.

I crept through the kitchen, periodically straining to listen, and finally circumnavigated into the living room, which was an extension of and right-angled from the kitchen. Still quiet. Nothing but the hum of the fridge and the air traveling through the HVAC vents.

Back in the small foyer, I turned on the overhead light and followed suit with the overheads in the other rooms as I passed through them again for one final look-see before heading back upstairs. Nothing notable except a slight wafting of sandalwood, and maybe cedar, but that was likely coming from the Okinawa shipment. I had purchased a couple of small Chinese Tientsin rugs while in Hong Kong and sent them back with my ditty goods. They had been, and obviously continued to be, aromatic with the scents of the Orient.

Satisfied I was not going to be hacked to pieces by an eight-foot-tall ax-wielding maniac or hugged to death by an eighteen-foot boa constrictor as I slept (at least tonight), I turned off the lights, returned to bed, and tried to settle back into sleep before the alarm woke me again at 0400. The only precaution I took was to shut and lock my bedroom door and place my baseball bat on the bed next to me before I closed my eyes.

Baseball bats are a good defense against zombies too, so I had all contingencies covered.

The next morning was Friday, our last day of company staff prep. The training schedule was considerably less structured and shorter (securing by 1200) to allow myself and my fellow SPCs time to prepare for the arrival of the lieutenants who would be our focus for the next six months. A free afternoon meant family time or an opportunity to run errands before the insanity of training commenced.

Since most of the lieutenants did not yet have an designated MOS and were unfamiliar with the range of specialties from which they could choose, the Marine Corps assigned SPCs from a variety of fields representative of some of the options. At this time, women were not yet serving in combat MOSs like infantry or artillery, so almost all were combat-service support, myself included. In my case, however, I was an anomaly. I was a motor transport officer which, admittedly, was kind of a grassroots and dirty MOS, and there were not a lot of women Marines, officer or enlisted, assigned that specialty.

I had been the first female platoon commander in a motor transport battalion and was truly fortunate, as my first battalion commander didn't see me as a woman but a motor transport officer. Period. End of story. I got my butt chewed out when I deserved it (and as a then-second lieutenant MTO, I deserved it a lot), but when I did something right, it was publicly acknowledged. His treatment of me was no different from his treatment of my male peers.

Note: It wasn't until later that I acquired my colorful mastery of salty language. My battalion commander could swear but seldom did. My fellow male platoon commanders, however, embraced profanity and used it more in my presence in order to get a reaction. They didn't get it. By the time I was a captain, I could string together more expletives and profanity than most Marines, and maybe even convicts, could imagine. Thanks to a particularly profane first sergeant when I was a company commander, *and* my maternal grandmother, I now considered myself a master of trash talk. Thanks to her and her example, however, I knew when to employ it and when not.

Anyway, I was an MTO. My fellow SPCs were two infantry, one artillery, and one tanker, along with the company XO, who was a logistics officer. I got along with all my peers, but the one with whom I got along best was Neil Giese, Fifth Platoon commander. Neil was physically imposing, a tad over six feet (like many of his fellow infantry officers), and already tending toward baldness, so he shaved his head. Despite being well regarded and experienced in his specialty, he didn't take himself too seriously, and since I didn't think I was God's gift to the Marine Corps either, we got along great. Neil was a new parent, proud father of a baby girl, and a pretty balanced guy, considering he was only getting an average of four hours of sleep a night.

His only shortcoming (some might not consider it so, but I did) was an obsession with all things Elvis Presley. When you walked past his office, there was always some Elvis melody wafting out the door or thrumming down the passageway.

The tune today, as I sauntered into the Elvis shrine, was "Hunka, Hunka Burnin' Love." Ho, boy. Neil was perched on the couch in the sitting area of his office, spit-polishing a pair of boots, and *twitching* (there was no more appropriate term) with the music. Since we had secured for the day, we were both in civvies. Neil's T-shirt read "Bad to the Bone," and a smushed-up baseball cap with "Freaks Unite" stenciled across the bill rested on his head. Except for the bald head and jeans with knife-sharp creases ironed into the legs, Neil could have been a Deadhead. I said as such, and his face immediately twisted in horror.

"Oh, no, no, no, you heretic!" he roared. "The King is still the King. Renounce your heresy, and we can again be comrades in arms!"

Did I say usually rational Neil was totally transfixed by anything Presley?

"Okay. Please accept my apologies for the sacrilege. But I refuse to kowtow to your Elvis poster," I conceded, gesturing toward the poster over the couch depicting the hip-swaying thin Elvis.

In response, Neil grunted and turned back to his polishing.

I got right to the point. "I wanted to talk to you about our additional duties. What the heck do you know about chorus? Doug got some kind of made-up thing called 'social interaction,' Dave is our human relations POC, and Scott is academics. Scott? Academics? He barely made it through college, and I know he doesn't even have a clue on something as simple as a five-paragraph field order."

Scott Zawicki was a sweet-tempered tank officer, a cross between a surfer dude and football jock. He gave the impression of laid-back California beach bum, but during our staff PT sessions, we'd glimpsed a completely different Scott—focused, aggressive, and determined to win. I suspected he'd coasted through college on an athletic scholarship, not sweating the little stuff like grades because he could be such a no-quarter animal on a playing field. Not a textbook Jekyll and Hyde exactly, but I'd hate to get on his bad side.

Neil paused in his energetic boot-buffing. "Well, at least you're a motor head and know how to read a map, so Land Navigation Officer makes some sense for you. But when was the last time you strolled through the woods with a compass?"

The assignments made by the company commander, Major Richard Mackey (we captains referred to him as "Dickey" among ourselves), didn't make sense. Instead of playing to our strengths, he had assigned us additional duties to what he probably assumed were our weaknesses. What a tool. This whole thing reeked of a setup for failure, and the assignments, in addition to the other BS he was already pulling, were slowly reinforcing a Mackey-versus-captains (SPCs and XO) situation. Not the best way to start six months of intense training and certain misery.

"Yep. I can read and orient a map, and I can get a convoy off-road to an LZ or otherwise, but I haven't done terrain association since I left here. But what do you know about chorus?"

"I know the King. That should be enough. The thought of leading a bunch of choir boys and choir girls in motivating song, though, makes my toes curl." Neil was just as unhappy as I was.

I had a plan. "Look. He's not going to let us switch duties. He wants to see us suffer. So we form a mutual support system that he doesn't need to know about. If any of us needs help, advice, or a stand in, he or she reaches out to the others, and we help. We don't go it alone."

What I was proposing was commonly called the CPA (Captains' Protective Association). These situational and ad hoc affiliations were not a new concept to a Marine. I think for my peers, though, having a woman as part of the federation was a new experience.

"I like it. Do we want to get together tomorrow and talk it out? We're stuck here for the day anyway, so we could sneak off someplace and plot. Should we let Bob in?"

Bob was the XO and probably disliked the CO more than the rest of us (though he was always properly military) since he had to deal with Dickey the most. His background was different from the SPCs as he had been enlisted for seven years before he entered MECEP (Marine Enlisted Commissioning Education Program) prior to becoming an officer. That meant he had almost the same amount of time in the Corps as Dickey, despite the latter's higher rank, and I think that made the CO uncomfortable.

Bob was sharp, but better yet, a great actor. When Dickey affected his bandy-cock posturing in meetings, Bob reverted to his deep Southern roots, assuming frustratingly slow speech and almost childlike sincerity. Really, suh. He was trying to get dis right, wasn't he? The CO was *obviously* smarter because he held higher rank, and Bob's part of the ensuing conversation would gradually reveal Dickey's proposal or soapbox for what it really was—a stupid idea wrapped in bombast to satisfy the CO's craving for notoriety. It didn't take much to derail that fantasy.

"I already talked to him. He's game, suggested we meet at 1100 tomorrow behind the motor pool. We don't want Dickey to see us, so we have to meet someplace other than this building. Bob will let the others know, and I'll stop by to see him after I leave you. I'll let him know you're in."

"Roger, copy all. See you then," Neil replied, focused again on his boots.

Later, as I pulled into my driveway at home, I noticed my nosy neighbor, Doris, a.k.a. Nebby Bitch, a.k.a. NB, lingering by the bank of mailboxes located across the street from our town houses. I glanced in my rearview mirror and wasn't surprised to see her look of surprise as she jumped away from what I knew was *my* mailbox. You needed a key to open your own box, but mine was easily jiggled open. I made a mental note to talk to the maintenance guy today about fixing that. I suspected since NB knew I didn't usually get home until the evening, she probably checked out my mail whenever she didn't think anyone was watching. Today she'd been caught in the act and knew it.

"Yoo-hoo, Abigail," she trilled as I dragged gear out of the back of my truck. "Just the person I want to talk to." Shit. She'd made me. I paused on my front porch without fitting the key in the lock. I didn't want her in my house, and I suspected if my door was open, she'd back me into my foyer and expect me to invite her in.

"What can I do for you, Mrs. Nolan? And I go by Abe, not Abigail. Not many people know Abe is short for Abigail. How perceptive of you to know." I plastered a phony smile on my face that even a three-year-old would see through, and noted her discomfort.

"Oh, I just know these things. And I'm Doris, by the way. No need to be formal with me!" Yeah, prescient all right. The only way she could have known my given name was Abigail was by snooping through my mail. My bills came to Abigail and not Abe. What a piece of work.

"Thank you, but I was raised to address old people by mister or missus, and my grandmother would never forgive me if I took liberties. So what can I do for you?" Sly slam dunk, Abe. NB couldn't be older than fifty, but I knew she'd pick up on the "old" comment.

Aha! Doris's heightened color and narrowed eyes indicated she'd noted the "old" designation, and she wasn't happy. I anticipated this discussion was going to be even bitchier than our usual exchanges, never pleasant to begin with.

I wasn't disappointed.

"Do you have anyone visiting? Not that it's any of my business, but I've heard some sounds during the day and knocked on your door to say hello. Nobody answers. If they're not able to come to the door, I just wanted to let you know it's all right for them to reach out to me. You have my phone number. I'm right next-door and would be happy to help if they needed anything."

Yeah, I bet. I wasn't about to tell her that there was nobody home during the day. I did want to know, though, what she had heard.

"Thank you. I'll remember that. I didn't know noise on my side would make it through the fire wall, and I'm sorry to have bothered you. What kind of sounds did you hear? Maybe the TV? Could it be the air conditioner coming on? It can be pretty noisy."

NB heaved a long-suffering first-Christian-martyr sigh. "Nothing too bad. Just something that sounds like furniture moving around, but not all the time. I'm not complaining, really, just curious about your house guest, I suppose."

Just curious? She'd probably been circling my house for days, maybe with a step stool, trying to see through my first-floor windows. I made another mental note to keep the blinds closed downstairs when I wasn't home. Then a thought came to me that would both fuel the rumor mill and get her off my back.

"Oh. That! *Now* I know what you're talking about. I have some kind of pest in my house. I think a snake might have sneaked into my household-goods shipment from Okinawa, and it's slithering around the house. Probably looking for a way out. Nothing dangerous. Not like a habu, but it's probably strong enough to push stuff around. I've got an exterminator coming next week, so you'll see the truck. I'm glad we had this discussion. It helped remind me to let you know. Now I have to get this stuff inside and get the washer going." With that, I turned around, unlocked the door, and threw my gear into the foyer.

When I turned to close the door, NB had advanced as far as the bottom step of my porch, a disapproving (or was it uneasy? I couldn't tell with her.) expression plastered on her face. She had to know my cover story was BS, but what could she do? I offered a toodle-oo wave and shut the door.

Breathing a sigh of relief, I hustled over to the phone and called first the maintenance man, and then the exterminator I had already found in the Yellow Pages.

*****

On Saturday, the other SPCs, XO, and I held an impromptu meeting behind the heavy hauler trucks in the motor pool. Bob had alerted the TBS MTO (a fellow captain) that we would be there (but not why. We didn't want to make him complicit.). All of us agreed that mutual support was the only way to survive the next six months, and the others all offered to spell me on remedial land navigation. We suspected at least twenty lieutenants would flunk the initial tested event. That meant I, the designated SPC, would be out every weekend, proctoring remedial land navigation until the last directionally challenged lieutenant obtained a passing grade.

At 1300, I met Master Sergeant Bennett and Kelly at the O-course. We spent an hour running the course (them as well as me), and they critiqued my technique (positive, by the way). Before we broke up, Kelly and the master sergeant ran the course for time, and Bennett beat Kelly by a minute. That was kind of noteworthy since Bennett had at least five years on Kelly, who took his defeat with his usual good grace.

"Well done, Top," he said, slapping the master sergeant on the back. "Too much time behind a desk. I need to work on my upper body. Rematch in a month or so?"

"No problem, sir. Let me know if you need any help with your technique." The master sergeant could afford to be magnanimous, but he was doing so with a hint of humor. He could have commented on Kelly's midriff, which had expanded a bit since we graduated from TBS, or allude (respectfully and playfully of course) to lumpy lawyers, but he didn't. I liked that.

We headed to our vehicles, and when I got to mine, I was able, despite my noodle arms (it had been a *long* hour), to pull out a case of Mountain Dew and heave it onto the bed of the master sergeant's truck.

"Ma'am, you didn't have to do that. I enjoyed it," he protested.

"It's the least I can do, Top," I responded. "Look at it as advance payment for help with my lieutenants if they need more coaching on the course. It's a graded event, so do you mind if they contact you directly if they have questions or need some help? You're a lot better on coaching this event than I'll ever be."

"No problem, Captain. Good luck with the company. Your life is about to get really interesting."

With a smile and a wave, he was gone.

Kelly followed me to my truck, which wasn't a typical MTO truck that would make a demolition derby driver envious. It was a kind of boring deep-blue F-150 that had been the Idiot's because he had gotten my sports car (the one my parents had given me when I graduated from college) in the divorce settlement. Where the truck was unremarkable, my car *was* memorable. I had named her Greta, and she was a 1971 Mercedes-Benz 280SE 3.5 Cabriolet, burgundy with tan leather interior. Oh, how I had loved that car! Particularly since my father and brother, JK, had painstakingly restored her from a veritable wreck to a beautiful gleaming showpiece that rode like a dream.

Remember I said the Idiot went after things I loved and that predated our marriage? Of all the regret I still harbored after a failed marriage, Greta's loss was still number 1.

Though I hoped Greta had refused to cooperate with Idiot, I didn't want it to the extent that he had sold or scuttled her.

"We're still doing dinner, right?" Kelly asked.

"Can we call it by ear? Why don't you head to your place, shower, and come back to pick me up? I think I get off at 1600, but you never know. If my truck's not in my driveway, just let yourself into my house, have a something to drink, watch TV, and we'll figure it out from there, depending on the time I get home. Or I can head to your place and pick you up once I clean up. Your call." I knew I was weaseling, but I didn't want to commit or lead him on. Meeting for a beer and pizza was one thing. Dinner sounded too much like a date.

"No problem. I'll swing by your place after I clean up and run some errands. Do what you have to do." I sensed, rather than saw, his disappointment. "See you tonight."

I watched as Kelly pulled out of the parking lot and onto the hardstand road. He was such a great guy. I resolved to have another discussion with him tonight to explain my reluctance not to get involved with anyone now or in the very immediate future.

*****

I finally pulled into my driveway at 1730. We had had a mix-up with the room assignment of one my incoming lieutenants, and the Training Officer, also a second lieutenant, but not part of the company, had been reluctant to venture into what he had referred to as "Lady Land" in order to correct the situation. He and I had an impromptu instructional session regarding that term. That is, he listened and I instructed that women Marines were Marines first, officers second, and happened to be women someplace down the adjectival list. I didn't scream or yell (not my style) and adopted the disappointed-parent treatment. Though I knew I hadn't entirely changed his perspective, I had given him some fodder to chew on.

Anyway I was home later than anticipated, and Kelly was again at the door when I came up the steps. This time, however, there was neither a Diet Coke in hand nor a smile on his face. It was just Kelly, and his face was beyond deathly white. It was literally gray. And this on a guy who, due to his insane addiction to hiking and white water rafting, usually looked like he competed in George Hamilton tan offs.

"You don't have a snake. You don't need an exterminator. Your house is haunted!" he exploded. I shushed him (NB was likely listening at her front door) and pushed him into the house.

"Okay, okay," I responded calmly. "You're acting very unlawyerly. Start at the beginning." I hustled through the living room into the kitchen, grabbed a beer for him, wine cooler for me, from the fridge, and sat down at the kitchen table. Kelly joined me, and I noted he sat with his back to the cabinets, all the while scanning his surroundings. Kind of like a watchman meerkat.

"I got here around 1630, and when your truck wasn't here, I came in, got a beer, sat down, and turned on the TV. I hadn't been here ten minutes when that middle box shifted outward. Not a lot. I ignored it. Figured it was my imagination. About ten minutes later, I had gotten into the movie again when I saw something just out of the corner of my eye. Person height, so it wasn't your mouse. When I turned to look, there was nothing there." His spiel complete, Kelly took a deep breath and drained his beer.

I waited until his rapid breathing resolved into a deep exhale and asked, "Anything else?"

"Abe, you have a ghost. There's no other explanation. Stuff moves, shadows flit around, next thing you know, you'll be seeing full-body apparitions."

Now where the heck had he heard that one? Was my buddy a closet paranormal junky? But I knew Kelly. He wasn't easily rattled, so there had to be something going on if he couldn't explain it other than attributing it to a haunting.

"Look, Kelly. I lived here on and off for a year before I went to Okinawa. I didn't experience anything. Maybe the renters invited something in? Just to be sure, I'll contact them and see if they noticed anything. They didn't seem the kind of people to be into that black arts stuff, but you never know."

"And check if they used a spirit board," he recommended. "They can invite things in you didn't intend to."

Whoa. Kelly Mr. I'm Not Afraid of Anything was terrified of the paranormal. Once we cleared up the current situation, I'd find out why. And then I'd use it as prank material.

"Think, Abe. Was this stuff going on before you had those boxes delivered from Okinawa? I know nothing happened when I was here alone and before your shipment got delivered." He paused. "You haven't unpacked any of the Okinawa stuff yet. Instead of going out, why don't we order delivery and empty out those boxes?"

I thought about it a minute, and it made sense. Maybe some Okinawa demon had inadvertently wandered into my stuff and been transported around the world and dumped here in Virginia. And he was pissed.

"I've been putting it off since I've been so beat at night, but it's about time I got the Great Wall out of my living room. Let's do it," I agreed. "I'll get some razor knives and something to pry the boxes open with and order from Antonio's while you get started."

And that's what we did. Two hours, two pizzas (Kelly was hungry), and a bottle of wine later, we had emptied the contents of the three boxes and piled the contents in related piles. Uniforms and military stuff here, a small heap of basic kitchen items there, and the by-far-largest gathering of curios, rugs, and Asian paraphernalia stacked in the dining room to go through later. I didn't remember if I had shipped intimate garments and was relieved to see what skivvies I had worn in Okinawa were already safely stowed in my dresser drawers upstairs. *Whew.* We paid particular attention to the rugs and curios as we unpacked them, and nothing had captured our attention as being even remotely sinister, but you never knew. By 2230, we were ready to call it quits. I surveyed the chaos we had created but just didn't want to tackle putting anything away tonight.

We stomped on the boxes to flatten them and loaded them into the back of my truck. I'd drop them off at the community dumpster when I headed to TBS in the morning.

As he pulled away from the curb, Kelly stuck his head out the driver's window and reminded me to call him to let him know if the unpacking had made things worse or better. I saluted smartly (well, smartly for me) and headed back inside.

At 0245, something startled me awake (again). This was starting to piss me off. I stumbled out of bed and was already at the door before I remembered my trusty baseball bat. As I turned to retrieve it, I stubbed my big toe on the bed-frame leg lurking under the covers I'd thrown off in my haste to confront my phantom visitor. Now I was *really* pissed off.

At the top of the stairs, I paused and listened. Nothing. Just regular house noises. This was getting really old really fast. Rather than repeat the nocturnal patrol I had performed for the past three nights, I stared down into the darkness below and yelled, "Beer and leftover pizza are in the fridge. Help yourself. Just keep the noise down and leave me alone." And with that, I turned back to my bedroom, slammed the door, and slid back into bed.

The next day was Sunday, and I didn't have to be in my office until 0800, so I was able to sleep in until 0630. I showered and dressed in PT gear and headed to the kitchen to make a mug of tea to drink on the way to base. As I passed through the living room, I spotted something on the kitchen table that had been clear and clutter-free when I had headed to bed last night. As I drew closer, I recognized what it was and why it was so out of place.

It was my unsheathed Marine Corps officer's Mameluke sword, the scabbard placed carefully below it, and positioned under that, my Sam Browne gear. Everything shone, smearless and smudgeless, in the light leaking through the kitchen blinds.

Change of plan. I'd pick up some weak tasteless tea at a convenience store on my way to work.

Oh, and Kelly was right. I had a ghost.

CHAPTER 5

Appearances

ON MONDAY, at 0700, Delta Company would muster for the first time. However, I, as well as my fellow SPCs, was expected to form my platoon no later than 0630, conducting roll call with a roster that had been compiled as lieutenants reported in during the weekend. Thankfully all of my new charges were aboard. Bad for me if I had to track down an errant body. However, worse and woe to the lieutenant who didn't make it to his or her appointed place of duty at the time and date assigned and in the prescribed uniform.

Today was a typical August day in Quantico. This early in the morning, it was already eighty-two degrees and 98 percent humidity with no rain in the forecast. Lovely. As I walked to the parade deck, a.k.a. the grinder, site of the formation, I was thankful the lieutenants had not yet been issued their combat gear. If that had been the case, I was certain Dickey would've directed we muster in flak jackets, helmets, and gas masks in addition to the utilities in which we were currently attired. The grinder is a huge open area of closely mown grass, used for conducting classes on close-order drill, parades, and formations like the one for which we were currently assembled. It afforded absolutely no shade. Though the sun was creeping up over the horizon, it would soon be strong enough to be not a little uncomfortable.

Not only was it hot and muggy with no breeze, there had to be a lot of anticipation and dread fueling the 250-plus students readying for their first TBS formation. That could spell trouble if the CO wasn't observant enough to notice their discomfort and cut short his remarks.

I wasn't optimistic.

My platoon of second lieutenants was already in formation, at parade rest, when I appeared at 0620. They were arranged in three squads, in alphabetical order. Billet holders—student platoon commander and sergeant, guide, and squad leaders—had been selected at random before their arrival and the lucky (or unlucky) officers apprised of the "honor" when they had reported in. SPCs didn't interface with their lieutenants until the first formation. Student billet holders were expected to have a basic understanding of what their positions entailed, but my observing whether and how they had done so was part of the training. All were OCS, PLC (Platoon Leader's Course), NROTC (Naval Reserve Officer Training Corps), or Naval Academy graduates. They understood the basics of a platoon's organization, but to this point, they had followed direction to organize. Now as commissioned officers, they were expected to form themselves and carry out the student billets assigned to them. Those not assigned leadership positions were expected to be good and cooperative followers. Heck, billet holders changed every week, and if you had been an uncooperative snuffy, you likely wouldn't get a lot of cooperation when you were a leader. Payback is a mother.

The company was comprised of five platoons, mine being the third. The other four platoons were anywhere from sixty to sixty-five officers. Third Platoon numbered a whopping twenty-five.

I was pleased to see the student platoon commander, Lieutenant Able, had lived up to her name in the organization and the immaculate appearance of her platoon. As I approached, she about-faced and called the platoon to attention, performed another about-face, saluted as I stepped in front of her, and reported, "Captain, all present and accounted for."

I returned her salute and put the platoon at ease, inviting her to accompany me in a walk-through roll call and meet and greet. All the lieutenants conformed to Marine Corps grooming standards with either short hair (that didn't go any lower than the bottoms of their utility collars) or, if they preferred a longer hairstyle, confined in a bun or twist with no visible bobby pins or hair clips. I marveled at those lieutenants who were able to handle longer hair without any visible means of support (my words, not the Marine Corps Uniform Manual's). Had it been me, I would've looked like Phyllis Diller during her schizophrenic hair phase.

Since all were attired in the uniform of the day (utilities), none wore earrings or more than one ring on each hand. Their uniforms were freshly pressed, boots buffed to a high gloss or spit-shined, and sleeves crisply rolled up with the inside out, forming a roll about three inches wide and terminating at a point about two inches above the elbow. That last was always a struggle for me when prepping my uniform the night before I wore it—attacking my starched utility jacket while still on its hanger, rolling and unrolling sleeves until the roll measured no more than the prescribed three inches. And hoping it didn't look too limp and bedraggled once I'd achieved the nirvana of three inches. I'd need to ensure that during uniform inspections, I was armed with a small ruler just in case my eye wasn't calibrated exactly to standards.

Attention to detail my ass. Sometimes enough was enough.

We had just completed our circuit when Bob appeared and announced that SPCs should stand by for the company formation. For this formation, SPCs would command their platoons and report to the XO, who would then turn the company over to the company commander, Dickey.

The CO made his appearance and, had they been available, would likely have had heralds announce his presence like a king taking his place at a medieval joust. Dickey was a little bit shorter than me but a dedicated weight lifter who needed gussets sewn into the sleeves of his utilities in order to accommodate his bulging muscles. I privately held that his brain was likely as muscular as his arms and, as I watched him approach, was reminded of a banty rooster—strutting and cocky, with the size of his brain inversely proportional to his build.

We knew that Dickey was long-winded and, full of himself, would ramble on about his illustrious background, expectations for Delta Company during the next six months, and generally bore the hell out of all of us. We knew we were in for at least twenty minutes of mindless drivel, and we expected he would put us at ease or, at worst, parade rest. We knew, however, that Dickey liked to do the unexpected and weren't really surprised he kept us at attention for his entire soliloquy. I prayed my lieutenants were savvy enough to keep their knees flexed and focused on staying upright for the duration of the diatribe. If not, I was certain I would get an earful about the unprofessional demeanor of whichever of my lieutenants was unfortunate enough to either drop out of the formation or drop in place.

Thankfully, none of them did.

On either side of me, Scott Zawicki, commanding second, and Doug Chavez, commanding fourth, were not so fortunate. I sensed, rather than heard, the stir as at least one lieutenant in each of their platoons hit the dirt. Did that catch Dickey's attention and hasten his ramble? Nope. In fact, living up to his name, he droned on another five minutes, emphasizing the need for officer bearing and setting the example.

So we were going to teach them how to make Marines' lives miserable? Good job, Dickey. It took you twenty-five minutes to say what could have been said in ten. At ease or parade rest.

He finally finished his spiel, ordered the SPCs to take charge of their platoons, about-faced, and strutted off. Probably to change into PT gear and to spend a couple of hours in the gym while his SPCs dealt with the detritus of lieutenants left too long in the heat.

All five of us immediately relinquished our platoons to the student platoon commanders and ordered them to get the students into air-conditioned spaces ASAP. Which, thankfully, they did.

While the lieutenants headed to class, the SPCs (except the First Platoon commander, Dave Keselring, who had the first watch as classroom monitor) retreated to their offices to review student records. The first week of training was relatively easy, focused on a battery of aptitude tests, assessing the lieutenants' physical status (physical fitness test), and reviewing basic military subjects. Once the company was secured (officially on liberty) each afternoon around 1700, SPCs would conduct introductory interviews with each of their students. With only twenty-five lieutenants at a half hour for each discussion, I figured I would complete my initial interviews by Thursday evening. The other SPCs would probably spend fifteen minutes with each of their platoon members since their platoons were considerably larger. We would all leverage the less-intense training schedule of this first week to get a better understanding of our lieutenants.

My MOS is almost entirely male, and I hadn't really interacted with female Marines since my own TBS class, almost seven years ago. All my lieutenants were college graduates, six of whom had attended Ivy League and second-string Ivy League schools, and two were Naval Academy graduates. So academics probably wouldn't be a challenge. Knowing the curriculum at OCS, I was confident they would all have basic familiarity with tactics, weapons, and drill. However, six months of fieldwork, twenty-mile hikes with full packs, and extraordinarily long hours was a lot different from the limited time and challenges they had experienced prior to their commissioning.

My platoon at OCS had started with seventy-eight women. Twelve made it to commissioning. What's that? An 85 percent washout rate? Attrition at OCS is particularly high for women, due to psychological demands to a great extent but more the downright brute strength required to complete training requirements. However, the twenty-five lieutenants I now had in my charge had met even more daunting physical challenges than I had, and I knew that in order for them to get to this point, they had to be determined to be Marines. They were the next generation, one which considered itself first as Marines, second as officers, and last as women. Based on my personal experience, I knew that part of their—and my—challenge in the next few months was to convey that perception to their male peers and facilitate the Marine Corps' vision of a unified officer Corps.

I had confidence in my fellow company captains' ability to realize this vision. I hoped somebody had shared it with Dickey.

At home at night, things had quieted down. I guess my challenge to beer and leftovers had worked, although the contents of my fridge hadn't been impacted. From that, I assumed the cliché about ghosts not eating was correct, though my phantom guest had made itself known with subtle shifts of furniture, books, and miscellaneous items. It seemed particularly interested in military paraphernalia like my framed commission and I-love-me stuff, such as end-of-tour plaques and photographs. None of that were on the walls. It was all stacked in the dining room until I made room in a closet in which to stash it. It wasn't that I was ashamed of this material, I just didn't think it should define what little interior design plan I had. I was more into signed seascapes and Civil War prints from areas I had visited or been stationed.

Despite telling myself (repeatedly) that it wasn't any big deal to share my quarters with a ghost, I was still pretty weirded out. I had no concept of why I'd been targeted or even if I *had* been singled out. Either way, I just hoped my unwanted roommate didn't escalate his/her activity. There had been nothing as dramatic as my sword on the kitchen counter—just barely discernable movements, like someone had moved the object to look at or appraise it.

I didn't consider the sword's movement threatening or an ominous warning that it might be used as a weapon against me. It *was* a beautiful piece of workmanship, styled after the sword presented to Lieutenant Presley O'Bannon, USMC, by the Viceroy of the Ottoman Empire, Prince Hamet, in 1805. Its curved shape, ivory-colored handle and intricate engraving are unique among American swords, and even my unmilitary brothers enjoyed pulling it from its scabbard to examine the designs etched along its length.

The sword is so distinctive and subject for comment that the 1987 Marine Corps recruiting commercial featured a knight on a horse riding into some kind of feudal hall, dismounting, and accepting a rapier from what one assumes is his king. As the sword transfers from king to knight, it transforms into a Marine officer's Mameluke. The knight then morphs into a Marine officer, in dress blues, executing the second movement of the sword manual.

He is sharp and breathtakingly military, and I'm sure the desire to be just like him has inspired many impressionable young people to enlist. But there's a catch—you have to invest literally hundreds of hours to get that good. The instructions in the *Marine Corps Drill and Ceremonies Manual* seem pretty straightforward:

> Draw the sword smartly, raising the right arm to its full extent, directly to the front at an angle of about 45 degrees, the sword in a straight line with the arm, true edge down; drop the left hand to the side. Pause for one count. Bring the false edge of the blade against the shoulder seam, blade vertical, back of the grip to the rear, and the arm nearly extended. The right thumb and forefinger embrace the lower part of the grip, with the thumb against the trouser seam, and the remaining fingers joined in a natural curl behind the end of the hilt as if holding a pen or pencil. This is the position of carry sword.

Executed quickly, sharply, and precisely, these movements are pretty impressive to an uninitiated audience. Heck, even to fellow Marines.

The general public has no idea that sharply bringing the "false edge against the shoulder seam, blade vertical, back of the grip to the rear" means you are flicking a piece of steel up alongside your head. And your earlobe has a tendency to get in the way of a sharply executed movement, unless you know what you're doing. Some sword brandishers involuntarily jerk their heads to the left to avoid contact, and it's obvious to the observer. Others, like yours truly, have learned to ever-so slightly shift our bodies to the left from the waist and usually avoid detection. Finally there are the other poor sods that just don't get it and inevitably wind up with bloodied ears for the duration of practices and ceremony that called for sword manual.

Only a fortunate (and talented) few can pull off the movements without adjustment or shedding of bodily fluids.

The sword is handsome and, even when not wielded as a weapon, dangerous. But not always in the conventional sense. My brothers learned the hard way and aren't quite as enamored of my sword as they were when I was first commissioned. In an impromptu visit to Stafford, prior to my departure for Okinawa, they'd spotted it in a pile of uniforms, earmarked for shipment abroad, and goaded me into demonstrating the movements from the commercial, which I had. When they'd had a good laugh at my pretty clumsy efforts (Hey! It'd been a couple of years since I'd had to wield my sword, and I was never going to be as awesome as the guy in the ad.), I invited them to demonstrate their prowess. Much to their mutual dismay, it wasn't as easy as it looked. JK managed to fling the weapon across the room as he whisked it from the scabbard. The sword, while slightly dented (even to this day), still fared better than the ceramic monkey it knocked off the mantel (I didn't like it anyway. I don't like monkeys, and it was a remnant from my previous life with the Idiot.).

Tad wound up with three stitches in his ear.

What *was* perplexing, however, was the fact that some invisible thing or body could move an object that weighed about four pounds, unsheathe the sword from its scabbard, and display it, with the Sam Browne, on my kitchen table.

And somehow, my unknown houseguest knew that the Sam Browne belt belonged with the sword despite its having been in a box already stowed away in my uniform closet upstairs.

I could coexist with that kind of presence. If it escalated into dining room chairs piled on the table or cabinet contents emptied onto the floor, however, we'd have another discussion. Or I'd get the house exorcised. Fair is fair.

*****

Friday evening, at the end of training week 1, I was enjoying my kinda-clutter-free living room from my spot at the kitchen table, having stowed the last of my trinkets away or hanging them on the walls when I'd returned home at 1730. I could work in chaos and noise at work, but I was most comfortable in an environment that was ordered and organized. That's not to say I was a neat freak (perish the thought), and I certainly wasn't at home in professionally decorated spaces (like the ones in which I'd grown up). Instead, I had surrounded myself in cherished stuff (but not too much of it) and comfortable furniture.

By choice, I'd lived like a hermit in Okinawa. My BOQ (Bachelor Officer Quarters) room was simply a touchdown space in which to sleep and get ready for work as I spent my waking hours in the office or traveling the island on battalion business. Weekends, I worked or went sightseeing alone, punctuated with biweekly Saturday dinners at my XO's home. He was in Okinawa on accompanied orders, so his wife and three children lived with him, in quarters, in Makiminato housing, just south of Camp Kinser. I looked forward to those dinners. The XO was great, but I absolutely loved spending time with his kids.

Makiminato (or *Kiramachiiji* in Japanese) had been the site of the Battle for Sugar Loaf Hill, where more than three thousand Marines had been wounded or perished in an attempt to take that higher ground. By American standards, *Kiramachiiji* was little more than a slightly elevated piece of real estate, but it commanded the terrain around it and, with two otherwise-innocuous elevations, considered key to taking the Japanese stronghold of Shuri Castle. The fighting had transpired over a week, wave after wave of Marine assaults, until May 18, 1945, when it was officially taken.

Every couple or so dinners at Major Manheim's house, the kids (the oldest was fourteen) had a story about a ghost—Japanese or American—showing up in someone's quarters. The Major, his wife, and I would poo-poo these claims, poking holes in the stories, and reassuring the younger set that ghosts wouldn't hang out around there. They'd be on rides at Disney World or slaloming in the Alps, the ludicrous pastimes for the spirits so diverting that the evening would inevitably end in laughter and reassurance.

Okinawa behind me, tonight I was enjoying being back in my own home, treasured things around me, and two days without 0430 wake ups ahead of me. I heaved a satisfied sigh and wiggled my bootless toes in contentment, then turned my attention back to the kitchen table, where I'd spread a lensatic compass, protractor, and terrain map in front of me. Oh, and a glass of wine at the ready.

Classroom instruction started next week, and land navigation would figure prominently among the classes, with the graded night compass event to follow during the fifth week of training. As Land Navigation Officer, I would be expected to provide additional after-hours instruction to the company's lieutenants should it be required. My fellow SPCs, time permitting, would provide assistance to their platoons but, should they be challenged for time, would send their lieutenants to me for additional instruction.

Remedial land navigation might very well run the duration of this class, failure-rate dependent. That's why it was covered so early in the syllabus. That and the lieutenants needed to demonstrate their navigational abilities before we launched them into the field on a tactical problem. There just wasn't any wiggle room in the training schedule to send out search parties for a platoon or squad led by a directionally challenged student billet holder.

I had just gotten into the zone and plotted my first coordinates on the map when I noted a change in the air around me. Nothing obvious. No strange smell. No breeze. Just a subtle shift in the house's atmosphere that wasn't attributable to the hum of the fridge or the sigh of the breeze coming through the air conditioner vents. I registered a slight buzzing between the back of my head and behind my eyes but figured that was just fatigue and my body barometer warning me that rain was likely before morning. Though I glanced up and around me a couple of times, nothing seemed amiss, and I returned to the task at hand.

The staccato rapping of my front door knocker disrupted what little concentration I had been able to summon on a Friday night, after a long training week. In my haste to make it to the foyer, I tripped over my backpack that was propped against a chair and smacked my knee against an end table. Great. Lame as well as pissed off. With a muttered oath and a resolve to decapitate my visitor (or at least send him or her away as expeditiously—not necessarily as politely—as possible), I stumbled to and flung open the door.

Who else? NB. She fell back a step from the sidelight, through which she was trying to peer (how inconsiderate of me not to instantaneously respond to her summons), and Cheshire-cat smiled at me. I had to admit a certain degree of grudging admiration for someone who, even caught in the act of snooping, had the bombast not to be embarrassed.

"Good evening, Abigail," she crooned, despite my having reminded her no less than a million times that I went by Abe. "I don't see you home very often and thought you might like to come over and have a glass of wine with me. I made some special munchies in case you haven't eaten."

Right. Special munchies that I was sure she had made and shared with her biddy buddies early this afternoon, and these would be soggy or burnt reheats.

"Let me take a rain check, Mrs. Nolan." Two could play the name game, NB. "It's already 2100, and I still have lesson plans to get through before I go to bed. I've been up since 0430, so it's already been a long day." What was she up to? I really wanted to slam the door in her face and get back to my land nav but was curious about what had happened now. Let her talk.

"Oh, I'm sorry, dear. I just thought you and your company might want to unwind a little, and offer some diversion." Did people really talk like that? *Diversion?* And what was her idea of diversion? Did she have a stripper's pole in her living room, and she was going to entertain me/us? And I had never confirmed I had company. Party line was the megasnake or mice.

"So the exterminator didn't work? I thought he had caught the snake. If you've heard anything else, that means there might be more than one."

"Hmm...I could have sworn I saw shadows moving around when I've walked Felicity"—her stupid insipid little rat of a dog—"A snake wouldn't be tall enough to cast a shadow I could see." You could if you had used your handy-dandy step stool to look in the windows, NB. Which I suspect she had.

"I'll look into it, but I don't have company, Mrs. Nolan. The house is only 1,600 square feet. I'd have noticed someone if they were here. Now if you don't have anything else, I really need to get back to work." Message delivered, I moved to shut the door.

NB's voice had lost all semblance of false friendliness as she delivered her parting shot. "I'll figure it out and let you know when I do."

I shut and dead-bolted the door, then turned back to the kitchen. "And miles to go before I sleep" ran like a closed loop through my head as I settled back into my chair.

Almost immediately, the air started to change. Not exactly heavy, more anticipatory, like Christmas Eve. I continued to work for another fifteen minutes or so and decided to call it quits for the night (and the weekend). As I stood up, shoving materials into my backpack, something caught my eye at the head of the table, closest to the living room.

Instinctively I clamped my eyes shut and told myself that whatever I thought I'd seen would be gone when I reopened them. I was likely overtired and maybe just a little tipsy (Really? After one glass of wine? True, it *was* a ten-ounce water tumbler, but I'd only sucked down, at most, half.). I counted to one hundred, inhaled deeply, and reopened first my left then right eye.

I wasn't drunk, and I wasn't hallucinating.

Sitting across from me was a Marine gunnery sergeant clad in plain-green utilities, complete with helmet and ammo belt. I glanced under the table, noted the leggings that covered his lower legs to his boots, and it registered that he looked a lot like the pictures of WWII Pacific Theater Marines I had seen in books and at the annual Marine Corps birthday pageant.

Huh?

I was more startled than frightened. Maybe a little unnerved. But more than anything, pissed at having to deal with something like this when I was bone-tired.

We stared at each other for a full minute, neither of us speaking nor moving. Oh, so it was going to be a stare down, was it? I didn't have the time or the energy for this tonight. I wanted to go to bed.

"Well, it's about time you showed yourself," I said, finally breaking the silence. "What took you so long?"

CHAPTER 6

Unwelcome Visitors

THE ALMOST-DEATHLY (ha!) quiet that followed my welcome was deafening and lengthy as the mantel clock on the fireplace in the living room ticked off the seconds, then the minutes. I wondered if the Marine and I would still be sitting there in the morning, staring at each other and neither daring to move. Maybe I'd be found dead next week (or later), still seated in my kitchen chair (or fallen to the floor), smelling of urine (or worse), sightless eyes glued to something no longer there. After all, the Marine was obviously already dead because he was a ghost. He could probably appear and disappear as he chose. Was he doomed to wander the earth (more likely my town house), haunting hapless humans and either scaring them to death or driving them away? I did know I would be found alone, no evidence of foul play. What if I were ruled a suicide? What would Granna do? I hoped she wouldn't blame herself. Who would deliver my eulogy?

I was just imagining the turnout for my funeral when a deep, rumbling, faintly jeering laugh broke the deadlock.

"Why does a woman need a map and compass? That's a terrain map, and it isn't going to be any help getting you to the library or a restaurant."

So not only a ghost but a chauvinistic, opinionated, and arrogant one to boot.

"I know that. Obviously you don't know how to read one since you're about seven thousand miles away from where you're supposed to be. Do I need to call you a cab?" Take that, Casper.

"I know how to read one *and* use a compass. I just want to know why *you* have one."

While I struggled to frame a response that was scathing but wouldn't end our conversation before it started, he pushed back his chair and unbuckled his ammo belt and canteen, dropping them to the floor with resounding *thunks*. His helmet followed with a muted metallic *thud*. The noises I heard indicated his gear seemed real enough, even if he wasn't. His weapon was leaning against the French door that opened onto the deck outside. If he dematerializes, will that stuff stay behind? Or does it have to be attached to him? My inquiring mind wanted to know.

He was tall—I guess a couple of inches over six feet—and lean, almost painfully so. His face and arms, where the sleeves were rolled back up over his elbows, were tanned a deep brown. He had died, after all, in the South Pacific and obviously spent a lot of time in the relentless Okinawa sun. What drew the eye, however, was his eyes, deep set and a peculiar light sea green. At the moment, those eyes squinted at me as though I were some kind of weird arachnid specimen that needed to be squashed.

"I teach remedial land navigation at the Officer's Basic School in Quantico. And since you've been pawing through my stuff when I'm not around, you already know that I'm a Marine captain. And you're obviously a gunnery sergeant," I concluded, gesturing to the insignia stenciled on his sleeve. I was not rank conscious but figured we might as well establish boundaries. He was an uninvited guest, and admittedly, it was a little late in the game to assert myself. But then, I hadn't had a chance to know what I was dealing with until now. "You can call me 'ma'am.' I won't insist on 'Captain.' And I'll refer to you as Gunny or Casper."

"Where I come from, women might be officers, but they do admin. Some of the troops drive trucks. But they aren't tactical. And they don't have swords, and they don't teach land navigation." He tapped his finger on the tabletop to emphasize his words, and the sound was real enough. "And where did Casper come from? Wasn't he one of the wise men?"

Didn't they have cartoons or comic books when he was alive, or was he just ignorant?

"That was Caspar. I'm referring to Casper, the Friendly Ghost, which you aren't, by the way. Friendly, that is." He still looked puzzled. "If not Casper, then what *is* your name, Gunny?" I figured I'd throw him a bone and use the affectionate diminutive of gunnery sergeant.

A momentary shadow of uncertainty—or was it fear?—flitted across his face and, just as quickly, disappeared.

"I don't know. All I remember is the smoke and gunfire from everywhere. The lieutenant dead. Trying to keep the platoon together and moving forward. That's it."

"Nothing else? The name of your unit? Your CO's name?"

"I remember the objective—high ground—the smells and sounds as if it were yesterday, but nothing else. I can't even remember my own damn name!" The last was uttered in frustration, bordering on anger. Not at me, obviously.

"I don't know. I've never been dead. And I'm pretty sure you are, by the way," I responded. Rather than get bogged down on something I couldn't control (at least for now), I continued, "Okay, I'll just call you Gunny, Casper when you piss me off. But in the meantime, we have to figure out why you're here so we can get you back to where, and when, you belong."

He rose, grabbed his ammo belt, canteen, and helmet, donned them, and turned to retrieve his rifle, which he slung over his shoulder. "I don't think that's necessary. I suspect I just needed to appear to you and then be free to leave." He turned toward the front door. "I'm sorry I scared you and your friend. I didn't know how to get your attention." This last was offered apologetically, if gruffly.

"Just appearing like you did tonight would have been enough," I replied, following him to the foyer. I didn't catch what he muttered in response, though I was certain it wasn't to wish me a fond farewell.

By the time I caught up with him, he was standing in front of the door. I figured he couldn't turn the doorknob to let himself out. How the heck could he move boxes and swords, even a kitchen chair, but couldn't manage a doorknob? To speed things up, I pushed past him (he seemed solid enough) and opened the door with a small fanfare of *ta-da* and stepped aside. Leave already. I want to go to bed.

Still he stood there, studying the welcome mat (mine said "Beat it") and my truck in the driveway. He didn't seem inclined to move, so I gave him a little shove to help him along. He just looked down at me and didn't budge. Argh. I was sure we were on prominent display to NB's cronies across the street, who were likely competing to be the first to call her and report the latest developments in my nonexistent sex life. So rather than still be eminently visible when she "happened" to appear walking her rat on a string, I pulled the Gunny back into the house and slammed the door.

"Okay. What's the problem? I thought you were leaving. You can't be that attached to me yet!"

He turned away from the door and headed back into the living room, where he stowed his gear next to an easy chair, collapsing onto it like he was some kind of colloid. That one got my attention. I knew he didn't have any bones. He was *dead*, for cripes' sake, but that kind of liquidly crumple was unsettling, to say the least.

"I can't. And I think it's because I *am* attached to you, but not in the conventional sense." Where the hell did that one come from? *Conventional sense?* Even Kelly, erudite and articulate pundit that he was, didn't use terms like that. Well, maybe in a courtroom but not in casual conversation.

"What do you mean attached to me? Was your spirit caught in one of the carvings or Shuri fabric I brought back from Okinawa? That just doesn't make sense. All that's relatively new, not forty-four years old."

"Forty-four years? What do you mean? That would make it…1989." He abruptly switched focus. "You were in Okinawa?" For all his posturing, my ghost still hadn't processed that the furnishings and appliances around him weren't vintage 1940s.

"Well, duh. Take a good look around you. Take a good look at me. Do I look like a pinup girl from WWII?" Okay, that last part wasn't quite fair. With my very-short blond hair and sweats, even on a good day, I didn't look anything like an Ingrid Bergman or Lauren Bacall. However, his surroundings of the past two weeks, even the music I played when I was home (let alone the CD player on which the tunes were played) should have clued him to a change in time, let alone place.

"All right. I don't know why I'm here. I don't know why I've been...nowhere...for forty-four years. I only know I can't leave this house unless I'm with you. And I don't know what I have to do to get back to wherever I was." With that, he sank back in his chair again (that liquid collapse again) and closed his eyes, apparently resigned to life with a banshee captain.

"We can finish this discussion in the morning," I offered.

His response was a grunt. I wasn't sure if it was in agreement or resignation.

"Before I go to bed, though, let's establish some ground rules. You don't come upstairs, let alone into my bedroom, and you stay out of the bathroom when I'm using it. And that's any bathroom, upstairs or downstairs. Got it?"

"Roger, copy." His eyes remained closed, like he didn't want to acknowledge his surroundings or, most likely, me.

"Do I need to leave you a bottle or box or something for you to...ah...slip into at night?"

"I don't need a box or a container, or even an amphora," I heard as he drifted out of sight. "Sweet dreams. Captain."

Amphora? Holy crap. I'd have to look that one up. I knew it was some kind of Greek thing, but I was too tired to consult a dictionary (even if I could find one) or boot up my computer to surf the Internet. I'd think about it tomorrow.

*****

The next morning, I woke to another hot and hazy, albeit cloudy, day and contemplated rolling over and going back to sleep. I had planned to be in bed by 2200 last night and up by 0600 in order to take a run before the heat and humidity got too nasty. However, the previous evening's events and turning in at close to 0100 had derailed those plans. Not that I was a dedicated runner, mind you. In my head, I set limited targets of opportunity for PT, especially during the summer months, and as it was close to 0830 (according to my alarm clock), that door had blessedly closed. Ah, shucks. A couple of BLTs with extra bacon might help console me.

And I had a ghost to deal with.

Resigned to a PT-less day—*yes!*—I threw back the covers, shrugged into my discarded sweats, and headed into the bathroom for relief of the immediate bodily situation. I trusted the Gunny to keep to his word and not visit me in either my bathroom or bedroom, but I did verify he was not in the shower before I went about my business.

Mission accomplished, I headed downstairs and inhaled deeply but was disappointed not to catch the sweet aroma of frying bacon or toasting bread. What was the value of a roommate who didn't cook? I knew he could move stuff. Why couldn't he move bacon into a pan and light a stove? Did I need to show him where I kept the pots and pans? I discarded this last idea. Of course, he knew where the pots and pans were, probably better than me.

Maybe I should show him how to operate a microwave? I quickly discarded that notion. He likely didn't even know what one was, let alone try to explain how it nuked stuff.

The house remained quiet as I went about making breakfast and tea. I turned on the television as I started in on the first of two enormous BLTs (I had made them with multigrain bread, since I am so health conscious), figuring I could catch up on the news that I hadn't been keeping up with due to the training schedule.

Newscasters are one of my pet peeves (and there are many). They are a necessary evil, though I really do get tired of the gravitas they convey to the camera when tossing serious news pearls to their porcine viewers (like me). Heads nodding solemnly, they listen to pseudoexperts, stretching two minutes of news into thirty minutes of driveling commentary until I've forgotten what the subject was when they break for commercials. Five to eight minutes later, after being bludgeoned with ads about everything from toothpaste to feminine hygiene products, the talking heads returned, now perky and upbeat, as they turned to the weatherman for his shtick. At least weather people are right 50 percent of the time, so at least worth a listen.

I had just stowed the last of my dirty dishes and pans in the dishwasher when I heard a voice behind me say, "Behind you."

Despite knowing that I had an intermittent housemate, it was still startling. I turned to find the Gunny, sans belt, helmet, or weapon, leaning against the counter behind me. There was that buzzing/ringing thing in the back of my head again. I wondered if it was associated with his appearances.

"We've got to work out how you materialize or whatever it is you do. Just announcing you're here behind me is probably more disturbing than seeing you appear in front of me." Might as well get this straight from the get-go. "But I have a question. Where is your deuce gear and rifle?"

"I think I imagine it gone, and it's gone," he replied with a shrug. "Is that bacon I smell? I so miss bacon." He moved closer to the microwave (where I had nuked the meat) and sniffed. "What is this? I smell bacon, but I don't see a burner."

"It's called a microwave oven. It cooks things. Quickly. If you plan to stick around here long enough, I'll teach you how to use it." I moved to the kitchen table and sat down, motioning for him to join me. "We need to talk. But first, I need another cup of tea. I can make you a cup of coffee if you want." I jumped up and headed to the stove. "If you can even drink it. I know vampires can't eat human food, but can ghosts?"

"First of all, I don't think I can eat or drink but not because I'm a vampire. I don't know why not. I can't. I *can* smell, and being able to smell but not eat is more frustrating than you can imagine." He gazed longingly at my tea mug, shook himself, and continued. "Second, I never could drink coffee. I liked the smell of it perking, just didn't drink it unless I couldn't get tea. Which was seldom. Couldn't drink that green sh—stuff that they called tea either. I got a lot of teasing that I was too hoity-toity to drink coffee, but I had a sweet tooth, and tea with lots of sugar was a lot better than coffee with a lot of sugar." He seated himself at the table, kicked back in the chair, and balanced it on the back legs. Would he get an owie if it slipped out from under him, and he fell? I'd make sure to watch closely, just in case. "I'd trade my C-rat coffee for sh—chocolate discs when I could. Shave 'em and pour hot water over 'em, and it made an okay cup of hot chocolate."

"Hey, we called them shit discs too, until C-rats were replaced by MREs," I offered. He didn't need to tiptoe around me where language was concerned. "My gunny in Okinawa told me I wouldn't pick up field grade if I didn't drink coffee, so he tried to convert me by adding hot chocolate powder to the coffee he gave me. No matter how much hot chocolate powder he put in it, I couldn't drink it. Finally he just waved the coffeepot over a cup of hot chocolate, asked me if that would do, and I admitted it was great. He gave up. Guess I'll never be a major. Boohoo." I didn't share that it had been a hard-fought battle with that gunny over a period of six months.

"I don't think it's our mutual love of tea that brought us together," he observed wryly. There it was again. The archaic maybe-1940's speech pattern, but not what I expected to hear from a WWII Marine gunnery sergeant.

"Did you do something really horrible when you were alive that you're being punished for now? Think. You were a 1940's Marine gunnery sergeant. Wouldn't God get a kick assigning you to a 1980's female Marine captain to work out your penance? Maybe He really does have a sense of humor."

"Very funny," he snapped, glaring at me in a way I was sure had struck fear in even field grade hearts. "I wasn't always a Marine, but I've always had a sense of duty. Our world blew up with Pearl Harbor, *Captain*. Millions of us wound up doing things we never thought we would or could do. Myself included. But I don't think I did anything bad enough to deserve *this*."

"You wouldn't know, *Gunnery Sergeant*," I shot back. "Your generation got my generation into a place called Vietnam and killed a lot of the best and brightest of us off. We wound up doing things we didn't think we'd ever do either, but we did and had nothing to show for it. That 'conflict,' as they called it, wound up in a stalemate, and the US withdrew with its tail between its legs." I was on a roll. "Oh, and since you were already dead, I guess you don't know we won WWII. Bombed Japan with something called nuclear bombs. That's a whole other can of worms."

He was just revving up to blast me back when the doorbell rang, unnecessarily punctuated by brisk rapping on the door. Nobody did that except NB. I knew if I didn't answer, she'd just keep on ringing and rapping until it kept time with the pounding in my head, and I gave in. My truck was in the driveway, so she knew I was home, and I'm sure her buddies had given her the lowdown on last night's drama on the porch.

I headed to the door, with the Gunny hard on my heels. "She might as well see you," I conceded. "The damage is already done." He stopped behind me, in full sight of NB, as I opened the door.

"Oh, Abigail. Are you all right?" As always, the nosiness was wrapped in a cocoon of false concern. "Jeannie and Wendy across the street—you know my good friends, Jeannie Thomas and Wendy Chandler—both called me last night and said you were standing on your doorstep talking to someone they couldn't see and poking at the air. They were afraid you were some kind of hostage. When I didn't see any movement around here this morning, I decided to come over and make sure you were still alive!" Translation: I didn't come over last night because I was too drunk to move, but now that I've sobered up, I want to get the skinny on your typically bizarre behavior.

"Who is this piece of work, Captain?" I heard over my shoulder.

"Shush," I warned, glancing behind me. I turned back to NB. "I apologize. He's a little short on social skills."

"Who, dear? Your snake?"

"No, him." I gestured behind me.

Too late, I realized she couldn't see or hear the Gunny, but *he* could see and hear *her*.

NB's expression morphed from politely perplexed to mildly alarmed, and she took an involuntary step backward. That, in turn, threw her off balance and precariously close to falling backward down the other two stairs to the walk. I lunged to grab her arm to assist, but she waved me off and somehow managed to make it down to the walk without landing in a crumpled heap. I knew she was putting as much distance between us as she could without actually leaving. For sure, there was juicy gossip to ferret out, and she wouldn't rest until she'd ferreted it out.

"She's a busybody. You don't have to take her sh—nonsense. Do you want me to handle this?" *Now* he was being accommodating and helpful but in a hey-little-lady-I'm-the-big-strong-man-and-don't-trouble-your-pretty-little-head way.

Shit. I frantically grasped for an explanation. "I was on the phone, Mrs. Nolan. It's work. The OD is on the line, and I guess he thought you were one of the lieutenants. I really have to get back to my call. Thank you for checking on me, but I'm really okay." I moved to close the door, but she was back up the steps in a heartbeat, not two feet from me.

"Abigail, I'm concerned! Do I need to call the police?" Throwing caution to the winds, she moved to get around me into the foyer, and I sidestepped to keep her from going any further.

"She's going to bully her way in here, Captain. Let me at her."

"*No to both!*" I bellowed in what I hoped was a no-nonsense command voice. Okay. Maybe it was bordering on hysteria. "I'm fine, and I don't need any help. Good morning."

With that, I firmly closed the door, not exactly in NB's face but with a finality that brooked no further conversation or intrusion.

Dead bolt shut, I turned, leaned against the NB portal, and regarded the Gunny, who was hovering uncertainly at the entrance to the living room.

"Don't you go disappearing on me," I advised him. "We have to figure out where we go from here."

CHAPTER 7

Cronies and Compasses

ON MONDAY, the training schedule really took off. Since these were not officer candidates, they were expected to get themselves to the mess hall for breakfast (if they were so inclined) and make formation by 0700, prior to marching as a platoon to class. On PT days, and since it was the height of summer, formation went at 0600, followed by "the daily seven" (calisthenics) to warm up (despite the oppressive heat and humidity), then off for a three to five-mile run on either hardstand road, washboard, O-course, or other assorted challenges.

Though I ran a first-class PFT, I was not particularly studly, and as I've already shared, running was not a favorite pastime of mine. We had not yet gotten into the field-operations phase of training. That would mean admin movement (hiking) out to "the problem," a.k.a. practical application, for a tactical phase of instruction and walking back. We wouldn't do organized PT on those days. Just formation misery, hiking anywhere from five to seven miles to get to the field classroom, conducting the tactical problem, then hiking back. Later training would necessitate two to five days in the field, sleeping in tents at night, and conducting tactical training during the day. Hiking I could do. Hiking with approximately seventy pounds on my back was doable but not fun.

Got the impression that a lot of TBS is physical training and developing stamina?

Anyway, much of the first three weeks of training entailed intermediate land navigation (both day and night), five-paragraph field order, introduction to Platoon in the Defense, and ready? PT.

I was getting to know my platoon members better each day, not in a getting-to-know-you way but through their actions and reactions to daily challenges. Currently the O-course figured prominently among those challenges as it required technique, upper-body strength, and managing the fear of some downright-scary obstacles like the combination. One lieutenant, who had started a company more than a year ago, had fallen from the combination, sustaining a pretty serious injury. She was back now, and though she would never achieve the fastest time when she ran the O-course for score, she tackled it with courage and determination. I made sure I stood at the obstacle whenever she ran the course, there to encourage but also there to watch in case there was a misstep that could cause her to fall and wind up back where she had been last year. I figured if nothing else, I would provide a softer landing zone than the ground or, at least, a suitable body block. I was pleased to see her fellow platoon members would follow my example, standing with studied nonchalance at other obstacles "just in case." Good on 'em.

They would need that mutual support when we started the serious hiking with full packs and a platoon radio, machine gun, and SAW (squad automatic weapon).

*****

As I went about my duties, I was seldom alone. I had my own unlikely companion, unseen and unheard to those around me, commenting on everything from the quality of the training to the weapons we carried and employed. I assumed he was less loquacious at home but just assumed so since I usually headed straight to bed when I got there.

The Sunday after NB's gossip-gathering visit, the Gunny and I had conducted some run-throughs to ascertain what he was or wasn't capable of doing. He couldn't leave the house unless he accompanied me. We figured this out when we tried to get him over the thresholds of the front, back, and side doors. Unless I went out, he couldn't. The downside of this (at least for me) was his not requiring my permission or knowledge to accompany me. After I'd come downstairs a couple of mornings and made what I thought was a Gunny-less escape to my truck, he'd appeared in my office, classroom, and even grocery store, judging or commenting. I realized if I wanted to be more situationally aware of his presence, I should listen for the annoying buzzing/ringing that seemed to announce his manifestations. Until I broke the code, I'd be spending a lot of energy not acting crazy or, at best, eccentric.

I was already under a microscope at TBS due to my sex (I was only one of two females on staff) and MOS (women truckers were still an anomaly) and didn't relish further attention by talking to someone not evident to anyone else. Though I'd made it *very* clear that Gunny should keep his comments to himself and not distract me while other people were around, I wasn't optimistic he had that much self-control. I'd have to be the adult and school myself to ignore his comments, no matter how outrageous, and reconciled myself to a lot of pinching and literal tongue-biting to refrain from responding.

Heck. Who was I kidding? I wasn't confident of my own self-restraint when provoked.

We had a tacit understanding that he would not accompany me to my lieutenants' rooms, and if there were a gray area on what was authorized and wasn't, I made the call. Or at least I thought I did.

He could move objects that were around when he was alive, like my field gear and sword, and general-purpose items like my kitchen chairs. He could not, however, turn doorknobs (no idea why not) or operate the TV and microwave (obviously).

We still hadn't figured out why were bound together. I really didn't have the time to give it much thought, and he seemed content to go with the flow for now. After all, this was new and different for him, and I sensed that sometimes he was even enjoying himself. Often at my expense—occasionally at others'—but always with an ironic gradually less-archaic perspective. We both knew, at some point, we would have to address the why and how of this situation, but for now, we had drifted into a routine, albeit a quirky one.

Despite the Gunny's and my uneasy truce, I didn't invite Kelly to the house. I suppose I didn't want an escalated repeat of the previous incident. Training often stretched into late Friday night, and I spent the weekends frantically doing laundry and running errands, so we hadn't connected except for a couple of phone calls. Heck, I barely managed my weekly phone calls with my Granna, and even those were brief, more often rushed. I hoped that once the training schedule settled, I could carve out time during the week for myself, but a nagging voice told me Dickey would eat up any free time the SPCs had with meetings and chest-thumping.

And then there was land navigation. I dreaded the final graded examination because that meant my Saturdays disappeared until all the land navigation failures had successfully passed the practical application. I knew my fellow SPCs would assist with the Saturday babysitting. However, I didn't want to cash that check too early on, as I'd be relying on the two infantry officers (Neil and Doug) to lend a hand on the five-paragraph-field-order phase of instruction. I could write one, but it was more an infantry tool, a means of organizing information about a military situation for a unit in the field. I anticipated some of my lieutenants would find its construction a bit challenging, and I knew my peers could clarify its murkier aspects better than me. The five-paragraph-field-order final exam was half the lieutenants' tactics grade, and they'd regularly employ it as we transitioned to the field-operations phase of training.

The closest wolf to the sleigh (you know, the most immediate challenge) was land navigation, which is important to Marines, especially officers. There is nothing quite as pleasant as being stuck in the woods with no idea where you are and confronted with twenty-plus Marines who already think you're clueless, let alone lost. Yup. Manipulating that map and compass (and nowadays, GPS) is a pretty important skill.

Officers are introduced to land nav in OCS. They learn the basics, but TBS ups the ante with more challenging courses and more in-depth orientation. Though the day and night land-navigation exams are conducted in two obviously different conditions (duh, like light and dark), students must, "without the aid of references, given a military map, lensatic compass, and a minimum of an eight-digit grid coordinate, locate specific points on a land navigation course."

Day land navigation (the all-day event I was really dreading) is conducted in a five-mile-by-five-mile area, bounded by hardstand (roads). Lieutenants must locate six designated points correlating to ammunition cans mounted on engineer stakes and with numbers painted on the sides. There are three letters and numbers painted on the can's sides corresponding to three courses (*A*, *B*, and *C*). Example: The lieutenant is assigned course *C*. He/she notes the numbers for that course on his/her scorecard (C11, C45, etc.). He/she does *not* copy down the number for *A* or *B* courses.

The exercise starts in the classroom where the students plot their assigned points on their maps. They figure out at what stop and at which boundary road they want to start, planning their course in a logical sequence so they don't run all over the training area like blood spatter on a wall. They also plan at which road and stop they want to be upon completing the course before they even leave the classroom. Points plotted, they're transported via cattle cars (a tractor trailer configured with wooden bench seats to transport personnel) to the training area and disembark at predesignated drop-off points.

The students spend the rest of the day stalking the elusive ammo cans, relying on terrain association, accurately shot azimuths, and maps to correctly identify the numbers of the cans correlating to the points. Their searches complete, the lieutenants make their way to the egress hardstand road they had chosen before they had departed the classroom. Here, they flag down one of the trucks that regularly circumnavigate the twenty-five-square-mile training space and travel back to the staging area where their cards are graded by the TBS Land Navigation Officer. They return to the BOQ in trucks once sufficient numbers have assembled to make the trip worthwhile (yeah, like cargo staged for transport) and await the last lieutenant's return to the staging area. The company is secured only after the last lieutenant checks in. Lost students (that is, those who have to be tracked down) are automatic failures. If an officer is late to the staging area, his/her grade is reduced correlating to the amount of time he or she was overdue.

The course is truly challenging. It is long, arduous, and frustrating and further complicated if the weather is foul or hot. Since it is a graded event, the already daunting requirements are complicated by the desire not to fail and be stuck tromping around the boonies every Saturday—in the case of Delta Company, with *me*—until passing the event.

In cases of snow, the test can be "called" if it is forecast to be over two inches, so the Tactics staff pays particular attention to weather reports. Heavier snow transforms the landscape, covering fallen trees, foundations of abandoned buildings, and myriad rocks and ditches. There's no sense pressing forward with the test if you stand to lose lieutenants to broken legs and concussions. On the plus side, ammo boxes are clearly visible due to lack of leaves and climbing vegetation.

Spring, summer, and even fall classes struggle in groves of tanglefoot (just what it means—barbed vegetation that catches the foot and impedes forward progress), and there are enough leaves to make ammo boxes disappear in surrounding foliage unless the lieutenant is carefully following his/her compass's azimuth and pacing distance. In the summer, the heat and humidity are oppressive. Lieutenants wear helmets and harnesses (a five-and-a-half-inch wide heavy-duty belt with suspenders carrying two canteens and first aid pouch), in addition to their standard utilities, T-shirts, and boots. Not nearly as well ventilated and lightweight as a Hawaiian shirt, shorts, and shower shoes but eminently more practical for scrambling and scrabbling through heavy vegetation and rocky terrain. Not to mention combating mosquitos, chiggers, and (ugh) ticks.

Lieutenants struggling through land nav really don't have the time or inclination to appreciate the beauty of their surroundings. They pass through woodlands of hundred-year-old secondary growth and fields in spring that are awash with wildflowers. It is so desolate that wildlife abounds with foxes, myriad varieties of birds, and even coyotes and bears. The former are seldom visible, but the bears sometimes make an unannounced and kind-of-scary appearance before they disappear back into the woods.

Leveraging the remoteness of the area, the Tactics staff enjoys deploying Lieutenant Wolf, one of their bubbas dressed in utilities with butter bars (second lieutenant rank insignia) and sporting a wolf mask. During their land-nav classroom instruction, the lieutenants had been warned about a student who had gotten hopelessly lost during *his* final and never heard from again. Except, that is, when he confronts unobservant lieutenants, absorbed with finding their next ammo box, and unaware of their surroundings. Lieutenant Wolf would unexpectedly appear, dancing around, thumping his chest, and then disappear back into the woods.

I really wanted that job.

The actual-day land nav is not without its comedy (for the observer, not the participant). It is exceedingly comical to observe a lieutenant standing under a power line or next to an armored vehicle, wondering why his/her compass is spinning crazily. When I was in TBS, I had encountered a couple of members of my company in just this situation, but since you aren't permitted to talk to your fellows while undergoing the land-nav ordeal, I had to wave and continue on my way without offering advice.

I knew another challenge would be terrain association, as many students misread terrain maps and mistake hills for draws (lower elevation). Using your compass alone won't get you to the right ammo can. Going down where you should have gone up can mean missing the objective. I'd make sure the remedials I'd have to wrangle were reminded of these pitfalls. I'd be just as anxious for remedials to pass as they would be.

For night land navigation, students start at designated points and are provided azimuths and distances, but no grid coordinates. Since they cannot use their flashlights, students can only use the compass's bezel ring, luminous magnetic arrow, and short luminous line to find their objectives. Heaping insult onto injury (after all, who wants to stumble around in the dark when they can be sipping a cold one in front of the TV?), the course is laid out in such a way that the officers must cross a stream (in this case, Beaver Dam Run) both on the first leg of their course and its return. Luckily, if there were failures on this course, remedial testing would be conducted by the TBS Land Navigation Officer since it required coordination of TBS assets, both personnel and training areas, and the FBI Academy, located to the north of us.

Finding lost lieutenants is a lot harder in the dark than during daylight.

So the fifth week of training, here I was sitting on a lawn chair, in the dark, along Beaver Dam Run, listening to splashing and muttered oaths as two-hundred-fifty-plus Marine second lieutenants made their way through the startlingly icy water to the opposite shore. The ammo cans for the night compass were only numbers (since there was only one course), and the one in front of me was labeled "12." Neil, forty yards to my left, sat just behind a can labeled "11." If a lieutenant was either slightly off in his/her azimuth, he/she could wind up at the wrong point.

I wasn't alone, however. The Gunny reclined on the ground beside me, laughing his ass off and marveling at the deviousness of the Marine Corps' ensuring the training of its junior officers was as miserable as he was currently witnessing firsthand. Without having to endure it himself, of course. Despite his taunting, though, I detected a grudging respect for what these young officers were willing to do in order to be lieutenants of Marines.

I'd been pretty successful controlling myself from responding to his disparaging but frequently funny commentary. The Gunny knew this and was taking full advantage of my situation, regaling me with mostly caustic but increasingly amusing commentary. The asshole.

"Can I cross here?" The male voice floated over the stream, directly across from where the Gunny and I waited in the dark. It was now late September, and the temperatures had cooled somewhat but were not yet autumnal. Almost daily summer thunderstorms had kept the stream's water level about five to six feet, and it was chilly despite the night temperature of approximately sixty-five degrees.

"Yep," I responded. It was fordable. Just a little cooler and deeper than the lieutenant probably anticipated. I heard Neil giggle softly off to my left.

"You have some mean streak, Captain," the Gunny observed. "I like it."

"The course is laid out, so they have to ford twice. I had to do this course in February, and it sucked when I hit the water. He's lucky it's only September," I murmured. Softly enough to be undetected, I hoped.

The lieutenant hit the stream with a resounding splash and equally resounding string of obscenities. Instead of stepping tentatively to test the depth of the water, he had mistaken my words to indicate the water was shallow and had plunged straight ahead. *And down.* Obviously his first foray across Beaver Dam Run had been upstream, where the water was only knee-high at best, so he had anticipated the same here. The TBS Land Navigation Officer made sure the crossings were safe and the ammo cans intact before each land-navigation problem, night or day. He did have a wicked sense of humor, however, and made certain each course contained at least one fording challenge.

Gunny howled as the lieutenant struggled up from the streambed, sliding back down as often as he made progress forward. It took a good five minutes before I heard a *humpf,* as he landed on solid ground. I saw him rise, his silhouette darker than the shadows surrounding him, and noted he was halfway between Neil and me, who stopped him short of our locations.

"Stand fast, Lieutenant," he barked. "Which is it? Left or right?" Neil knew, with all the foundering around, slipping and sliding, and anxiety to finish, the lieutenant had likely lost track of his course (if not his compass). He had a 50-50 chance of getting it right. When there was no response, he repeated, "Left or right?"

Thinking Neil was doing him a favor by speaking out (and I had betrayed him by telling him he could ford), the lieutenant took a chance with the friendly. "Right, sir."

"Come over here and let me see your card."

The lieutenant sloshingly obeyed. He was so wet, the squelching sound he made as he moved toward Neil drowned out the creek's gentle murmur but not the Gunny's chuckle.

Neil turned on his flashlight, the lens covered with a red filter to less impact night vision, aimed it downward, and compared the card to his master key.

"Wrong guess, Batman. It was Captain Rush's point." I couldn't see it but assumed he marked a red *X* through the appropriate block on the card before he handed it back to its owner. "Before you head over to her so she can set you back on the right course, let me give you a word of advice." I *could* see Neil slowly rise from his lawn chair, snapping off the flashlight as he did so. His shadow loomed over that of the unhappy lieutenant. "You want to be an infantry officer, right?"

"Yes, sir."

"Let me tell you something. That stream was fordable, just like Captain Rush told you. But you were cocky, and instead of seeing how deep it was, you jumped right in. That was reckless." Neil paused before he made his point. "There's a difference between reckless and bold and audacious. Reckless gets Marines killed. Got it, Lieutenant?"

Neil's use of *lieutenant* to punctuate his last comment was uttered sarcastically, with a sneer in his voice. It reflected his disgust with the officer's behavior and that he had slipped somewhat in Neil's estimation. Gone was the easygoing Elvis-loving SPC. In his place was a professional Marine who took his profession as an infantry officer and role model very seriously.

Neil's knowledge of the lieutenant's preferred MOS indicated this was probably a member of his platoon, and I suspected this was the first time this student had experienced Neil's serious side. Even I hadn't, for that matter, and I was impressed with how he had leveraged the lieutenant's blunder into a serious teaching point. Neil's stock—already high with me—multiplied a thousandfold. Night land nav wasn't just blundering through a forest at night. It was about how you *applied* that skill to being a better Marine.

"Yes, sir."

Gunny had practically been in hysterics at the lieutenant's watery and muddy trek from the stream but ceased his braying to hear Neil's admonishment. Though there were further splashes and comedic moments for another hour or so, he remained uncharacteristically silent. I wondered what kind of snide comment I'd get when we returned to my office. None was forthcoming.

He had evaporated.

Later, as I started my truck, he appeared in the passenger seat. I was so startled, if I hadn't already fastened my seat belt, I probably would have hit my head on the overhead from my spastic reaction. Damn it! I *really* needed to be more aware of what my noggin was trying to tell me.

"I wish you'd give me some kind of warning before you do that," I snapped. "If I'd been driving, I could have gone off the road." I was bone-weary, it was 2330, and I still had a twenty-minute ride home, so I was not in the best of moods.

"My apologies, Captain," he offered. Nothing more meant something was up. I was not going to scratch that scab, and focused instead on driving.

Back at home, I dropped my gear and headed upstairs to shower. "Captain?"

I turned and looked down at him in the foyer. "Yeah?"

"Uh...I...uh...good night." With that, he disappeared. I was too tired to try and figure out what he'd intended to say. Like Scarlett O'Hara, I'd think about it tomorrow.

CHAPTER 8

Donuts and Daughters

THE DAY land nav practical application had been exactly as I recalled it from my previous sentence to TBS. Terrain wise, it remained rolling hills, vast open meadows (doubling as fire-breaks and power-line easements), wooded areas (with plenty of tanglefoot, ready to trip up inattentive lieutenants), and streambeds (wet and dried up). In addition to the power lines soaring overhead, there were still some occasional abandoned sheds, nondescript ruins, and rickety footbridges. Probably the best way to describe this twenty-five-square-mile piece of real estate was simply *desolate*.

This time, though, I was able to take my truck onto the tank trails, park, and watch what action transpired. I had checked with the TBS Land Navigation Officer to find out which would be the most traveled routes, stationed myself in that general area, and waited. It wasn't long before a lieutenant appeared in the clearing in front of me, eyes glued to his compass, and obviously pace-counting (calculating distance) to his next objective. I was leaning against a tree, about four feet from an ammo can, making sure I didn't block it from his view, but he about fell on me before he realized I was there. Of course, he apologized profusely (Captains are gods to second lieutenants, and he should be happy that I didn't chew his nose off.). I just moved aside for him to jot down the number for his route, B18, and wished him fair winds and following seas. He started to salute before he moved onto his next objective, then remembered that we didn't salute in the field.

Instead, he proclaimed, "Semper Gumby, ma'am!" and he went on his way, focused again on his compass and map, stumbling over rocks and tree stumps as he made his way back into the woods. I was confident he would be successful, though I wasn't as comfortable with some later arrivals who clearly didn't understand that they should be seeking a draw (lower elevation where this ammo can was actually located) and mistakenly looking for a finger (higher elevation). I was pretty sure I'd be seeing at least one of them for remedial.

Sure enough, fifteen lieutenants flunked day land nav, and my Saturdays would soon center around remedial for the foreseeable future. The maggots. I think fourteen of the miscreants had deliberately flunked the course just to make my life miserable. The fifteenth failure, Lieutenant Meyerson, was one of my lieutenants, and she couldn't navigate her way out of a wet paper bag. I feared I'd be tramping around the training area with her until she graduated in February. Though my fellow SPCs had agreed to spell me, I knew Meyerson would be the last lieutenant standing, and I considered it my responsibility that I, as her SPC, would escort her every Saturday until she passed. Holy chicken farts. By the time she graduated, she should have memorized every ammo can in the twenty-five-square-mile training area. I saw admin officer in her future. They usually don't have to know how to read a map.

*****

It was my last free Saturday before remedial-land-nav hell commenced, so I had invited Kelly for a run at Prince William Forest Park. Adjacent to the Marine Base, this beautiful area, over sixteen thousand acres, is the largest protected natural area in the Washington, DC, metropolitan region. Kelly and I had decided to meet there, despite the literally hundreds of running trails aboard Quantico because the park was convenient, roughly halfway between my house in Stafford and Kelly's place in Woodbridge.

And there was a conveniently located Dunkin' Donuts not far from the entrance to the park.

Gunny, noticing a change in my Saturday routine (namely, trying to sleep in as long as I could), had followed me around the house, nagging me like a six-year-old pestering for ice cream money.

"You're *not* invited, and you're *not* going," I barked. Almost as soon as it was out of my mouth, I relented. Maybe I should take a more *conciliatory* approach. "Please promise you won't go all invisible on me and tag along."

"I get bored sitting around here. Your life is much more interesting. And I'd like to get to know Kelly better."

"First of all, you don't have a life because you're dead. Second, you are not—repeat *not*—going." Gunny had heard me talking about stopping for donuts when we finished our aerobic torture, and all he could chant was "jelly donut, jelly donut, jelly donut," despite my repeatedly reminding him he couldn't eat because he was a vampire.

His whining followed me up the stairs as I entered the no-Gunny zone of my bedroom (really the whole upstairs was forbidden, but I was willing to cut him a huss to get him off my back). Time to change into PT gear and then on to meet Kelly.

The Gunny hovered at the doorway, still stating his case for accompanying us. Ugh. Would he never give up? This was like dealing with my younger brothers when I started dating.

"So you don't want me to go because this is a date?" Could he read my mind or was he just trying another tactic?

"No, it's not. He's just a friend. That's all. I want to talk to him about you. Explain that he isn't nuts. Because I want to be able to invite him over for a beer or glass of wine instead of going to his place or a restaurant. He's still trying to figure out what's going on. And football season is coming up. I have a bigger TV." I took my gear into the bathroom to change. When I emerged, clad in shorts and T-shirt, running shoes in hand, the Gunny's face reddened so much, I thought he might be having a stroke. Wait. He was already dead, so it couldn't be a stroke. But how could his face get so red if he'd been dead almost fifty years?

"What the Sam Hill do you have on? Or should I say, what the Sam Hill *don't* you have on?" he erupted. He was still watching his speech with me. I wondered when that would change. Probably not until our first field operation when weapons jammed or lieutenants in the attack got tear-gassed.

"Hey, upstairs is a no-Gunny zone, remember? And it's PT gear, Casper. You've seen people wearing it in stores when you snuck a ride. You've seen it on TV. You've seen us run PT at the base. What's the problem?" Ah, that was right. He hadn't seen *me* in PT gear when I wasn't with a formation. When I went to work, I wore slacks or, at worst, sweatpants and shirt. Oh, showing a little leg was embarrassing to him. Guess he'd have to get over it.

"You're going out in that?" He was affronted and incredulous. I pushed past him and headed down the steps, and he was right behind me. "You look...fast."

I knew he was saying I looked slutty (by his standards), though I responded, "No, I'm an incredibly slow runner." Then I moved into the living room and perched on an ottoman to don my shoes. "Get a life, Casper. Or get an unlife. It's 1989. This is what I wear to run. And it's pretty conservative, considering. Fast? Really? Why don't you just say *hooker?*"

Okay. That one set him off.

"Fine. Leave your television on when you go," he huffed. "I like that ESPN channel." With that, he evaporated.

You're lucky I don't leave it on cartoons, Casper. I know you haven't quite figured out the channel knob yet—oh, that's right! You can't operate the TV!

Kelly and I struggled through our run. Since he had about ten inches on me, he could kind of lope to my stagger, but his breathing was still ragged as we stopped running and walked the last quarter mile back to our vehicles in order to cool off. Me? I ran at least three times a week, both with and without the platoon in tow. Despite this, I was now barely upright when we finished. Humidity, pace, and the seven miles had gotten to me.

In fact, I am probably the only Marine officer whose time for a physical fitness test run is timed by a calendar and not a stopwatch. Have I mentioned how much I hate running?

At Dunkin' Donuts, Kelly secured us a place outside at a picnic table while I got our tea and coffee. And a dozen of the store's fluffiest, fattiest, gooiest confections. I had deliberately offered to order and buy because I was planning on taking three jelly donuts home to wave under my houseguest's nose. He could smell, right? He smelled bacon even though he couldn't eat it. Then I was going to leverage this torture to get him to try to remember who he had been and/or why he was bunking in my house.

We'd made no progress on this one in the four weeks since he had appeared. This couldn't go on forever. There *had* to be some kind of time clock counting down days or even hours that we were working against to determine Gunny's name and origins. I just hoped we didn't unknowingly run out of time, and I came downstairs one morning to find Gunny had morphed into an ectoplasmic blob. Gross! How do you explain *that* to a cleaning service?

Admittedly I'd slipped up a couple of times in front of an audience, muttering a comeback to one of his more sarcastic remarks I'd found impossible to ignore. I was getting too accustomed to his being around, and I think my initial impression as eccentric to others had progressed to borderline crazy. I could see my sanity hearing now. "Tell me, Major Mackey"—or any one of probably two hundred and fifty-plus witnesses—"why are you so hard over on having Captain Rush relieved of duties and committed?"

And then good ole supportive Dickey responding, "Because she's friggin' nuts! All the time having one-way conversations with—"

"Whoa, Abe. I told you I only wanted three. Figured three or even four at most for you since you're a glazed-donut freak. But a dozen of glazed *and* jelly?" Kelly grabbed his coffee and gestured toward the other six (likely five) orphan donuts in the box. He knew you'd sneak another donut, Abe. You're not getting anything over on Mr. Prosecutor.

"That's what I want to talk to you about."

"Donut addiction? It's not chargeable under the UCMJ (Uniform Code of Military Justice). Now being overweight is something else. That's administrative, and I don't do that." Kelly was so focused on poking fun at my appetite, he hadn't noticed my voice take on a serious note, and my face probably looked intense. At least as intense and serious as I could muster, given my sweaty red mug that I kept wiping with every available napkin. And I probably sported gobs of jelly dripping off my chin.

"I want to talk to you about the last time you were at my house," I started. "I found out what's going on." I had downed an entire donut before Kelly responded. Maybe he really didn't want to know?

"Okay. This sounds serious. Were your tenants into the occult? Is your entire town house block haunted? Do you have a recently deceased relative that wants to hang around?" Cripes! Was he cross-examining me?

"No to all three. At least as far as I know. It's a…it's a…WWII Marine Gunny," I blurted out. There. I'd said it. No taking it back.

I sat back on the bench and feigned nonchalance as I crammed half a donut into my mouth.

A range of emotions passed over Kelly's face in a matter of seconds. Disbelief. Puzzlement. Fear. Finally amusement, demonstrated by a broad smile.

"You're yankin' my chain, right? Really. What's going on?"

I proceeded to fill him in on the events of the last few weeks. Everything from the nighttime noises to the current situation where Gunny accompanied me when I went to work and sometimes tagged along when I didn't know he was with me. While I delivered my soliloquy, Kelly sat back on his bench, munching a donut and slurping his hot coffee. However, as my story stuttered to a close, he leaned forward, a concerned expression on his face. I hoped it wasn't to make the recommendation that we head to base and check in with medical.

"So…he could be with us right now, and we wouldn't know it?" Bless his heart. He believed me! But he was also leery of what invisible baggage might have accompanied us on our run and might just as easily be sitting beside me, eavesdropping on our discussion.

"I've gradually noticed that I hear a funny sound in the back of my head when he's around, whether I see him or not. It's kind of like the sound people say they hear when they have tinnitus. Kind of a ringing buzzing. Not enough to block my hearing. Just…there."

"And?"

"He's not here."

"Okay. So he doesn't know who he is or how he died. And clearly, neither of you knows why he's here or how to get him back to where he came from. Where do we go from here?"

I didn't realize I'd been holding my breath, but with these last words, I exhaled, relieved that Kelly believed me and was offering his help. I was uneasy, though, that he might think my sharing raised him to a status above friendship. We were friends. Okay. Becoming a bit more, and if I wanted more than that from any man at this point in my life, it would be Kelly. But I didn't. At least, for now.

"Can you swing by my place, and I can introduce you? You won't be able to see or hear him, but I can act as interpreter. And since you're a lawyer, you might be able to coax some answers from him or help him remember. I'm not good at that type of thing."

Kelly frowned. "I can't today, Abe. I have to go into the office at 1700 for a strategy session with our prosecution team. We start that court-martial on Monday, and we're working on and off all weekend. Sorry."

Kelly was what the civilian sector would call a second chair on what was becoming a very public military court-martial. The trial involved a Marine accused of viciously bludgeoning his girlfriend beyond recognition. She would require years of surgery before she resembled something even close to human. Even worse, she was a fellow Marine and extremely attractive (if the pictures of her published in the newspaper were to be believed). Her beauty, and the disillusionment that one of America's finest could commit such a horrific act, had aroused media coverage at a national level. I only knew what I had seen on TV or in the papers. However, I was certain that even though this seemed like a slam dunk for the prosecution, just one false step by the lawyers would be the subject of intense media commentary and, likewise, public outcry. I was lucky Kelly had been able to spare the time for our run.

"That's okay, Kelly. I understand. Do what you have to do. We'll catch up again when you're not living in a fishbowl." I rose from the table, gathered up the trash, and tucked the box with the remaining donuts into my gym bag. "And before you ask, the donuts aren't for me. Well, I guess they'll wind up being mine. Gunny loves jelly donuts. He can't eat them because he's dead, but for some reason, he can smell. After I torture him with the smell for a few hours, I'll eat them, one by one."

"And you're doing this because…" Kelly queried as we headed toward our vehicles.

"It's so fun to screw with him."

Later that afternoon, I settled down to actually read a non-Marine Corps book, with Gunny's beloved ESPN providing background noise. Luckily there was a football game on, and he was parked in front of the set, commenting and haranguing the refs' calls. He loved football, and if you thought about it, except for some upgrades—and TV coverage, of course—it hadn't changed much in almost fifty years. He seemed particularly fond of the Philadelphia Eagles (I'd have to check and see if they even existed in the 1940s), and his remarks seemed insightful enough that he might have played before the war. For me, there's a sense you get when you actually play a sport, and the commentary some sportscasters spout, though informed, is not the same as from those who have actually been there, done that.

"Did you play football before the war, maybe professionally?" I asked, looking up from my book. You really don't want to open that can of worms right now, do you, Abe? He's like a little kid. He's finally wound down from his donut tantrum. Let him alone and enjoy the quiet. It was a logical question, at least from my perspective. "We've got to figure out where you came from and what you did before the war. Should we start with looking up pros, cross-reference against those who went into the Marines, and see if any of the names sound familiar?"

He briefly acknowledged me with a grunt, eyes still glued to the screen, and waved me off with, "Next commercial." Well, that didn't take long. He's a guy, and he's getting too comfortable. He had become one with the TV.

I was just gathering my wits to fling back a pithy but blistering response when the doorbell rang.

"You are so lucky, brother. Literally saved by the bell." As I headed to the door, I wracked my brain for a veiled irascible comment I could deliver to the likely visitor, NB.

"Yes? What is it?" I asked before I even had the door all the way open. When I looked up, I was truly taken aback. *I've always wanted to use that word.*

Standing on the top step, big black rented limousine looming in my driveway behind her, was my mother, Pru.

So much for my relaxing weekend.

CHAPTER 9

Mother

I N *MATILDA*, Roald Dahl wrote that mothers love unconditionally, and that "even when their own child is the most disgusting little blister you could ever imagine, they still think that he or she is wonderful."

Though I respect Dahl's sentiment, he obviously had never met my mother. Mother. Not Mom or Mamma or Mommy. Mother. Growing up, I had envied other kids' pet names for their mothers. Heck. I envied other kids' relationships with their female parents, let alone the names they used.

Mother (Pru to her friends) had been born in the early days of WWII, almost exactly nine months after my grandparents had married. In a totally uncharacteristically impetuous move, her father, Jebediah Peabody Drinker, had left Princeton after the attack on Pearl Harbor, following his lifelong friend to enlist in the Marines. Jeb and my grandmother were already engaged, but the huge wedding being planned for June 1945 (after my grandmother would graduate from Bryn Mawr) was moved forward to a small tasteful ceremony and reception in January 1942. My grandfather shipped out to boot camp less than two weeks later, and my mother was born that October.

Mother "came out" at the Bellevue-Stratford Hotel in December 1960 and married my father shortly thereafter. Unlike my Granna, who had also married young but eventually returned to college and earned her BA and MBA, Pru had no desire to go to college, go into her family's business, or pursue a career. Don't get me wrong, I have no issue with women who want to stay at home as wives and mothers. I want to eventually have kids and look forward to that challenge. In Pru's case, however, marriage and children were just to cement her *perceived* place as a society mover and shaker.

I won't mince words; unlike her egalitarian, smart, and kind of quirky mother, Granna, my mother is the personification of the snooty bitch. Though there is no physical similarity, she reminds me of a Bette Davis character with her disparaging attitude and supercilious comments. Maybe my opinion of my mother is so negative because I've never quite measured up to her expectations, and admittedly, the more she snipes at me, the more I reinforce the behavior that had provoked the derogatory comment.

In my thirty years of life, there had been a plethora of derogatory comments. I guess I just relish being a horse's patootie.

No matter how much I achieved, no matter how hard I had tried to meet (let alone exceed) her expectations, I couldn't quite meet the mark. No, I couldn't even figure out what the mark was, let alone approach it. She had been somewhat easier on my older brother, JK, and, compared to her previous demonstrated behavior, had become downright indulgent in her dealings with my younger brother, "baby" Tad.

Mother wasn't always distant or censoring. When we were sick, she was attentive. When we (even I) suffered cataclysmic failures, she could deliver sympathy. But not for long.

She was like her mother, Granna, in many ways. However, where Granna could and would take a strategic pause, negotiate, and adjust her messaging, Mother was 100 percent my way or the highway.

Needless to say, I took the highway a lot.

As I got older and finally resigned myself to the fact that I was never going to be a pewter, let alone golden, girl in her eyes, I tried to figure out what her problem was. It had to be *her* problem, right?

Something motivated her to treat me like a second-class citizen from my earliest awareness. True, as I grew more comfortable with being a miscreant, I insisted on doing things that I knew would set her teeth on edge. I'm only human. Like, I'd deliberately mispronounce the word *detritus* despite knowing better and having been corrected a dozen times. Or though I preferred sweet German wines, I'd drink beer at the dinner table. Not only beer but declining a glass and drinking from the bottle.

It wasn't until after a particularly nasty confrontation with her, while I was on leave and bound for Okinawa, that I got an idea what her problem with me might be. Mother hadn't liked the Idiot and was certainly relieved when I divorced him. However, my divorce had added yet another arrow to her quiver of my lifetime failures.

The family, including my Granna, had gathered together for a farewell dinner (my father and grandmother's idea, I'm sure), when my mother made the "innocent" observation that she hoped my divorce wouldn't impact my chances for future promotion. She had been furious when I joined the Marine Corps and still nursed that grudge, and she continued to loathe the Idiot. It just seemed so disingenuous a comment that I snapped back with something like, "Now wouldn't that be good for you?"

In response, she and I exchanged "terrible icy glares," as my father referred to them, and she abruptly left the table with the comment, "It won't be a divorce that ends your career. It will be comments like that." My brothers, their wives, and my grandmother prepared to depart soon after.

So much for the party mood.

"I'm very disappointed in you, young lady," Granna murmured in my ear as she wrapped me in a farewell hug. "Haven't you figured it out yet? Do the math. You were born nine months after your parents married, and your mother could have done something about it when she found out she was pregnant. But she didn't. She had you instead and never looked back. Did you ever think that she might have had dreams, too?" With that, she turned and headed to her car.

That had gotten to me. She seldom chided, but when she did, Granna was a master. I closed the door behind her, a dejected and deflated warrior.

A year and some later, here I was on my front porch, confronted by the gorgon. I resolved to be upbeat and polite, remembering my grandmother's admonition. You better behave yourself. Gunny will take his cues from you, and if you're snarky, he'll be all over it.

"Good afternoon, Abigail!" Mother greeted, offering her cheek for a kiss. I dutifully did so and threw in a tentative hug to demonstrate (more to myself than her) my new resolve to behave daughterly. The hug obviously surprised her, but I saw something more than shock in her eyes. Was that a tear? "I had to come down to DC for lunch with a friend who was passing through and thought, 'Abigail's only a half hour away. Why don't I stop and say hello?' I hope I'm not imposing."

"Hi, Mother. Thanks for thinking of me. Please, come on in."

As she glided by me, the past came rushing back, triggered by the scent of her Chanel. It seemed like a lot of the bad things in my life were associated with that perfume, though there had been some good ones. I would strive to dwell on the good memories for now. Face it, Abe. The road to hell is paved with good intentions, and you are a weak and twisted creature.

Mother stopped short at the entrance to the living room. For a minute, I panicked, certain she had spotted the Gunny perched on the ottoman, eyes glued to his football game. How was I going to explain that one? When her head turned, obviously in her survey of the room (and my pile of 782 gear [personal combat equipment] stacked by the fireplace), I realized she was doing her usual assessment of my habitat and, just as usual, finding it not up to her standards. *Whew.* At least I didn't have to explain the dead guy watching TV.

As always, she was impeccably groomed and dressed, though she was obviously slumming since she had on a tailored pantsuit instead of her usual skirted business ensemble. So the driver couldn't get a glimpse of too much as he handed her in and out of the limousine? Stop it, Abe! Play nice. Despite the less-formal attire, she was still elegant and looked decidedly out of place in my currently messy (but clean) digs.

As she seated herself on the edge of my easy chair (afraid you might catch cooties, Mother?), the Gunny roused from his focus on the TV and, finally aware that we had a visitor, directed his attention to Mother.

"Wow. Who's this?"

"Mother, would you like some coffee or a glass of wine?" I figured if I prefaced my question with her title, it would answer his question as well as demonstrate my newfound hospitality.

"Coffee would be nice, Abigail, but I know you don't drink it. Do you know how to make it?" I would take that comment at face value and should be flattered that she remembered my preference was tea. The Gunny was on his feet, poised to participate in the discussion.

"Well, la-di-da. Doesn't think much of your cooking abilities, does she?"

"I make it for friends that drink coffee. I use a French press and grind beans, and they tell me it's pretty good. If you want to sit at the kitchen table, we could talk while I make it." Keeping up a conversation with a living person while regaled with comments by a dead one had become easier for me, but that was usually for short periods and/or surrounded by other people. One-on-one with my mother with the Gunny's Greek chorus in my ear was going to be exhausting.

"I'd like to freshen up first. I know where the powder room is." True, she had been here before I went to Okinawa, so she knew the layout of the first floor. I also knew she would be checking the bathroom for cleanliness or any indication of male habitation. Ha! Got ya! I had cleaned the bathrooms when I came back from my run with Kelly. Abe 1–Mother 0.

Gunny hovered next to the kitchen island while I busied myself filling the kettle and grinding beans. "Is she going to be here very long? I'd like some peace and quiet to watch my game. I'd prefer not to double-task watching TV and listening in on your conversation."

Where had he heard *double-task*? Sometimes it was like living in a badly written soap opera.

"What? This isn't any of your business. Sit down and watch your game," I hissed back.

"I think it *is* my business. After all, I'm here for a reason. Maybe she's the reason. And besides, she smells good."

"You'll keep your comments to yourself. This'll be stressful enough without you chiming in. If you don't behave yourself, I'll turn off the TV."

"What was that, Abigail? Do you have a visitor?" My mother had reappeared, glancing around the kitchen to see who I might be talking to.

Busted.

"Oh, I was just thinking I might turn off the TV so we can talk. But I like to keep track of scores, so I'll just turn down the volume." I headed over to the set, glared at the Gunny, and turned down the sound. He had repositioned himself between the living room and the kitchen so he could eavesdrop on my mother and me as well as keep track of the game. As I passed him, he put a finger to his lips, indicating he would be quiet. I wasn't confident he'd be able to control himself, and my only leverage was the TV. He was probably still irritated by the jelly-donut incident, so who knew what he'd try?

Mother and I settled down at the kitchen table, she with her coffee, me with a cup of really strong tea. Maybe I should have spiked it with bourbon. We busied ourselves with cream and sweeteners and then chatted about essentially nothing for a half hour. Who back home was doing what. JK and his wife were trying to start a family and Mother obsessed about what a future grandchild should call her and my father. Grandpa and Grandma sounded too old (and in my mother's defense, she was not yet fifty, so that didn't register on the age scale). Tad's wife, Chelsea, unexpectedly headed home to Boston as her father had suffered yet another heart attack, and this time, his prognosis was bleak. I tuned in and out, making a concerted effort to focus on her chatter, but I seldom talked to my parent and even less often listened to what she had to say.

I really *was* a miscreant.

I didn't share anything about my world of tactics-and-weapons familiarization. She wouldn't have understood and likely would have been uncomfortable with such a macho subject.

As our conversation limped toward awkward silence, I offered a subject that I knew was dear to her heart.

"How are things going with your charity projects, Mother?"

"People just don't seem to understand that there are others less fortunate than them," she responded, immediately warming to the subject. "Potential donors seem to want something to reward them for opening their wallets. Plaques. Mention in the newspapers. Sycophants. Perks at restaurants. I really could use someone like you to speak at these fundraisers. You always had the touch." My initial reaction was to bridle at the comment. But since I was on a be-nice streak, I actually considered the spirit in which she had made it. She wasn't belittling me. She was genuinely trying to be complimentary. What a concept!

"I really won't have much free time until after the company graduates next February, but I'll do what I can until then. I should have some solid downtime in between companies. Will that do?"

Gunny definitely had his own ideas on good works, and it was evident he was not impressed so far with my mother's role in that regard. "Do-gooders need to get to know the people they think they're trying to help. Instead of the poor in Africa, why doesn't she get familiar with the needy here? When was the last time she volunteered more than an afternoon at a soup kitchen? Is she willing to roll up her sleeves and work or just get contributions from fat cats?" I shot him a shut-up glance, but his eyes were fastened on the television. I wasn't fooled.

"That would be lovely, Abigail. JK does what he can, and even though Tad works with the poor, I don't think he sees the even worse side of their situations. People with not enough to eat or too proud to apply for food stamps. Young teenage girls getting butchered in illegal abortions. The list is endless, and my group just doesn't know how to get donors' attention. They're more focused on children in South America or third-world flood victims."

I was flabbergasted, and I guess my incredulity was evident. Typical Mother, she mistook it for disapproval or censure on my part.

"I'm not blind to what goes on in the world, Abigail," she sniffed. "But I notice and want to help the unfortunate around me. You and your grandmother never give me any credit for having any compassion. Just because both of you went to Bryn Mawr, you think you or that school have cornered the market on good works. You couldn't be any more wrong!" True, my grandmother had returned to Bryn Mawr a few years into her marriage and completed her degree, and I had attended college there because she was an alumna. However, despite its Quaker origins, Bryn Mawr's focus these days was more on high-caliber education than good works. It was a shame my mother attributed Granna's and my sympathies to an institution rather than a natural sense of caring.

"Well, isn't she the noble one," drifted over from the TV set. "Your mother might just be the next Mother Teresa."

How did he know about Mother Teresa? I surreptitiously flipped him the bird (did he know that wasn't a term of endearment?) and turned my attention back to my mother.

"That's not what I meant. I guess I never really thought about what charities you supported or why. I'm glad you're so passionate about your work. Really."

Somewhat mollified, she drained her coffee with a, "Surprisingly good coffee, Abigail," and rose to leave.

"Well, at least you got some kind of compliment, even though it was backhanded." As expected, Gunny's attention was avidly fixed on the TV, as if there were no way that comment had come from him. But he'd voiced exactly what I was thinking. Hadn't he?

"I'm concerned about you, Abigail. You seem distracted," Mother observed as she paused at the front door.

Distracted? That ain't the half of it. I live with the ghost of a WWII Marine gunnery sergeant who goes just about everywhere with me and has something to say about everything. If I told you about him, you'd be in line behind Dickey to have me committed.

"It's probably coming back from Okinawa and right into a training company. Kind of hectic, but it will settle down." Yeah, when I figure out why I got saddled with a ghost and how to send him back to wherever he came from.

Gotta admit, though, he kept me on my toes.

I walked her to the limousine (I was sure NB and her friends were glued to their windows with binoculars, and I would be subjected to interrogation at the earliest opportunity) where the driver waited to settle Mother into the back seat. There she paused, offered her cheek for a kiss, and—*surprise!*—initiated a hug. "I'll let your grandmother know that you're all right. Just a little stressed."

"Thank you. Please give her and Dad my love," I said.

As the car drifted down the driveway, Mother lowered her window, waved, and advised, "Don't work too hard, Abigail." And she was gone.

Gunny met me at the front door. He had had the courtesy to let me say my goodbyes to my mother in private. Maybe we were making progress on the boundaries issue, but I was not optimistic. It was like training a child on touch and no-touch areas.

"She doesn't have a clue about what you do, does she?" he exploded. "'Don't work too hard.' You're training Marine officers. It can't be easy! Ever! It has to be hard!"

As I closed the door, I smiled to myself. Progress with my mother. Acknowledgment from the Gunny that Marine officer training was relentless. For both sexes.

All in all, it had been a good day.

CHAPTER 10

Never a Dull Moment

ACCORDING TO *Merriam-Webster, dumb* means, among other things, "Lacking intelligence; showing a lack of intelligence; and not having the capability to process data."

Conversely *stupid* means "given to unintelligent decisions or acts; acting in an unintelligent or careless manner; marked by or resulting from unreasoned thinking or acting; lacking interest or point."

I would argue that junior officers, particularly second lieutenants or ensigns, are in no way dumb. By any definition. After all, they *do* require a certain measured level of intelligence to be accepted into a commissioning program or military academy.

Those commissioned through NROTC and OCS programs have lived and learned in a civilian world with regular forays into the military environment. Once commissioned, that occasional contact becomes daily routine for the foreseeable future. It is an adjustment, and it takes time. What makes sense in the civilian sector doesn't necessarily translate into the military, and it's only when they daily don a uniform after commissioning, and the military environment becomes their primary environment, that it becomes a daily challenge. Often it is a clash of two cultures and their associated rules and thought processes.

So junior officers aren't dumb, but they do tend to do stupid stuff.

When I was an officer candidate, I'd been a captain's wife. Since Idiot was the Mess Officer, I and the rest of the company saw him at meals as we shuffled through the chow line. My fellow candidates soon noticed the messmen's conspiratorial comments to me as they dished out entrées and potatoes, asking me how I was doing and if I needed anything. My platoon also noticed a female messman who, whatever she was serving, managed to splash it on me, or ladle a noticeably smaller amount than anyone else's on my tray. Her sneer when she did so was deliberately insolent in order to provoke me into making some kind of retort or even a physical retaliation, like smacking her (which I desperately wanted to do). Obviously the latter would have been assault and immediate termination from the program. Talking would have earned me a chit, written notification that I had committed some kind of infraction. Either way, she'd have won.

Here I go again. Off topic. Anyway the long and short of it was my platoon mates (and eventually the entire company) figured out the "Maxwell" nametag on Idiot's uniform was the same one stenciled on my utilities, and that somehow endowed me with vast and relevant knowledge into OCS mind games. This is where that civilian background with limited military frame of reference comes to mind. I really had no insight into the terminology, training, or expectations for officer candidates. The Idiot hadn't shared, and I didn't know to ask.

After PT one morning, we were finishing up an individual-effort exercise (it might have been a circuit course). Our platoon sergeant, Gunnery Sergeant Parker, barked at those of us who had finished (about fifteen candidates) to "get on our gear" as she stalked away to round up the other forty platoon members who were still struggling at the various stations. We were in perhaps our second week of training, and our initial platoon numbers had already dwindled from seventy-eight to under sixty. Though just short of our third week, we still had only limited frame of reference to what she wanted us to do. Fifteen heads looked toward me for guidance, but heck, I didn't have any more idea what she meant than they did. I thought putting on our sweats was too obvious (there was always a catch). So I stood on my ELB (Executive Laundry Bag), which contained my notebook and sweats (we had gone to PT after a first aid class). The rest shrugged and followed suit. As more platoon members joined our numbers, they took a look at us, perched precariously on our ELBs, and did likewise. By the time Gunny Parker returned with the last two stragglers in tow, she was greeted by the student platoon sergeant, at attention, standing on her ELB, reporting that that all were present and accounted for.

Though she seldom did so, all Parker did was laugh, but she didn't clarify what her expectations had been. A week later, we were finishing up rifle-cleaning in our squad bay when the platoon sergeant marched in and snarled, "Secure your rifles and get on your footlockers," before she turned and marched back to her office. We knew what securing our rifles meant, so we hustled to lock our weapons in our wall lockers. Since we were still unclear on the "get on" thing, we complied with the second part of the order by climbing onto our footlockers and standing at attention.

When she reappeared, Parker took one look at us and roared, "Why the hell do you keep doing that? What about standing by your stuff don't you understand?" Hands on hips, she glared at us while we repositioned ourselves.

That was the first in the long process of culture clash and adjustment. Not just terminology but a different way of thinking. As an SPC who had experienced my own personal adjustment challenge, I actually understood why our lieutenants didn't always make intuitively obvious leadership decisions.

I was looking forward to the shits and giggles Major Manheim had predicted. I just hadn't anticipated experiencing them with an old-school Gunny commenting on every misstep.

We started fieldwork during the sixth week of training with Platoon in the Defense. This exercise was to be our first overnighter field problem (in tents, of course), and the exercise required us to be in place, ready for instruction, by 0730. True to his promise (or was it a threat?) to "make real grunts out of Delta Company lieutenants," Dickey refused transportation in cattle cars out to the field. *We* wouldn't muster at 0645 to make what would have been a fifteen-minute truck ride to the site; *we* would muster at 0415 in order to step off at 0430 and start the six-mile admin movement to the outdoor classroom.

While I advocated acclimating lieutenants to the harsh realities of their profession, I also understood that they would be seriously tired when they got to their destination. Ridiculously early start time, distance to cover, and the sixty pounds they carried on their backs (not to mention the flak jackets and helmets they would wear and the machine guns and radios each platoon had to carry) would take their toll. It certainly wouldn't enhance their learning experience. However, all I could do was project a positive attitude that I didn't feel and encourage them to rest whenever we stopped for a fifteen-minute break.

Gunny was almost apoplectic when he heard that Dickey had turned off transportation in order to hike to the field exercise.

"What the f—heck is the matter with that idiot?" he bellowed in my ear. "Why walk when you can ride? You never turn down transport. Never. Nobody needs to practice being miserable. Believe me. I know. You're a motor head. Turn it back on!"

"No." It was 0400, and we were in my office. I backflipped my pack onto my back and groaned as I pulled on the straps to draw it further up onto my shoulders. It was heavy, but I could handle it and my flak jacket. However, I positively hated the Kevlar helmet that pushed my neck down until I looked like an upright two-legged turtle. A Teenage Mutant Ninja Turtle I was not.

"You've got to make him see that this is stupid." Gunny attempted to help me with my helmet chin strap, but his hands couldn't connect. How come he can move my sword and not be able to help me with my chin strap? *Hmm.* My chin strap was attached to the new-style helmet not in use during WWII. Or does he have to concentrate in a different way? Make a note to ask him about it. Maybe he can do more around the house.

"TBS CO knows we're walking to all problems. If he hasn't put a stop to it, I for sure can't. It's not illegal, it's not unethical, so

I can't protest. All I can do is make it as bearable for my platoon as possible." I opened the door to my office and headed down the hall toward my waiting lieutenants. "They can do this. You'll see. They're tough."

As I stomped down the passageway, Gunny was at my shoulder. "I know you can do this, Captain. But I'm not sure about your ladies."

"They are *not* ladies, Gunny. They're Marine officers," I snapped. "Just keep your mouth shut so I can concentrate on being miserable."

When I got outside, I observed my platoon, packed up and ready to go. The shortest of them was barely 5'2", the tallest almost 6', and Lieutenant Rawley, the student platoon commander, had already directed the tallest lieutenants to shoulder the radio and machine gun. Good thinking. I had worked out how we would redistribute gear at the first rest stop in order to accommodate the additional weight, but if Rawley had planned ahead for rotation, we'd employ her plan. We'd reallocate personal weapons (they carried rifles, I carried a 9 mm, but I wouldn't relinquish my sidearm), pack contents like MREs and sleeping mats and sleeping bags to alleviate the stress on those shouldering the radio and machine gun. Since the smaller platoon members were already carrying more than half their bodyweight, they would do their fair sharing of the misery, but we would relieve them of as much additional gear as possible. I wasn't exempt. I had intentionally packed the minimum in my pack so I could shoulder my share of the load. All of us would have to at least wear our flaks and helmets since personal protective gear was required to be worn at all times. Oh, and the gas mask. The flippin' gas mask. I knew it was an essential piece of gear, but its slamming against my leg every time I took a step about drove me nuts.

"This is bullshit, Captain. They're women. They're not cut out for this." I had to remind myself that Gunny's world hadn't included women in combat, let alone women Marines in combat roles. As a gunnery sergeant in the South Pacific, he had likely never seen a woman officer either.

"Give it a rest, Gunny," I muttered as we stepped off. As Third Platoon, we were starting off in the middle of the company.

I knew what all the lieutenants had had to go through in order to be commissioned, and this hike would be the first of many. I wouldn't be surprised, but I certainly hoped the Gunny would be.

And he was.

Neil's Fifth Platoon, last in line for the march, started their first chant with "Blue Suede Shoes," and the other platoons joined in. We would be regaled with a continuous stream of Elvis songs, sung as jodies, for the duration of our admin movement.

We reached the first rest stop forty-five minutes later. I dropped my pack and walked the line, encouraging my lieutenants to hydrate and helping Lieutenant Rawley redistribute weight among the platoon. I had to hand it to her. She had already organized redistribution of equipment and had enlisted her squad leaders to assist with her plan, so I didn't intervene with mine. When we stepped off fifteen minutes later, I carried a rifle (in addition to my issued 9 mm) and was satisfied that we would make this hike intact.

At 0700, we reached the training area and staged our gear by dropping packs and switching out helmets for soft covers. The platoon was hot and sweaty but motivated. As my lieutenants gathered around the student company commander, I wandered over to where my fellow SPCs were gathered (platoons had rotated order during the movement, and we were last in the formation when we reached our destination).

"Damn, Abe. Your platoon is a bunch of animals," commented Scott Zawicki, Second Platoon SPC. "And I don't mean that in a bad way."

Captain Doug Chavez, Fourth Platoon commander, was just as impressed but guardedly so. "No drops. And they're half the size of some of my lieutenants. Hope they can keep this up for another five months."

"They did okay, I guess," Gunny conceded. "It wasn't that far, but you did have one lieutenant that straggled a little, Captain."

"Gents, they're Marine officers. I appreciate your comments, really. But instead of expecting them to fail, why don't you just expect them to meet the standard and go from there?" I responded.

I had to hand it to my peers. They were great guys and didn't mean to be condescending, but positive. Since all were combat-arms officers, they had likely never served with women, let alone women toting packs and crew-served weapons and operating field radios. The sooner they just accepted my platoon as lieutenants and not female lieutenants, however, the sooner they'd treat them like their male counterparts. And they'd be able to unself-consciously laugh at the stupid stuff they'd do. Just like their male counterparts.

The other SPCs smiled and agreed, but before we could join our platoons, now seated around their instructor, we paused since Dickey and Bob were headed our way.

"Ah, geez. Spare me," Neil muttered.

"No salutes, Captains?" Dickey greeted us as we rose from our perches on fallen logs and rocks.

Bob was on that in a heartbeat. "Suh, we're in the field. No salutin'," he drawled. Bob always affected his Southern drawl in a deep baritone voice when Dickey was on his soapbox.

Dickey obviously had other business to conduct, so he immediately changed the subject and glared at Neil.

"Captain Giese, what is with the Elvis jodies? And I saw your entire platoon had blue material with 'Elvis' stenciled on it attached to their packs. Not very tactical." I, as well as the other SPCs and Bob, had noticed the blue tags and thought nothing of it. We had also sung the Elvis songs along with Neil's lieutenants. Leave it to Dickey to squash lieutenant enthusiasm, but hey, he was living up to his name.

Before Neil (who was turning kind of magenta around the mouth and eyes) could explode back, Bob jumped in again, "The Elvis tags are a kinda platoon identifier, esprit de corps thing, suh, and they come off 'fore the company starts th' exercise. And I was *not*"—this uttered in a really distinctive Southern drawl—"aware that there were approved jodies. Do y'all have a list of acceptable ones?" Bob's comments, uttered basso profundo, were innocently offered and maybe covertly disrespectful, but not quite, and by his words, he had publicly drawn the battle lines of captains versus dictator. We all knew that as XO, he dealt more with Dickey than the rest of us, and we appreciated that he had gradually interjected himself as body block between the SPCs and the company commander. Also thankfully in this instance, his intervention had afforded Neil time to get control of himself and bite back something that *would* have been downright disrespectful.

"We'll discuss this later, Bob," barked Dickey as he turned away.

"Stand down, Neil. They didn't do anything wrong. I'll handle this." Uttered in a lighter bass and without a trace of the long vowels and relaxed pronunciation of a Southern accent, Bob shot us a wink and sly smile and followed our earless feeder to a waiting HMMWV.

Dickey would return that evening to spend tonight and tomorrow night in the field with us, but Bob would return main side and hitch a ride back our final morning to make the movement back to the BOQ. His job was more logistical and behind the scenes than ours, and *his* additional duty was major buffer. None of us envied him his responsibilities despite our days being longer and more physically exhausting.

With Dicky and Bob safely out of earshot, Dave looked querulously at the rest of us. "Is it just me or does Bob sound like James Earl Jones meets Gomer Pyle when he talks to Dickey?"

We all paused in the process of shouldering packs, picking up helmets, and stowing canteens, exchanging looks as realization dawned—Bob was playing Dickey. Playing dumb but always a step ahead of him. Neatly done.

"God love 'im," muttered Dave.

As I walked toward my platoon, a voice in my ear remarked, "Your CO is a real piece of work, Captain. I think his butt is so tight, his mouth is really his asshole." Despite his inclination not to swear around me, the Gunny was obviously incensed enough to blurt out exactly what he was thinking. I appreciated his candor.

And he and I were on exactly the same wavelength for a change.

Much later that day, the SPCs hiked the short distances to where our platoons were settling into their various defensive positions. Each platoon was assigned a different zone that it would defend, and they were separated by as much as a quarter-mile. My lieutenants were emplaced in two-man fighting holes (three in one case, since the platoon numbered twenty-five) in lightly rolling forested terrain about a half-mile from the outdoor classroom and site of our bivouac.

SPCs, though not instructors, were expected to reinforce the lesson through visual reconnaissance of the emplacements, verifying that the student platoon commanders' actual layout reflected the plan that had been approved by the Tactics staff. Our inspections included checking whether the fighting holes were deep enough to shelter their occupants and sufficiently camouflaged that they could not be detected by the EIs (enlisted instructors) who were acting as enemy aggressors.

I envied these guys. They were usually operationally experienced infantry NCOs (non-commissioned officers) and SNCOs assigned to the Tactics department at TBS, and their role was to be the lieutenants' enemy, whether as aggressors or defenders. They provided a modicum of realism to the classroom lessons, but they didn't just assault emplacements or platoons on patrol. They made their assaults—usually winning, of course, because they knew the lay of the land—but before they moved on to terrorize another platoon or support another company's field problem, they gathered the students together to critique their performances. This is where they transitioned from being the enemy to an invaluable asset.

Assembling the platoon in a circle, the EI spokesman would cover the highs and lows of the lieutenants' performances, particularly that of the student platoon commanders and sergeants. They were true professionals and agilely walked the tightrope of maintaining respect for the lieutenants' ranks while honestly critiquing their performance. Where a billet holder had planned or performed poorly, they hit the wave tops in the more-public forum, reserving their sometimes-bitingly negative comments for one-on-ones with the recipient. Poor performers took note of their failures and learned from the experience, hopefully resolved to do better in their next leadership role. Those whose performance was praised basked in the positive glow for hours, if not days.

These guys got to experience, firsthand, lieutenants doing stupid on a larger scale than the SPCs because they got to witness the entire company's faux pas. Though they took their jobs seriously, I suspected when they had beers at Tin Tavern (the TBS enlisted club) after a field operation, they exchanged stories and had a good laugh at the lieutenants' expense.

As I approached, Lieutenant Rawley met me, prepared to accompany me on my inspection. As she handed me her layout, I studied her camo. Face and ears were striped green and brown with an artful touch of black, and I noted that despite the heat, her sleeves were rolled down and her hands covered in black gloves, according to tactical guidelines. I paused at the greenery festooning her helmet but didn't comment, making a note in my pocket notebook to take a good look at brush surrounding the platoon's fighting holes.

"Did you see what was in her helmet, Captain?" Gunny almost danced around us, a quizzical yet gloating expression on his face.

"I did," I muttered back.

Like the rest of the platoon, Lieutenant Rawley was accustomed to my talking to myself, and ignored my muttering. Dang it. Slipped up again. I was going to really have to rein in on my discussions with my invisible friend. After all, I was supposed to be a role model (yeah, right), and impressionable lieutenants might just start murmuring to themselves, thinking it was the norm for more cerebral officers (which I certainly wasn't).

We walked the defensive area for twenty minutes, chatting with the lieutenants and confirming their understanding of the scenario and their roles. However, despite the actual layout conforming to the plan, we could not locate the three-person fighting hole assigned to Lieutenants Campbell, Carter, and Casio. Couldn't see them, couldn't hear them. Since we still had another hour until the start of the daytime assault, I located myself in the center of the defensive area, blew my whistle, and called the platoon to rally on Lieutenant Rawley and me. Twenty-four heads appeared, to include the elusive lieutenants. I soon realized why I couldn't locate them.

"How're you going to handle this, Captain? Yell? Ream them out? They've got most of the basics right, but the devil's in the details."

"Stuff it," I retorted from the corner of my mouth. I should consider ventriloquism if the Marine Corps didn't work out. Maybe use a blockhead dummy that I'd call Gunny.

As they all took a knee around me, I critiqued their work and their understanding of the upcoming exercise. I was pretty impressed and said as such, happy to offer praise because the next message was not quite as positive.

"Lieutenants, you've done a great job digging, settling in, and camouflaging. It's obvious you've learned that the foliage on your fighting holes and in your helmets needs to blend in with the greenery around you." I gestured to the three amigos and asked them to join me at the center of the circle and to face their fellow lieutenants.

"Greenery tends to dry out and change color once it's cut, particularly in hot weather, and it can make your location obvious, but you *can* plan on it staying green around ten to twelve hours, less in heat. If you can dig in around fir trees, that's even better. That greenery usually stays fresher longer." All twenty-five heads nodded in agreement.

"BOHICA," the Gunny murmured, anticipating my next words. Bend Over, Here It Comes Again (BOHICA) was a common military term for warning that a previously experienced bad thing was about to recur.

"Some vegetation naturally stays...uh...greener longer. It screams 'Pick me! Pick me.'" Here I paused and turned to the lieutenants standing beside me. "Like poison ivy. Are any of you allergic? Because that's what you have in your helmets, and I suspect you dug your condo fighting hole in a pretty big patch since you blended in so well." Three pairs of eyes strained upward to view the garnish in their helmets.

"Shit," observed Lieutenant Casio. "It was my idea." Lieutenant Rawley looked like she wanted to be swallowed up in a sinkhole, *her* poison ivy-festooned helmet included.

Argh...We could do this. I got on the radio, let the corpsman know that we needed him at our site to assess the situation and take action. Hopefully, within the next hour, he could clarify what needed to be done.

For those of you who haven't watched *Sands of Iwo Jima* or any WWII or Vietnam War movie featuring infantry Marines, a corpsman is a Navy "enlisted man trained to give first aid and minor medical treatment." The Marine Corps has no organic medical support. It's provided by the Navy, whether as hospital medical staff or support to operational Marine Corps units in the form of field or line corpsmen. Marines value these men (and now, women) as they often mean the difference between life and death for fallen combatants.

If you're fortunate enough to watch a Marine battalion or regimental parade, you'll easily spot the corpsmen. They're the ones sporting small packs centered at the bottom of their backs and, more markedly, *not* carrying rifles. Their weapons (by this time) were 9 mm pistols, ostensibly to protect themselves and their patients. No heavy-duty firepower. No wonder then, that Marines, even today, guard these medical assets so zealously.

Our second evening in the field, the company prepared for a nighttime assault. That afternoon, the lieutenants had struck their tents, moved to a new location, and dug in again. This time, however, their fighting holes were long enough to accommodate lying prone but not deep enough in which to crouch without being detected. Their unused shelter halves were laid as a base with their gear on top. They'd position their ponchos over them once settled, with rifles at the ready, waiting for the enlisted aggressors' attack sometime in the early hours of the next morning.

Lieutenant Rawley and I dug out our fighting hole and set up our little piece of real estate along with the rest of the platoon, but we wouldn't spend much time there. She would be coordinating the defense with her platoon sergeant and squad leaders, and I would circulate throughout the evening, checking on lieutenants and generally visiting.

As Lieutenant Rawley and I chopped away at the drought-hardened soil with our e-tools (entrenching tools), muttered oaths and shimmying from the direction of Lieutenants Campbell, Carter, and Casio's emplacement indicated that they were already in position. And already itching, it would seem.

Since we were in the field and wouldn't return to garrison for two days, the afflicted lieutenants, Carter and Campbell, weren't able to change uniforms, apply cold compresses, or take warm skin-soothing showers. All the corpsman had been able to do for them was provide calamine and advice not to scratch the rash, thankfully limited to the backs of their hands right now.

As the afflicteds' muttered but muted oaths floated our way, Lieutenant Rawley stifled a laugh and paused in her digging. "I am *so* glad I'm not allergic but sorry they're having a hard time. I'll ask the platoon sergeant to check on them once things settle down, ma'am."

I nodded. "It's a good teaching point." I gestured toward our "workmanship" (for lack of a better term). "I think this hole is deep enough. Why don't I get our gear in place, and you go do platoon commander stuff?"

"Thanks, ma'am. Appreciate it," she said, grabbing her rifle and notebook and heading toward the assembly area.

Gunny materialized and peered down at me as I stowed our packs in the fighting hole and refastened my harness onto my flak jacket. I groaned as I climbed out of the depression. At least the platoon was a sufficient distance away from me, attentive to Lieutenant Rawley's five-paragraph field order instructions for the night. If Gunny said something argumentative enough, I'd be able to respond without their observing me. And I sensed he was going to make an unpleasant announcement.

"It's going to rain," he announced. "And the temperature's dropping. I wouldn't be surprised if it started sleeting after midnight. It's going to be *M-I-S-E-R-A-B-L-E*." He gleefully spelled out the last word to emphasize his bad news.

"It's only the beginning of October. I doubt it."

"I can feel it. I can smell it," he pronounced sagely.

"You're dead. I don't know how you can feel or smell. Okay. I know you can smell. You can smell jelly donuts and bacon. But I'm not so sure about the weather."

"This is God punishing you for your jelly-donut stunt, you know. Payback, as you say, is a mother."

"Oh, bugger off," I grumbled. "You're as funny as a root canal without Novocain." The put-down didn't faze him in the least, and his taunting laughter lingered in my ears long after he had faded from view.

He was right. Well, not really. The cold rain that started about 2100 turned into sleet by 2330. I knew (the lieutenants didn't) that our attack would commence around 0200, and I had made hourly rounds since sunset. At 2400, as I prepared to make my next and final pass through before the attack, I contemplated the click of ice on the ponchos above me and seriously considered staying put. I couldn't (all that role model BS I was supposed to demonstrate) and sat up enough to shrug into my helmet and field jacket, staggering up and out of the comparative dryness of the fighting hole. I still had to hunch over as I made my way from position to position, thereby (hopefully) limiting my profile to observant aggressors who might already be scouting the area.

At 0045, I duckwalked to the last fighting hole, that of Lieutenants' Lopez and Lee. I was surprised to hear muted, barely discernible laughter drifting toward me from under the ponchos. This wasn't like them, usually the most reserved and solemn members of the platoon.

They were an unlikely pair; Lee was a first-generation Korean American, daughter of two PhD parents. She was a kinda "homey," graduate of the University of Pennsylvania, and, like me, had become a Marine despite considerable parental disapproval. *They* had planned for her to attend law school, and she likely would, either postmilitary service as a civilian, or while still in the Corps, earning her degree through the funded law program. For now, she hoped to be assigned an MOS as an air traffic controller. I thought she'd be an excellent fit—cool, calm, and collected even when stressed, and possessed of a boatload of common sense.

Lieutenant Lopez was first-generation Mexican American, who spoke no Spanish as her parents had forbidden it to be used in their household. They were adamant that their children assimilate into American culture and felt that a bilingual background would be a drawback rather than a benefit. I disagreed but wisely (unusual for me) kept my opinions to myself on that one. Lopez was bright, optimistic, and, like my brother Tad, saw the best in people and their motivations. My leadership challenge with Lopez, in the next five months, was to help her adjust her expectations without becoming bitter or jaded.

I quietly announced my presence and slid into the fighting hole. As my eyes adjusted to the interior (we were tactical and not permitted flashlights), the lieutenants readjusted their places to afford me space to lie down on my stomach next to them. Their temporary shelter was not as deep as it really should have been, as they had started digging late, both having been assigned to stringing concertina wire. I made a mental note to talk to Lieutenant Rawley about assigning both officers from a fighting hole on a detail. One should have been free to start digging.

"What gives, Lieutenants?" I whispered.

"Lieutenant Lee was just telling me about a movie she saw last weekend called *Child's Play*, and she does the voices and everything." I could still hear the laughter in Lopez's voice.

"Don't let me stop you. Just keep it down." I glanced at the luminous dial on my watch, 0100. We still had time. "Go ahead. I'll listen."

So Lee continued her account of the maniacal doll, Chucky, and his relentless deadly progress through the movie. I had to quietly laugh. She really did have a repertoire of voices and probably mannerisms (which I certainly couldn't see).

"Damn. Don't they take anything seriously?" I heard in my ear. "If this were real, you'd be ambushed already." I knew I couldn't respond, but I didn't even have the opportunity before Lee sat up (which pushed the poncho up about twenty inches above the edge of the fighting hole).

"And then he kind of robot-walked over to the mother, waving a butcher knife in his doll hand, and said, 'Chucky says you're a bitch.'"

The heightened profile and movement must have attracted the attention of the aggressors, already in place, who opened fire (blanks of course) and swarmed toward the platoon's positions.

They were almost an hour early. Figured. The positive was that we would actually eventually get a couple hours of sleep.

Despite a dogged and pretty lengthy resistance, my platoon was overwhelmed. It was going to happen anyway, but they did put up a good fight. Of course, the sleet didn't help either defender or aggressor. What had fallen on the ground was at first slippery, then slippery and muddy. Within ten minutes of the assault, the defensive area had been transformed into a slimy churned-up mess.

It was a relief when the senior EI finally blew his whistle to end the attack and signal the aggressors' withdrawal. As they passed by the lieutenants emerging from their fighting holes, I caught snippets of laughter from both sides, with EI comments of "Well done, Lieutenant," and "Good fight," met with the defenders' responses of "We'll get you next time!" and "Payback's a mother!"

Lieutenant Rawley rallied the platoon sergeant and squad leaders, directing them to gather their charges and head to the assembly area for the EI debrief.

I heard, more than saw, them as they made their way toward the fly tent that served as our CP (command post). Their boots made peculiar *thwup* sucking noises when they managed to get purchase, but more often than not, they just about skated over what had previously been dry packed earth. All carried their weapons upside down from their shoulders in vain attempts to keep them dry (it had transitioned into an icy rain) and muck-free. All were more mindful of their rifles and SAWs than they were of their own faces, uniforms, and boots.

I lingered behind them, checking fighting holes to ensure there were no abandoned flares or other pyrotechnics. In this rain, I doubted they'd be usable but did it anyway, out of habit.

Second squad, responsible for starting the camp's fire once we turned administrative (we were no longer tactical now that our war was over), had wisely stashed dry kindling and firewood underneath the tent and had a healthy blaze going by the time I rejoined the platoon. I guessed they were my lieutenants, as they were all encased in mud from boots to helmets, their faces, except for areas surrounding their eyes, obscured by layers of mud and camo. They looked like twenty-five oversized lemurs.

I bet I didn't look any cleaner.

Our debriefing EI, Sergeant Chance (who looked remarkably tidy, by the way), was already seated, a bit removed from the lieutenants, shuffling papers and making notes by the light of a penlight held between his teeth.

"I'll be ready in ten minutes, ma'am," he managed to say around the penlight, so I doffed my flak and, as I sank to the ground, positioned it as a backrest behind me. Then I unhooked my helmet's chin strap with fingers stiff from the cold rain, removed the cursed turtle bucket, and quickly replaced it with a soft cover before my matted hair was detectable.

Keying on my movements, the lieutenants followed suit.

If not exactly comfortable, at least we were out of the rain and seated rather than prone on our stomachs and wet.

At the conclusion of Sergeant Chance's debrief, I thanked him for his support, then congratulated Lieutenant Rawley on her positive evaluation. As we moved from under the tent, Rawley was hailed by Lieutenant Lee, who was determinedly slogging back through the mud toward us. I excused myself so they could chat privately.

True, Lee's voice and movement from the fighting hole had attracted the aggressors' attention and triggered an early attack. However, she wasn't responsible for the platoon's defeat. Even if Lieutenant Rawley had had an additional two hours to prepare, the aggressors' victory was inevitable. I was pleased to see that Lee recognized her faux pas, though. I'm sure there was an apology in the offing.

The return trek was much easier than out as Bob had arranged transportation to haul our packs back to garrison. We still wore flak jackets and helmets and carried gas masks, and personal weapons, as well as the machine guns and radios, but lack of the packs made for an easier journey. Well, easier for all the platoon except Lieutenants Campbell and Carter, who squirmed under their utility jackets (the rashes had spread to their necks) despite the application of massive amounts of calamine lotion provided by the laughing corpsman.

At the first break, I reminded the platoon that the pack amnesty was not the norm and shouldn't be expected the next time we hiked back from a field problem. Apparently our reprieve was due to an early armory closure (1900), and we'd have to get the weapons cleaned and accepted before they shut down for the weekend. Lack of packs meant we could move quicker, and we arrived at TBS at 1630. Platoons recovered their gear from the trucks, slid out of flaks et al, and substituted soft covers for helmets. Lieutenant Rawley had them detour past the BOQ to drop gear before heading to the armory to clean weapons.

Like the lieutenants, SPCs swung by their offices in the BOQ to deposit packs and miscellaneous equipment. Unlike the lieutenants, who secured their rifles in lockers in their rooms, SPCs would turn in their sidearms at the armory when they met their platoons for weapons cleaning.

We wandered over separately to the armory, checked our weapons back in with the armorers, and then gathered around an empty cleaning station. Doug's "Ah…my flipping legs and feet are *killing* me" was answered by the rest of us with groans of concurrence.

"Hey, Dave," Neil opened. "What happened with your platoon's radio? And are you missing a couple of lieutenants?" He gestured toward Dave's First Platoon, dipping and scrubbing weapons in the cleaning vats directly in front of us. Neil was right. There did seem to be fewer than there should be. We all turned back to Dave for an explanation.

"I sent five of them in a POV (privately owned vehicle) back to the bivouac area to retrieve the radio." Dave's disgust was evident.

"Huh?" I said, "didn't you have a radio on the way back?" I paused to reflect. "Come to think of it, I noticed your student platoon commander stationed himself in the back of your formation when you guys rotated in front us. Was that to use our radio if he had to?" Whichever lieutenant was carrying the radio was expected to stay pretty close to his/her platoon's SPC during troop movements, administrative or tactical. Mine had always been in position, so I hadn't thought anything about it.

"They forgot their radio, Captain. *Your* platoon didn't forget *its* radio," Gunny observed over my shoulder. Did I detect suppressed laughter in his voice?

"Yep," sighed Dave. "After we made our first stop, I noticed I didn't have a radio within reach, and called the platoon commander forward to tell me what was going on. My damn hoopleheads left the radio back at the bivouac area. So my platoon commander got with the rest of your platoon commanders to cover. If he had told me sooner, I could have sent Bob back in a HMMWV to get it, and Dickey wouldn't have been the wiser. Now Bob is in *his* POV leading the idiot hoopleheads back to the site so they can pick it up and turn it in before securing. Oh, and they'll be cleaning machine guns for the rest of the platoon until they graduate."

Dave Kesselring hailed from western Minnesota and was the stereotypical Nordic—tall, blond, and slender, with piercing blue eyes and an even more startling vocabulary. That is, extremely profane to extremely erudite. Until you got to know him, he seemed aloof and reticent, even condescending, but we other SPCs were gradually getting to know the man behind the facade, one who had a keen sense of humor and a quirky way of looking at the world. *Hoopleheads* was just one of the monikers he called his platoon, which, usually uncertain where he was coming from, jokingly (and somewhat reverently) referred back to him as Herr Field Marshal."

"Hoopleheads," repeated the Gunny. "I like that one."

"Mine camo'd in poison ivy, then laid in it," I offered. "I've had the corpsman checking on them, but a couple already have enough rash around their ears and chins that it looks like I'm running a leper colony."

"None of them will be winning any beauty contests for a while," Gunny commented. He was really starting to bug me, and I vowed to retaliate. I was going to watch cooking shows all weekend just to spite him. Unless he had figured out how to change the channel to ESPN, of course.

"There'll be a run on calamine at the Exchange this weekend," observed Scott. "At least your platoon commander didn't change the platoon defensive layout for the first day at the last minute. Mine didn't think his setup was defensible enough, so where he had had interlocking fields of fire, he changed positions so one squad would have wound up shooting at the other two. We did a crazy quick repositioning and had just gotten settled in—not too dug in, but at least not set up for friendly fire—when we were attacked. It was a massacre."

"I had an entire squad leave their MREs back in the BOQ because they didn't want to handle the weight. They figured hots for evening and morning chow were enough to keep them going. When the hots didn't make it out last night, there was a lot of stomach rumbling while they waited for the attack. 'Surprised you guys didn't hear that and their pissing and moaning from where you were." Neil's platoon always had a different angle on things. "I didn't let the other squads share their MREs. Good lesson for next time."

As one, the rest of us turned toward Doug Chavez who, to this point, had not contributed his stupid-lieutenant experience.

He didn't disappoint.

"I've got a conspiracy on my hands and still wrestling with how I'm going to squash it. For two days, I've been finding Taco Bell tacos everywhere. In my pack. In my gas mask case. In my sleeping bag. I must have found forty tacos, still in their wrappers, in my gear." Doug had done an exercise with the air wing where he had acted as the infantry liaison. His fellow officers—all pilots—had call signs, and since Doug was likable, they wanted him to have a moniker as well. Being obviously Latino, he was christened Taco Vendor, or TV, and the nickname had stayed with him.

"Too bad my doofuses didn't know about them," Neil said. "What'd you do?"

"Ate 'em. At first, I thought it was one of you, but when I realized the rest of you were too far away to keep sneaking them over, I knew it was *my* doofuses. So whenever they were all together for their five-paragraph field orders or debriefs, I made a big show of eating and enjoying them. I am *so* sick of refried beans I could scream, but I'll figure it out. They'll pay. Do any of you know where you can buy cans of methane?"

Scott, always helpful, offered to find out where Doug could buy methane. Surprised (but not really) that he didn't get Doug's joke, the rest of us studied our feet, the weapons cleaning, even the rafters, rather than look at one another and laugh.

"Maybe a local farm?" offered Dave. "Does anybody know how to process pig shit?" It was like he had signaled an all clear, and we laughed (Scott joined in too, though he probably didn't understand what the joke was.).

"Not pig shit. Something...unique," Doug responded, deep in thought. He was already planning his revenge, and I was sure it would be more memorable than forty tacos.

With that, we broke up, each joining his/her platoon. It was time to resume being adults.

*****

"Those armorers accepted filthy weapons. We wouldn't have tolerated that on my watch," Gunny muttered as he accompanied me back to my office. "And Marines who did stuff like that taco escapade would have gotten court-martialed. What's happened to the Corps?" He sounded like he was on the verge of a meltdown. I found myself again wondering if ghosts could have fits. Too bad I couldn't consult a paranormal PDR (Physicians' Desk Reference) to get a read up on symptoms.

"Don't start on the old-Corps line, Gunny. Doug will handle it in a memorable way that those lieutenants won't forget. And old Corps just means you joined before me. Oh, and I believe the punishment should fit the crime."

"What's that mean to me?" His tone was wary.

"You've been particularly snarky the past couple of days. I see a vacation from football in your future."

His response was to snort and disappear.

When I got to my office door, Lieutenant Myerson was waiting for me. Aw, crap. Having enjoyed the time with my fellow SPCs and happy to be back to civilization and in anticipation of a shower, I had forgotten that my workweek didn't end with the company securing tonight. Since it was a weekend, and I was running remedial, I'd called 0730 as the start time. We'd meet in a designated classroom where I'd hand out the coordinate cards. They would calculate their routes, and then use their POVs to travel out to the starting point where I would launch them off on their second remedial experience. Seven had actually passed last week (thankfully), which left eight to still demonstrate their mastery of the subject by correctly identifying five of seven boxes at the end of six hours (remedial mastery was not quite as challenging as the actual land-navigation graded event). Obviously Lieutenant Myerson wasn't one of the lucky seven.

"Ma'am, can I get a ride out to the course with you in the morning? I kind of had a fender bender before we headed to the field, and my car's in the shop for repair."

Lieutenant Myerson was like herpes. The gift that kept on giving. "No problem, but did you report it to the student platoon commander? I don't remember her mentioning it to me." TBS policy stated that all accidents and traffic tickets had to be reported to the responsible SPC, no matter how trivial it seemed to the offender.

"Uh, no, ma'am. I forgot." She had the grace to look embarrassed.

"Put the relevant points on paper and have a copy of whatever citation you might have gotten to me when you get to classroom *B* tomorrow. We can talk then." With that, I turned to unlock my office door.

"Thanks, ma'am. See you in the morning," she called as she half-ran down the corridor to her BOQ room.

"Good grief, Captain." Guess who had reappeared, and where the heck had he heard *good grief*? Had he been watching Charlie Brown specials when he wasn't with me at work? "What MOS does she want? I hope it isn't motor transport. Her platoon would always be lost."

He had a point.

"Air traffic controller." Before he could explode, I added, "I'll make sure she doesn't get it. She has public affairs or admin written all over her." I smiled as I unlocked the door to my office and stepped inside, Gunny close on my heels, attempting to follow me in. I held my hand up like a traffic cop.

"I've gotta shower and change. You know the rule. And then we're gone. Why don't you pop into the guys' rooms on your way to my truck? You might get an education." From current and past experience, I knew that a number of lieutenants, particularly the males, had plans in DC tomorrow night. It was already 1930, and I suspected that by the time they showered and changed, they'd be heading to the Hawk for beer and food, then in the rack by 1200. It would be interesting to hear what their plans might be, and even more interesting to get the Gunny's take on them. I knew I'd get an earful.

"I know just which rooms I'm going to visit," he remarked as he disappeared from view. "First Platoon has some real operators." Operators? Maybe he was catching on quicker than I had thought.

We really needed to figure out who he had been and where he had come from, and soon. I contemplated whether I was living with the 1940's version of an operator and just as quickly discarded the notion.

I had a hunch that my roommate had been a nerd.

CHAPTER 11

Non Sequitur

AT THIS point, I've spent a lot of time talking about me and my job and only lightly touched on life with a dead guy—a mysterious WWII Marine gunnery sergeant with no knowledge of who he was or how he died. I did know something about where he was likely killed—Okinawa. Despite being a Marine, I actually *could* read, and the Corps really does ensure its people—both officer and enlisted—have more than a passing familiarity with their heritage. It's awareness of that heritage, and the desire to uphold your end of that long dress blue line, that distinguishes Marines from other branches of the Department of Defense. And Marine Corps leadership counts on that sense of obligation.

That's not to denigrate the roles and contributions of our sister services. They all have missions, responsibilities, and traditions they uphold and about which they are justifiably proud. We respect that. But the little voice inside my head still chants, even thirty years later, "We're still the best."

Despite my "osmotically acquired" knowledge, I knew it wouldn't be enough to unravel the mystery of Gunny's origins and death. I needed to access firsthand accounts, sources other than Marine Corps-approved texts. So I searched what we now call the web, which, in those days, was simply the Internet, and what I learned was more than unsettling. I didn't know where he had died, but I now knew it would not have been clean or neat. No banners flying and trumpets sounding. It would have been up close and personal and *horrific*.

The Battle of Okinawa, code-named Operation Iceberg, was fought by Marine *and* Army forces and initiated on April 1, 1945. It was the largest amphibious assault in the Pacific Theater and waged until June 22, 1945. Okinawa culminated a long campaign of island-hopping, its key objective to secure Kadena Air Base as a base of operations for the planned invasion of the Japanese homeland. The fighting was fierce, and casualties included not only Japanese and American forces but civilians, many of whom took their own lives rather than be subjected to the atrocities they had been told the invaders would impose on them. The Japanese propaganda machine was still alive and well even at this late stage of the war.

Since we didn't know in what part of the campaign Gunny had died, we talked instead about how he came to be in the Marine Corps. And we were no further along in the who and what department than we had been when he appeared more than two months ago.

I originally attributed the difference in his speech to the fact that he had lived (and died) almost a half-century ago, but as time went by, I noticed something else. He had an extensive vocabulary and comfortably employed it. Frankly, Gunny didn't speak like a run-of-the-mill Marine (myself included). His speech could be colorful enough, and he could string together expletives so inventively that even I was impressed. However, he conversed (and I mean conversed, not talked) like someone with education. When he wasn't making caustic comments—and as I have demonstrated to this point, they could be snarky and truculent—he was easily the most knowledgeable and insightful person, albeit dead, with whom I had ever spoken.

So how had he landed up in the Marine Corps? There was a draft during WWII, and despite common belief, the Marine Corps did draft men into its ranks for that conflict. It also increased its numbers during Korea and Vietnam through conscription. Had he been in college or the son of a wealthy family, he likely wouldn't have been drafted, particularly into the Marines, so I assumed that he had joined voluntarily. But why? And from where?

He had no trace of an accent, speaking what we were then calling Walter Cronkite English. With no Southern drawl or Midwestern "you betcha," I pegged him as either mid-Atlantic East Coast, or California-born and raised. But hey! I wasn't a linguist, grammarian, or even Henry Higgins. I just wanted some idea of where he hailed from in order to help him remember, so rather than recite every major city in the United States at him, I narrowed my search to what seemed the most logical.

Initially I was relentless in my investigation of his origins, but after a couple of weeks of twenty questions every time we had a quiet moment, he had exploded and disappeared for two days. During that time, he was just a disembodied voice that chanted "no see-y, no speak-y" at odd moments (usually when I was engaged with my platoon or fellow SPCs).

When he finally offered, "Can I come out now?" I knew he was bored with the game, and I agreed to let up on the interrogations. I had another ace up my sleeve, though—television.

When the weekly TV guide came out, I marked upcoming shows and movies relevant to WWII on the calendar and made sure the TV was set to the correct channel in case Gunny was going to be home during the day. We still hadn't figured out how he could move some stuff around, but I suspected that he could only move items that were associated with his time. I sought titles like *Guadalcanal Diary*, *Sands of Iwo Jima*, *Battle of Okinawa*, and *Okinawa*. Though I focused on WWII in the Pacific documentaries and movies, particularly Okinawa, it didn't stop there. I figured some of the female stars of the period—Rita Hayworth, Carol Lombard, Veronica Lake, even Katherine Hepburn—might pique something, so if there wasn't anything war-oriented on, I chose their movies. Conversely, I selected Philadelphia, Delaware, New Jersey, and California-focused travelogues if they were available. There weren't a lot of those, though.

I did have a heart. I left him to his Philadelphia Eagles if it was Sunday afternoon or Monday night.

The Saturday evening after we returned from the Platoon-in-the-Defense exercise, I was wearily scraping mud off my boots on my back deck. Despite the time suffering in the field, I'd been up since 0600 in order to conduct remedial land navigation (Ooh! Sleeping in!) and meet the lieutenants at the classroom. Thankfully six had actually passed today (and there was much rejoicing, at least on my and the successful lieutenants' parts). Two repeat failures remained, and you guessed it—Lieutenant Myerson was one of the two still standing. The other student was from Doug Chavez's platoon, and when I called him at home to inform him that his Lieutenant Patterson had failed (again), Doug stepped up to the plate as advertised and promised to take the two amigos out next Saturday. He also observed that the other SPCs suspected Myerson was going to be an ongoing challenge, and they were working out a schedule to stand in for me so I didn't have to spend all my Saturdays tromping around the training area. I'd take them up on some of their offers. I suspected Myerson, however, was Delta Company's *Flying Dutchman*, and she (and I) were doomed to wander the training area for eternity.

Or at least until the Company graduated the end of February.

Anyway, as I scrubbed the yuck off my boots, the Gunny appeared on one of the patio chairs and had the audacity to ask me how my day had gone.

"It rained. You know that. And rain means mud. And Myerson always gets lost, so I had to tromp through mud for an hour trying to find her."

"Well, did you?" he smirked back.

"You know I did. I couldn't leave there without her. Was about to radio range control and get somebody out there in a HMMWV to search with me, when I found her sitting in a dry streambed trying to figure out where the ammo can was. She *always* confuses draws with fingers, no matter how much I tell her to study the elevation numbers and the terrain. *Of course*, the can wasn't in the streambed. It was on the finger above it. *Argh!* To top it off, I had her shoot an azimuth to the staging area, and she got us back with no problem. I give up."

"You'll figure it out," he offered. "You always do." What? Support from Gunny Snarky? I needed to record the date and time.

"She has admin, maybe supply, written all over her. Anyway what did you do today?"

"I watched that movie you set up for me. I knew Canadians were strange but had no idea that beer was such a motivator. I laughed my ass off." Ass off? He had obviously been eavesdropping on either lieutenants or staff.

"What Canadians? What beer?" I had no idea what he was talking about. I had put the TV on channel 5 and told him that *Sands of Iwo Jima* was on at 1000.

"*Strange Brew.* I loved it. Thanks for the break from war and harlots."

Harlots? Katherine Hepburn was *not* a harlot. A little brazen, perhaps, but she only projected what Bryn Mawr was known for—the walk and outspokenness. Did I mention that my grandmother and I were Bryn Mawr alumni?

I obviously had not set the channel to the one showing *Sands*, but Gunny's enjoyment of what was one of my favorite movies was telling. He had a sense of humor, and he appreciated dumb stuff, as did I. "You're welcome." I was *not* going to admit I had flubbed that one.

"Your friend next-door has been sniffing around again," he offered, and I knew he was referring to NB.

"What did you do?" I dreaded the answer, but the perverse part of me wanted to know.

"I tossed your gas mask case around the living room and kitchen while she was 'casually' glancing in your patio doors. So she got a show of the mask case moving around with nobody throwing it. What a hoot."

Oh no. I would hear about that the first chance she had to track me down. I resolved not to go out or answer the door for the rest of the weekend. Thankfully during the week, I left before NB got up and got home late enough that it would have been impolite, let alone impolitic, for her to stop by late in the evening.

"Can you behave yourself for the rest of the weekend? I have to prep for a class on Monday, and I'll make sure you have a football game on tomorrow afternoon. Eagles aren't playing, but the Redskins are. It'll top off your comedic weekend."

Gunny clearly rooted for Philadelphia or New England if the Eagles weren't playing. I didn't have a preference (I didn't even understand football rules), but since Kelly, a Green Bay fan, referred to Washington as the Foreskins, I delighted in referring to his team as the Fudge Packers. Certainly not politically correct, but it irritated him, so I persisted in my reference whenever he denigrated Washington. "I can see if Kelly is available, and you two can dump on Washington for the afternoon. I'll interpret."

Obviously Gunny could hear Kelly, but Kelly couldn't hear or see Gunny, and since I had admitted to Kelly that I had a ghost, he had managed to make a couple of uneasy abbreviated visits to my house. I knew he still wasn't comfortable with the situation, but he was a good friend and didn't want to let something as trivial as my living with a dead guy interfere with our relationship. So I acted as interpreter if Gunny was around when Kelly visited.

"I like Kelly. Even though he's an officer...and a lawyer. And despite University of Chicago Law, not Harvard."

"Were you a lawyer when you were alive, or are you just a snob?" I asked. Sheesh. A Harvard Law-trained lawyer in my house? Tad would cringe. He was Rutgers. But maybe Gunny just knew of Harvard Law and considered it a standard. Who knew?

"Nah, I wasn't a lawyer. I do know that. Besides I'm too nice and honest to be a lawyer." There was that quirky sense of humor again. I had no idea if he was honest, but I would certainly dispute the *nice* adjective.

"Gag me with a spoon," I shot back as I quietly made my way upstairs to change clothes. My truck was in the driveway, so NB knew I had come home. However, I figured if I didn't make a lot of noise, she might assume I had been picked up and wasn't in. Feeble, I know, but I could dream.

Early evening, I sat at the kitchen table, reviewing the questions for Monday's guided discussion with my lieutenants. This was the first of four books from the Commandant's Reading List that we would discuss, and thankfully, Scott Zawicki, the Company

Academics Officer, had chosen an easy read—Jeff Shaara's *Killer Angels*. I had enjoyed and appreciated the writing the first time I read the book, as it not only accurately recorded the events at Gettysburg but managed to depict the characters as people and not just historical figures. I particularly admired Joshua Chamberlain and wasn't alone in my veneration for that scholar/soldier. A lot of my peers fancied themselves cut from the same cloth but not necessarily from the intellectual or academic perspective. Rather they admired his bold and audacious actions at Little Round Top as well as his prior and subsequent quiet and competent performance throughout the Civil War despite having been wounded eleven times.

Though I would thoroughly prepare for the class, my expectations were limited. I just hoped my lieutenants (1) had actually read the book, (2) would share their impressions of the tactics employed, and (3) stay awake for the hour discussion.

Gunny was also sitting at the kitchen table, but he was focused on the filigree that embossed my officer's sword. I didn't understand his fascination with that sword, but since it was like those in use by Marine officers during WWII, he could move it, so he had brought it over to the table when he joined me there.

"If you like it so much, and since you can move it, why don't you polish it for me?" I offered. "You don't leave smudges since you don't have fingerprints, but it could use a good buffing."

All I got in response was a glare and a flip of the sword to the reverse side where my maiden name, Abigail Drinker Rush, was engraved in script that mirrored the "U. S. Marine Corps" embossed on the other side. I was glad I had waited to have my sword inscribed. Had it been done when I was commissioned, it would likely have read "Maxwell," since I was married to Idiot when I entered the Corps. As it was, I had waited (more an oversight than deliberately waiting) until I was in Okinawa to have it engraved.

"Shaara did a good job describing the chaos of the battle without losing the storyline," I observed a couple minutes later. "Kind of the essence of the fog of war without getting bogged down in detail."

"Clausewitz."

Startled, I glanced over at him. He was, and wasn't, at the table with me. His hands remained on the sword's pommel, paused as if he were about to heft the weapon back into its scabbard, but his eyes were focused elsewhere, fixed on something, someone, or sometime other than here, now, and me.

Gunny had to be remembering.

I suspected I was going to experience Clausewitz's fog of war without actually seeing the sights or hearing the sounds that simple term conveyed.

"The smell," he murmured. "The smell. Everywhere. In your nose and clothes. Everywhere." His gaze drifted my way, and though he seemed to direct his next words to me, he was talking to someone from his past. "We can't get them. Not right. It's just not right."

Finally eyes closed, as if in prayer, he sobbed. "I don't need to go to hell. I'm already there." As if released from some kind of spell, he sagged forward, head cradled on his arms, now folded over the sword.

What I had previously known as a vibrant sassy ghost was transformed, now a husk of a man, defeated and haunted. The change was so overwhelming, so gut-wrenching, I found myself at a total loss of words for either the Gunny or those others he could not save or whose bodies he couldn't retrieve. History books could never convey the horror and carnage to which this man, and countless others, had been subjected. For a fleeting moment and second hand, I had glimpsed into the hellish abyss that had been the Battle of Okinawa.

I scrutinized the wilted Marine in front of me and realized he was not just a reluctant roommate and annoying sidekick. He had been a living, breathing human being who had died not only violently, but terribly. For the first time in over two months, he was finally real to me, and I was not sure how to process my thoughts and the turmoil his agony created in me.

I sat in the darkening room, watching over the Gunny. I knew he was dead and beyond my help physically. The anguish in his voice had spoken to me, however, telling me that I had a role to play in easing his pain. I didn't know how, I just knew.

So I just sat there, lost in thought, maybe even dozing off a couple of times. It was almost an hour before the Gunny stirred in what was now total darkness. I heard the rustle of his uniform and the clang of the sword entering its scabbard before it registered that he was with me again. He must have been aware of me as soon as he came back to himself. Heck, as a ghost, he had abilities I didn't share.

"Sorry, Captain. I kind of lost myself there." His voice was strong again, but raspy. Like he had been weeping.

"Not to worry, Gunny. And call me Abe. I think it's about time we cut through the horse shit."

I stood, and he must have sensed that I was about to turn on the kitchen light behind me. "Please don't turn it on, Abe. I just want it to be dark right now."

"Understood. Do you want to talk about it while it's fresh in your mind?" I asked, returning to my chair. "Sometimes remembering and talking about it is good for the soul."

"I don't know if I have one anymore, but I think I have to." He sighed. "Let me get my thoughts together. Can you give me a minute?"

"No problem. Take all the time you need. I'm here."

I'd waited approximately ten minutes when I heard, "It'll be jumbled." He was back with me. "'Kind of impressions as I remember them. And a lot of them shocking. It might help us figure out who I am and why I'm here, though."

"Go ahead. I'm listening." I knew this was going to be hard for me to hear, but it would be significantly harder for him to tell.

"The stench was unbelievable," he started at a slow deliberate pace. "You could smell the front lines before you saw them. It must have been what the First War soldiers saw and smelled at Verdun and Passchendaele. Two forces fighting desperately over a relatively small piece of earth. It was hell. It was worse than hell. The weather—rain—turned the slopes into a slanted mudslide. Just walking would have been tough, but who could walk?"

He paused to gauge my reaction. "Go on," was all I could manage. I was already transported back almost fifty years to a gruesome, bleak landscape I could never have imagined on my own. Even more frightening, his words, though matter of fact and emotionlessly delivered, were creating a slowly gathering whirlwind swirling around us.

"Both the Japanese and Americans made it into that hell. Sweat, piss, shit, and blood mixed with the stink and texture of the mud. You didn't want to touch it, but they made sure we did. We tried to dodge bullets and shells by burrowing into that unholy…substance…like some kind of demented gophers. We had to slither up that damned hill, shooting and sobbing, hoping enough of our buddies could get there so we could hold the ridge. We must have gone up that hill a dozen times, and eleven times those of us left got driven back down. And there weren't many left."

The whirlwind increased in strength, the banshee moans and screams rising, circling around us, like being in the eye of a terrible hurricane.

"And all the time, that fucking hellish mud and crud was everywhere…on your rotting clothes, your weapon, your face, and up your nose. You spat it out, since it got in your mouth when you dove to avoid incoming, but you just sucked it in, again and again. I can still smell it, taste it. It smells like my dead platoon. Too many of them… gone. And at the end of it all, too many of my Marines, my friends, never left that cursed piece of real estate they called Sugar Loaf."

Spent, he must have sagged back into his chair again. With his last words, the shrieking force abruptly crescendoed and died, and we were once again in the present, with only the ticking of the clock and the hum of appliances breaking the silence.

I was not an emotional person (my mother would never have tolerated that shortcoming in any of her children), but as I struggled to hold back tears, I wondered if this was why Gunny and I had been thrown together. Was I supposed to be some kind of messenger of what total war was and could be? Or was there something deeper, less obvious, but just as *profound*?

"I could say I understand, Gunny, but I can't because I have no concept of what it was like. All I can say is I'm sorry. I'm sorry this horror happened to you, I'm sorry Marines had to live and die like that. I'm so, so very sorry."

My words were met by silence.

126

I desperately hoped I hadn't overstepped my role as audience or inadvertently said the wrong thing. I waited, barely breathing, for a reaction.

"I appreciate that, Abe. Thank you for listening," was the weary response. I heard him gather himself and push back the chair. "I think I'll leave for now. I have a lot to think about."

I waited five minutes, then rose to turn on the light. As my eyes adjusted to the brightness, I noted that the Gunny was gone. My sword still lay on the table, but it was not completely sheathed, despite the sound I had noted earlier. Instead, the scabbard was pulled back enough that I could read my name engraved on the blade.

What was it about that sword? Why was he so fascinated with it?

*****

The next afternoon, Kelly showed up with beer and wine coolers (for him and me) and jelly donuts (to tease the Gunny).

"Is he here, Abe? Are we gonna watch the game together?" Kelly said as he plopped the donut bag on the counter and reached for a bottle opener for the beer. "I've been thinking. I'm not really creeped out with this. It's kind of...cool. And I really need the break from reality."

Kelly's case had ended with a conviction for the accused Marine (a victory for Kelly's team) but a black eye for the Marine Corps. True, the case against him had been airtight and well argued, but whenever a Marine committed an atrocity, particularly to another Marine, the Corps loses some of its sparkle. The press had had a field day with the trial, judging and condemning the accused even before opening arguments. The victim, after all, was a beautiful and vivacious young woman, savagely beaten and left for dead in her barracks room. The Corps didn't consider the guilty verdict a victory. Instead, it blamed its corporate self over how it had failed *both* of its service members. Kelly, though victorious as a lawyer, shared in kicking himself for our lack of training in not seeing the signs of the young Marine's mental state or providing a safe haven for him, or his victim, to vent. We all knew it could happen again. However, we needed to anticipate and provide resources *before* the act instead of scrambling to understand afterward.

Gunny hadn't made an appearance that morning, but I suspected/hoped that hearing Kelly's voice and a football game on TV, not to mention detecting the siren smell of jelly donuts, he would join us.

I had no intention of sharing all the details of yesterday's developments with Kelly. I'd provide the Sugar Loaf information without revealing the angst and anguish that had accompanied its disclosure. Since Kelly was pretty perceptive, he would guess that this was a sensitive subject and would refrain from badgering me about how I had obtained the information. It was yet another thing I appreciated about him.

"He's around somewhere, I guess. He gets bored when I'm doing classwork and goes off somewhere and plots his next reign of terror." I went on to relate yesterday's NB incident, and Kelly roared with laughter, imagining what might have been the look on her face.

As Kelly's laughter faded, Gunny appeared and headed over to his favorite football-watching chair.

"So now he's in on the harassment too, I see," he grumbled, gesturing toward Kelly, draped over the couch, guzzling beer and munching a jelly donut with noisy lip-smacking appreciation. Yuck. Jelly donut and beer. Even for a lawyer, he had serious issues.

"He's here, Kelly, and he's pissed about the jelly donuts. Why didn't you just get bacon-flavored while you were at it?"

Kelly guffawed and saluted what he knew wasn't really an empty chair with his almost-empty bottle of beer, and we all settled down to watch the game.

Later that night, I pulled out a couple of my Marine Corps history books and searched for the Battle of Okinawa, Sugar Loaf Hill in particular. Knowing what I knew now, the words, while terrible on paper, could in no way capture the horror, helplessness, and despair of the actual six-day ordeal.

As I turned out my bedside light, I wrestled with what our next steps should be.

We didn't have a destination yet. But I guess we had a direction—find out the units that had fought at Sugar Loaf and if any of the reported dead had been gunnery sergeants. If so, names? It was a beginning.

And the clock was ticking. I *knew* it.

CHAPTER 12

The Job Doesn't Get Any Easier... But It Can Be Fun

DESPITE THE weekend's angst, Gunny was raring to go on Monday morning. Maybe sharing his experience in the abattoir that was the Battle for Sugar Loaf Hill had been therapeutic for him. Can ghosts undergo or benefit from therapy? Or maybe he thought we had made progress in our search for his identity. True, knowing his rank and where he had died would help me in my search for his name, but where could I find the time? Weekdays, training stretched as late as 2000, and Lieutenant Myerson's land-nav challenge took up the bulk of my Saturdays, so I wasn't quite in a position to either make phone calls or visit archives.

Then again, he might just have enjoyed Sunday afternoon, watching football with Kelly (despite the jelly-donut nudge) and taxing me to the max in my translator mode. Fun for them. Exhausting for me.

Unlike the Gunny, I didn't greet Monday morning with any sense of anticipation. It was more like dread. I had no idea how our *Killer Angels* discussion would play out. Though I was well prepared, I had never conducted a guided book discussion before and wasn't really confident in my ability to not only cover the material but hold my lieutenants' attention. What if they were talked out in fifteen minutes? How would I fill the other forty-five allotted for the class? Should I plan on charades to kill time, or should I just dismiss them early?

At 1600, I entered our assigned conference room with a high degree of trepidation. I was sure my Charlie shirt (short-sleeved khaki wool shirt) was sweated through to the outside despite the dress shields sewn into the underarm seams. When I felt droplets down my back, I prayed the lieutenants I passed on the way to my chair didn't note it. Never let 'em see you sweat. Right. Easier said than done in an overheated room wearing wool and sweating bullets. Give me fifteen minutes, and I'd smell like a wet dog.

I could not, for the life of me, figure out why this was causing me so much torment. As a fundraiser for my mother, I had addressed auditoriums full of distinguished and discerning potential donors and never batted an eyelash. Even during my limited time as a management consultant, I'd facilitated discussions with high ranking military personnel and government officials and done so with ease and confidence. Heck, mastering the O-course was nothing compared to facing the twenty-five faces turned my way as I entered the conference room.

Being good and respectful officers, they all rose and stood at attention as I made my way to the seat allotted to me and waited until I signaled them to be seated. I almost didn't, so focused was I on getting into and out of this situation that I forgot they were standing, waiting for me, until I looked up from organizing my materials.

"At ease. Please take your seats." At least I got that out right as I settled into my chair and prepared to fail.

"Before we begin," I started, "I'll remind you that we're here to discuss the why and how of Gettysburg, not refight the Civil War." Twenty-five heads nodded in the affirmative. That was good. "That said, what did you think of *Killer Angels*?"

"I think it had too much of a Union focus, ma'am. It was well written, and I really got into it, but there should have been more from the Confederate perspective," volunteered Lieutenant Beauchamp. She was from Charleston, and though not exactly a belle (well, she had gone to Sweetbriar), she did tend to personify her Southern roots. Not to the point of "The South Shall Rise Again," but you were never in doubt from what part of the country she hailed.

"With all due respect, what's that supposed to mean?" challenged Lieutenant Morrow. "Did Shaara provide enough for us to get into their heads? I think he did."

"We needed more insight into Lee. There had to be a reason he assigned Longstreet the charge on Cemetery Ridge and not A. P. Hill. I think Longstreet begged for the honor, and Lee agreed in order to shut him up. Hill would have made sure he was successful. Instead, Shaara focuses on what he *says* were Longstreet's misgivings, but I think Longstreet set Lee up for failure." Beauchamp's perspective, though deviating from documented facts, was certainly tenacious.

Too late, I realized that Beauchamp had either been steeped in or certainly advocated the Lee apologists' Longstreet-stomping school of history.

However, before I could intervene, Morrow diffused the situation with a noncommittal, "I disagree, but that's why we're here, isn't it? To discuss the different perspectives."

The other officers visibly relaxed, and Beauchamp, realizing she had been neutralized, settled back in her chair with a barely suppressed scowl on her face. I'd have to chat with her about controlling her facial expressions as well as her tendency to argue rather than discuss. This wasn't the first time she'd escalated a benign situation into a confrontational one. And Morrow needed to be reminded that, in my experience, when "with all due respect" prefaced a statement, it was usually followed by a disrespectful one.

Catastrophe averted, for the next hour and a half, my lieutenants—almost all of them—offered their positive opinions on Shaara's writing, his portrayal of the characters, and the way he made history come alive. Those that didn't initially speak up were quick to jump on the other questions I threw at them.

I was admittedly impressed. They had actually read the book, and the discussion was so lively that I extended our discussion for almost another hour at their request.

At 1745, I dismissed them so they could get to evening chow before the mess hall secured but asked Lieutenant Morrow to hold up before she cleared the hatch.

"The Twenty-Fourth Michigan was under the command of a Colonel Henry A. Morrow at Gettysburg. Any relation?"

"My great-grandfather, ma'am."

"You have big shoes to fill, Lieutenant. By all reports, he was a fine commander. Wounded, captured, and escaped on the Fourth of July."

"You know your Civil War history, ma'am!" I didn't, but Gunny did. He'd noticed her last name on my platoon roster and asked me where she was from. When I answered that she was from Michigan, he'd told me about Colonel Morrow. Another clue that Gunny might have been a history teacher before the war.

"Thanks for backing off on an argument with Lieutenant Beauchamp. Company is secured, and you need to get to chow."

"Aye, aye, Captain." She mimicked a salute and turned toward the hatch. There she paused, turned back toward me, and announced, "And, ma'am, remember Fredericksburg."

"Get out of here," I shot back with a laugh.

Neil's door was ajar as I passed by, so I stuck my head in to see what he was up to, and surprised to see Scott Zawicki and Doug Chavez were with him. All three were already in civvies, guzzling bottles of the cheap beer Neil kept in his minifridge. I had forgotten that my discussion group had gone longer than scheduled, so the company had to have been secured since 1700.

"Hey, Abe. Something to drink?" Neil offered. "It's about time you got done." Neil gestured toward his fridge, which I opened, looking for a wine cooler. Ah! One left, which I grabbed. Despite all the references I've made to beer-drinking so far in this story, I'm not really a devotee. And when I *do* drink it, it wouldn't be Neil's brew (now I sound like a Dos Equis commercial). "Scott couldn't leave until all SPCs reported that they'd finished. Dave already left. Probably going to a lederhosen fitting." We all chortled at that one, the words conjuring up an image of tall, seemingly haughty Dave in leather shorts and Tyrolean hat.

"Or his field marshal's baton," I observed to another round of laughter.

I took a deep slug of my cooler, grateful I wasn't sharing the others' "Neil swill." A couple of weeks ago, Neil had noticed that I either didn't accept a beer or didn't finish it, and asked if I didn't drink. I'd confessed I preferred plain sweet German wine, spritzers, or coolers, and he'd surprised me a couple of days later with the coolers. I knew Neil's was a single-income family, hence the cheaper beer, but he deserved better if he was going to continue to host our ad hoc gatherings. I made a mental note to pick up some decent beer for the guys when I got wine coolers for myself. That or they'd all (to include Bob) die of ptomaine before the company graduated.

Scott tossed his empty bottle into Neil's trash can and retrieved another from the fridge. "It sucks to be the Academics Officer," he sighed. "I barely made it through the book myself, and leading a discussion about it? That was a ball breaker." Surprise, surprise! Scott made it through an entire book! He looked my way. "How did your discussion go? You guys were in there an extra hour. What did you talk about?"

"What color nail polish is best when you're tactical. What kind of moisturizer to use after you take off your camo stick. Which is better, waxing or shaving?" I waited for Scott to take the bait, and by the stunned expression on his face, I could see he was wrestling with how to respond. I decided to take pity on him. He *was* a good guy. Just a little dense.

"What do you think we talked about? The book. They read it. They liked it. They had a lot to say." I was not going to volunteer what an uncomfortable start we'd made.

Neil choked on a swig of beer. "You had him there, Abe." He turned to Scott. "Admit it. You kind of thought they were just doing girl talk, didn't you?"

"Nah. I thought they might not have read the book, and she had them doing bends and mothers for the extra hour." Scott slumped back in his chair. "Sometimes you're scary, Abe."

Huh?

"Anyway, let me tell you what my guys did this time. What does Dave call his platoon when they screw up? Hoopleheads?"

Oh boy. Doug must've had a challenge with his platoon, and we were about to hear about it. Neil smacked his lips in anticipation. Scott and I nodded and settled back to hear what Doug's bad boys had done this time.

The Taco Vendor incident wasn't the only stunt Doug's criminals had pulled. Delta Fraternity from *Animal House* had nothing on these guys. It seemed like every week, there was something they had done, either singly, as a squad, or as a platoon, that merited a caustic comment from Dickey or heart-to-heart conversation with Doug. And that was just the stunts Dickey heard about. Thankfully Bob did a daily scrub of the reports of their antics and forwarded only the most outrageous onto Dickey for information. Doug and Bob spent a lot of time together, with and without the guilty lieutenants, but were slowly making progress on curbing the platoon's rowdy behavior. They weren't bad guys and would eventually transition into fine officers. They just did some stupid stuff.

"Only four of the sixty-five of them read the book. Four. And I don't think they really *read* the book. I think they just glanced at chapter headings. I listened to them dance around my questions for around fifteen minutes, and then I started asking them about what insight the book gave them into the Battle of Antietam. Stuff like, what do you think of Jackson's heroic stand on the Confederate right flank which earned him the nickname Stonewall? And what do you think of Joshua Chamberlain's charge over Burnside's Bridge? Hell, it was bad enough about Jackson—he was already dead—but they even got the battle wrong. The book was about *Gettysburg*, damn it."

Throughout his monologue, Doug had gotten more noticeably agitated to the point that he was as red as a beet (seemed to be a common characteristic of most of the men, living and dead, in my life), and his neck muscles bulged from clenching his jaw. Laid-back Doug was certainly not laid-back now. If he weren't so nauseatingly fit and healthy, I'd fear he'd stroke out. And *that* seemed to be happening a lot around me these days.

By this point, we were rolling in our chairs, Scott laughing so hard he slid out of his and onto the floor.

"And?" he finally gasped.

Doug swallowed his mouthful of beer before answering. "Henshaw tried to deflect the discussion to Chesty Puller and his role in WWII. Not only the wrong battle but the wrong war! It was pathetic. At 1630, I called a halt to the idiocy. I couldn't take it anymore."

"So what memorable teaching point are you going to do this time?" I asked. Just as Doug's platoon was inventive in their transgressions, he was even better at retaliation. His "lessons" always focused on the infraction and a suitable response. Usually it was a private counseling, but when he did publicly react (well, publicly within the platoon), it was targeted on the offense so that the guilty parties understood how far was too far. He never openly aired their dirty linen in front of the rest of the company's lieutenants (SPCs were a different matter, as he knew we wouldn't share the latest escapades with our own platoons), and he never put his guys in jeopardy.

Doug's response to the Taco Vendor incident had been to replace both of his platoon's hot chows during the last overnighter with refried beans. Each meal featured four gallons of refried beans and nothing else. I don't know how he arranged it with the chow hall. I don't know where he got that many refried beans or if he and his sainted wife had made them (Doug was not standoffish about "women's work" and was probably the better cook.). All I knew was his guys had looked kind of green on the hike back.

"We're going to do the discussion again. But this Saturday night at 1900. In dress blues. My wife's gone this week. I have all the time in the world to be a good role model."

"Good night, Chesty, wherever you are," Neil guffawed. With that, our little group broke up, the guys to home and me to my office to change.

I enjoyed these impromptu get-togethers, and I think the guys did too. The first few had been awkward as none of them had ever served with a woman before, and they danced around profanity or any comment that might be construed as sexist. Neil's sense of humor and outgoing nature had been the catalyst for our loosening up, and I attributed my I-will-take-no-prisoners-if-you-say-something-stupid perspective as the breakthrough.

About three weeks before, Bob had called an impromptu SPC meeting in his office. I can't remember the purpose, but I do remember Scott making a comment about the "guys and girls" in the company.

The room fell eerily silent, and I watched the other captains' eyes shift my way while they fussed with notebooks and coffee mugs.

"What did I just hear you call the lieutenants?" Bob queried innocuously, leaning forward over his desk. Uh-oh. His voice was the calm before the storm.

Before Scott could respond, I commented, "That's a really cool watch, Scott. I don't think I've ever seen one quite that…big."

As usual, Scott was oblivious to the comment he'd made as well as why I as asking about his watch.

"It's a diver's watch, Abe."

"Don't the recon guys wear them?" I continued.

"Yeah!"

"I've heard that the size of the watch is inversely proportional to the wearer's manly endowments. I don't have any direct knowledge, so I was just asking."

The room erupted into raucous laughter while I just sat, innocent and smiling. Scott glanced around at the other captains, struggling to figure out the source of the amusement when it finally hit him. You could actually *see* realization dawn on his face, which promptly turned a lovely shade of pink.

Ever the good sport, he turned to me and admitted, "Good one, Abe. I got it." He turned toward Bob and clarified, "The *lieutenants*, Bob. The *lieutenants*."

Something had started at that meeting. Call it camaraderie, bonding, whatever. I *do* know, though, that our signal phrase for stupid had become "big watch."

We used that term a lot when referring to Dickey.

Okay. I digressed (again). I do have a habit of doing that. Just thought it was time to explain how our group dynamic had transitioned from proper and professional to at ease and professional.

As I made my way back to my office, with armpits that had dried out at least an hour ago, Gunny fell into step next to me.

"I told you it'd be fine," he said. "With all the sh—er, stuff you have to do, why'd you think this was going to be so hard? I popped into a couple of the other platoons' discussions, and it was like their SPCs were pulling teeth. Your lieutenants seemed to enjoy themselves, and you got comments out of them that the other platoons probably didn't even think of. But then, I think your platoon actually read the book. And I gotta hand it to Captain Chavez. Next time, his platoon will probably memorize the reading assignment."

"Doug's certainly one of a kind. His guys are making progress, but it seems like it's baby steps. You're right, though. I don't know why I was so nervous. I guess I forget that some of the things I learned as a civilian might have some…relevance…to being a Marine. I get so focused on needing to do the hey-diddle-diddle-up-the-middle stuff, that I kind of bury what I was before. Does that make sense?"

"I get it. I don't know why I understand, but I do." He paused as I unlocked my door. "And I know you're going to change clothes, and I'm not allowed to watch, so I'll meet you at your truck."

With that, he abruptly vanished, and I was left alone in the passageway, marveling that I had not only been successful this afternoon but actually gotten an acknowledgment from Gunny Casper that I had done something right.

My happiness was short-lived. When I pulled into my driveway at 1840, I saw NB's front door open and a flash as she sped toward my truck. Well, maybe more a staggering flash. It was, after all, almost 1900, and I think she started happy hour each day no later than 1500.

Now what? Gunny had been with me all day, so she couldn't have heard any of my "visitors," and if she had, that meant I *did* have a big-ass rat or snake knocking around my house. Then again, she might want to report the floating gas mask she had sighted on Saturday. I'd managed to avoid her yesterday, saying goodbye to Kelly inside when he left and playing hermit for the rest of the evening.

Resigned to my fate, I got out of my truck, counted to ten under my breath, and turned to face her.

"Oh, Abigail," she trilled, her breath heavily redolent of gin and Cheez Whiz. "I have something for you." With that, she fumbled in her skirt pocket and drew out a card, which she playfully withheld from my proffered hand. "The most regal, and I mean positively *regal*, lady showed up this afternoon. Driving a Rolls-Royce. No chauffer. *She* was driving. And even though she was casual, she was so...*regal*. No other word to describe her. And how...nice!"

With that she finally relinquished the card. I didn't have to look at it to know who had come calling. My visitor had been Winifred "Fred" Shippen Drinker, a.k.a. Granna. Who else did I know who would drive her own Rolls, in this case, all the way down from Philadelphia, unannounced? Granpa had bought her that Rolls for their fortieth anniversary, and being a bargain hunter, he had bought it very used, so I had no idea how old it was. But it had obviously impressed NB, old or not. Granna's "uniform" was casual. When not in a board room (where she reluctantly conformed to the CEO image of a severe business suit), she gravitated toward khakis and a jean jacket. In cold weather, she inclined toward corduroys and a sable that had been passed down from *her* mother. *That* my great-grand-father had won in a poker game, so who knew how old it was either. It was understood that when Granna passed on or tired of it, my mother would inherit it, and then I, in turn, would be burdened with the old smelly fur. It was really warm, though.

"Thank you, Mrs. Nolan. Did she say anything?"

"Just hello and did I know when Abe got home? She made a point of calling you Abe, not Abigail. Since you keep such odd hours, I didn't want to commit you to a time, and offered her a cup of tea at my house if she wanted to wait. She was so *polite* but said she'd head back to Philly (that's what she said, by the way) before the traffic got too bad. She wrote a note on the back."

I was certain NB had already read the note, but she hovered over me, hoping I'd read it, and she'd be able to pass my reaction onto her cronies. Or maybe even have a heart-to-heart conversation with me on what she probably thought was my wealthy (*not*) family. *That* certainly wasn't going to happen.

"Again, thank you, Mrs. Nolan. You've probably guessed that she's my grandmother. I'll make sure to let her know that you passed on her message. Now if you'll excuse me, I've had a long day." With that, I scurried up to my front door and fitted the key into the lock. Miracle of miracles, she didn't follow.

I turned to wish her good night from my door. As she tripped toward her own entrance, her response was surprisingly, "Good night to you too, Abe."

Her door closed with only a whisper of its usual resounding *thunk*.

Throughout the exchange, the Gunny had hovered just at the edge of my peripheral vision and remained unsettlingly quiet. Inside, I dumped my laundry bag on the foyer floor (today's uniform needed dry cleaning, big-time), and he moved to his football (and kitchen) watching chair. He must have sensed that I'd head to the kitchen for a glass of wine before going upstairs to shower and get ready for bed. And he was right.

"So...what was her message?" he queried casually, as I sat down at the table with an extremely large water glass of cheap white wine.

I picked up the card from the counter where I'd left it and turned it over. Granna's bold, distinctive fountain-pen scrawl dominated the creamy background. I gulped and read aloud, "I want to talk to you YL. Tell me where, and I'll be there." No salutation. No heart or mushy sign-off. Typical Granna, but this was pissed-off Granna.

"YL. Young lady?"

"Yep."

"She mad about something?"

"I think very mad."

"You going to set up a meeting? Here, maybe?"

"Yep. Here. Weekends are too full of work and prep. I guess this Sunday."

"Do you know what set her off?"

"Nope. But I'm sure she'll let me know as soon as she shows up. She doesn't broadcast stuff ahead of time. She kind of...ambushes you."

"I am so looking forward to this. *Clash of the Titans*. Wish I could eat popcorn."

CHAPTER 13

Strategy and Conspiracy?

THANKS TO my grandmother's impromptu visit, I now had two mysteries on my hands: what was the Gunny's name and origins, and what had set off Granna that she'd hightailed it down to Virginia. I didn't have the time or resources to figure out the first puzzle, and I knew the second would be revealed when I welcomed her on Sunday. Or should I say, dreaded her on Sunday?

Tuesday afternoon, I summoned up the courage to call her house to set up a visit and was relieved to get her answering machine. I had purposely waited until after 0900, betting against the outcome that she'd be at her office (she had taken over as CEO of Granpa's family's two-hundred-year-old business when he had died) or elsewhere terrorizing what she perceived as overcompensated upper management. Don't get me wrong, I adored my grandmother, but I also had a keen sense of self-preservation, and I didn't willingly seek her out when she was in an open rampage, even one that had smoldered for a while. A couple of years ago, JK had been the target of one of Granna's fuming rages, and he'd likened it to the spectral librarian at the beginning of *Ghostbusters*: Tranquil and seemingly content one minute, eye-popping and terrifying virago the next.

I seriously contemplated a public meeting where she couldn't—wouldn't—castigate me too loudly (she *never* made a scene in public), but that would be like a harried mother threatening the misbehaving toddler with "wait till I get you home." It would be a hundred times worse when we were alone.

I resolved to offer this Sunday, my house, for the shootout.

On the fourth ring, the machine clicked on, and my grandmother's brisk, certainly not-melodic voice barked, "Hello. This is Fred. If you're selling something, don't leave a message because I won't call you back. If you think I might be interested in talking to you, leave your name, business, and telephone number, and I might return your call. If this is Abe, tell me when and where, and I'll be there." *Click.*

Oh, boy. This was going to be worse than I thought.

"Granna, this is Abe. Sorry I missed you yesterday. The training schedule is a bummer." I wanted to say a bitch, but she didn't appreciate profanity, despite her ability to swear like a Marine. "I should be home all day Sunday if you can make it down again. I'd love to see you. But it's all right if you can't. If I don't hear from you, I'll be sure to be home all day." I resisted the urge to ramble on and ended with "I love you," and hung up.

I had crossed the Rubicon, but I had no Roman Army at my back. It was in front of me, led by a sixty-nine-year-old berserker.

*****

"What do you think you did—or didn't do—that pissed her off?" Kelly asked around a mouthful of sweet-and-sour pork. "You have to have some idea. Think hard." He punctuated the last with a jab at me with the serving spoon before he dished out some more triflavored lo mein onto his plate. "You always say she's the most reasonable member of your family, so why is this different?"

"The only thing I can think of is my mother. I wasn't rude when she visited. In fact, I thought we got along pretty well. Maybe she had a different impression and mentioned it to Granna. Granna isn't a Prudence fan, but she won't tolerate disrespect or rudeness. Maybe she's playing avenging angel for her little girl."

It was Wednesday evening, and Kelly and I were meeting at the China Garden Restaurant in Dumfries for dinner. This wasn't a date but a strategy session to discuss the Gunny investigation and an opportunity for me to brainstorm what I might have done to set my grandmother off. When I checked my answering machine at 2100 on Tuesday night, it contained a single terse directive message from the monster matron of Bryn Mawr (Tad's words, not mine). "I'll be there at 1000 Sunday morning. Make sure you have plenty of my Earl Grey and Irish Breakfast mixed tea ready. It better be strong. We'll both need it." *Slam*. Not *click*.

Knowing Kelly went to bed pretty late, I'd immediately called him and set up dinner.

"That part about 'we'll both need it' doesn't sound like she's mad at you. It sounds to me like she has some bad news, or she wants to get you involved in something. I just don't think it's you. It's something else. She might want an ally. Your call, though. You know her better than I do."

I chewed on that thought along with my crispy egg roll and decided Kelly was probably right. No sense stressing out over something I didn't know and couldn't fix, so I moved on to the other subject for discussion—tracking down the Gunny's identity and maybe why he had followed me home from Okinawa.

"Like I mentioned on the phone, I want to talk about Gunny and how you might be able to help me figure out who he is."

Kelly paused in midbite, glancing around our booth and the empty seat next to me. "Is he with us?"

"Remember, when he's around me, I get this low-frequency buzzing and ringing. Kind of like a touch of tinnitus. He's not here. Anyway *The Alamo* is on tonight, and he wanted to watch it. He's a big John Wayne fan. Since he's been on his good behavior this week, I turned on the TV for him before I left."

"Okay. What's up?"

"Remember last Sunday when you came over to watch the football game? I mentioned that I suspected the Gunny died at Sugar Loaf Hill. I knew you wanted to know how I had found it out, but I just couldn't talk about it, particularly since I didn't know when he'd show up to watch the game. But before I ask you a favor, I want to explain how I figured it out."

"Got it," Kelly said.

"I was sitting at the kitchen table, prepping for the platoon's discussion of *Killer Angels.* He was sitting there too, kind of rubbing his hands over the engraving on my sword. I told you how he can move stuff that was around when he was alive, right?"

"Uh-huh. Go on."

"I mentioned how Shaara had really captured the characters without skimping on the details of the fog of war, when the Gunny came out with 'Clausewitz.'"

I could see this resonated with Kelly. "He's read Clausewitz. I've wondered. When you translate, it sounds like somebody pretty well educated. And I know you aren't that erudite." He offered the last comment with a smile and ducked, anticipating my smacking him in retaliation. I was too focused on my next words to bother.

"He went into a kind of trance for about an hour, and when he came out of it, I asked him if he wanted to talk about it. And he did." Though it had been four days since the Gunny's gut-wrenching revelation, the agony and hopelessness in his voice were still trapped in my head. For a moment, I was transported to another time, a hell of screams and smoke and the reek of blood and death. As quickly as it had come, the scene vanished. It was 1989, and I was surrounded by the noise and bustle of China Garden Restaurant.

Kelly sat across from me, silent and waiting. His face reflected his concern and the frustration of wanting to help me, but not knowing how.

"I've read about Sugar Loaf, Kelly. I read firsthand accounts of what it was like. The Marines couldn't retrieve their dead. They assaulted over and over again, in unbelievingly horrific conditions. The hill was slick from mud made up of dirt, rain, blood, and human waste. When they tried to avoid incoming, they buried their heads in that shit. And they kept it up until they took the high ground. He died at Sugar Loaf, Kelly. I know it. That gives us something to work off of, doesn't it?"

"Yeah, it does. Just like now, Marines then didn't wear unit insignia, but we can figure out what battalion, maybe even company and platoon, that he belonged to. I know you're stuffed for time and I can help, but I have some questions before I get started. You game?"

"If it'll help, absolutely! Do you need some paper to take notes?" I pulled out the spiral-bound notebook I'd tucked into my tote before leaving home.

"Nah, I'm pretty good at remembering basics. It must be from dealing with crooks so much and having to think on the fly. Okay. Was he a gunny or refers to himself as a gunny? What I mean is, is he a staff sergeant that got a battlefield promotion and his sleeves still show staff sergeant stripes? Think."

"He's a gunny. Gunnery sergeant chevrons stenciled on both sleeves."

Kelly pondered his next question but before speaking, grabbed an unused paper napkin off the table and pulled a pen out of his pocket. "I think I need to write all this down after all. Okay. Height?"

"How tall are you? About 6'5"?"

"It's really 6'4 1/2", but Marine Corps rounds up. So yeah, 6'5"."

"When he stands next to you, he's just a little shorter, so I'd say about 6'2" or 6'3"."

"What do you mean when he stands next to me? When has he stood next to me? What else does he do when he's near me that I don't know about?" This time, Kelly looked *really* uneasy as he squirmed around in his seat.

The opportunity to screw with him was too hard to resist.

"Well, it started with just standing next to you when I've said goodbye, but then he started kind of hanging around near you when you're sitting down. A couple of times he's sat down next to you on the couch. Rested his arm on the back of the sofa and maybe touched your hair or neck. You might actually have felt that." I was proud of myself for my deadpan matter-of-fact delivery. I tasted blood as I clamped down on the inside of my mouth to keep from laughing.

"Damn, Abe, that's...ugh!" he sputtered. "You've got to tell him I'm straight. I appreciate the interest, but...I'm not interested. I mean, even if he were a gorgeous dead woman, I wouldn't be interested. I'm flattered, really, but I'm not ready to be some dead guy's boy toy."

"Well, tell him yourself next time you come over."

Kelly's answering expression of horror was too much. I lost it. A snicker turned into a chuckle, and then snorting, which gave way to hysterical cackling. I don't think I had ever laughed that hard before and haven't since.

"You are such a shithead," he snarled, realizing I had duped him. "I will retaliate. I swear, you will feel the wrath of Kelly." With the last comment, he reared back and did a fake double-fisted chest thump. "You have been warned." I'd never seen this macho, even feigned, side of Kelly. Kind of interesting.

"Excuse me." A soft, timid voice drew our attention to our petite waitress, Joy, now hovering at our booth. "Is there a problem? Is everything okay?"

"Everything's fine. Thank you," I responded. "He doesn't chew well enough before he swallows, so he chokes. It's not the food. Really."

Kelly glared at me before he flashed a smile at the waitress. "Sorry. I didn't mean to make a scene." She breathed a sigh of relief and returned his smile with a sweet one of her own. He could be so charming. I wanted to slap him.

As she turned, she offered, "Can I get you anything else right now?" I knew she wanted to beat feet as soon as she could, but she was a good waitress and trained to be hospitable.

"Maybe another beer for me and an iced tea for her." He leaned conspiratorially toward Joy. "She can't handle alcohol," he confided, gesturing my way. "Need to cut her off. She's a messy drunk."

Joy beamed at Kelly but cast a surreptitious, nervous look at me, and headed toward the bar. I was sure she was conferring with the bartender as to how inebriated I might be, having only had one planter's punch. I just hoped I wasn't asked to leave before I got the Gunny's specifics to Kelly.

"Truce," I offered. "What else do you need? Hair, eye color?"

"Well, duh. If I can get pictures, I might be able to pick him out. I don't know how helpful SRBs (service record book) will be for personal data, if I can even get them. Idea of build will help too."

"Okay. Build…lean, but I guess that would be true of most of those infantry guys after months in the Pacific Theater. Hair. Maybe light brown, dark blond?"

Kelly scribbled some more and grabbed another napkin to continue.

"Why don't you just let me give you my notepad so you don't accidentally throw the napkins away?" I offered.

"No thanks. It probably has some kind of invisible ink on it that'll stain my fingers or my clothes. You are so in the doghouse. And by the way, I'm contemplating charges against you."

"You wish. What else? Oh, eye color. That's probably the most striking thing about him. He's pretty tan, so his eyes really stand out. Brilliant blue green. Like the Aegean, but light. And long thick black lashes."

"Women and eyes," Kelly muttered to himself and looked up from his notes. "The photos are usually black and white, so I'll key on any Marine that looks like Daddy Warbucks. Anything else about Gunny Dreamy Eyes?"

"Nope. What's your strategy?"

"I have some contacts at Manpower. I'll start there. Then maybe Marine Corps Archives, history division. Units that were at Sugar Loaf, then death records. That kind of thing. I'll warn you. Right now, I have more time than you to search, but it looks like I'll be nabbed for another complicated prosecution case, so I'll get done what I can before that heats up."

Joy appeared with Kelly's beer and my iced tea.

"Thank you, Joy." Kelly beamed. "Can we get the check now? Just one. The lady is buying." Joy smiled, glanced uneasily at me, and I nodded. After all, Kelly was doing me yet another favor, and I had certainly had a good time at his expense. He was a good sport, though I suspected there would be retribution.

"The sooner you can make progress, the better. I'm getting the feeling that we're running out of time. Like whatever cosmic influence sent him here is getting impatient, and I'll wake up one morning, and the Gunny's gone because I was given a mission and blew it. Does that sound paranoid?"

Kelly smiled and shook his head. "Nope. It doesn't. Even if it *does* happen, it's joint failure. I'm with you all the way on this one, Abe. I mean, he tried to get my attention first, didn't he?"

A loud *humpf* interrupted our discussion. I looked to see the burly beefy bartender beside our table, proffering the check and obviously sniffing my breath as I produced my credit card. Sheesh. I made a note not to come back here very soon. They probably wouldn't let me in anyway.

Later, as Kelly and I parted at the front door, curiosity overcame me, and I asked, "So what charges are you thinking of? Conduct unbecoming a TBS classmate? Disrespect to an officer of the court?"

"Disproportionate amusement at the expense of an officer of the court and disrespect to a far superior and illustrious officer. Don't you know anything about the UCMJ, Boot?" he retorted as he turned and headed toward his car.

"I'll make sure to pass on our conversation to the Gunny. You know, that part where you regret he's dead because you would've liked to have gotten to know him better. In your own special way, of course."

The only answer I got was a guffaw and an extremely audible raspberry.

*****

"What is an ALF?" queried Gunny as I came through the front door at 2130.

"Uh, I think it means alien life-form. Why're you asking?"

"After *The Alamo*, a sitcom called *Alf* came on, and I watched it. Couldn't change the channel or turn off the TV, didn't feel like reading an FM (field manual), and I can't turn the pages of anything published since 1945, so I watched *Alf*."

I sighed. Why did I think this conversation was going to last longer than I wanted? As I sank heavily onto the couch, I accepted

I might as well get this over with, or I wouldn't hear the last of it for weeks. "What did you think?"

"A man, or should I say puppet, or creature, after my own heart. Surprising how a character can be written so…insightfully. Maybe I can relate because we're both so new to this post-WWII world." His piece delivered, the Gunny watched me with interest and anticipation. I knew this was a setup. I was just too tired to think my way out of it.

"Okay," I managed to say. What did he expect? A literary analysis of a TV show based on an alien puppet? This was not *Killer Angels*. This was a sitcom, for heaven's sake.

"Do you want to hear what the show was about? I couldn't take notes, but I have a pretty good memory for this kind of thing."

"Gunny, it's a TV show about an alien life-form portrayed as a *puppet*. What is there to discuss? I'm glad you liked it, but I need to go to bed. By the way, how was *The Alamo*?" I figured if I could sidetrack him to John Wayne (a pretty straightforward topic), I could get to bed before midnight.

"The Duke is always great. The movie was a little historically shaky, but the duke is always stand-up. Now back to *Alf*—"

"No," I erupted. "No. I am *not* going to analyze a puppet show. Not now. Not ever. So good night." I rose and stomped toward the staircase, Gunny on my heels.

"Abe!" reverberated off the stairwell. "Abe!"

Reluctantly I turned and looked down at the bottom of the stairs where Gunny leered in a pretty good parody of Jack Nicholson in *The Shining*. He wasn't going to chant "Here's Johnny," was he?

"What?" I managed.

"I have good news. I think I know my name."

That got my attention, and I sat down on the top step. "What is it? This could be significant."

"Gordon Shumway."

Something familiar clicked in my brain, but I couldn't connect. "What? How did you figure that out?"

"Alf. I think he's the reincarnation of me. When I died, I floated into outer space and landed on Melmac, and my soul entered Alf as he was born. I still can't figure out how 1756 fits in, but I'll get there." Gunny beamed at me from the bottom of the stairway, and I flashed back to my discussion with Kelly this afternoon. Payback truly was a mother.

"I'm not even going to dignify that bullshit with a comment," I tossed back at him.

"Abe, Abe! Wait!" I popped my head out of the bedroom door and waited.

He was ready. "What's the kindest thing you can do for someone?"

"I don't know, and I don't care."

"Burp downwind…get it? I kill me."

With a resounding Alf-like guffaw, he was gone.

Though exasperating, I really did enjoy these interludes and would miss them when Gunny went elsewhere. I half-wished Kelly weren't successful in his search but knew we couldn't remain in this state of stasis forever.

CHAPTER 14

Doug Isn't the Only One with Challenges

I T WAS the end of October, and training continued at its inexorable pace. I was really looking forward to a five-day break at Thanksgiving and even more to a two-week operational pause for the Christmas holiday, but there were several significant events to get through before we could welcome the new year: the Commanding General's reception, the Marine Corps Birthday Ball, O-course for grade, and completion of the patrolling package.

With any luck, Lieutenant Myerson would have passed land navigation, hopefully by Thanksgiving, so I could start having weekends again.

Oh, and though not on the training schedule, I was wishing, for Gunny's sake, that the new year would bring resolution to his situation.

With the CG's reception looming on Friday, I had little time to obsess about Granna's upcoming visit. The reception was a big deal, as it would be the first time the lieutenants attended a formal function in dress blues, and it was a rite of passage on learning how to conduct themselves, if not as ladies and gentlemen, at least as somewhat socially adept junior officers. I had no idea why Dickey had scheduled the reception before the Marine Corps Birthday Ball on November 10th. For whatever reason, Delta Company would get a steady dose of tradition and restrained socializing for the next two weeks. Dickey, of course, would just show up, schmooze, and bask in the glory of his SPCs' and lieutenants' hard work.

SPCs had spent countless hours inspecting and reinspecting uniforms, providing instruction on military etiquette, and leading practical applications on the dos and don'ts of polite conversation. We were so tired of CG reception preps, we just wanted it done, but all of us knew if there was some way the lieutenants could muddle something up, they would. I didn't think even I would be exempt, and I knew Doug was planning on being particularly vigilant. The rest of us were placing bets on how long it would take for his hoople-heads' latest caper to be revealed.

When my alarm went off at 0415 on Friday morning, I slammed the offending button down with a groan and uttered another when I saw the rain pelting against my bedroom window. The only consolation on that front was knowing we wouldn't have to venture out in our wool uniforms once primped and spiffed up for the reception, as the Quarterdeck (site of the event) was directly accessible from the BOQ. Delta Company wouldn't smell like wet dogs, but our guests might not be so fortunate. The Quarterdeck was a large reception area, with access to the kitchen on one side and a wall of patio doors that opened into gardens on the other. The balcony that overlooked the room was called the Flying Bridge. Obviously whoever had named the two areas was totally enamored of nautical terminology.

"Abe! Get up! Today's a busy day! I think we need bacon before we go, so you need to get up and make it."

I glanced heavenward and prayed for patience and with a groan, shuffled to the top of the stairway where Gunny waited below, shifting from foot to foot in anticipation.

"You can't eat it. You can only smell it. What's with the bacon angle this morning?" Maybe I really didn't want to know. I did know, though, that I was *not* making bacon this morning.

"You need a good breakfast because it's going to be a *long* day, and you have to be strong enough to deal with whatever those lieutenants have cooked up. Come on. We have enough time before we have to leave."

As I slowly made my way down the steps, I searched for a motive for this sudden interest in bacon. *Alf?* Or did Gunny know something he wasn't sharing, like lieutenant plans to do something outrageous?

"Spill it," I grumbled as I stumbled toward the stove and the teakettle. "What do you know that I should know?"

Somehow Gunny Tough Guy managed to look small, innocent, and clueless. That was my surety that he knew something and had no intention of sharing it.

"Not mine to tell," he offered. Truculently. Then he evaporated.

"You asshole," I muttered as I measured Irish Breakfast into my tea press. "And just for that, I *am* going to make bacon. A lot of it. I hope you choke on the smell!" I yelled at him since I knew he could hear me, even if I couldn't see him. Then it occurred to me. Could Gunny, adopting his Alf persona, think he was drawn to bacon because it tasted like cat (Alf's favorite snack)? Cripes on a cracker.

I had to shut this down. "And cat doesn't taste like bacon. Believe me!"

All I got in response was a resounding guffaw from nowhere and everywhere.

At 1815 that evening, my student platoon commander, Lieutenant Reardon, reported to my office with an update on the platoon's "state of readiness" (her words, not mine) for the reception. SPCs and lieutenants were to be in place at 1830 in case any of our guests showed up early.

Really? "Just in case any of our guests showed up early?" Of *course* they would be early. These were Marines and their spouses, and to them, on time was late. Everyone but the Commanding General, who would be announced, would be early.

Lieutenant escorts would accompany VIPs (lieutenant colonels and above), ensuring their charges were well watered but not fed (grazing wasn't permitted until after the CG arrived). Even better, we expected the escorts to engage in *appropriate* conversation with their assigned guests until they could flag down a substitute babysitter.

Escorts were required to keep an eye on their charges even if they were not actually colocated, making sure their glasses were refilled (if desired) or another lieutenant or SPC attendant dragged over, introduced, and left to entertain the guest.

"Lieutenant Reardon, I'm sure the platoon's ready to go. No need to have them form up. Just have them head down to the Quarterdeck and be there by 1830."

"Yes, ma'am. Can do. I did think it was a good idea to know which lieutenants don't drink in case any of the platoon…uh…need to be escorted back to their rooms." Lieutenant Reardon had obviously considered the possibility that some of the platoon still hadn't transitioned from college party to proper Marine Corps social event. Excellent thinking on her part.

"Good idea, Lieutenant. It never hurts to plan ahead. Who are our teetotalers?"

She looked perplexed. Obviously she hadn't heard the term before, but then I remembered she had gone to Brigham Young University where she, and likely most of her classmates, were Latter Day Saints and religiously mandated teetotalers.

"Who are the nondrinkers?" I clarified.

"Oh, sorry, ma'am. Me, Lieutenants Price, Wykowski, and Lewis. Oh, and Lieutenant Myerson."

"Thanks for the info. Head on back to the platoon and tell them to get over to the Quarterdeck. I'll be there shortly." With that, Lieutenant Reardon about-faced (pretty good maneuver considering she was wearing two-inch-high pumps) and made for the platoon's area.

As I closed my office door, Gunny appeared on my couch and regarded my uniform with a critical eye.

"Abe, not to offend, but those dress blues are pretty plain. Where's the red piping? Where's the choker collar?"

He was referring, of course, to my dark blue jacket and skirt, starched white shirt, and red neck tab. The only bright spots were the rank insignia on my shoulders, gold and silver Marine Corps eagle, globe, and anchor symbols on the lapels, brass buttons, and ribbon bar. I glanced at the mirror on my wall and confirmed all was in order but realized he was right. It *was* a pretty plain dress uniform.

"I'm a female company-grade Marine officer, and that's the uniform. Male Marine officers' uniforms don't have red piping either. They wear a white shirt with starched cuffs and stand-up collar that you see instead of the red piping. If I pick up field grade, I'll get evening dress. That's a darker cutaway jacket and two lengths of skirts and a ruffled shirt with a black neck tab. Oh, and a red cummerbund. I guess that's kind of plain too. But it is what it is." I turned toward the door.

Gunny appeared at my shoulder as I moved down the passageway. "That's okay. I guess I just imagined something…different."

I turned his way to snap something back; he stopped and gestured a truce. "Not girly. I mean, you're a captain of Marines. You've paid your dues. You deserve something…grander."

"Good catch," I responded, mollified. He remained silent for the rest of our walk until we arrived at the door to the reception room where I stopped and observed. "Maybe we'll make a modern man of you yet. Now disappear and mingle. I have to go kiss babies."

By 2000, the reception was in full swing. Well, at least as much as a bunch of junior Marine officers in choker dress blues or two-inch heels could swing. The Training Command Commanding General had arrived promptly at 1915, *his* scheduled time to appear. All the company's staff captains (SPCs and Bob) had kowtowed, then resumed our circulating around the room. Dickey, as expected, hovered within whispered hailing distance of the general who, after handshakes and "happy to see you again/happy to be here," studiously ignored him, focused instead on chatting with lieutenants. It was, after all, *their* reception and their first opportunity to rub shoulders with a general officer. I decided I liked this guy.

The staff captains had decided to stick to nonalcoholic beverages this evening, since we were all on the lookout for aberrant lieutenant behavior and didn't want dulled senses to impede reaction time. I had just retrieved another diet soda from the bar when the CG's wife approached me.

"Captain Rush," she greeted me. "How do you think it's going?" She assumed a place to the right of me, smiling and nodding to other guests but obviously closely studying the room. "I know these young people must hate these functions. I know I did when Stan was a second lieutenant." Wow. A general's wife with a heart and a brain. We had never met, but I assumed she'd learned my name from Bob, with whom she'd been chatting before heading my way.

"As well as can be expected, ma'am." I glanced down at her left hand that was holding a can of beer. Not a glass of wine. Not even a glass of beer. A beer can. And she didn't have a fancy manicure. Her nails were blunt cut but clean and buffed, hands rough. Her makeup was flawless and cocktail gown simple but elegant. What an anomaly. It was like looking at a younger version of my grandmother.

"I've got my own life, separate from being a general's wife," she offered, acknowledging my eyes focused on her hands, both of which were devoid of rings or nail polish. "I'm a master gardener and have my own landscaping business. Always forgetting to put on gloves before I go mucking in the dirt. Sometimes I don't clean up so well." With this last comment, she wiggled her eyebrows in a mimic of Groucho Marx and took a dainty swig from her can of beer.

I *really* liked this lady.

"I think they rate this kind of thing up there with a double run of the O-course. But at least that's only ten or fifteen minutes of pain. Prepping for and enduring the formal social stuff is a lot longer to suffer." There. I'd said it. I hoped I hadn't overstepped myself.

"No argument there. I'd rather be someplace else too, though I do enjoy meeting the lieutenants. A barbecue would be more to my taste. Anyway I do have a question. Maybe it's an observation."

"Ma'am?"

"There certainly are a lot of Lieutenant Elvises. Or am I just seeing the same couple of lieutenants with the same last name?"

I glanced around the room, concentrating on Neil's lieutenants and their name tags, knowing they would be the culprits. At least three were within eyesight, and all had "Elvis" name tags pinned over their right breast pockets. *Argh.* None of the CPA had noticed this as we were focused on behaviors, not uniforms.

When I looked back at her, she was smiling, and I relaxed somewhat, knowing I was chatting with a friendly.

"We do have a couple of Lieutenant Elvises, ma'am, but since all the guys have short hair and are in dress blues, they do tend to look a lot alike. But just in case, I'll double-check. Thank you for bringing it to my attention." I excused myself and turned to start my search for the Elvis lieutenants, but before I stepped away, she stopped me with a gentle tug on my sleeve.

"Captain, I counted at least thirty," she whispered conspiratorially. "Though I think it's an entire platoon." With that, she winked and headed toward two lieutenant colonels' wives who looked happily abandoned near the patio doors.

Gunny appeared and kept step with me as I made my way through the crowd, searching for Neil. As I passed Elvis name-tagged lieutenants, I stopped and advised them (strongly of course) to head back to their rooms and get their legitimate tags, and if they passed other rebels, to have them do the same.

"It's the entire platoon." Gunny laughed. "This is priceless. Great idea, but I probably would have done it in a less-formal setting. I'd help, but you know, I can't intervene. Not that I'd really want to." Braying laughter accompanied him as he faded away.

Definitely no football games for him this weekend, I vowed.

I spotted Neil and steamed his way but drew up short when I saw he was chatting up some lieutenant colonel from the Tactics department that I absolutely loathed (inwardly of course). I gestured (coolly of course) that I needed to talk to him.

Neil, never cool nor slick, excused himself with, "Sorry, sir. Gotta go," and joined me.

"You—no, we—have a problem," I hissed as we made our way casually out the door to the passageway. We smiled and nodded at lieutenants and guests as we went, not stopping until we were well down the passageway and out of hearing distance of the Quarterdeck.

"Oh no, what did Doug's dudes do this time?" Neil groaned, leaning against the wall, taking a deep drag from his diet ginger ale.

"I know they're doing something but haven't seen anything yet. No, it's your guys. They all have 'Elvis' name tags on. I've flagged down the ones I've seen and told them to spread the word that they have to put the right ones on, but I don't think I got them all."

Neil straightened, choking on his drink. "What? *All* of them?"

"Yep. And I didn't notice until the CG's wife brought it to my attention. Don't freak. She'll keep her mouth shut. But if *she* noticed, more will too. We've got to do damage control. *Now.* There's still another hour to this goat-roping." My last words were lost on Neil, who was already on the move back into the reception room. I hastened to catch up with him.

"Thanks, Abe. I've got it from here. If you see any of my gang still with Elvis name tags on in ten minutes, kick them in the ass and send them back to their rooms," he directed and disappeared back into the Quarterdeck.

I continued my way back to the reception to roaring laughter only I could hear.

"Can it, Gunny. I'm busy," I responded, strolling past groups of guests and lieutenants, all engaged in socializing and nibbling assorted finger foods. One of the dishes caught my eye, and I casually remarked to the owner (one of Scott Zawicki's), "Hey, Lieutenant. What's that brown stuff on your plate?" I already suspected what the mystery substance was, but hoped I was wrong.

"I don't know, ma'am," he said. "I thought I'd try it, but it's kind of nasty. I'd stay clear of it if I were you."

I thanked him and made my nonchalant progress to the buffet table where I immediately acquired the target—a white serving plate of artfully displayed refried beans with crackers tastefully arranged around it like Druid worshippers venerating a squatty Stonehenge megalith.

I glanced surreptitiously to my right and left, and since no one else was close to or looking at this end of the table, I casually draped a cocktail napkin over the plate and picked it up.

Before I could turn and make off with my treasure, I heard, "Hey, Abe. Are they clearing the table already? They were supposed to keep it stocked until 2030." I glanced to my right, prepared to talk my way out of why I was making off with a buffet platter, and heaved a sigh of relief.

Bob.

"Do you think you can get this to the servers without anyone noticing?" I asked, handing him the offending plater. As an SPC and one of only two female officers in the room, I was notable, and my moving around with a serving dish in my hand would likely attract attention. Bob, on the other hand, blended in better and was not so sought out to engage in idle chitchat. "And ask Doug to find me if you see him first."

Bob didn't even glance down at what I was offering. Somehow he knew.

"Sure. And I'll let Doug know." With that, he proceeded leisurely toward the double doors leading into the galley or whatever the food preparation staging area was called.

Having averted another catastrophe, I strolled back into the social, pausing to chat with lieutenants and guests but mainly scrutinizing name tags to verify that Elvis had indeed left the building. It seemed he had, and I heaved a sigh of relief that we had successfully averted *that* train wreck. Thanks to the CG's wife, of course, who deserved an update and thanks. I had noticed her eyes on me as I flagged down Neil and later as I made my way to the buffet table, so as I approached her, she excused herself from chatting with three lieutenants' spouses and offered her hand (neither hand encumbered with a beer can this time) for a firm shake.

"Congratulations, Captain Rush," she smiled. "I see you've had your hands full. I haven't seen any more Lieutenant Elvises, by the way. And thank you for taking care of that very…interesting… hors d'oeuvre on the buffet table. What was it anyhow?"

"Refried beans and crackers, ma'am." In response, she threw her head back and let loose an almost ribald laugh. I continued, "And thank *you* for the heads-up about the name tags."

"My name's Ellie, Captain, and no thanks necessary. I've certainly enjoyed watching the action. By the way, when did you become the company fixer? Or do you captains share the additional duty?"

"It's shared. Whoever spots the mess handles it and informs the impacted SPC. It helps keep the platoons off the skyline."

"You can be sure I want to hear the story behind the refried beans, but it'll have to wait until the Marine Corps Ball. It seems that it's time for Stan and me to leave. Thank you for an entertaining evening!"

And with a swirl of silk, she was gone.

A half hour later, all the guests had departed (as had Dickey, thank goodness), and the staff captains gathered in a corner of the Quarterdeck to heave a corporate sigh of relief and indulge in adult beverages. We deserved them.

"Hey, Abe," observed Scott, pointing toward a group of lieutenants obviously having a good time near the patio doors. "Is that Lieutenant Myerson the center of attention over there? Whatever she's doing, it must be pretty funny."

I glanced behind me and confirmed that it was, indeed, Lieutenant Myerson, saying and doing something that had the other members of the group in hysterics.

"Oh no!" I groaned. "She's supposed to be one of the sober ones, but she's acting like she's drunk. Let me see what's going on." My fellow captains laughed and resumed their discussion of the night's events as I made my way to the jolly gathering.

Not stealthily but not exactly noisily, I came up behind Lieutenant Myerson. The other officers, catching sight of me, immediately stifled their laughter. Myerson failed to notice their abrupt silence and continued, oblivious to me behind her. One of Neil's lieutenants (he wasn't sporting an Elvis name tag) desperately tried to catch her attention, but it seemed Myerson was on a roll. I didn't smell anything. However, her slurred speech and the loose way she moved (she tended to be pretty uptight) was a giveaway that something was significantly different about her.

"Really, I don't think she's nuts. Not even eccentric. She's really talking to somebody that we can't see. It's a ghost. I know it. I mean, I probably spend more time with her than anybody else. I should know."

"Come on, Kate," Lieutenant Reardon interjected, attempting to shut down the one-woman show. "Captain Rush isn't haunted. She's a Yankee blue blood. They're all a little eccentric." Well, gee. I guess I should be thankful you're attributing it to inherited eccentricity, Lieutenant Reardon. But I'm not a blue blood and certainly not odd because of it.

"No, no. I've *seen* him," Myerson protested. "Really. He's a Marine. His uniform's old. Can't place it. But—" The last was lost as she staggered backward.

Into me.

"Lieutenant Reardon, please help Lieutenant Myerson back to her room," I directed, catching Myerson by the shoulders and handing her over to her student platoon commander. "When you're done tucking her in, stop by my office. The rest of you, the fun's over. Head back to the BOQ."

Though I was shocked at what I had overheard and, admittedly, had not yet processed, I needed to disperse the group and return to my office. The lieutenants disbanded with mumbled "Good evening, ma'ams" and made for the doors as I rejoined my fellow captains.

"So what gives?" Bob asked. "I didn't think Myerson drank."

"She doesn't," I confirmed. "I've got to get back to my office and talk to Reardon. Between Myerson's getting drunk and her story that I've got a ghost companion, something's not right. I've gotta get to the bottom of this."

Dave chimed in, "The drunk thing, yeah. But hey! Half the company's convinced they've seen you with a ghostly Marine. I think somebody came up with it as a joke, now everybody's 'seeing' him. Face it, Abe. Neil has Elvis, Doug has refried beans, Scott has something unmentionable, and I'm the field marshal. They've got to have something on you. You were too...vanilla. So *you* have a ghost."

The other captains nodded in agreement. They obviously didn't think anything of it.

"You mean you guys heard this and kept your mouths shut?"

"It's not a big deal," Bob reassured me. "We thought you knew. You're clearly in good company. With my luck, I'll be haunted by Dickey when he gets toasted by friendly fire on the rifle range."

"Thanks, gents, but this really concerns me. Makes me mad too. I'm not a paranormal freak show." I struggled to shrug off my mounting anger and angst. "Anyway see you Monday, guys. I've got to talk to Reardon before I go home. And, Doug, could you take Patterson out on land nav tomorrow? I don't think Myerson is going to be up to it, and I want to be available in case she has any problems besides a killer headache." Doug nodded, then he and the other SPCs offered their good nights, and the group disbanded.

Bob lingered behind.

"Don't sweat it, Abe. It's not a big deal. I'd be kind of flattered if I were you. It's not like they're targeting you because you're a woman. You're one of us. Now I admit, the ghost thing *is* kind of unusual. If it's true, though…" He paused and raised an eyebrow, inviting me to respond.

I wasn't going to lie to him, but I couldn't admit to the Gunny either. "I don't know how, so I'll be more situationally aware and make sure I don't have any ghostly cling-ons."

He knew I'd avoided answering his question directly and didn't comment. I was certain Bob knew there was something else, though, but he was doggedly patient. He was likely convinced he'd ferret it out of me, if not tonight, then not too far in the future.

We made our way off the Quarterdeck, shooing lingering lieutenants to their rooms and thanking the waitstaff, who were clearing up the reception's detritus, for their support of the event.

We reached Bob's office first, three doors up from mine.

"Good night, Abe. Thanks for the help with the Elvises and the bean-dip mess. And let me know if I can help on…the other thing. After all, 'Wo' I comes from in Goja', we be used to h'ants.'" The last was offered in his best James Earl Jones/Gomer Pyle voice, and I laughed, just as he had intended.

"Thanks, Bob. I'll keep that in mind."

Twenty minutes later, I answered my office door to not one but two lieutenants. I was surprised to see Reardon accompanied by a member of Dave's platoon, Hale, according to his name tag. I stood aside, directed them to sit on the sofa, and shut the door firmly behind me. I was tempted to make a production of locking it so we wouldn't be interrupted, but who was I kidding? It was 2230, the company was secured, and tomorrow was Saturday. The BOQ was a ghost town.

I assumed the chair opposite the two lieutenants and waited. I can be very still when I put my mind to it, and for the target party, it can be pretty unnerving. So I just sat and looked at them. After five minutes of uncomfortable silence (for them, not me), Lieutenant Hale glanced at Lieutenant Reardon and then back at me.

"Ma'am, you're probably wondering why I'm here."

"The thought had crossed my mind. Why don't you clue me in?" I suspected he had had a role in Myerson's bender but wasn't sure how or why.

"Lieutenant Myerson's pretty stressed about not passing land nav yet, so I thought I'd help her relax. You know, another Friday night when she's facing another Saturday out in the boonies with you." He immediately realized how his comment must have sounded, and lamely clarified, "I mean, you're stuck out there every Saturday with her, too. It must get kind of old."

"Psychoanalyzing Lieutenant Myerson and me isn't any of your business, Lieutenant Hale. Get to it. Now."

He shuffled uncomfortably on the sofa, drawing an irritated glare from Lieutenant Reardon.

"When she put her glass down to go to the head, I slipped in some grain alcohol from a flask I had tucked in my sock. Not a lot. Just enough to loosen her up. I guess it was too much."

Message delivered, he sank back on the sofa, deflated. A flask in his sock? I'd seen Marines carrying cigarette packs there but never a flask. I knew he couldn't have had it in his blues blouse (jacket). They were tailored to conform to the body, and a flask would have been pretty obvious.

"How many times did you spike her glass? It had to have been more than once." He squirmed, knowing I was onto him.

"Just twice in all, ma'am. And not much either time."

I turned to my student platoon commander. "Lieutenant Reardon, did you know about this before it happened? And I want the truth. Covering for Lieutenant Hale is *not* an option."

"No, ma'am. I did not."

"Lieutenant Hale, you can go. I'll take this up with Captain Kesselring tomorrow. This isn't over."

He rose, offered me a head nod and a barely audible "Good night, ma'am," and departed, closing the door quietly behind him.

I turned to Reardon.

"I've sent a corpsman to Lieutenant Myerson's room, and he says she's okay but should have someone stay with her for the night to make sure she doesn't throw up and suffocate in her own vomit. Please arrange a couple of watches. You can go, but tell whoever is with her now that I'll be up to check on her before I secure."

"Got it, Captain. I guess she's not going to land nav tomorrow?" she asked as she opened the door.

"No. She needs to sleep it off, and I don't feel like spending a day 'in the boonies' waiting for her to sober up, throw up, or pass out on me. Good night, Lieutenant Reardon. We'll talk about this Monday."

"I'm sorry, ma'am. I really had no idea."

"If it hadn't been so obvious that she was drunk, this could've been really bad. She could have fallen into her rack, puked and choked on it, and died. It's happened here at TBS before. An enlisted Marine celebrated his twenty-first birthday with too many drinks. Puked in his rack, rolled over into it, and was too far gone to wake up. He didn't live to see his twenty-second birthday." Lieutenant Reardon sagged against the wall, obviously unaware of how badly this could have played out. "We'll talk about it on Monday. Hopefully you'll think about this over the weekend and figure out how—or even if— you could have prevented it. Good night."

I changed out of my uniform, warning the Gunny (who seemed, but wasn't necessarily, absent) that he should stay away until I let him know I was done. He didn't appear when I announced the all clear either. Strange.

When I checked in on Lieutenant Myerson, the door to her room was slightly ajar, and there was a soft light glowing on the bedside table. Instead of Lieutenant Niley (she and Myerson were roommates), the other rack was occupied by Lieutenant Reardon, who looked up from the book she was studying. I nodded and returned the door to its slightly open position and noticed a piece of paper containing a schedule posted on the outside. Watches were assigned in two-hour shifts through 1100 the following morning. Reardon was signed up for every other watch.

It certainly had been an enlightening, entertaining, and certainly eventful evening.

CHAPTER 15

Tidying Up

SATURDAY MORNING, I awoke to sunshine, thoughts of the CG's reception fresh in my mind, and remembered I needed to call Dave and also check on Lieutenant Myerson. Since I wasn't committed to a morning of terrain appreciation, I had allowed myself to sleep until 0700.

What luxury.

There had been some unlikely moments last night, and I smiled, recollecting Neil's platoon of Lieutenant Elvises and Ellie's assistance and, not so surprisingly, Doug's hoopleheads' refried bean appetizer. Not as amusing, Myerson's interpretation of Captain Rush and her invisible muse did strike a chord (I was spending entirely too much time with that young officer). I needed to be more vigilant on how I responded to the Gunny. Even more concerning was the Gunny ghost sightings and the company's acceptance that I was haunted.

My grandmother insisted that there were haunted people, not haunted places, and I wondered if I was one of the fortunate few who not only saw ghosts but lived with them. I cringed, dreading that this might be a permanent arrangement (much as I had come to kind of like the guy), but I needed to find out why he was with me, a way to get him back to *wherever* and not have to worry about being regarded as a Marine Dr. Doolittle, talking to ghosts instead of animals.

When I was first diverted to TBS, I spent a lot of time resenting the assignment there because it kept me from what I had really focused on the year I was in Okinawa—applying my master's in acquisition management to the modernization of the Marine Corps' tactical wheeled fleets. As a motor transport officer, I had spent more than my fair share of time nursing along Korean-era trucks, peppering radiators so they didn't leak, or waiting on flight lines, munching bubble gum like a cow chewing its cud in order to plug seepages and leakages to get my vehicles accepted by a loadmaster and underway to some foreign hotspot. MCRDAC was my ticket to having an impact on the Marine Corps during my tenure and beyond.

This morning, however, I wasn't quite so bitter. My life was interesting, and as they happened, I had started capturing my experiences in my platoon commander's notebook. I had toyed with eventually committing them to a novel, but who would believe the part about living with a ghost and the unbelievable escapades of second lieutenants in training? Browsing in a bookstore, I'd pick something like that up, maybe even buy it, but I certainly wouldn't consider it nonfiction. More like fantasy.

Anyway, I heaved myself out of bed and headed for the stairs. All was stillness below. The uncommon silence continued as I made my way through the foyer and into the kitchen, but just because it was quiet didn't mean I was alone.

Okay, enough was enough. As my tea water heated up, I rattled the frying pan and announced, "I'm in the mood for bacon. And I think I'll watch the home shopping channel all day." Surprise! Guess who appeared, sprawled on the kitchen island, a scowl plastered on his face?

"It's Saturday. That means football. Why aren't you out with your directionally challenged lieutenant?"

"You know why I'm home. You saw and heard it all. Why didn't you warn me what was going on? And get off the counter. I don't want ghostly germs near my food."

He grudgingly slid off the counter and relocated to his kitchen chair. Just in case, I sprayed Lysol on the surface he had occupied.

Gunny immediately jumped to his Nuremberg defense. "Honestly, Abe"—oh, that was good—"I didn't see that happening. I was too busy watching the Lieutenant Elvises and the refried-bean-mess sideshows. You know your platoon is usually pretty restrained, not that they're boring, and I don't want you thinking I'm some kind of creeper (where did he get that term?), so I don't hang around them unless I'm with you. I swear, if I had seen the Lieutenant Myerson thing, I would have found a way to do something, especially if I couldn't get your attention." His tone of voice was sincere, his eyes pleading that I believe him, and despite knowing that he had visibility on more than I did, I trusted him.

"Yeah well, you should've warned me about the Lieutenant Elvis thing. That could've had serious consequences if Dickey had found out," I reluctantly conceded.

"Oh, I noticed the CG's wife watching them, and she seemed like a good egg. I knew she'd play along."

Before I could reply, the phone rang, and I answered it with a sense of foreboding. This early on a Saturday morning? It couldn't be good.

"Ma'am, this is Lieutenant Reardon. I hope you don't mind my calling this early. I got your number from the OD (the D Company Officer of the Day)." Hearing it was Lieutenant Reardon and not the TBS Duty Officer, I relaxed somewhat. Had it been the latter, this would have assuredly been bad news.

"Not a problem, Lieutenant. What's up?"

"Lieutenant Myerson is awake. She puked a couple of times last night but got to the head before she blew cookies on the bed. Lieutenant Price is with her right now but wants to know if she can give her some aspirin. Kate says she has a headache that feels like a tank is driving through her skull."

"Aspirin is fine if she can tolerate it. Big thing is hydration." I paused, trying to remember the textbook antidotes for alcohol after-maths. "Water, Pedialyte if someone can go out and get it for her. Try to get her to eat some eggs later on." Though I was sure Lieutenant Price had her own miracle hangover cure, I appreciated her holding off and sending Lieutenant Reardon my way for guidance on an acceptable remedy.

"Got it, ma'am. Thanks. I'll get the Pedialyte, and somebody will stay with her today. She still looks pretty green."

"Sleep and hydration today, and she should be better tonight. Do I need to pop in now or later this afternoon?" Reardon seemed to have the situation well in hand, but I wanted to offer her support if she needed it.

"No, ma'am. I've got this. If it's okay, I'll call you early evening and let you know how she's doing. By the way, Lieutenant Hale's been by just about every hour to see how she's doing. Just letting you know."

With a thanks for contacting me, I rang off and regarded the Gunny, who was trying to look nonchalant but failing miserably. He had heard every word from Lieutenant Reardon's end.

"Everything okay?" he asked innocently.

"You know it is. Now give me space while I call Dave and talk about Lieutenant Hale's little joke from last night."

Dave and I spent the next half hour discussing what had happened with Lieutenant Myerson and Hale's role in her drunken spectacle. I offered, in mitigation, that he'd voluntarily confessed to spiking the drinks and that he'd probably not gotten any sleep, having kept tabs on his victim throughout the night. Dave was surprised about the spiking behavior. Apparently Nathan Hale (yes, named for the Revolutionary War hero) was a straight arrow and the platoon's corporate conscience. We conjectured that maybe he had a thing for Myerson, and maybe the grain had been provided with good intentions that just happened to backfire on him (and her). I offered that he could tutor Myerson on land navigation and accompany us on what had become our weekly sojourns into the training area, and surprisingly, Dave concurred and thought it a fitting recompense. We agreed we needed to make the point without grinding Hale into submission, and land navigation just might be an appropriate penance.

I spent the rest of the day cleaning up and tackling laundry, all to the background noise of college football games. Though Gunny preferred professional ball (the Eagles still being his favored team), he really got into the college games, further indication that he might have played when he was alive.

At 1700, Doug called to inform me that Lieutenant Patterson had passed land nav. As predicted, Myerson was last man (woman) standing.

By 1800, my house was sparkling clean, laundry folded and put away, dry cleaning picked up, and groceries stowed in the kitchen. It was time to have a heart-to-heart with the Gunny about Granna's visit tomorrow.

I waited until the game he was watching was at halftime, then asked him to join me at the kitchen table. I wondered who the guys in white and burnt orange were. University of Texas or Texas A&M? I had no idea, but Gunny seemed to prefer the team with the longhorn cattle. Was he from Texas? To my uninitiated ear, he didn't seem to have a Texas accent, but then, all I knew of Texas accents was TV and movies (not the most reliable sources of information).

I was already concentrating on my covers when he assumed his usual chair. That morning, I'd washed them and, having just stretched them on metal frames, was preparing to coat them with watered-down starch in order to make them presentable again.

"What's up, Cappie?" Gunny asked, settling down across from me. "Make it quick. I like to watch the marching bands. All those designs they make while they march and play musical instruments. Amazing."

"This won't take long. I just need to ask you a favor."

"Fire away."

Cappie? Fire away? Too much TV. I needed to be more careful about what I let him watch.

"You know my grandmother's coming tomorrow, right?" I opened, laying down the brush I was using to spread the starch. I needed to focus on this discussion and press the point home that this was serious. Couldn't have Granna thinking I'd totally lost it. Gunny's behavior was critical to her leaving tomorrow assured my faculties were intact.

"Yes, and I know what you're going to say. I can watch, but I have to keep my comments to myself. Well, at least until she leaves. Got it."

"Thanks. I appreciate it. I don't want this to be like the Kelly experience. I don't get to see her much and won't have an opportunity to set things right like I did with Kelly. Besides, something's going on with her. Not sure what, but I don't want to add to whatever it is. She means a lot to me."

"Aye, aye, Captain," Gunny responded solemnly. "Now if you'll excuse me, I have halftime activities to watch."

With that, he sauntered into the living room and resumed his preferred TV viewing chair. That used to be my favorite chair. What would happen if I just sat down on him when I wanted to read or watch TV? Would he dissolve into vapor or would I even feel anything? I decided I didn't want to find out.

Sunday morning, I was up at 0600 knowing Granna was inevitably early, so I was showered, dressed, and fortified with two huge cups of strong tea by 0900. I rearranged mugs, Earl Grey and Irish Breakfast teas, lemon and sugar (Granna refused to use artificial sweeteners and called them gritty granules) for the umpteenth time. I didn't know why she thought sweeteners were gritty, they seemed pretty powdery to me, and the granules part was always uttered with disdain. Wasn't sugar usually in granules? As I pondered the basis for Granna's term, I watched Gunny out of the corner of my eye. He seemed nervous, pacing back and forth from the front window to the patio door. Heck, it wasn't like he was going to be introduced to her or anything, but I figured it was probably a flashback to his previous life where grand old dames were ladies to impress with good manners and attire. He was batting zero on both counts, whether she met him or not. He was attired, as usual, in his WWII utilities, and though his manners were still somewhat intact, his language was now peppered with a lot of popular jargon speak. I resolved, again, to monitor his TV viewing and set him up with more PBS specials.

"Relax," I said. "It's not like she'll be able to see you or anything. Just behave yourself and let *me* look good."

He turned from his vantage point at the living room window that overlooked the driveway and announced, "She's *here*...Game time!" And he hightailed it to the front door to watch the action. He was ten times worse than a dog greeting company.

But he was right. Showtime.

Granna had just reached the front porch when I opened the door, anticipating one of her effusive welcomes. For the entirety of my life, she had always greeted me with a smile and arms spread wide in a warm and welcoming hug. This time, however, her arms fell to her sides, eyes opened wide, and mouth falling open in disbelief. And I realized Granna was focused not on me but on something behind me.

The Gunny.

"Who the Sam Hill is *that*?" she managed to sputter. "*What* is that?"

"Just come in, Granna. I can explain," I managed to get out, glancing next-door and across the street as I frantically gestured my grandmother into the foyer. Grabbing and physically hauling someone like Winifred Shippen Drinker into my house was *not* an option.

However, responding to the urgency in my voice, she did, indeed, hightail it through the door, slamming it behind her, finger pointed accusingly at the Gunny, who'd backed up into the living room and looked like he was about to pass out. Okay. I had never actually *seen* a ghost pass out but couldn't summon up a better comparison. Maybe a heart attack or stroke? But how could he since he was already dead? Before I could conjure up any more analogies, Granna's voice brought me back to my surroundings.

"*Who* or *what* is he?" she repeated, this time without the frenzy but with considerably more assertiveness. Granna, master of every situation, had regained her composure and was quickly moving onto the bottom line.

"So you can see him?" I didn't know how else to respond. "Why don't we go sit down, and I'll make some tea." Lame, Abe. *Let's drink tea like civilized people while we ignore the dead guy in the other room.*

"Of course I can see him," she snorted, shrugging out of her jacket (it was still too warm for the sable) and handing it to me.

"We'll drink tea and talk about him after I wash my hands. I'll meet you in the kitchen."

She took a couple of steps toward the powder room and stopped abruptly, turning toward the Gunny. "You can join us as well if you can behave yourself," she directed and disappeared down the hall.

After exchanging looks—mine quizzical, Gunny's stupefied— we made our way to the kitchen where he seated himself on his usual chair, back to the living room. I stumbled around, busying myself with the kettle and tea things, and readied for the inevitable tribunal to which I was about to be subjected.

Granna emerged from the passageway and, seeing I didn't need any assistance at the counter, moved toward a kitchen chair and eyed the Gunny as he respectfully rose from his. Once she was settled, he resumed his seat, and unlike his usual two-legged perch, all chair legs were in contact with the floor. *Dang!* I still hadn't asked him how he could move the chair but couldn't turn the channel selector on the TV. Note to self: Get to the bottom of that tonight after she leaves.

"Well, it looks like someone taught you some manners." Granna sniffed, studying him while I placed a mug of tea, lemon, napkin, spoon, and sugar bowl in front of her. "Thank you, sweetie." The latter comment was directed at me, by the way.

I seated myself across from her, with Gunny to my right, and took a nervous sip of my tea that sounded, even to me, like a noisy slurp. I'd doctored it with "grainy granules" while I was still at the counter rather than get Granna's usual lecture about my good taste in tea and questionable selection of sweetener. The slurp drew a disapproving glance from Granna, but she quickly refocused to the base of the table where Gunny was perched primly on the edge of his chair.

"Can you talk?" She peered at the Gunny, took a sip of her tea, and nodded her approval at me. "You make a great cup of tea, Abe, even though you use that horrible artificial sweetener. I hear your coffee is adequate too, but since I don't drink coffee, who cares?"

Oh, so she *had* been talking with Mother, who had obviously changed her tune about the quality of my coffee. Nuts to you, Mother. I thought we were getting along better.

Gunny cleared his throat and squirmed in his chair. "Yes, ma'am, I can. I suppose you're wondering what I'm doing here." So the gorilla in the room was going to bring up the gorilla in the room. Interesting tactic.

"Direct, aren't you?" she parried. "Well, so am I. Then let's get down to business. I suspect you're a ghost since you look kind of... shimmery, but I'm curious why you're haunting my granddaughter." She turned to me. "From the beginning, Abe. I didn't see him before you went to Okinawa, so I assume he followed you home like a stray cat or dog."

Holy crap! She could actually see him, put two and two together within minutes, and was already trying to figure out why he was here. I obviously hadn't gotten her intuitive or interrogative genes. I did wonder what Gunny thought about the stray cat or dog comment, but he remained impassive.

For the next hour (broken only by two tea refills for Granna and a head call for me), I related the whole mess, from Kelly seeing the boxes move to Friday night's reception where others reported having seen my ghostly companion. Gunny periodically interjected his understanding of the situation (or lack thereof) but also drew guffaws from Granna when he touched on Kelly's reactions, the lieutenants' antics, and my role as either Bluestocking eccentric or ghost whisperer. I concluded with Kelly's efforts to gather some kind of information from Marine Corps sources and my, to this point fruitless, attempts to provoke memories through movies and travelogues.

"The only certainties we have are that he...passed...at the Battle of Okinawa, and he was a gunnery sergeant," I finished, gesturing toward Gunny's sleeves, still faintly bearing his rank insignia.

"All right." Granna raised her hands, palms out to indicate she had the floor. "Before we go any further, let me share a couple of insights. Abe, you've heard me say people are haunted, not places?" I nodded in agreement, wondering if she was just going to reaffirm that I was haunted. Which I knew, of course. "When I said haunted *by* a ghost, I meant people that could sense spirits. Those other people that have seen Gunny are sensitive, maybe even a little bit like you and me."

Well, that would explain why others had sighted him, and her, to a certain extent. But why could she talk to him, and why was he attached to me? Anticipating my questions, Granna held her hand up again to hold me off until she was finished.

"I've had glimpses of people that aren't really there my whole life, but it seems it's clearer for me when they're my contemporaries. Gunny, you'd be about my age if you hadn't…moved on. I'm sixty-nine. Am I correct?"

Gunny and I had never talked about how old he might be today, and I saw him do some quick mental math (which had to be kind of hard since he didn't know when he was born) before he responded, "I think so."

"For now, just accept that you're here and enjoy your time making Abe miserable!" She cackled. Gee, thanks, Granna. "I'm confident Kelly will be able to answer some or all of your questions. Eventually. And somehow, the three of you will figure out who you are and how to help you move on."

Granna turned to me and, having obviously finished with the Gunny topic, abruptly (albeit politely for her) dismissed him with, "Could you excuse Abe and me for a bit? I need to have some time alone with her. Then I'll catch you up on all that's happened since the war. That is, before the football game comes on. I understand the Eagles are playing today."

Surprisingly Gunny offered no protest and nodded, first toward Granna, then me. "Not a problem. I'll be back," he intoned, slowly dissolving.

Arnold Schwarzenegger he wasn't, but no matter how many times I witnessed that kind of exit, it still creeped me out.

"Kind of eerie when they leave like that, isn't it?" she commiserated, observing my reaction. "Thankfully you only have one to deal with. I've been seeing them for years, and it still makes me uneasy. But let's get comfortable in the living room so I can tell you the reason for my visit."

Settled on the couch together, Granna took my hands in hers and fixed me with now-sad and serious blue eyes. She lost no time in getting to the point.

"I'm pretty sure I'm dying, sweetie, and I wanted you to hear it from me before I tell your father and mother." *That* got my attention.

Before I could respond, however, Granna provided the background. A few months ago, she'd starting experiencing severe shortness of breath and a heart "racing like a train out of control." She'd consulted her GP (an eternal pessimist, in my opinion), and he'd referred her to a local specialist who'd tentatively concurred with her doctor's prognosis that the condition was extremely serious. This guy, though, had had the presence of mind to send her to a leading cardiologist at Johns Hopkins. I wondered what kind of specialist referred a patient to another specialist, but since the patient in question was Granna, it kind of made sense.

She'd swung south to Stafford after her first visit to Baltimore, where she'd met her new cardiologist, Dr. Proctor. Granna confessed that *he'd* flatly told her not to jump to conclusions and forget whatever line her GP had fed her. He'd mentioned possible conditions such as cardiac arrest, coronary heart disease, cardiomyopathy, and sick sinus syndrome but was adamant he couldn't—wouldn't—posit *any* diagnosis until he'd had a chance to study the results from blood, stress, and other tests ordered at the initial consult.

Dr. Proctor sounded like just what the doctor ordered (excuse the pun) for someone like Granna, who had already decided she was dying. It was obvious she disliked him, and despite her claims that he didn't know what he was doing, he possessed impeccable credentials and an excellent reputation (I researched him later, but even until I did, I suspected he was probably, at least, competent given his association with Johns Hopkins). Granna's aversion could only be attributed to a clash of personalities. As she continued her vitriolic rant about Dr. Proctor (her dire death announcement forgotten for the time being), my mind wandered, and I imagined a battle of the gorgons—Dr. Proctor as lab-coated King Kong, perched atop the hospital's roof, fighting off an attack from a Godzilla figure clad in sable. And King Kong looked like he was winning.

Granna had made her announcement in typical businesswoman mode. She'd gotten my attention (like, duh) with the worst-case scenario and *then* dangled a glimmer of hope that perhaps all was not lost.

Kind of like the initial position in a negotiation. Come to think of it, I'd learned the technique at her knee and unsuccessfully employed it when I told the Idiot I wanted a divorce and wanted everything—house, cars, savings. As you already know, that hadn't necessarily worked to my advantage. I'd almost turned everything over to the drooling ass-hole just to get out of the marriage before I came to my senses.

Granna obviously knew how to drop a bomb and back off from it, where I could only drop the bomb and get blown up. To quote David Niven in *The Guns of Navarone*: "There's always a way to blow up explosives. The trick is not to be around when they go off."

Talked out (was that even possible?), Granna rose, brushed her hand across my cheek, still moist with the tears her first words had provoked (boy, she could be bitchy, but I adored her just the same), and excused herself with a bright, "Ugh. You shouldn't make such good tea. I've drunk too much and have to answer the call," and disappeared toward the powder room. I suspected she'd delay her return from the bathroom to afford me time to get myself together and process her news, incomplete as it was.

And then it occurred to me—I think she still clung to the pur-ported bad news because she didn't want to hope. And *that's* why she'd been so adamant to see me.

She needed a cheerleader.

At 1215 (twenty minutes after she'd departed to "answer the call"), Granna re-emerged, flashed me a brilliant cagey smile (the old bat noting, I was sure, that I wasn't overwhelmed with grief at her imminent demise), and seemed taken aback that I wasn't the blub-bery mess she'd anticipated.

"When's your follow-up appointment, Granna? Do you need me to go with you? If we're not in the field, I can probably make it." I was matter-of-fact, almost brusque.

She visibly relaxed, the brave show forgotten. "November 10."

"I have the Marine Corps birthday ball that night, Granna. I can't make it. Why don't I call Mother and see if she can go with you?"

She brightened. "You'd do that? I know you and Pru really don't get along, but at least it's better than I do. I'd appreciate it. I *do* under-stand that you have those lieutenants to spiff up for the big event, so don't feel you're letting me down." Her words were genuine, and I realized that, though I'd had to rescind my first offer, my backup position to call my mother was proof enough that I wanted to help.

She again changed the subject (and this time, mood), catching me unaware. "Almost game time. I'm starved. What do you have to eat?" Shit. It was like dealing with the girl from *The Exorcist*, head swiveling 360 degrees. I just hoped there wouldn't be any pea soup vomit.

"When Kelly's here, I order pizza and Chinese. We call it the Sino-Italian pig out. I hadn't planned on anything since I didn't know how long you'd be staying." Okay. I had my feet back under me again.

"Sounds good to me. Take out or delivery? Is he coming over?" She came to stand by me and offered a happy hug, reassured with the knowledge she had my support. I snuggled into her familiar scent of lavender but certainly not old lace. "Why don't you see if he can join us? I'd love to see him again. He's a good guy. Especially since he knows you live with a ghost, who is, by the way, where?"

Before I could respond, Gunny materialized in a ta-da kind of pose and proclaimed, "*Here's* Gunny."

"Can it, big guy." Granna laughed. "Abe and I are discussing matters of importance. Food, which I assume you can't eat, so more for me. Abe, why don't you call Kelly, order food, and while you pick it up, Gunny and I will catch up." She turned to him, winked, and offered. "I can tell you what went on in the '50s to the '70s that isn't in the textbooks."

"Okay, you're right. Gunny can't eat, but he can smell bacon and obviously had some kind of obsession with jelly donuts when he was alive. So I'll order a couple of pies with sausage and pepperoni, some Chinese, and call Kelly." With that, I trudged upstairs to wash my face and use the phone in my bedroom to call him. He picked up halfway in the first ring.

"Hey. How did things go with your grandmother?" were his first words.

"Great. She's staying to watch the Eagles game and wants to know if you can join us. For some reason, she likes you. Probably because you were so steady during my divorce. Wanna come down? I'm ordering pizza and Chinese."

"Sure. Does she know about...you know?"

"Didn't have to warn her. She saw him when she came in. I guess since they're from the same time, there's a connection. Otherwise, I have no idea. I'm just going with the flow at this point."

We agreed that he'd pick up the food on his way down from Woodbridge, and I headed downstairs. Granna and Gunny were seated on the couch with their heads pretty close together like coconspirators, obviously conversing about Granna's experiences since the World War. From their hoots and laughter, I could only assume she was talking about her audacious exploits during the late '60s and early '70s, most of which my mother insisted hadn't really happened. I had no doubt they had, though. Nobody could make up the stuff my grandmother had actually lived.

Forty-five minutes later and post kickoff, I answered the door to Kelly, burdened with more food than I had ordered and more than we could possibly eat that afternoon (considering one of us was dead and couldn't). As he stepped into the foyer, and I relieved him of some of his burden, he studied me and simply offered, "You don't look too bad, so it probably could have been worse. I can stay longer if you want to talk later." I nodded, and we proceeded into the living room with enthusiastic greetings from the Gunny (which Kelly couldn't hear) and Granna (which he could).

Granna departed at 1915, and despite its awkward start, it had been a wonderful visit.

"I'll call to let you know I arrived intact," she promised, despite my offer for her to spend the night. She'd already said her farewells to the Gunny and Kelly, who politely stayed behind in the living room, seemingly enthralled with post-game interviews and commentary. Not.

Granna kissed me on the forehead and enveloped me in a huge hug. "I love you, sweetie. Thank you for being there for me. We'll be in touch."

We headed, arm in arm, down the walk together, and when I relinquished her at her car, she turned for one last hug and offered, "Kelly's a keeper, Abe. Don't let him go. Let him in." And with her usual aplomb, she settled herself behind the wheel, started up the car to the magnificence of Beethoven's "Eroica" coming through her vehicle's superb sound system, and was gone.

"I'll share with him, Granna," I remarked to her as much as myself. "But I'm not ready for anything else yet."

When I returned to the living room, the TV was off, and Kelly was alone. He gestured for me to take my chair (Hey! No Gunny butt!) and said, "Talk to me, Abe. I'll listen."

I chose, instead, to join him on the couch, where I shared Granna's potentially devastating news.

And he did. Listen.

*****

The phone rang at 2330 that night and I hoped it was Granna checking in. Though I had to get up at 0430 the next morning, I had only slept fitfully after Kelly departed. I didn't want to sleep through the phone ringing in case Granna actually remembered to call when she got back to Philly.

"Abe, it's me," she thundered into my unsuspecting ear. Yep, Granna was back to her old self. For the umpteenth time, I wondered why she treated a phone like a child's tin-can receiver.

"Hey, Granna," I managed, instantly wide awake. "Thanks for calling."

"It was a good run. I love driving that car at night. Makes me feel like I'm in a spaceship. Anyway I know you have to get up early, so I won't keep you. Just wanted to let you know I got here in one piece, and I enjoyed spending the afternoon with you and your guys." Me and my guys? Sounded like a verse from a 1940's song. Wait. Granna *was* from the 1940s. "And I'll try to find a way to help you figure out who the Gunny is. Anyways, good night. And I love you."

Message delivered, and before I could respond, she hung up. Though always overwhelmingly polite in person (all right, to non-family members), Granna's phone etiquette left much to be desired.

"I love you too, Granna," I whispered to dead air. "I love you too."

CHAPTER 16

Round-Robin and Roundhouse

S TILL COGITATING over Granna's bombshell, I faced the upcoming week with dread. Not so much the Myerson-Hale issue but spending Wednesday through Friday in the field, in increasingly colder weather, with high probability of sleet or, hopefully, snow.

On Monday, Dave and I dealt with Lieutenant Hale, whose punishment consisted of a stern lecture in private (delivered by Dave and me), an apology to Lieutenant Myerson (witnessed by Dave and me), and the requirement to tutor her in land navigation. I hoped the last requirement would be resolved shortly.

With Patterson now a pass, I only had Myerson's land-nav challenges with which to deal.

Tuesday was a short training day to afford the company preparation time for the three-day round-robin, starting on Wednesday. Taking advantage of the abbreviated schedule, I gathered up Lieutenants Myerson and Hale, stuffed them in my truck, and ferried them out to the training area for yet another remedial land-navigation exercise. Myerson had traversed this area almost every week for eight weeks, so there was no doubt that she could hike the distance in the prescribed time. Therefore, since we only had five hours before it got dark, I was authorized to transport us in my truck through the twenty-five-square-mile area. We had a field radio, and Hale would call in our whereabouts whenever we stopped.

My plan was to drive to the road closest to her objective (per her direction, of course. I wasn't going to do her planning for her.), dismount, and Lieutenant Hale and I would follow behind her as she made her way to what she thought was the right ammo can. Of course, he carried the radio, and the only time he would speak was to transmit our whereabouts.

Thankfully Gunny maintained his own radio silence.

Myerson directed us to her first drop-off point, and we all dismounted. As I shrugged into my harness and buttoned my truck keys in my side trouser pocket, I used this last opportunity to provide instruction, reinforcing what I had been repeating for the past two months, and hoping this time, it might sink in. Once Myerson started the practical application, I couldn't provide any prompting.

"Lieutenant, remember what I've been telling you, *pay attention to the elevation numbers on your terrain map.* If the numbers are going up, you search *up.* It's a *hill or finger.* If they're going down, you're headed down a *draw.* And if you're looking for a stream as a terrain feature, and it isn't there, what are you looking for to confirm that it might be dry for now but could become a stream?"

"Ferns," she promptly replied. Lieutenant Hale nodded and flashed her a thumbs-up. It's not like we hadn't had this exchange before, but I wanted to start her off on a positive note. I did *not* want to be out here, still, in January.

"Right. You can do this. Let's start."

For the next four hours, Lieutenant Hale and I strolled along behind Lieutenant Myerson as she stumbled through tanglefoot, mumbling paces and azimuths. After she found an ammo can and noted it on her card, she'd direct us to whether the next point required our driving or whether we could access it easily by foot. She had planned well. We only had to move the truck twice.

By 1635, Myerson had completed her last objective, turned her scorecard over to me, and we headed back to garrison to check the results. She was understandably nervous, but I was probably more so. If she failed, I'd be doomed to wander the land-navigation area for what had already become to feel like eternity.

Myerson and Hale hovered outside my office door while I graded her scorecard. I dreaded what I had become programmed to see—another failure—but stared unbelieving and aghast at the grubby piece of cardboard upon which she had entered her ammo can numbers. I rubbed my eyes and checked again—*all* her answers were correct. Just to be sure, I double and triple-checked the box numbers—100 percent accurate.

Myerson had passed land navigation. Finally.

Relieved and extremely happy that I wouldn't have to spend any more Saturdays trudging around the land-nav course, I gathered up my gear and headed toward the hatch, outside of which the lieutenants shuffled from foot to foot in anticipation. I was inclined to extend the drama, so I slowly (almost ponderously) closed and locked my door.

I moved toward the training office, two doors down from my own, as I had to record Myerson's score. When I emerged, Myerson and Hale were still positioned at my office door, looking perplexed and antsy.

"You passed," I announced as I made toward the exit and my truck. The dual whoop behind me confirmed they had heard.

Not surprisingly, Gunny appeared at my shoulder. "You finally have your get-out-of-jail free card. Congrats. Now you'll be home on Saturdays and can change the channel for me. I'll be able to watch more football games!"

"Keep it up, and you won't have *any* football games to watch. It'll be back-to-back cooking shows." He just snorted and evaporated.

I don't think he knew I was dead serious.

The next day, we headed out to the round-robin site. This activity was advertised as being an "easy" week since the lieutenants wouldn't be either attacking or defending, just experiencing. But the weather had turned cold, and I was not looking forward to sleeping in a freezing tent and waking up to frost on my combat gear.

Unlike the textbook definition of "a tournament in which each competitor plays in turn against every other," the round-robin we would experience was a series of hands-on training, like grenade toss and familiarization and firing of various types of machine guns and other weaponry. True, the next three days were potentially lethal, but the Tactics staff so closely supervised this type of exercise, we would be as safe as unfamiliar hands handling dangerous weapons could be. Well, unless one of the lieutenants was the arms-challenged equivalent of Lieutenant Myerson.

Though tense for SPCs, it would be interesting and a welcome break from the routine of classroom duty and paperwork, punctuated by PT.

Oh, did I mention that we'd be doing grenade work? That is, each SPC, one-on-one with a lieutenant and an EI, in a cement bunker, reinforcing the class on the fundamental carrying, proper handgrip, and three basic hand-grenade throwing techniques. *And* supervising the activation and throwing of a grenade over the bunker wall.

Lovely. Cold *and* the opportunity to be blown up if the lieutenant dropped the grenade before lobbing it over the concrete barrier.

Per usual, Dickey had declined transportation to the field operation, and we set out Wednesday morning at 0500 in order to make it to our tactical classroom by 0730. Our packs were particularly heavy since the weather was forecast to be unseasonably cold, and we had additional clothing. But at least we were only carrying one machine gun per platoon. We were, however, still burdened with a radio, wore flaks, helmets, and gas masks and carried packs and individual weapons.

Delta Company pulled into the bivouac area at 0700, and the Tactics staff directed us to areas where each platoon would establish an administrative bivouac. Administrative bivouacs don't require the occupants to set up and man defensive positions. Campfires are authorized but necessitate fire watches throughout the night.

My student platoon commander for this exercise was Lieutenant Grabowitz, with whom I would share a tent since, with me, the platoon numbered twenty-six. We each carried a shelter half, and once married up, there would be thirteen platoon tents.

We made our way to our assigned bivouac site, grounded our gear (that is, dropped our packs), and Lieutenant Grabowitz directed the platoon on where to establish their tents around a to-be-built firepit. While the rest of the platoon set up their structures, she and I erected our tent, staged our equipment, and, using our e-tools, carved out a shallow ditch around our tent in case it rained (or snowed). The ditch would capture water runoff, but going was tough. The ground was frozen, and digging was like chiseling marble, without the beauty or aesthetics.

E-tools are exceedingly handy. The modern version (or at least, what was currently modern and employed by the American military at this time) is made of lightweight metal, with one end shaped as a serrated-sided shovel and the other a handle. They are collapsible and, once deployed, can be either used for digging or sawing.

They can also be used as a weapon, using the wickedly sharp point on the shovel end like a clumsy spear.

At 1000, the platoon and the rest of the company gathered at the impromptu classroom, and I set about establishing our firepit—carving out a trench, positioning rocks, collecting brush, and chopping firewood. My fellow SPCs were doing likewise. I had brought a hatchet (heeding Neil's advice) since using an e-tool to chop wood could be pretty frustrating and time consuming.

"Doing a great job there, Abe," I heard over my shoulder as I hacked away at the frozen soil with my e-tool. "I wish I could help, but you know, I'm dead."

I glanced around to ensure we weren't being observed, and glared at the Gunny reclining against a large fallen log. His words belied his actions. This was a romp in the woods for him, and he was enjoying my having to dig into the frozen rocky soil and fetch firewood and rocks for the fire ring.

"What did I tell you about going visible around other people? Granna says sensitives might be able to see you or, at least, sense you. And there were e-tools when you were alive, so you should be able to help."

"Now don't you think a levitating e-tool *might* just attract a bit of attention?" Unfortunately he was right. Just as he was enjoying my breaking a sweat in twenty-five-degree weather.

"Stuff it," I shot back. "Slime over to the company and listen to what the instructors have planned for the day. When we're on the grenade range, I'll make sure the lieutenants are aiming your way when they lob their grenades. Even though they can't see you, I'd like to see what exploding ectoplasm looks like."

He disappeared, but I assumed he was relocating to the assembled lieutenants, and I returned to my excavating.

By 1100, the firepit complete and firewood staged, I joined the platoon for chow prior to departing for our first station of the round-robin.

While the company had been busy establishing the bivouac, in typical Dickey fashion, our intrepid leader had pitched a tent and commandeered a HMMWV to take him back to his office for the day. He'd return that night with the chow trucks, rested and warm, while we traipsed around in the cold all day. The next morning, he'd return to garrison to shower and linger in a heated office while we continued the field operation in frigid temperatures. And I knew he'd thump his chest to the other company commanders and talk about how he'd shared his lieutenants' discomfort overnight.

As a motor transport officer and logistician, I was accustomed to being treated like a second-class citizen. My MOS's role was support to combat arms, and I'd dealt with my fair share of prima donnas (usually infantry officers) who expected me to produce miracles of sustainment—crudely put, to pull fuel, ammo, food, vehicles, and maintenance out of my ass, with little to no notice or justification.

Dickey's behavior, however, was over the top, even for me.

I was relieved to hear my fellow infantry SPCs complaining about Dickey's conduct when we gathered prior to the afternoon's activities. We hoped that Dickey got caught in garrison and not able to hitch a ride back out to the field but, in our guts, knew he'd be back tonight.

Lucky us.

As I had anticipated, we were the first platoon on the grenade range, but my fears were unrealized, except when Lieutenant Negly's grenade didn't immediately explode after its toss over the reinforced wall.

The enlisted instructor and I had taken our stations on the opposite side of the cement pit, with Negly in the *tossing zone* (my term, not the Marine Corps'). She grasped the grenade, pulled out the pin (keeping the handle compressed against its body), and lobbed it over the wall. Instead of an immediate bang, however, we heard nothing. Not even a pop. Then despite repeated warnings during class not to do so, Negly headed toward the wall to peer over the side. Holy shit. I performed the quickest duckwalk on record, scuttled over to Negly's legs, and just about pulled her utility trousers off as I wrestled her to the cement floor. Meanwhile, the EI, seeing I was dealing with Negly, was on his radio, notifying the range officer that we had unexploded ordnance. Transmission complete, he directed us to low-crawl back to the wall adjacent to him and remain in place for another fifteen minutes until they could verify that the grenade was a dud.

We all settled back on the floor, backs to the concrete walls—Negly and I on one side of the pit, EI on the other—and awaited the all clear. The EI made good use of this downtime, launching into a thorough, respectfully delivered dressing down that reddened Negly's face while she fought back frustrated and embarrassed tears.

"Don't cry," I hissed at her. "Don't you dare cry."

She didn't. Good on her.

With the all clear sounded, the three of us made our way back to the platoon, standing by outside the grenade fortification. Negly returned to her squad. The EI and I collected the lieutenant in the bullpen, who had been "snapping in" with another EI, and headed back toward the concrete bunker.

"Ma'am," I heard behind me. Negly.

"Can we talk when I finish with Lieutenant O'Reilly?" (the officer I was escorting into the grenade pit and last to complete the exercise).

"Can do, Captain. But I think you need to know something before you go back into the bunker." Negly was still shaky from her experience, but there was obviously something that bothered her more.

"Staff Sergeant," I called to the EI. "I'll be there in a minute. Give me five." He nodded, and he and Lieutenant O'Reilly disappeared into the bunker.

"What's so important you need to talk to me now, Lieutenant Negly?" I asked, studying her ashen face and glassy eyes. "It's over. Just don't do it again. Got it?"

She shook her head. "It's not about my being stupid. It's about what I think I saw after you dragged me down from the wall." She nervously glanced over my shoulder, and in response, I glanced behind me but didn't see anything.

"What?"

"I saw him. I saw the ghost gunny. He was...hovering...over you and me. Like he was protecting us in case the grenade went off right outside the wall. Myerson's right. He's like your guardian angel. He's real."

Think fast, Abe. "I don't have a guardian angel, Lieutenant. When I'm really stressed, I focus on my grandfather. He was a Marine during WWII and kind of my...totem. Maybe my feelings and thoughts get so intense they...project...him to not only me but others." I paused, wanting to disengage from the conversation but deciding to leverage it for a credible explanation of my ghostly comrade. "It was pretty stressful in there. I think you saw what my brain was conjuring up. It happens, and it's not a big deal. And I'd appreciate it if you kept what you think you saw to yourself. We wouldn't want the platoon on the lookout for a ghostly protector every time they screwed up, would we?"

Thankfully, Negly was a credulous trusting audience, and she nodded so emphatically the chin straps on her helmet (which should have been secured) flapped back and forth. She wasn't John Wayne, for cripes' sake). "Got it, ma'am."

I hustled toward the bunker and heard Gunny's laughter echo through my head.

"She's got public affairs written all over her, Abe. She'll believe anything a more-senior officer attests is true." As quickly as it had come, his voice was gone.

"Damn you," I muttered and ducked into the bunker.

*****

By Friday afternoon, the company was absolutely exhausted. Though the training had been varied, and sometimes enjoyable, the days had been long. We were accustomed to long hours, but it was the weather that made this exercise seem interminable. In our time in the field, temperatures had seldom gone over thirty degrees; nights had all been in the low teens. We'd intermittently struggled through sleet and freezing rain to get to our training problems or wallowed in mud as we settled into machine-gun emplacements.

Since the weather was so extreme, the Tactics department erected warming tents at every station so lieutenants could have temporary respite from the elements as they waited for a problem to begin or end. We SPCs steered clear of the tents, convinced that we were just colder when we emerged from them but didn't share that with our lieutenants. They were here to learn, and we weren't. We knew numb brains, feet, and hands didn't help mental osmosis.

It started to snow, hard, as we formed up to start what would likely be a three-hour administrative movement back to garrison. Bob, who had been in and out of the field for the past three days, sauntered over to me as I zipped up my flak jacket and prepared to hoist my pack onto my back. As I've mentioned, Bob's job was to stay in the rear and ensure we had the logistics support we needed while in the field, though he inevitably shared the other captains' pain as we hiked to and from field operations.

"Dickey won't let us load packs in the trucks for the hike back, Abe. I tried," he offered. Bob and I had discussed the possibility the previous night when he brought out evening chow.

"Yeah, I guessed that. We all heard him yelling at you. We appreciate your trying, though."

"I've got six five tons to pick up lieutenants if they drop. With this snow, it's going to be slippery, and we're probably going to be full up by the time we get back to garrison. And it's going to be bad going over the tank trails."

Tank trails ran throughout the TBS training areas. Where they intersected with established roads, the road was elevated, like a shallow bridge, over the tank trail. However, like any bridge, they froze quickly and could be very slippery for traffic (and the people) traversing them.

Bob would be hiking at the tail end of the formation. If a lieutenant straggled or fell too far behind the formation, Bob would nudge him or her along, but if he or she continued to straggle, he would order the lieutenant into one of the trucks. He tried not to resort to this measure, as once committed to a transport, the lieutenant was there for the rest of the hike. For them, a shameful return that they struggled to avoid at all costs.

Dickey's priority, upon reaching TBS, would be to note who had ridden out the hike. Physical status was considered an excuse only if there was blood or a broken leg.

What a dick.

"See you on the other side, Bob," I said as my student radio operator gestured that we were starting. "I'll try not to send you any passengers from my platoon."

Bob laughed and headed toward the rear of the column. "March or die," he hollered as he passed by, and the lieutenants within earshot responded with oorahs in typical Marine fashion.

Two hours later, at our second rest stop, I dropped my gear and walked the line, encouraging my lieutenants to drink water and, since we were slogging through ankle-high slush and mud, change their socks. When I noticed Lieutenant Wagner drinking from her canteen but not changing her socks, I stopped and inquired why.

Always respectful, she started to struggle to her feet to respond, and I gestured for her to remain seated. I raised my eyebrows, inquiring.

"Please, ma'am. Don't make me take off my boots."

"Because?"

"I don't need to change my socks. Please, ma'am. I just need to keep my boots on."

Gunny's voice sounded in my ear. "Let her be, Abe. She's a Marine officer. Respect her judgment."

I *did* respect Lieutenant Wagner's judgment and, knowing we only had another hour of hiking, decided to back off. I nodded and returned to the head of the formation just as we got the whistle warning we were starting.

For this final leg, we would be last in the formation. Not easy considering we would be slogging through now-churned-up mud and slush. And to top it off, it also meant three tank crossings. They'd be slick, and they'd be slippery.

By this time, the snow was pelting down in earnest, mixed with sleet and freezing rain. We'd rotated carrying the machine gun and radio, and as the going got worse, Lieutenant Grabowitz and I walked alongside the formation, directing the lieutenants to grab the packs of the officers in front of them in order to make it up the inclines over the tank trails. I guess we looked like a giant slinky from above, but it worked.

Gunny walked next to me, chanting Bob's "march or die," intended, I assumed, to make me smile and keep me going. It did.

Meanwhile, we passed stragglers from the other platoons. Many would wind up in the trucks and, when we arrived, subjected to Dickey's scrutiny and derision.

When the lights of TBS appeared around three-quarters of a mile ahead, I dropped back to survey the state of my own platoon. All, except Wagner, were keeping pace with the main body. She was about twenty feet behind the formation, walking with Bob.

"She won't drop," Bob warned me. "But Dickey will notice she's so far behind. He'll label her a straggler. What do you want me to do?"

"Can you take her pack?" Bob's pack was lighter than the rest of ours since he hadn't stayed in the field for two nights. "I'll take her rifle and gas mask. We'll get her caught up, then put her pack on her so she finishes with her gear and with the company."

And that's what we did. Wagner doubled her pace, and a quarter-mile short of our stopping point, Bob returned her pack, I relinquished her rifle and gas mask and hustled to the front of the platoon. True, she was a bit behind the formation when we halted, but she was technically with the platoon.

Did I happen to mention that Wagner was all of 5'3", weighed about 105 pounds, and carrying 70 percent of her body weight?

Dickey decided to forego his usual posthike pep talk, dismissed the formation, and hustled toward the waiting five-ton trucks, almost drooling in his anticipation of denigrating those who had dropped from the hike.

Imagine his surprise and disappointment when he noticed there were no female officers aboard those trucks.

Of the thirteen lieutenants in the five tons, three required stitches of some number, five had heavy chest colds (you could hear the rattle as they breathed in), two likely had pneumonia (and had avoided detection by their SPCs in order to finish the exercise), and three had some kind of fracture or severe muscle pull. Thankfully Bob had been relentless. As he had observed lieutenants struggling, he'd pulled them out of the formation and into the trucks.

Helping Wagner finish pretty much with the formation could have been construed as cheating. However, if any of my fellow SPCs had had the same opportunity, they would have done the same for their platoon. And none of us, to include Bob, would say a word to Dickey about the technical straggle.

Was my platoon tougher? Nope. Were they more motivated? Maybe. I knew they unanimously disapproved of Dickey and, though always respectful of his rank, had little to no respect for the man. Did they have more to prove? Absolutely.

I ditched my pack in my office, secured my sidearm, donned a soft cover, and headed up to my lieutenants' rooms to check on them before they headed over to the armory to clean machine guns and the other automatic weapons used during the round-robin. Lieutenant Grabowitz had requested a corpsman accompany her to Wagner's room, and that was my first stop.

When I arrived, the corpsman was cutting Wagner's left boot from her foot; the right was already on the floor, slit open from tongue to toe. The reason was obvious—Wagner's socks were saturated in blood, probably from a severe case of blood blisters that had burst. No wonder she had been reluctant to change her socks.

The corpsman confirmed that Wagner should just stay close to her rack and didn't require hospitalization, so I excused her from heading over to the armory to clean weapons.

I was just short of my office, where I intended to drop my flak, shrug into my field jacket, and retrieve my sidearm to return to the armory, when I heard Dickey yell, "Rush, get in here." Damn it. Damn it. Damn it. I had no patience for his pontificating tonight.

As I crossed over the threshold into his office, I knew this meeting was going to be worse than I had thought. I smelled alcohol. Even though the company was not yet secured, Dickey had had a drink. Likely more than one.

"Go easy, Abe," Gunny's warning echoed in my head. "Dickey's spoiling for a fight, and he's drunk."

I had only stepped three paces into his office when Dickey planted himself in front of me, deliberately positioning himself in my personal space. Just as deliberately, I refused to back up. His location was calculated to intimidate me but he'd forgotten that I was at least an inch taller than him.

I leaned forward from the waist and he, not I, backed up a step.

Dickey launched his assault with "Fuckin' Wagner. She straggled. You and she'll report to me on Monday morning for counseling along with the other stragglers and their SPCs."

I caught a whiff of his breath. Whew! He *had* been drinking.

"That's if the corpsman clears her for duty on Monday. She's on bed rest for bleeding blisters. And I'd appreciate it if you'd drop the profanity." I had no problem with swearing, but coming from Dickey, it just sounded dirty and demeaning. "If you'll excuse me, sir, I have to head over to the armory."

I moved to depart, focused on relaxing my right hand, which had somehow formed itself into a fist.

"Not so fast, Rush."

Crap. He hadn't gotten a rise out me so he was going to take another tack.

I reluctantly turned and faced him. "Sir?"

Dickey had followed and was again only a pace in front of me, jaw cocked upward like Popeye confronting Brutus. I concentrated on assuming a neutral expression but more importantly, unclenching my fist. Those damn fingers just weren't cooperating.

"You think Wagner hiking with bleeding blisters makes her a Marine?"

"I don't think—I know—she's a Marine. Sir." I offered the title as an afterthought.

"You don't know shit. Wearing a flak and helmet and toting a rifle doesn't make a woman a Marine. You and your platoon are no more than grown up girls playing little girl dress up." He settled back on his heels, eyes fixed on my face for a reaction, convinced he'd delivered a killing blow.

I again started to turn, intent on departing, but thought better of it. Well, maybe not better and certainly not thinking. Instead, I delivered what I now know is a roundhouse punch ("a circular attack using a closed fist as the attacking tool that connects from the side, relying on momentum and centrifugal force to generate power") to Dickey's jaw.

He dropped like the rock he was.

As he scrambled to regain his feet (not easy considering the floor was highly polished and buffed, he was drunk, and very likely seeing stars), I extended my hand to help him up. He slapped it away of course, and finally managed to stand, albeit unsteadily. Behind me at the open doorway, I heard a titter, but it was empty by the time I figured out we had been observed. Unfortunately, somebody (or somebodies) had witnessed the incident, and I was in deep shit.

I forced myself to saunter to the door but not before I heard behind me, "The next time I see you, Rush, it'll be at your court-martial. You can count on it."

I slowly, almost ponderously, turned (I was starting to get dizzy with the back and forth) and regarded his bright-red face now with an even-deeper-red splotch on his jaw where my fist had connected with it (oh, that was going to leave a mark). "And I'm going to request a jury of infantry officers. You can explain how and why the 140-pound WM motor transport officer knocked the big bad weight lifter grunt major on his ass."

I continued down the passageway to my own office, which I entered with a sigh of relief, closing the door behind me.

By this point, I was shaking so violently I couldn't unzip my flak jacket. Instead, I sank into my desk chair and called Kelly at home. Though it was 2130 on a Friday night, I knew he was prepping for his latest case and likely there eating pizza with his TV on mute as he reviewed his prosecution notes.

Not surprisingly (but oh, so thankfully), he answered on the second ring.

"Kelly, it's Abe," I managed between chattering teeth.

"Hey, Abe. Back from the field? Thawed out yet? I was going to—"

"Kelly, I decked Dickey. I think—no, I know—he's going to court-martial me. What do I need to do?"

"First, tell me what happened."

And I did. Every last detail. But before I had finished, Kelly was laughing.

"Calm down, Abe," he soothed. "Dickey's not gonna do anything."

"Easy for you to say. He's royally pissed. And I think a couple of lieutenants either saw the whole thing or at least part of it."

"First, he'll sober up and realize he'd look like a wimp if he accused you of anything. Afterall, you're just a girl playing dress up, aren't you?" He paused, expecting and receiving my nervous titter in response. "Second, the lieutenants? They'll gossip among themselves and conjecture about what they *think* they saw but that's about it unless they're questioned directly. If they are, they'll tell the truth but that would mean Dickey's making allegations. Which he won't. And last but not least, you were provoked. And sexually harassed. Big time. If he'd said something like that to another guy, he wouldn't have been able to get up."

I relaxed somewhat. "I've gotta go. Weapons cleaning. Talk to you tomorrow."

"Hey, Abe," Kelly added before I hung up the phone. "If it came to a court-martial—and I'm certain it won't—I'd defend you. You *know* I'm a great defense counsel. Relax!"

And he was gone.

I smiled to myself and hung up too, shed my flak, and struggled into my field jacket. Chicken farts. My right hand hurt like the dickens and was starting to swell.

Gunny appeared at my side as I made my way down the hall, making for the armory. "Great roundhouse punch, Abe. I'm proud of you. That pig deserved it."

"I'm not proud of myself, but enough was enough. I just hope it doesn't go any further," I admitted.

"You might be surprised. I'll listen to chatter when we get to the armory and report back to you. Deal?"

"Good to go," I murmured, hoping most of the company was over at the armory, and nobody was around to overhear my part of the conversation.

I emerged from the BOQ into the frigid cold and ambled toward the armory. I really wasn't in any hurry to get there. I knew that, by now, whoever had witnessed the incident had shared the intel and likely the entire company was aware of my behavior. Might as well get it over with.

The rise and fall of more than two hundred and fifty-plus voices—booming, tired, and almost giddy—became louder and clearer as I made my way across the parking lot. However, as I stepped into the light that illuminated the walk adjacent to the outdoor cleaning area, the chatter stopped. Abruptly and totally. Two-hundred-plus voices stilled and waiting.

I gulped and stepped into the brightly lit and busy cleaning area.

A company of eyes followed my progress as I made my way to the corner where my fellow SPCs were gathered, and the noise slowly escalated to its previous cacophony as I settled back against the wall with my buddies.

Neil didn't waste any time getting to the point. "Is it true?" he opened.

"Yep."

"He was already drinking?"

"Yep."

"He's too chicken to do anything to you. And you did us *all* a favor," Doug observed. "'I just wish I'd had a chance to deck the bastard." With that, he headed toward the armorers' window where one of his squads was lined up to get its cleaned weapons inspected and accepted. The other SPCs nodded their concurrence, and we disbanded to join our own lieutenants.

I finally exhaled and headed toward my own platoon.

*****

Kelly and Doug were right. Dickey did nothing about our little encounter. In fact, I think it helped as his only response was to avoid any contact with me unless we were in a meeting, and then he studiously avoided meeting my eyes. Maybe *some* good had come of the incident, though I didn't want to get too comfortable with Dickey's lack of action. A year ago, I was fat (figuratively), dumb, and happy in Okinawa, focused on making it back to the States, and here I was, living with a dead guy.

In my experience, things could always go south when you least expected it.

CHAPTER 17

Everybody Loves the Holidays?

ON NOVEMBER 10, the official founding of the Marine Corps, regardless of where Marines are stationed or deployed, you will always hear, "Happy birthday, Marine." The birthday is a big deal for us. In November of 1775, the Continental Congress formed a committee to draft a resolution to establish two battalions of Marines to be employed on ships as well as shore. The committee met at Tun Tavern, Philadelphia. *Of course* the Corps was formed in a bar. The resolution was approved on November 10, 1775, and the Continental Marines were born. By early 1776, the first increment of troops was ready for action and almost immediately engaged, during March, in the Corps' first amphibious action at Fort Nassau.

In September of the same year, Marines were issued green coats with white facings (lapels, coat lining, and cuffs) with high leather collars, ostensibly to protect against cutlass slashes. Since Marines were often deployed aboard Navy ships, this would have made sense. Another theory is that the almost three-inch-high stock (as they were called) kept the wearer's head high during parade. Personally, I think it's a blending of the two, but for whatever reason, the high collar is still part of the dress blue uniform, and Marines are still often referred to as leathernecks based on their original attire.

In 1921, General John A. Lejeune, the thirteenth commandant, issued Marine Corps Order No. 47, Series 1921. This order summarized the history, mission, and tradition of the Corps and further directed that it be read to all Marines each year, on November 10, to honor the founding of the Marine Corps. Soon after, Marine commands began to not only acknowledge the birthday but celebrate it.

The first formal birthday ball took place in—you guessed it—Philadelphia, in 1925. Since that time, the annual event has grown from a simple fancy dress party to a formal event where civilian women wear gowns, civilian men wear tuxedos, and military members don evening dress or dress blues. The ball is a big deal as it affords spouses and significant others the opportunity to dress up along with their Marines, share the pomp and circumstance of a formal military event, and party (the last usually after the higher-ranking officers and VIPs have departed).

In 1952, then-Commandant, General Lemuel C. Shepherd formalized the cake-cutting ceremony, which has become not only part of the birthday ball proceedings but any celebration of the birthday. The cake is cut with a sword, either an officer's Mameluke (ivory-colored pommel) like mine or the M1859 NCO/SNCO sword (black pommel), which is the Marine Corps drill and ceremonial sword. When a single piece of cake is cut (sometimes there are three, one each for the youngest and oldest and guest of honor), tradition mandates that it be passed first to the oldest Marine present and then on to the youngest Marine. This represents the passing of tradition from generation to generation. Today it is customary that in addition to the cake-cutting, General John A. Lejeune's order and the current Commandant's birthday message are also read to those assembled.

A great parody of the Marine Corps cake-cutting is captured in Pat Conroy's *The Great Santini*, though there are a lot of Marines who consider the depiction sacrilegious. I, however, find it hysterical.

By November 11, Marines are usually partied out, and eyes become focused on the four to five days off at Thanksgiving.

Fortunately the company managed to get through the Marine Corps birthday ball with only a few lumps, bumps, and speeding tickets. Thankfully no DUIs.

This year, I made the pilgrimage to Philly for the formal Thanksgiving dinner—always hosted by Granna—and would then hightail it back to Virginia early Friday morning to assume duty as the TBS Command Duty Officer. None of my family disputed my claim of military commitments that precluded my staying longer, nor did I share that I had traded duty with another captain in order to work the day after Thanksgiving. Things were better with Mother, but I didn't relish four days in close proximity and biting the inside of my cheek rather than blurt out some kind of rejoinder or snide comment. Then there was the Gunny.

Gunny, of course, opted to accompany me north. This was his first experience traveling anywhere except the base and local spots, and he was absolutely enthralled with the number of cars and lanes of traffic. There were a few drawbacks. He spent an almost-apoplectic hour as we sat in bumper-to-bumper traffic in Maryland for no apparent reason, and when he spotted his third driver applying eye makeup in the rearview mirror while whizzing along at 60 mph, he resolved to keep his eyes closed for the rest of the trip. I knew he wouldn't, and he didn't.

I did spend considerable time and effort emphasizing the necessity of good behavior on his part and ignoring even his funniest comments on mine. Yeah right. Like he was going to keep his mouth shut, and I was going to play sphinx.

We arrived at my parents' home late Wednesday night. It was late enough that my mother had already gone to bed, and my father kept watch until I arrived. We exchanged abbreviated hellos, and both of us headed up to bed, while Gunny remained downstairs. The last I saw of him, he was heading toward my father's study, intent on the wall of books behind the desk.

On Thursday, I drove to Granna's a couple of hours earlier than showtime for dinner so we could visit. Mother had already come and gone, having prepped the turkey and committed it to the oven. She'd be back in an hour to consult with Granna on times, doneness, and final preps.

Granna's holiday dinners had always been, and continued to be, out of the ordinary. Anybody who could cook—male or female—was invited to do so, with the understanding that the joint turkey-stuffing effort (Mother's bird, Granna's savory stuffing) was already spoken for. Dad made a killer potato casserole, and JK's wife usually provided a sweet potato soufflé that was so tantalizing even I ate it (I detest any orange vegetable except carrots, since I associate their color with squash, which is up there on my yuck scale.). Tad and Kelly would appear with something trendy. My Aunt Hannah and Uncle Jeb (Granna's younger child) could be relied on to bring at least three mouthwatering desserts. Their three sons didn't contribute since the twins were in their junior year of college. Now legal, they just might bring alcohol. The youngest son was struggling through his last year of high school, so he just brought himself. I always contributed booze and Lynchburg Lemonade.

It wasn't the food that distinguished Granna's holiday meals, however. It was the serving and cleanup of dinner that was unconventional. The men, whether family or guests, were responsible for getting the meal on the table, clearing, and cleaning up.

Some might consider this sexist and punishment, particularly on Thanksgiving when men traditionally eat and retire to the television set to belch and watch football. Frankly it wasn't Granna's brainchild. My late grandfather had launched the tradition the first year of my mother's and father's marriage. Granpa insisted that women doing all the work just made them bitchy, and the men's temporary refuge in food and football was just that—temporary. They paid for it all holiday weekend as "abused and neglected" women embraced their cloaks of martyrdom.

Thanksgiving cleanup usually conjures up visions of mountains of dishes, leftovers to address, and hours of scrubbing and stacking. Granpa's vision included this scenario but with a twist. Half of the huge kitchen was focused on a state-of-the-art chef's workspace with Sub-Zero fridge and freezer, Viking stove, and a mile of marble countertops. The other half featured a walk-in fireplace, always crackling away on the holidays, two groupings of overstuffed comfy chairs and sofa, and a bar complete with a Kegerator and full-size refrigerator. It was the TVs, though, that put the kitchen over the top, a seventy-inch mounted on the wall opposite the workspace and two smaller ones within view of the seating areas. All could be viewed from anywhere in the room, and particularly on weekends or holidays, all featured different football games. The seventy-inch TV was inevitably tuned to an Eagles or college game that my grandfather (now grandmother) favored that year.

As a kid, I had preferred to be out in the kitchen with the men, fetching them beers and running the washed-and-dried good china into the dining room to be put away later. In addition to the TVs, there was cigar smoke and continuous off-color jokes. It was always bright, busy, and noisy. More importantly, it would be a far different atmosphere later this afternoon than the more-refined movie the ladies would be watching while they addressed Christmas cards or planned holiday parties and benefits.

Gunny and I entered through the kitchen door as I knew Granna would be inside, drinking wine and keeping an eye on all three football games as she sliced or diced or just dawdled.

"Well, if it isn't my favorite granddaughter and her pet Gunny," exclaimed Granna as we appeared. "Come on in! I know at least one of you can have a drink, so get yourself something, Abe." She flung my coat into a nearby chair and enveloped me in a hug, then turned to Gunny. "What's with you? Cat got your tongue?"

Gunny was almost drooling as he scanned the room, focused on the games playing on the three televisions. I didn't know if the Eagles or one of his favorites was playing today. Whoever it was, I suspected he would likely spend mealtime and later out here in the kitchen, in football nirvana.

I just hoped he wouldn't pester me to convert my entire downstairs into a sports bar, but I wasn't optimistic. I'd be captive to his haranguing and brainstorming on how it could be achieved all the way back to Stafford.

He managed to turn, regarding her with an almost-ecstatic smile. "I think I'm finally in heaven."

Granna wasn't flattered. "Humph. Just behave yourself today. Abe's aunt, uncle, and three boy cousins will be here too. That makes seven men and Abe for cleanup. Don't do anything that she'll have to respond to. They already think she's barmy enough without you helping her along." When she turned back to her stirring, I shot the bird at Gunny. Just to reinforce her point, of course. Gunny responded with a cross-your-heart-and-hope-to-die gesture (Wait, he was already dead. Who was he fooling?) and turned back to the larger TV to scrutinize halftime's scantily clad female vocalist and equally half-naked backup dancers.

As it turned out, it wasn't Gunny who disrupted our holiday cease-fire. It was Granna.

The holiday meal this year had actually been pleasant and not the ordeal I'd dreaded. I wasn't sure if Mother had mellowed (well, mellower for *her*), or maybe I was trying to make Granna's holiday as stress-free as possible, so I bit back some of the caustic comments I might otherwise have verbalized.

I hadn't seen my cousins in almost two years, and besides the obvious growth and transition to baritone voices (the latter more the baby than his older brothers), they had transformed into amazingly funny quirky young men. I found myself relaxing and actually enjoying myself. What a strange sensation!

Everything was fine until we moved to clear the table.

"Abe," Granna said as I removed her place setting. "Tell Gunny he can help with the washing up. I know he didn't eat, but he can still con…" Her words trailed off as she realized her flub. I flinched but didn't acknowledge the comment, hoping no one had overheard.

I was wrong.

"Who's Gunny, Granna?" JK asked, pausing by the swinging door into the kitchen. Before she could respond, he had pushed the door open and glanced into the other room. "There's nobody there. Were you expecting someone?"

Granna and I exchanged panicked looks, and as she struggled to stammer out some kind of response (a circumstance alien to her, in my experience), I knew I had to pull something out of my butt, or the conversation would devolve into further interrogation.

"Not here, JK. Granna's visited a couple of times since I got back from Okinawa, and she's gotten used to my friend…a gunny… hanging out in the kitchen while she and I visit. I guess it's just an uh…established pattern now." It sounded lame even to me, but I wasn't known for my improvisation.

"Oh, cool," offered my youngest cousin (I think he was George). "A real Marine gunny? Wasn't Great-Granpa a Marine, Granna? Was he a gunny like Lou Diamond or the guy in *Full Metal Jacket*?"

How the heck did my cousin know about Lou Diamond, unless he was familiar with Lou Diamond Phillips, named for the famous WWII Marine?

My, JK's, and George's exchange had provided Granna enough time to collect herself. She stood up, and her napkin trailed, unnoticed to the floor. She was once again cool, calm, and collected.

"Yes, he was a Marine, George, but I don't think he was a gunny. Isn't that term short for something, Abe?"

I jumped in rather than let the conversation drift back into dangerous waters. "Yes, it's a gunnery sergeant. We call them gunnies. They're kind of the backbone of the Marine Corps." My tutorial delivered, I hightailed it into the kitchen before I had to deal with any more gunny discussions. I planned to remain there for the foreseeable future.

Gunny was ensconced on the couch avidly following yet another football game on the larger TV. I took the opportunity, while we were alone, to whisper, "Granna flubbed and said something about the gunny in the kitchen. Can you go invisible or whatever you do for a while so she doesn't see you and blurt something out again? You can watch the football game. Just not be so…evident…to her and me."

For once, he dissolved as requested. Just in time. Granna led a procession of menfolk through the dining room door, and as she directed us on leftover packaging and recycling items, she surveyed the kitchen. Satisfied she wouldn't have any visuals to further provoke her, she nodded her approval and departed. She'd reappear a couple of hours later to supervise dessert and coffee.

The eight of us scraped and stacked, scrubbed and loaded, and within an hour, the twin dishwashers were humming as we helped ourselves to soda or alcohol and settled on the couch and chairs.

Uttering a satisfied groan, I had just propped my feet on an overstuffed ottoman when I heard Gunny in my ear.

"Your mother suspects something. She's pulled Fred aside, giving her the third degree. Maybe you need to intervene." *Intervene.* What Gunny uses words like *intervene* in casual conversation?

I didn't deserve this and contemplated leaving Granna to her own devices but knew Mother could be a ruthless interrogator. So I pulled myself out of my chair, warned my brothers and cousins that it was not up for grabs, and made my way out of the kitchen.

I didn't have far to go. Mother and Granna were huddled in a corner of the huge dining room, engaged in an intense—likely heated—whispered conversation. Mother glanced up guiltily as I approached and went silent.

"What's up? Aren't you supposed to be in the family room watching *Rain Man* or something?" I was not about to swing for the fence unless pressed to do so.

"Not now, Abigail," Mother retorted. "This doesn't concern you."

Granna looked incredulous. "It most certainly does." She turned to me so that my mother couldn't see her face. My grandmother's expression—a go-with-this look—indicated that I should play along with her. "Abe, your mother thinks I've fed you too many stories about your Granpa and put ideas in your head. That I've been encouraging you to believe that he's come back from the dead as a WWII Marine and that he's living with you."

"Mother? Really?" That seemed like a safe response.

"Abigail, you've always had a vivid imagination. And when you'd get together with Granna, you two would conjure up all kinds of imaginary…creatures." She struggled to collect her thoughts. "For almost a year, you and she had the rest of us believing there really was a life-sized pig in a vest living with us." Here she paused and seemed to gather herself for what she was about to say next. "This time, though, it's so real even I can see glimpses of something that isn't there."

Okay, Mr. Porker had been a fantasy Granna and I cooked up (could this be the bacon thing coming back to haunt me?) the year my grandfather died. We knew the pig wasn't real, but we delighted in convincing the rest of the family that *we* believed he was. I know now Mr. Porker and his adventures helped us deal with Granpa's death from a sudden massive heart attack. Inventing uncomfortable situations for others precipitated by Mr. Porker focused our thoughts and softened our grief. And as we healed, he appeared less and less. One day he was just *gone*.

The upside was that Granna's and my relationship, always close, had emerged even stronger.

The expression on Granna's face went from pleasantly neutral to immensely irritated. Before I could process that the playing field had changed, she spat. "Prudence, you are so off base here. I have *not* stuffed Abe's head full of Marine bullshit. She lives it every day, and you might as well resign yourself to that. And if you've seen anything, then it's on you. Maybe *you* need to get your head examined." Message delivered, Granna turned and sailed regally (but determinedly) toward the family room.

Mother shrugged and gestured for me to come closer, and I did. I knew she wouldn't slap me, but just in case, I stuffed my right hand in the pocket of my wool slacks. I didn't need a repeat of the Dickey incident.

"I sense something around you, Abe." Huh? She was trying to get along? "I've seen something with you. I don't know what it is." Surprisingly she reached out and hugged me, and I hugged her back. "I just hope it's a good thing. If it's not, I'm just a phone call away." She released me and pushed me toward the kitchen. "Now go hang out with the guys. And don't eat too much mince-meat pie. You know it gives you nasty reflux."

Nothing more of note happened that evening, and I went to bed early since I had to be on the road by 0330.

Gunny and I hadn't been in the truck fifteen minutes when it started.

"You know, all you have to do is knock out a couple of walls. The one between the dining room and the foyer is a good start. You already have a pretty open flow between the living room and the kitchen. Then the TVs…"

I knew it. Why did I take him to Granna's for Thanksgiving dinner?

It was a *long* ride back to Stafford.

*****

After Thanksgiving, we were on the downslope to the two-week holiday break. Well, not really the downslope. SPCs psyched the lieutenants up for the graded O-course, and with that event completed, the lieutenants truly were cruising toward Christmas. SPCs, though, continued with PT, classroom monitoring, and enduring Dickey's biweekly staff meetings. The latter I was kind of enjoying.

Just as Kelly'd predicted, Dickey had made no move to charge me for my indiscretion the evening we'd returned from the round-robin. Quite the contrary. Instead of popping into my platoon's meetings or formations to monitor my lieutenants' knowledge base or performance, he studiously avoided them and me. When they ran the O-course for grade, he was absorbed observing another platoon's warmups prior to their run. During staff meetings, his eyes never met mine, and any comments or responses I offered were wholeheartedly approved or complimented.

When I mentioned this treatment to Kelly, he wasn't surprised.

"He's afraid *you're* going to do an end run on him, Abe. He was overheard making really sexist remarks. And I bet not one officer in Delta Company would support his counterallegation that you slugged him."

With that reassurance, I was enjoying the hell out of Dickey's discomfort.

As for my platoon, I could almost feel their relief that they were no longer subject to Dickey's intense scrutiny. They obviously had heard about the confrontation in his office the night we'd returned from the round-robin and drawn their own conclusions that I had acted on their behalf. For whatever reason, it was evident that Dickey had changed, and it truly was gratifying to see lieutenants finally being treated as Marine officers rather than uniformed Barbie dolls.

*****

After we returned in January, the syllabus called for a couple of days of rappelling. When I'd first noticed it on the schedule, I'd thought we SPCs were in for a couple of quiet days; lieutenants would have some classroom instruction the first day, and the second, we'd monitor them as the Tactics staff supervised abseiling down the rappelling tower. No sweat.

I hadn't read the fine print. Or should I say, I hadn't completely read the class description. The part that stated in order for the SPCs to instruct and monitor their platoons, we had to complete our own training to be at least entry-level rappel-master qualified. For my fellow SPCs, this wasn't a big deal. All were combat-arms officers, and the infantry officers, in particular, had advanced training and experience in this area. I, on the other hand, had absolutely none.

Have I mentioned that I have an intense fear of heights? Like stand-on-a-chair-and-get-sick kind of fear? Like driving on a suspension bridge, and I have to focus on the road so that my eyes won't wander upward, obsessing on the people who had to work on the steelwork overhead?

SPC rappel training would happen the week we returned from the holiday, and I found myself dreading the new year, preoccupied with what I knew was going to be, for me, a horrific experience.

That preoccupation was interrupted, however, by, of all things, a Christmas tree.

CHAPTER 18

Oh No... Christmas Tree

AT 1900, the Sunday after the O-course event and one week before the beginning of our holiday-leave period, Dickey called all five SPCs and Bob into the office for an emergency meeting. As the six of us cooled our heels in the conference room awaiting His Majesty's arrival, we grilled Bob on what was so important that we had to drop everything (like watching football games, actually spending time with families, or drinking copious amounts of beer) with thirty minutes' notice. Gunny sat beside me, grumbling his own protests on why we had been pulled away from a Vikings game. I'd tried to dissuade him from accompanying me, but he was certain that the news we were about to get was something truly catastrophic, like declaration of war, so he had tagged along as I hightailed it over to the base.

"I have no idea what this is about," Bob finally said as we quieted down. "I got a call from the CO, was told to assemble you— uniforms not required—and that was all."

Before he could offer anything else, the conference room door slammed open, and we all stood as Dickey strutted in, counted heads, and magnanimously gestured for us to retake our seats. He settled himself at the head of the table and scrutinized us, one by one. Well, in my case, he kind of glossed over me and focused on Dave before settling on Doug.

"I won't mince words." (Yeah, that would be a first.). "We have a very serious situation."

That got all of our attentions. "I *told* you it was either war or a police action," Gunny murmured in my ear.

I didn't think I had heard Dickey correctly when his next words, deliberately and solemnly spoken, were, "The O Club Christmas tree is missing."

Message delivered, he settled back in his chair, folded his hands, and let us absorb the seriousness of the situation.

"Ah'm sorry, suh. I mighta mishud you. I thought I heard ya say the O Club Chris-mas tree is missing." As usual, Bob played sacrificial anode and affected his basso profundo sharecropper voice.

"I did, XO. This is *very* serious. Last night, the tree disappeared. It's decorated with the base CG's wife's personal antique ornaments. Tree and ornaments gone. The only thing left behind was the tree skirt."

"With respect, suh. Why was this so imponnant that ya dragged us in on a Sunnay night when we coudda heard 'bout it in less 'en twelve hours? What are we s'posed to do? Shit the tree ovahnight?" Uh-oh. Bob was on a roll.

I intervened. After all, I was kind of bulletproof right now.

"Sir, I don't think we understand why this is relevant to us. Is one of us suspected of taking the tree? Our lieutenants? Are there any witnesses? Could you fill us in on why we're here?"

"Good questions, Captain Rush." Of course, he was still in suck-up mode. Two months ago, he would have told me to sit down and shut up. "The O Club staff reports that there were several young officers in the club Saturday night, obviously happy and several drunk. They're the likely suspects."

"Short-haired young officers actually having a good time at the club. That's bizarre enough," Doug muttered what the rest of us were thinking. Thankfully, Dickey didn't catch it.

Junior officers tended not to gather at the main side club because MPs hovered not far from the building on Friday and Saturday nights, ready to pounce on unsuspecting officers who might (or might not) have had one beer too many and were potential DUI candidates.

"So among TBS, Amphibious Warfare School, and Advanced Communications School, there are probably a thousand young fit short-haired officers aboard this base. Why does the O Club staff think it was Delta Company lieutenants, sir? Were they singing Elvis songs?" As I said this, I glanced over at Neil, who covertly shot me the bird.

"This isn't funny, Captain Rush." Ugh. Maybe I had been too logical and offhanded in my observation? "Whether it was Delta Company or other TBS lieutenants, we will find the tree and the offenders. I called you all here tonight to give you the heads-up and to pass the word tomorrow morning at your formations about the theft. Have your lieutenants form up at 0630. I'll address them first, then expect you SPCs to reinforce my messaging. Encourage them to go to you one-on-one if they have any information." Translation: encourage them to snitch.

What? We had transitioned from mandatory morning formations at least a month ago. We formed for PT or admin movement, sure, but student platoon commanders handled reveille and getting their platoons to morning chow and class. SPCs were expected to be in their offices at least a half hour before their platoons headed to class so that student platoon commanders could check in, receive any last-minute instructions for the day, or report any "challenges" that might have occurred the night before. That is, issues or information that needed to be shared, though not serious enough to have contacted the SPC during the night. Likewise, SPCs remained in their offices at least a half hour after the company was secured to be accessible to the student billet holders or lieutenants who wanted to converse privately.

Since attending chow was not a requirement, student platoon commanders usually mustered their platoons thirty minutes before class, and they marched together to the classroom. Class tomorrow wasn't scheduled to start until 0800, so Dickey's 0630 formation was not only harassment but interfered with any plans I might already have made with my billet holders or those lieutenants who did want to go to breakfast.

"With respec', suh." Bob leaped into the fray again. "The SPCs can handle gettin' the word out to theah platoons without mustering them so early. I rec'mmend they set theah own times to talk to theah lieutenants and—" He got no further. Dickey drew a hand across his throat in shut-up-and-stifle motion.

"Formation. On the grinder, 0630 tomorrow morning. You will *not* discuss the reason for the formation with your platoons. I want to maintain an element of surprise. This matter is important enough that I will stay personally involved. I expect all of you to do the same. You're dismissed."

We all sprang to attention as Dickey swaggered from the room.

Scott, closest to the door, glanced down the passageway to ensure little Napoleon was gone and not hovering nearby. Bob gestured for him to shut the hatch, and we all sank back into our seats.

We sat in stunned silence for a couple of minutes, each of us contemplating how we could mitigate this idiocy. A little more than one week until the holiday break, and instead of the hundred-plus tasks we had to wrap up before we could secure for Christmas, our priority was now locating a Christmas tree that might not even be at TBS.

"Well, stick a banana up my ass and call me Susie!" Dave exploded. *Where* had the king of Norway picked up *that* Southern saying? "How the fuck did this become *our* priority? Just so he can be some kind of hero!"

"We'll go through the motions, but that's it," Bob said. "Who has room inspections tomorrow morning?"

"Me," I replied.

"Who has classroom monitor?"

Neil waved his hand. "I do."

"Okay. We need to hit every room, and we need to get it done before noon chow. Dave, Scott, and Doug, you're going to help Abe. Make sure you hit *every* room, gang. If you spot an ornament or a branch, or anything that looks suspicious, you come to me. Don't go through their personal effects—drawers, suitcases—but gear adrift and closets are fair game. It might take all of us to handle it, but we've got to do it quietly. Got it?"

We all agreed and headed toward our platoon areas to alert our student platoon commanders about the early formation.

"Stick a banana up my ass and call me Susie. Never heard that one before." Gunny would seize on the expletive. "I know it's unlikely you'll find the tree in your company's rooms, but even a blind squirrel finds a nut once in a while."

Cripes. Now he was off on a Southern aphorism kick. "Just shut up and let me figure out how I'm going to announce the formation and act like I don't know why we're even having a formation," I retorted, heading up the ladder to my platoon's spaces.

"Just trying to lighten the mood. See you at the truck." Gunny disappeared from sight.

"Holy grape nuts. See if I butter your butt and call you toast," I muttered to myself, reaching the landing.

"I heard that," floated up from below. "I'll consult Alf for an appropriate rejoinder."

"Bite me," was the only response (childish, I know) that I could muster.

*****

The next morning, after the lieutenants were safely committed to their classroom, and Dickey headed main side for a meeting—probably a brownnosing session with the TECOM (Training and Education Command) staff—Dave, Scott, Doug, and I met outside Bob's office, gathered master keys, and divided up rooms for inspection. We would all start with our own platoons, but since mine was less than half the size of theirs, I would start inspecting Neil's spaces after I completed my own. If we hadn't hit all the rooms by 1100 (an hour before class ended), the four of us would finish off Neil's rooms.

I completed my platoon spaces around 0930 and, as expected, had not found any indications of a tree or ornaments. I'd encountered piles of wrapped Christmas gifts obviously intended for transport or mailing to family or friends, but as expected, no Tannenbaum.

I hadn't expected to find anything. After all, the O Club staff had reported young men, not women, being the culprits. I had still been thorough in my search, though. Or at least without invading personal spaces. That didn't mean my lieutenants were necessarily blameless. They might have aided and abetted their male counterparts with hiding the tree and/or its contents, but complicity wasn't currently evident in their rooms. Now maybe their cars…

As I unlocked the door to room 308, home to Lieutenants Schmidt, Shaw, and Solkowitz of Neil's platoon, I was greeted by the distinctive almost-astringent scent of pine, and I hoped it was just deodorizer or incense or even Pine-Sol. I carefully closed the door and confirmed my suspicions: directly in front of me was an at-least-eight-foot Christmas tree, beautifully shaped, and resplendently decorated with perhaps as many as three hundred tiny handblown glass ornaments. They caught the windows' light and wrapped the tree in a diaphanous glow that danced and winked and twinkled, invading even the darkest corners of the room.

It was absolutely breathtaking, and I could only imagine how even more gorgeous it would be with the lights on. And I could only imagine how imminently pissed off and probably heartsick the base CG's wife must be about the tree's disappearance. I just hoped that none of the ornaments was broken or missing.

"So it *was* Delta Company." Gunny's voice, flat and dispirited, bespoke his disappointment that our lieutenants were responsible for the rip-off. "I just don't believe it. I don't want to believe it."

"You can go through walls, Casper. Why didn't *you* just flit around and save the rest of us the trouble of searching for this?" So much time wasted searching when we could have already developed a course of action.

"You didn't *ask* me to snoop, or I would have." There was something else, and I sensed he wasn't inclined to share it.

Realization dawned. "I get it. You wanted the chance to go to *my* platoon spaces since I don't let you visit without me. You're just plain nebby."

Before Gunny could respond, a key sounded in the lock, and I planted myself in front of the tree, hoping to block what I could from direct view. I knew it was stupid and hopeless, but I guess it was just reaction.

The hatch opened, and Dave appeared.

"Hey, Abe. Did you get to—" His eyes focused over my shoulder, and he slammed the door, shaking the floor and causing the glass ornaments to sway and tinkle.

"Holy shit! How did they do it? *Why* did they do it? Dickey is going to make Neil's life miserable if he finds out. Hell. He'll have the lieutenants thrown out of the Corps or at least go to summary court-martial." His babbling finished (for now), Dave sank onto one of the racks and just shook his head as he stared, open-mouthed, at the tree.

"I have no idea how or why, okay? But we have to do damage control. And quickly. Send Bob up here and replace Neil in the classroom. Remember to tell them that it's room 308. Got it?"

Dave rose and hustled out the door, punching the button on the knob to relock it. I pulled a chair from under one of the desks and did my best to prop it under the doorknob. It wouldn't stop someone from entering, but it'd slow him down.

"You know that's pointless, don't you?" Gunny observed, indicating the chair and moving toward the tree, regarding it in all its glory. "This is really something."

We silently admired the tree for about five minutes when three sharp raps sounded at the door. Bob identified himself and I moved the chair, opening the door only wide enough for him to enter. He relocked the door and replaced the chair.

"Merry damn Christmas," he muttered, sinking onto the same rack Dave had occupied as he regarded the spectacle before us. "Thank God Dickey won't be back until 1400. He's having lunch with some lieutenant colonel he knew from Eighth Marines. Knowing Dickey, this isn't something the colonel wanted to do. Probably accepted to just shut Dickey up, but it gives us time to figure out a plan."

Silence once again settled on the room as the three of us cogitated the matter at hand. I figured the Gunny was frantically trying to come up with some solution as well as Bob and me.

When Neil arrived, he was surprisingly calm.

"Look," he began, "there're some extenuating circumstance here."

Bob's face went from dark brown to eggplant, and the veins on the sides of his neck bulged. "*What?* Why do you even think there are extenuating circumstances when we have overwhelming proof of theft right in front of us? Are you high? This is at least CG's office hours or even a summary court-martial!"

Neil settled himself on another rack and gestured for Bob and me to take seats as well. Bob hesitated but complied, and Gunny settled himself next to me on the third bed. Great. I knew I was going to be subjected to his old familiar harangue on how the Marine Corps had gone to the dogs.

"Solkowitz asked to talk to me during the first class break this morning," Neil began.

"Well, I hope you did," Bob barked.

"Yeah, I did. And the story is too bizarre to be made up."

Bob responded with a roll of the eyes and a gesture for Neil to get on with it.

"According to Solkowitz, he, Schmidt, and Shaw *were* at the club on Saturday night. Solkowitz was the duty driver and doesn't drink anyway, so Schmidt and Shaw were free to knock back a few. There were other Delta Company lieutenants hanging out too, celebrating the end of the O-course and Shaw's setting a new record for time. Everybody was buying him beers, and Shaw got pretty fu—screwed up."

"Surprise, surprise," Bob dryly observed. The whole company (except Dickey) knew Lieutenant Shaw was Delta's super athlete despite being a party animal. None of us could figure out how he could drink as much as he did and still run circles around his peers. And he was near the top of the class in academics. Truly a golden boy.

"Anyway the three of them left the club at last call. They were parked out back, and when they hit the cold air, Shaw said he had to toss cookies. Even though it was pretty dark Saturday night, Schmidt knew the barfing might attract attention, maybe even from a senior officer, so he pulled Shaw into the shadows next to the building to do his thing. Shaw finished heaving chunks, Solkowitz and Schmidt

216

each grabbed one of his arms, and they were ready to leave the shadows and make for the parking lot when the kitchen door opened, and they saw two men and a woman dressed like kitchen staff carrying the tree outside and positioning it by the door. The woman's voice carried, and they caught something about how it was hidden well enough that the other staff members leaving wouldn't see it, and they'd be back to get it after everybody else was gone." Neil paused and regarded Bob and me.

"Does he think the XO just fell off the turnip truck?" Gunny observed.

"Go on," was all Bob managed. I glanced his way, and his face didn't betray what he might be thinking. Or planning. Strangely enough, crazy as the story sounded, I could see where this was going. Not that I entirely believed it, but I refrained from commenting until Neil finished with the why and how the tree had gotten into room 308.

"They flagged down two other Delta lieutenants that were getting into their car and told them what was going on. The four of them—Shaw was pretty out of it—decided that if they tried to report the cooks or whatever they were, the lieutenants would get blamed for moving the tree. After all, the staff was obviously taking advantage of a bunch of drunken and rowdy lieutenants that would likely get blamed for the theft. They figured the ornaments were probably valuable and were going to be sold, so the junior officers were good scapegoats. Kind of damned if they did something, damned if they didn't. So they did. Something."

Bob harrumphed and once again gestured for Neil to get on with it.

"They made a snap decision to get the tree away from there and figure out the rest later. One of the other lieutenants had a couple of tarps in the trunk of his car, and he ran back and got them. Since Solkowitz has a pickup with a camper shell on it, he pulled up short of the door but still in the shadows. They wrapped the tarps around the tree so the ornaments didn't get broken, and loaded it into the truck. Schmidt sat in the back with the tree to keep it from shifting, and they headed back to TBS, going just under the speed limit.

Solkowitz figured if he drove too slowly, the MPs were more likely to pull him over because they'd suspect he was drunk, and maybe check the back of the truck. The other lieutenants followed in their car. When the five of them got back to TBS, they secured the truck and dragged Shaw up to his rack. The rest of them sat around, drank coffee, and waited until 0300, then brought the tree in through the side entrance here at the BOQ. They spent most of yesterday trying to figure out what to do next."

"Why the hell didn't they just leave the tree in the truck? If they were so innocent, why didn't they call you and give you a heads-up? And who were the other two lieutenants?" Bob was obviously not yet convinced.

"They were afraid if they left the tree on its side, under the tarps on the metal floor of the truck, that the ornaments might break. You can see they're pretty delicate. I don't know more than that. Before I could get more details, class restarted. Fifteen minutes later, Dave showed up, and I hightailed it over here."

With a sigh of either resignation or disgust, Bob rose and headed toward the hatch and moved the chair but turned back to Neil and me before departing. "This all sounds crazy enough that it might be true. It's 1100. They'll be breaking soon for noon chow. Neil, get back to the classroom, relieve Dave, and tell Solkowitz I want to see him, Shaw, Schmidt, and the mystery lieutenants in my office at 1145. You too, and the other lieutenants' SPC, once you find out what platoon they're from. After we're done, all SPCs will meet in the small conference room on second deck at, say, 1230. I don't want Dickey coming back from his brownnose lunch and seeing all of us in my office. He'll get suspicious." Neil nodded, moved past Bob, and disappeared out the door. "Abe, let Doug and Scott know what's going on." He opened the door that Neil had closed behind him. "And start thinking about how we're going to get this fuckin' tree out of this room. More importantly, what are we going to tell Dickey about the search without downright lying? I won't lie, but I do need a believable spin."

We walked silently back down the passageway, Bob to his office, me toward Scott's to fill him in on the morning's developments.

I heard the subtle buzzing that preceded Gunny's materializations as he appeared at my side.

"Do you want me to listen in on the discussion with the lieutenants and Bob?" he offered.

I was tempted to refuse, but curiosity got the better of me.

"Go ahead and listen in, and let me know what they say and give me your call on whether it's bullshit or not. We'll have to deal with the tree no matter what, but I'm curious about where Bob will be coming from at 1230."

"Aye, aye, Captain. At your service. Of course, your interest is purely professional and not nebbiness." He sniggered as he mock-saluted and evaporated.

By the time we gathered at 1230, Gunny had reported back on Bob's discussion with Neil's and, unsurprisingly, Doug's lieutenants. This time, though, it seemed Fourth Platoon had engaged to help, rather than harass.

Gunny's impression was that all parties were telling the truth, and their failure to alert their SPCs was due to obsessing too long on how to extricate themselves from the mess. At this phase in training, they were more or less leading themselves and had been encouraged by SPCs, curriculum, and instructors to develop their problem-solving skills since in two months, they would be faced daily with what-now-lieutenant situations. Obviously they hadn't conducted an ORA (Operational Risk Assessment) on Saturday night or even Sunday.

Bob updated Dave, Scott, and me on what had transpired at the 1145 meeting and professed his belief in the lieutenants' story. He was equally convinced that the staff had intended a rip-off, but he was stymied on how we could expose their culpability. Before we went down that rabbit hole, however, we needed to figure out what to tell Dickey upon his return and how to get the tree—ornaments intact—back to the club.

We handled the easier problem first—getting the tree out of room 308 and back to where it belonged. The club was closed on Mondays, and today was Monday. We couldn't get the tree *into* the club, but we wouldn't have to worry about dodging staff either. Neil, Doug, and their lieutenants would do essentially the reverse of Saturday night, but they would first remove all the ornaments (with their dress uniform white gloves on, of course) and wrap and pack them in cardboard boxes. Obviously the MPs would become involved, but we weren't sure if they would waste the time and effort trying to lift fingerprints, but you never knew. Tomorrow was an early day, so the BOQ would be quiet by 0200. That's when the tree, once again wrapped in tarps sans ornaments, would be transported to the club and positioned at the same place it had been found. The boxes of ornaments would be placed alongside it. Once that was done, Neil would call the MPs from a pay phone off base and report suspicious activity at the club.

I know, it seemed cloak and dagger and rife with possibilities, even probabilities, for detection and failure, but it was the best we could come up with since it was now 1330, and Dickey was due back at any moment. He'd monopolize the rest of our afternoon collecting our statements and tediously outlining next steps in pursuit of the phantom tree.

Which brings me to what line we'd feed Dickey.

Though classroom monitor duty was usually a morning or afternoon (but not both) assignment, we replaced Dave with Neil as that afternoon's duty SPC. We all knew that if Dickey got hold of Neil, he wasn't verbally facile enough to dance around questions or accusations. Neil would trip up, Dickey would smell blood, and he'd ferret out the truth.

All six captains had either sighted or had firsthand knowledge of the tree, so we couldn't state that there was no tree in Delta Company spaces. Scott, Dave, Doug, and I could all honestly confirm, however, that there was no tree in *our* platoon spaces.

We'd try to keep Neil out of view or occupied for the rest of the day. He'd check in with Dickey in the morning, and by then, he'd be able to truthfully affirm that he had walked his rooms, and there was no tree.

As soon as we disbanded, the Company Training Officer would receive a call from Captain Dicerbo's (Bob's) wife that he had a domestic emergency that required him to head home. Since Bob lived an hour away in rural Spotsylvania, he likely wouldn't return today. He wouldn't be available should Dickey telephone (he had caller ID) but *would* respond when I contacted him.

I would be acting XO since I was the senior SPC and had often filled in for Bob when he was out of the area. More importantly, since I had experience as a fast-talking consultant, I'd have the best chance of deflecting Dickey's questions. *And* I'd leverage his current reluctance to deal with me to my advantage. Or so I hoped.

By 1400, Neil was in the classroom, Bob had departed for home, and I was installed in my office shuffling paperwork. Gunny was wandering the halls and classrooms in an attempt to determine how much the rest of the company knew about the tree's location. 1500 came and went, and no Dickey. At 1530, Dickey's office door was still closed and secured (I tried the knob.), and I checked in with the Training Officer to confirm that Dickey hadn't returned or called. He hadn't. I reminded him that any calls from Dickey or Bob (or the TBS XO or CO) should be forwarded to me and returned to my office.

Hmm, where was Dickey?

At 1615, my phone rang, startling me enough that I jumped up, crashing my chair back against the wall behind my desk. At the second ring, the Training Officer appeared at my door, pointed at the phone, and mouthed *CO* and departed. I gulped and picked up the receiver.

"Delta Company, Captain Rush."

"Captain Rush, this is Major Mackey." He sounded kind of upset. Please, please don't let him know already.

"Yes, sir. How can I help you?"

"The Training Officer said Captain Dicerbo had to leave to handle an issue at home and left you as acting XO. Have you heard back from him?"

"No, sir. But if it were catastrophic, I'm sure he would have called and let you or me know what was going on. He has three kids under the age of eight, so it could be anything from a broken leg to—" I was prepared to babble indefinitely, but Dickey cut me off.

"Got it. I won't be back this afternoon. My car slid into a ditch on my way back from main side, and I had to get it towed to a service station. My wife picked me up, and we just got home. What's up with the—"

"Oh geez, sir. Sorry to hear that. I hope you weren't hurt. Maybe you need to get checked out at sick bay. I had an uncle who crashed his car and walked away from it. Two days later, he dropped dead from a brain aneurysm. You don't want to risk your health when dealing with an automobile accident. Too many unknowns—"

"No, I'm not going to sick bay. It wasn't that serious. I'm fine. What happened with the room—"

"Okay, sir. Whatever you say, but I recommend you get checked out. After all, we've got the holiday break coming up, and you don't want to be stuck in traction in a hospital because you didn't take precautions. You know, being a motor transport officer, I've seen more than my fair share of what a big hunk of metal can do to the human body. While I was in Okinawa, I ran a convoy of five tons from Camp Schwab down to Camp Kinser, and a civilian car T-boned one of my trucks. The civilian ran a red light as my convoy was passing, and—"

"Thank you, Captain Rush. I'll see you in the morning. Call my home if you hear from Captain Dicerbo. Tell the Training Officer to have the XO call me if he contacts the company office after you secure." With a slam, Dickey was gone.

"Nicely done, Abe." The Gunny was back, reclining on my couch. "That must have been hard for you. You really don't talk very much, let alone babble." At that one, I looked up, flattered and surprised. A *compliment!* "But you just confirmed Dickey's impression that you're a twit."

I pulled my chair back to my desk and collapsed into it. I felt like a wet dishrag. "Double shit. That was exhausting. And if the price I have to pay for not lying is confirming Dickey's thinking I'm a twit, then fine. Did you hear anything? Anybody suspicious?"

"Nope. They all seem to think that it was lieutenants from Charlie Company since they graduate next. That's January, right? Delta graduates in February?"

"February 21. We are definitely on the downslide."

"Who's on the downslide?" Neil strolled into my office and glanced around, trying to locate my companion who, of course, wasn't visible. Gunny slid over to the side of the couch closest to me as Neil threw himself onto the side nearer the door and propped his boots on the coffee table. "Talking to yourself again, Abe? You've got me doing it too. Maybe you're a bad influence. Anyway what's this about Dickey not coming back this afternoon?"

Obviously he had checked in with the Training Officer at the company office before he headed to mine, so I filled him in on my conversation with Dickey and my impression that he had seemed out of it on the phone.

"Training Officer thought he sounded like he had had one too many. What do you think?" he asked.

"I was too busy tap-dancing to worry about how he sounded. Let's just be happy he didn't come back, and we can get that freaking tree gone. And since you're here, I assume class is over." I checked my watch, 1645. "I'm going to secure the company, and then you and I can call Bob." I buzzed the company office and instructed the Training Officer to announce over the PA system that the company was secured, then turned back to Neil. "Let's call Bob and fill him in."

Neil closed the door, slid over the couch to be closer to the speakerphone and, unknowingly, squarely onto Gunny's lap. Affronted and disgusted, Gunny dissolved but didn't reappear. I'd hear about that all the way home, but the look on Gunny's face was worth the diatribe I'd have to endure.

I stifled a laugh as I dialed Bob's number. Since we were on speaker and didn't want to be overheard, I quietly informed Bob, who answered after the prearranged number of rings, about my conversation with Dickey, confirming that the ornaments were packed and the tree staged for transportation.

"I'm going to have my wife make the phone call from a pay phone," Neil concluded. "Less likely that Dickey will try to figure out who made it."

"He probably won't hear about the tree's recovery until late tomorrow morning at the earliest. He wasn't in charge of the search.

He was just a self-appointed investigator. But once he hears, he might give you, Abe, the third degree," observed Bob. "I don't think he'll go after your platoon, though. He's been pretty hands-off lately. What we *should* be prepared for is an inquisition first thing in the morning. What and when is on the training schedule tomorrow?"

I checked the schedule on the wall behind my desk. "At 0700. Classroom. Introduction to convoy operations. I'm teaching it, with help from Ray Turner. He's a logistician and never done one, so I agreed to lead the class, with him in support instead of the other way around. Then we're going over to the motor pool and get up close and friendly with the rolling stock."

"Okay. I'm not calling Dickey tonight, so pass the word for all SPCs to be in by 0600. We need to be on deck when he gets here and all of us able to swear there is no tree in our spaces. When he finds out later in the day that it's been recovered, he might suspect we got rid of it, *but* we'll have had the advantage of time to give us credibility. I know you guys think I'm overthinking this. Remember, I deal with that…guy every day, and you have no idea how controlling and paranoid he can be."

Neil and I confirmed our understanding and rang off.

"Abe, if you could let Dave, Scott, and Doug know about the 0600, I'd like to head home and get some sleep before I have to be back here at 0200. Is that okay?" Neil requested, opening the door.

"No problem. Good luck tonight." Neil waved and was gone.

As expected, my ride home was dominated by the Gunny's ravings on the lack of courtesy demonstrated by not only my generation but the entire Marine officer corps. It was truly amazing how he had assessed and judged millions, if not tens of millions, of people around the world *and* the *entire* Marine officer corps. Imagine! I was so beside myself with embarrassment and shame that I laughed hysterically for the half hour it took to get home and almost ran my truck off the road twice.

Unlike Neil, I was able to get a decent amount of sleep before my phone rang once at 0315—the signal that the tree had been successfully delivered and phone call placed to the MPs.

Bob's prediction was spot-on. When Dickey arrived (Surprise! In his wife's car) at 0615 the next morning, all of us were already in uniform and awaiting the summons that came at 0620 for a 0630 meeting in the conference room. If Dickey was disappointed that he hadn't caught us, literally and figuratively, with our pants down, he didn't show it.

We were subjected to thirty minutes of interrogation, the same information demanded in various ways to catch us up, and we were all able to answer, truthfully, that we had inspected the entire company spaces, and there was no Christmas tree. As a snarky epilogue before we were dismissed, Bob suggested a search of the armory since it had restricted access, and really, you never knew what those armorers were up to because they worked under lock and key. I kicked him under the table before I rose to leave, but the CO didn't register Bob's responding oath and glare my way.

Dickey was already reaching for the phone as we filed out. I suspect he was contacting the TBS XO (who might or might not already be in his office), reporting his company clear of any involvement in the tree-napping, and heavily suggesting that a search of the armory might be in order.

CHAPTER 19

Transition

ENOUGH OF captain conspiracy and lieutenant lunacy. We need to get back to the gorilla (or is it ghost?) in the room. It had been more than four months since Gunny had made his presence known, and all I had to show for it was the knowledge he had likely died at Sugar Loaf.

I was certain of two things, however: more people were glimpsing him (and I didn't think they were *all* sensitives), and when he did appear, he seemed slightly less *there*. Not exactly dissolving or fading, but less sharp, less in focus. It was almost as he became more visible to a larger audience, he was less tangible. I didn't know if Gunny was aware of these subtle changes, so I kept my thoughts to myself, even as I searched those online Marine Corps sources that I could access on my office desktop. In a rushed phone call the previous week, Kelly disclosed he'd made some progress in his research, but with the upcoming holidays, our schedules were frantic, and we'd not been able to further connect.

We'd have time to compare notes and cogitate, though, on the upcoming ski trip we were taking with friends to the Poconos.

*****

The company managed to get through the rest of the Christmas tree week and through the following abbreviated one before the holiday break. Since Christmas this year was on a Monday, we essentially did nothing (some PT half-days) until the Wednesday before, when the holiday-leave break would commence. Lieutenants didn't have a lot of vacation on the books, so most wouldn't head out until Friday or Saturday, likely returning the next weekend and spending New Year's at TBS. Or the reverse. Those who were married were authorized to phone in if not on leave since we still had to account for them. Officers who remained in the BOQ were required to swing by the company office and verify that they were still alive. We SPCs had worked out a duty roster to accommodate our leave plans (as captains, we had more on the books), and I opted to stand watch until Saturday, when I'd head first to Philadelphia for Christmas, then onto the Poconos for four days with Kelly and other friends, skiing and just relaxing.

Christmas was the usual Christmas, but my sights were set on skiing. I can only do cross-country since I'm kind of a klutz going downhill. The holiday did bring good news—Granna's situation wasn't as grave as she'd originally feared. As long as she slowed down (was that possible?), had an implantable defibrillator installed after New Year's, and modified her diet (among other things, that meant no more huge supercharged and caffeinated Irish Breakfast mugs of tea), her prognosis was very good. Despite her good fortune, however, she complained constantly about that "quack at Johns Hopkins," Dr. Proctor. I think the grumbling was more to save face than lack of confidence in his care (confidence that seemed to be increasing proportionately to her whining). He was just as blunt and uncompromising as she was, and I suspect she had met her match.

Gunny reluctantly opted to accompany me to the Poconos once he realized that even if he stayed back at my town house with the TV on, he wouldn't be able to change the channels. When I shared with him that Kelly had some possibilities regarding his identity and wanted to discuss them some evening during our vacation, he was all in. Once at the lodge, he spent one day observing my cross-country endeavors and the others' more practiced downhill skiing, but

I sensed he had been an accomplished skier while alive and found our pursuits amusing but, more obviously, boring. I understood and supported his spending the rest of the stay hanging out in my room with the TV tuned to ESPN. Surprisingly I didn't need to explain to my roommate, Darlene, a fellow captain and the TBS adjutant, why I was tuning into the sports channel each morning. She didn't even comment, and I assumed one of my fellow SPCs had filled her in on my often-bizarre behavior and/or invisible friend.

Sigh. If I had had any hopes of making a career of the Marine Corps, they were slowly diminishing while my reputation as an eccentric was growing. True, the Corps valued its 1 percent lunatic fringe—Marines who conformed physically and operationally but danced to another drummer, challenging groupthink and proposing innovative alternatives to tactics and procedures. I longed to be a valued lunatic. However, I had to face it. I was increasingly viewed more as crazy (or, at the least, daft) than a revolutionary thinker.

Kelly was a pretty good downhill skier and spent three of our four days in the Poconos with Darlene and his buddies, hitting the slopes. He did spend one day skiing with me. I warned him that he should dress in, at most, long underwear, wind-resistant pants and light jacket, shirt, and maybe fleece, despite the current biting wind and forecast of a high of twenty-five degrees. Instead, he showed up in several clothing layers topped by a hat and heavy parka. Though it was pretty cold, we'd soon work up a sweat, and when I chided him about his attire, he trustingly ditched the parka with the guy handing out skis and borrowed his windproof jacket. Since Kelly is a sturdy six feet five inches, and the rental guy was only around six feet and more on the slender side, it was a tight fit but would do the job of blocking the wind.

Quickly realizing that cross-country wasn't for him, Kelly commented, within fifteen minutes, that it felt like he was slogging through quicksand. He just couldn't get the hang of the arm/leg movement, nor was he built for this type of exercise, and I sniggered every time I glanced back at him. Due to his height and bulky shoulders, he resembled more a bear on barrel staves than a man, trudging along the alternately uphill and downsloping paths, emitting impressive combinations of expletives and pleading for me to shoot him. He hung in there, though, and actually trudged the entire eight-mile loop. Sure, it took us a more than four hours, and when we returned to the lodge, Kelly flashed me a weak smile and mumbled something about heading to the sauna.

When he didn't show at dinner, I feared he had fallen asleep there, but his roommate, Chuck (a fellow lawyer from Headquarters), reported that when he had come back from the slopes, Kelly was already in bed and refused to move any further than the bathroom, and then, only if necessary. When Chuck returned to their room after a postdinner drink around the fire with the rest of us, he carried two cheeseburgers and a couple bottles of water just in case Kelly was still alive and hungry.

The food and water must have hit the spot as Kelly was recovered enough the next morning, our final day in the Poconos, to again attack the slopes, albeit a little stiffly.

Darlene spent two days with Kelly and his friends downhilling, and one day with me on the cross-country course. By the last day, however, she had tired of snow, and I was now noodle-legged and armed, so we drove into the nearby town that boasted kitschy specialty shops (which proved more tired than trendy) but which did host an excellent German restaurant with great food and beer.

When Darlene and I returned to the lodge, Kelly hailed me from the bar. He was sitting at a sheltered table, a bit removed from the others but which afforded him a view of the lobby. I assumed he was waiting for me to return from town.

Strangely, whether Kelly knew it or not, Gunny was languidly draped on the chair across the table from him. I excused myself to Darlene, who nodded knowingly and offered, "Get him, Tiger," as she headed toward the stairs. Sheesh. Everybody was an expert on my behavior these days.

"Wine or beer, Abe?" Kelly asked, rising from his chair (as did Gunny) and pulling one out for me.

I shucked my coat, threw it on the chair not occupied by the Gunny, and sank down in the proffered seat. "Diet Coke. Darlene was the duty driver, so I had two glasses of Auslese at the German restaurant. I feel pickled."

He headed toward the bar to get me my drink and, I assumed, another beer for him. There were already two empties on the table, so he must have been waiting awhile.

"Does he know you're here?" I murmured to the Gunny.

"Strangely enough, I think he does. He was already sitting here when I drifted down about an hour ago. He kind of...startled... when I sat down, like he felt a chill. By the way, do you feel cold when I'm around you? I mean..."

"I've got it. Nope. All I experience is your warm and generous personality. And either a buzzing or ringing."

Kelly rejoined us and placed my drink in front of me while he pushed another beer for himself across the table. "I ordered some nachos to help sop up the pickling." He settled back in his chair and observed, "He's here, isn't he? I think I felt him earlier, and you're not very good at hiding that you're talking to yourself."

Gunny flashed me such a smug smirk that I longed to kick him but stopped myself midmovement. It'd just be like him to anticipate my plan and dissolve, leaving me with a toe stubbed on a chair or table leg. Worse yet, toppling out of my chair.

"He is."

Kelly looked relieved. "I thought so, and that's good." He fiddled under the coat I had dropped on the chair, fished out a notepad from under it, and brandished it in the air. "We're going to need him for this conversation, but we need some privacy. Let's eat our nachos and then head over to the library when we're done. There's never anybody there."

We chatted over drinks and the nachos once they arrived, and while Kelly settled the bill, Gunny and I wandered down the passageway to the library which was, as Kelly predicted, deserted. I collapsed into an overstuffed chair, one of a grouping of four, in an alcove and far enough from the entrance that we wouldn't be overheard and only casually observed. I didn't care if strangers saw me talking to someone who wasn't there (all of our group seemed to accept that I was touched), but Kelly was a lawyer. He needed to maintain some semblance of credibility, and he didn't need me to endanger his current reputation and our future relationship (whatever it may be) because I was an acknowledged crazy.

"Do you think he's found something?" Gunny, no longer nonchalant, nervously leaned toward me from the chair he had taken. "You're going to translate for me, right?"

At this point, Kelly appeared at the door and sighted me in my corner. Before he sat down, though, he nodded quizzically toward the chair in which Gunny was sitting. I pointed to another one that was unoccupied, saying, "This one is vacant."

Kelly sat, opened his notebook, cleared his throat, and began, "I have five possibilities. I started with MIAs and KIAs. Initially. There were a lot due to the explosions and collapsed caves. At this point, they've accounted for all but three Marines. Then I came at it from the other direction. Since we know he was at Sugar Loaf, I focused on gunnery sergeants that were verified killed there. And geez, Abe, there were several. I was pretty surprised."

"When the lieutenants bit it—and a lot of them did—gunnies were fleeted up to act as platoon commanders." Gunny's voice caught, and he struggled to continue. "You can't lead from behind."

When I passed this comment on to Kelly, he nodded his understanding and agreement. Leading from the front is instilled in every Marine, whether enlisted or officer. If you're in charge, you don't coordinate or manage from the rear. This concept becomes harder to ignore as you advance in rank, but generals on the front lines are more liability than asset.

"Based on what he remembered about the assault, I assumed he didn't die early but probably toward the end of the action. That yielded five possibilities. Gunny, do you want me to continue?"

Gunny, eyes glued to the floor, raised his thumb in the affirmative. I nodded his assent to Kelly.

"Okay. Here we go. Jack Keller—and that's Jack, not John—John Alexopoulos, Frederick Salton, Calvin Mercer, and George Rodriguez."

As Kelly rattled off each name, I repeated them and studied Gunny's face for any signs of recognition. There was only disappointment there.

"A couple sound familiar, but nothing rings a bell," he said.

I gestured a thumbs-down.

Kelly studied his notebook and looked back up at me, nodding that he had a plan. Of course he had a plan. He was a lawyer, for cripes' sakes. They always had a plan, just like the trains in Germany always ran on time, and the English were known as notoriously bad cooks.

But I digress.

"Let's approach this by process of elimination. First, we'll rule out George Rodriguez. The stereotypical Hispanic is shorter with darker coloring. Since Gunny is blond, kinda green-eyed, and lanky, it's unlikely he's of Mexican or Puerto Rican extraction."

I glanced at the Gunny who was nodding in the affirmative.

"Wait just a minute, you two," I interjected. "His father might have been Hispanic and his mother Anglo, which could explain his coloring."

Gunny shook his head. "That's not the way things usually worked in my time. I agree with Kelly. It's not me." Damn men. Always sticking together. I didn't share this comment with Kelly.

"Fine, nix to Rodriguez. We should eliminate Jack Keller and John Alexopoulos too," I countered. Both Gunny's and Kelly's faces registered their puzzlement (and probably disagreement) with my pronouncement.

As if on cue, both barked, "Explain."

"He's well educated and speaks like a preppy. Wealthy people don't call their sons Jack unless it's a nickname. He would be a John if he came from money. So Jack Keller is out."

Kelly considered this for a minute and said, "I'll put him in the maybe category for now, and if I have the time, I'll try to get the skinny on him." Gunny nodded in concurrence.

"John Alexopoulos sounds Greek." I turned to the Gunny. "You might think you look like a Greek god, but in the '40s, there weren't a lot of affluent Greeks enlisting in the Marine Corps."

"I do *not* think I look like a Greek god. I don't even know what I look like. I'm dead. I can't see myself in the mirror. But I'll go along with your somewhat-flawed reasoning. For now." Gunny crossed his arms over his chest and looked peevish.

I passed his words and actions on to Kelly, who hooted his amusement.

"Pissed you off, did she?" he chided Gunny, whose reaction was to flip Kelly the bird. Interesting. From buddy to nemesis in the blink of an eye. I didn't share the gesture with Kelly.

I moved on. "Cut it out, kids. It's Salton or Mercer. Frederick sounds lofty, and Calvin might be for Calvin Coolidge. Those are the two to focus on, Kelly. And if you have time, take a look at Keller." I turned to the Gunny and commented, "It'd be nice if you had ID tags (Naval service dog tags). That would've been helpful."

Gunny pulled his jacket collar aside and gestured toward the empty cord at his neck. "Don't you think I thought of that? Hell, I don't even know how I *died*, but let's just assume I did! Do you see any blood on my uniform or me, for that matter? I don't even know what I look like because I can't see myself in a mirror…and not because I'm a vampire," he quickly added.

Chagrined (and rightfully put in my place), I muttered, "Sorry. My bad."

"And just to educate you, my tags were oval and worn on a heavy cord, not oblong and on a chain, like yours. It wasn't unusual for the cords to break or the entire thing pulled off the dead. I have no idea what happened to mine." I relayed this last comment onto Kelly.

"I wondered about that, Gunny, but didn't feel comfortable asking."

We sat in awkward silence for a couple of minutes and collected our thoughts.

"Okay, enough contemplating our navels," I announced, breaking the stillness. It had become so quiet in the library, my voice resounded like a fart in church. "Kelly, you're going back to Manpower archives then and try to find homes of record, photos, anything that might help with zeroing in on who the Gunny might be, correct? Is there any way I can help?"

"Not until I have more information. Give me a couple of weeks, and I'll run anything I've found past you two."

"Wait. I just had a thought. Granna can see him. I'm not sure if it's because she's from that generation, can see ghosts—which she claims she can—or recognizes him and isn't saying. She can be pretty secretive when it suits her and might know him but isn't sharing it with me because it's something she'd rather not remember. Think, Gunny. Does she look at all familiar?"

"Not a clue," he responded. "But I assume she can see me for several reasons, not least of which is her close relationship with you, Abe. Could it have been her preoccupation with death last fall? Remember, she hasn't seen me since she got the revised diagnosis. At Christmas, I had to make myself scarce so neither of you screwed up and talked to me in front of the rest of the family. You didn't want them to think you and she were pulling another Mr. Porker bluff." As usual, I was taken aback by his proper manner of speaking. He sounded like a cross between a professor and Princeton Seminary-educated Presbyterian minister.

Kelly shot me a quizzical look. "What's he saying?"

I did *not* want to discuss the Mr. Porker phase of my life with Kelly right now. It was enough that he had taken the leap of faith in believing that the Gunny was, indeed, real. Telling him about Mr. Porker might shake that confidence at a time when we were actually making progress on identifying the Gunny. "Nothing important. And his answer was no to recognizing Granna. I'll press her anyway once she has the defibrillator implant and is back on her feet. I don't want to stress her any more than she is right now. Between the procedure, cutting back on her work hours, and lack of caffeine, she's got enough on her plate." Gunny shot me a scrutinizing look. "And besides," I finished (lamely, I might add), "with rappelling coming up in ten days, I have enough stress of my own without pissing her off."

Both the living and the dead nodded sagely, obviously in agreement on how intimidating Granna could be when provoked (or even when not). I stood, gathered up my stuff, and headed toward the door. Kelly and Gunny did likewise.

"See you at dinner, Kelly," I said as we parted at the second-floor landing, he to his room and I to mine. "And thanks. I appreciate all you've done and are doing. It means a lot. Even more, *you* mean a lot."

Kelly flashed me a happy, hopeful smile. "You are certainly welcome. I'm actually enjoying the search." With a backward wave, he disappeared down the passageway.

Gunny had gone invisible, but I could distinctly hear him singing, "Abe and Kelly sitting in a tree. *K-I-S-S-I-N-G.*"

"Jealous?" I challenged under my breath.

He appeared long enough to respond, "Nope. He's been sweet on you for a long time, even before I came into the picture. Besides, who's going to keep you out of trouble when I move on?" With a wink and a flourish, he was gone.

Then it hit me. I felt more alive than I had in years, and all because of a dead guy, and I wasn't so sure I wanted him gone. True, my life had become pretty complicated, and I was likely at my terminal Marine Corps rank because of him, but it was interesting. And he kept me on my toes. I woke up each morning wondering what he was going to pull next, sometimes with dread, others with anticipation. I knew I would miss him however, and whenever, Kelly and I helped him move on.

Meanwhile, my gut still told me there was a timer ticking down. I just hoped we were able to help him before time ran out.

CHAPTER 20

Rappelling Is Repelling

G RANNA'S IMPLANT was postponed until the end of January. She claimed it was because she hadn't finished the turnover she needed to accomplish before Christmas, but Dr. Proctor saw through the flimsy excuses. Though he rescheduled her procedure as requested, he did threaten removing himself as her physician if she "tried to play him again" (his words, according to Granna and Mother). I suspect her request for delay was a combination of fear that she'd die on the table with unfinished business, and just plain fear (Dr. Proctor's call on it). True, while the implant was a pretty standard procedure by this time, it still carried risks, though I think the Quack would take it very personally if she "croaked" (Granna's words, not mine) on his watch. Mother planned to remain in Baltimore with Granna throughout her pre and post-op stay in the hospital, and I anticipated at least one visit from her while she bulldogged Granna, Dr. Proctor, and Johns Hopkins.

For me, there was no plea-bargaining with the Delta Company training schedule. We returned to work on Wednesday, the third of January, and SPCs were scheduled for rappelling training that Thursday and Friday. Thursday morning was primarily classroom instruction where we'd be introduced to technique and tying a Swiss seat, with a visit to the rappelling tower in the afternoon. Friday, we'd spend the whole flipping day climbing up the sixty-foot tower and rappelling down. Climbing back up. Rappelling back down. Repeat. Repeat. Repeat.

Thursday was fine, until the afternoon when we drove over to the tower. I dreaded making my way to the top, let alone jumping off the side of it, but we'd been told we weren't going to *actually* rappel that day, so I trudged doggedly up the bazillion steps to the top, my eyes focused upward rather than on my feet. Open risers provided an increasingly higher, and disturbing, view of the ground below.

We reached the top and got a tour of the rappel stations where SPCs would be tied in as they supervised rappelling and belaying lieutenants. Fine by me. I was ready to go home. Before we headed to the ladder, however, we stopped at an approximately four-by-four-foot hole with padded edges. There were two ropes disappearing down the middle and tied to heavy steel-anchor points affixed to the platform.

Our instructor, Gunny Lambert, welcomed us to the hellhole. My fellow SPCs murmured their understanding and anticipation. I, however, had no idea what was in store for us.

As directed, my fellow captains and I gathered around the hole to wherever and watched one of the instructors rig the ropes to his Swiss seat. He allowed himself maybe twelve feet of slack in the ropes, stepped over to the hole, yelled downward that he was on rappel (receiving an answering, "staff sergeant Murray on belay"), and sat on the edge of the abyss with his legs dangling. Then he calmly slid off. Into nothingness.

Standing about a foot from the edge of the hole, all I could see was the bottoms of his boots, and then his head, as he jerked back up and recovered from the free fall. He then made his way to the ground guided by the staff sergeant on belay.

I knew the hellhole was supposed to simulate free fall roping from a helicopter. I knew it looked scary but was perfectly safe (if you executed it as directed). I knew I only had to do it once. The rational part of me understood all of this, but I was still scared shitless.

So I volunteered to go down next.

I won't belabor the terror, and then exhilaration, I felt when I walked away from the tower. Reality struck heading home, though, when I remembered I still had to spend all day tomorrow climbing and rappelling, climbing and rappelling.

Gunny accompanied me to work the next day. He'd stayed home on Thursday, glued to a John Wayne marathon on TV. He professed interest in observing SPC training on Friday, however, and I figured, if things went wrong, I could very well be joining him in the land of the dead by the afternoon. I was silent as we made our way to base. When the Gunny tried to reassure me that rappelling could be fun, I shushed him like a mother silencing a kid in church. I didn't want a pep talk. I didn't want any kind of discussion. I needed to focus on where I had stashed my will (drawer or safety deposit box?) and if I'd drawn up and signed a power of attorney.

All too soon, we were at the tower. The instructors had us seat ourselves on the ground around them in an open school circle but facing the tower, where we focused on two staff sergeants already in place there, one atop the tower in a Swiss seat and tethered onto a rope, the other on the ground, rappelling rope in hand, awaiting his fellow's descent. At a signal from our instructor, they started the descent until the rappeller was halfway down the tower wall, at which point, our instructor yelled for him to halt. Which he did, maintaining his place, feet braced against the wall with his body in a crouch, right hand clasping the rope right behind his butt and his left clasping the rope just above his head.

And he hung there for the next half hour while our instructor continued his remarks and finished with his safety brief, whereupon he signaled for the two staff sergeants to finish their rappel and belay.

I understood they'd stopped the rappel to demonstrate how proper form and vigilant belay ensured a safe descent. The whole time, however, I thought, *I am so flippin' glad that's not me.* Neil must have sensed my unease because he nudged my shoulder with his and mouthed, *Not a problem.*

Huh. Not for *you*, Neil. You've done this three million times. And from hovering helicopters, no less. But I appreciated his support and mimed hanging myself in response.

Before I knew it, I was making my way up the ladder to whatever fate awaited me.

Gunny was there to observe my first tenuous rappel, then increasingly confident descents, and, by the fifth time, flashed me a thumbs-up as I, once again on the ground, detached myself from the rappelling rope and backed away from the tower. Since the wind had started to pick up, we'd skipped lunch in order to complete the required number of rappels for certification before the weather turned too breezy. I was happy I'd already completed the requisite number of rappels. Those officers still bounding down the tower walls were finding it increasingly difficult to descend in a relatively straight line.

Before I knew it, it was time to secure. I was comfortable, not necessarily happy, with the whole process and sure enough of my newly acquired skills that I could hold my own during the lieutenants' training next week.

"Are you the only SPC who never rappelled before?" Gunny asked as we headed home at 1600.

"Yep. We didn't do it when I was in TBS and not a lot of motor transport officers need to drop out of helicopters or scale walls. Why? Was it that obvious I was a newbie?" I glanced over at Gunny in the passenger seat and noticed he was avoiding catching my eye.

He squirmed a bit and then blurted out, "No. In fact, you looked pretty well-heeled there at the end. But don't be surprised if the instructors use you as a demonstrator."

"Did you hear that, or are you assuming it?" Sheesh, what did this mean?

"Didn't hear anything, but it's a good move on their part. I'd say a good number of those lieutenants are going to be terrified to head up that tower and slide down the side, let alone the hellhole, if they have to tackle that. I don't think the instructors will have you demonstrate the hole, but I think they'll introduce you as a novice and have you do something. The fact that you're inexperienced but doing the rappel thing anyway will reassure the ones that are scared." He smiled conspiratorially at me. "That's what I'd do if I were an EI."

I didn't waste any time that weekend worrying. I mean, how bad could it be?

It was worse.

*****

The Company spent Monday in the classroom, receiving detailed instruction on the how and why of rappelling, spending three hours learning to tie, untie, and check their own and someone else's Swiss seat. Though many lieutenants seemed excited to rappel the next day, Gunny was indeed correct—there were many who were smiling gamely and obviously not at ease with what they would be doing on Tuesday. In my platoon, several seemed anxious, but I was confident they'd make their two rappels with, at first some trepidation, and then confidence.

One officer, Lieutenant Howard, was notably fidgety, and I wasn't surprised when she showed up at my office that evening as I prepared to secure. Gunny was already marching down the passageway to the exit but turned around and headed back my way, having heard me talking to someone other than him.

"Ma'am, do you have a minute?" Howard asked. I waved her back into my office where I gestured her toward the couch. I took a chair and watched her, saying nothing but scrutinizing her body language. I knew what was coming, and oh, I was not going to enjoy what I knew I would have to do.

Gunny floated through the door and took the other chair. I suspected he knew what this was going to be about too.

Before I go any further, I need to explain something else about myself. I'm extremely empathetic and constantly struggle with what sometimes seemed to me to be the Corps' unrelenting and intractable code of conduct. It could best be summed up in the simple statement "Marines don't do that" when offered taking the easy way out of an ethical dilemma. The Corps wrapped that mantra around itself like a hair shirt, and I often wondered what the difference would be if we *did* do something like that. Usually the question was answered within days, even hours, when I witnessed what was becoming increasingly acceptable behavior in our society. And it wasn't pretty.

For the lieutenants, there were the endless physical challenges. They tackled O-courses with intimidating obstacles. They gutted out five-mile formation runs in boots and utes, enduring shin splints and stress fractures. They regularly hiked in sleet and high heat and humidity because their CO refused transportation (that was my pet peeve as an MTO). But I got it. Shared misery forged camaraderie, for sure. *And* "that which does not kill us makes us stronger," according to Nietzsche. Ditto. I could master (if not embrace) the physical challenges and help my lieutenants do the same.

It was the mental, or maybe it was psychological, trials we put them through, however, that often made me uncomfortable. I frequently dealt with situations where my lieutenants were uneasy about a tactical problem or physically tasking event, and I wrestled with what the appropriate motivation might be—empathy or a slap in the face? I found myself adopting and projecting the middle ground of businesslike demeanor when confronted with weakness, knowing I wasn't doing any of them a favor by encouraging them to feel.

And I wasn't proud of myself for often taking that approach.

Lieutenant Howard was going to confide her fear of heights and profess her inability to complete the rappel class tomorrow. I shared her terror (and for me, there was also a paralyzing fear of the dark, which I had confronted every time we had gone patrolling), but I knew I couldn't—shouldn't—share my personal challenges with her. Running away wasn't an option, so why revel in weakness?

Holy cannoli. I was starting to sound like some kind of Nazi propaganda machine. And I'm also straying off topic. Again.

I must also admit that I didn't particularly like Lieutenant Howard. I'm not big into appearances, not being a beauty myself, but there was something about her that was off-putting. Her skin was sallow, her mouth pinched, and her too-close-together eyes were constantly assessing the action around her, weighing her options and aligning herself to whatever was most advantageous to *her* agenda. She was small and wiry and had few problems with the physical challenges we sent the lieutenants' way. I had noted, though, that she never voluntarily shouldered additional gear during hikes. There was always a reason why she couldn't do so, and the student billet holders had just given up trying to make her share the burden. When she was a billet holder, Howard was abrupt and dictatorial; when she was a snuffy, she was reluctantly cooperative. Consistently at the bottom of peer rankings, her platoon mates obviously shared my impression that she wasn't, nor did she even try to be, a team player.

I had absolutely no idea how she had gotten commissioned.

Howard squirmed and nervously clasped her hands, tenting her fingers and resting her elbows on her knees. I silently watched and waited.

Finally she confided, "Ma'am, I am deathly afraid of heights. I can't rappel tomorrow."

I studied her for a couple more minutes. She refused to make eye contact.

"Do you have a medical reason that precludes your participating, Lieutenant? A doctor's note, maybe?" Cripes. I sounded like Dickey.

"No, I don't. I just know I can't. I didn't sign up for this kind of thing when I got commissioned. I want to be a supply officer. They don't have to slide down walls. Have you ever had to do that kind of thing as an MTO?"

"Nope, but I learned how last week, and when I go to my next command, and the commanding officer decides to take us rappelling, I'll lead by example and instruct my company or section how."

"Captain, you don't understand. I'm totally terrified. I can't even climb that tower to get to the top, let alone slide down a rope. You don't understand." She repeated this aimlessly and was, by this point, crying. I anticipated it would soon transition into full-blown sobbing. Okay. I had hoped for more self-control this far into her training but was obviously wrong. Or maybe too Pollyanna.

"Yes, in fact, I *do* understand. Do you think being a Marine officer is like a Chinese menu—do what you're comfortable with, ignore what you don't want to do? Do you think you're the only officer in this company, our platoon, that doesn't like heights? That there aren't others who would rather pass on tomorrow?"

Howard's eyes remained glued to the floor. The only response I got was a headshake.

Gunny let loose a derisive snort and commented, "Uh-oh. Here it comes."

"Lieutenant Howard, we're having an informal discussion, but I still expect proper military courtesy and an affirmative or negative, followed by a ma'am or Captain. Do you understand?"

"Yes, ma'am. No, I don't think I'm the only lieutenant that doesn't want to rappel tomorrow." At least she was looking at me now.

I drew a deep breath and did what I had to do. "Lieutenant, are you refusing a lawful order to participate in tomorrow's rappelling class? Because that's what I'm doing right now, I'm ordering you to accompany the platoon to the rappelling tower tomorrow, and I'm ordering you to climb the tower with your classmates and to complete two rappels. There is no negotiation on this." I abruptly rose, as did she. She was now in full sob. "Commissioning and a training syllabus aren't subject to negotiation. But right now, I'm ordering you to participate. Do you intend to obey, or should I start the process *now* for administrative or legal action? Refusing could likely result in losing your commission."

"I'll try," she blubbered, wiping her eyes—*and yuck, her nose*—on her sleeve despite a box of tissues setting on the coffee table in front of her. "I'll try."

"There's no *trying*, Lieutenant Howard. You either will, or you won't. If you get to the tower and refuse to climb the ladder or refuse to attempt a rappel, you've disobeyed a lawful order. Do you understand me?" I opened the door to my office, gesturing for her to leave, which she did, albeit in a dragging defeated manner.

"See you tomorrow. Don't dwell on it tonight. It'll just make it worse. And please tell Lieutenant Myerson (student platoon commander for the week) to report to me at 0630 in the morning." With that, I closed and sank back against the door.

"Whew! You are *not* empathetic, are you?" Gunny observed as I gathered up my gear. What did *he* know? I was as mushy as two-day-old milk toast. "Why didn't you tell her that you were scared too but did it anyway? And with a much-less-sympathetic audience."

"Just like you said, Gunny. A lot of that company is scared or, at least, apprehensive, but they'll do it anyway. They're Marine officers. It goes with the territory. If she wants sympathy, she can find it in the dictionary between *shit* and *syphilis*." I made for the door. "Let's go home. I need a glass of wine and a brainless TV show."

"You do know that it's Monday, right? I don't think *Alf*'s on, but there's sure to be football," was all he offered in reply.

*****

The next day, we admin moved to the rappelling tower where we spent an hour and a half tying, retying, checking, rechecking, and rerechecking Swiss seats. Neil and I were the first platoons to get the final upcheck from the Tactics staff, and the principal instructors, Gunny Latimer and Staff Sergeant Reynolds, approached us as we directed our platoons to be seated on the ground in a school circle for the final hour of instruction before ascending the tower.

"Captains, could we have a minute?" Gunny Lambert requested. Oh no, this was what the Gunny predicted. Was I going to have to demonstrate the hellhole?

Neil and I nodded our assent, and the four of us moved away from the students.

Gunny Lambert continued, "We need some assistance for the rappelling demonstration. Could you help?" I *knew* it.

"Sure, Gunny. What do you need?" I hoped he didn't notice the hesitation in my voice. I certainly did. Neil nodded his concurrence, but he didn't look at all anxious. Then again, he had been rappelling since he was commissioned. Heck, I wouldn't have been surprised if he had rappelled from the top of the Grand Canyon.

My hopes that I would be on belay and Neil on rappel were crushed when Gunny Lambert continued, "Captain Rush, I'd like you to demonstrate the *L*-shaped position on the wall and how the brake hand works, either in a stationary position or in the descent. Captain Giese, I'd like you to be on belay at the bottom of the tower. Typical procedure, before Captain Rush begins her descent, she'll announce her rappel, you'll announce your belay, and the company will see how both ends of the rope work as a team."

"Gunny, maybe it's better if I rappel and Captain Rush belays," Neil countered. He remembered my reaction to the staff sergeant suspended on his rappelling rope and against the wall for a half hour the previous week. "I'm experienced. She just learned the basics last week." In that moment, I dearly loved Neil.

"With respect, lady and gentleman, it's *because* she's inexperienced that we want her to be on the tower." Gunny Lambert turned to me. "Ma'am, I know you were scared shitless last week when you watched the hellhole demonstration. When Staff Sergeant Murray dropped through the hole, I thought you were going to puke. But you didn't. You volunteered to go next. We guessed you were probably afraid of heights and never rappelled before. Am I right?"

I sighed and nodded.

"By the time we finished on Friday, though, you looked like you'd been rappelling for years. That's why we want you on the wall. We know a lot of those lieutenants are edgy, maybe even scared to death, and if you don't mind, my voice track will include that you had never rappelled before last Friday, and you're not comfortable with heights. I'll make the point that rappelling is perfectly safe if you follow directions and trust your belay."

"You can mention that I'd never rappelled, Gunny, but not the fear of heights. It's not relevant."

He nodded his understanding. "So can you help us with the demo, ma'am and sir?"

Neil and I agreed. He headed to the side of the tower nearest where the company was seated, and I trudged up the ladder to meet Staff Sergeant Murray and the rest of the EIs who were overseeing the rappels. Gunny Lambert headed to the assembled lieutenants and started the final hour of instruction.

"Okay, ma'am," Staff Sergeant Murray offered, giving a final tug on my rappelling rope.

Shit. Shit. Shit.

"I'll be with you, Abe," Gunny murmured in my ear. "You'll only see me if something starts going wrong. Which it won't. But just in case, listen to what they tell you. These guys are good. And they chose Neil to be on belay because you two are buds."

To make a long (very long) story short, I hung on the side of that tower for forty-five, not thirty, minutes. I bounced and waved when instructed, and by the time I was directed to descend, my right hand was numb from braking in place. When I finally landed back on the ground, Neil waited for me to unhitch myself, but my hand wouldn't work, so he stepped in and did it for me. It was thirty degrees outside, I had been locked in place for more than a half hour, and I had been terrified the whole time. No wonder my hands didn't work.

Once I was free, he grabbed my right hand, tore off my glove, and vigorously massaged my fingers and thumb. After what seemed a lifetime (but was only about five minutes) of his spirited rubbing and my flexing my fingers, my hand had regained some feeling.

"You've gotta be frozen, Abe," he commiserated. "I think Dickey kept asking questions just to make you hang there longer. What a fuckin' asshole." Returning my glove, he observed, "They're sending the platoons up the tower. Here we go."

The other platoons would bring up ten lieutenants at a time. Since I was the newbie and wanted to ensure I did everything by the book, I would work slower until I was comfortable with roping mine in and preparing for their rappels. The students wouldn't have to negotiate the hellhole unless they wanted to, and only after all of them had completed two rappels down the tower. They could stay behind and free fall under the instruction and watchful eyes of the EIs, but I didn't think we'd have enough daylight once all the company had finished the basic requirement.

I climbed the not-stairway to heaven with Neil and the other SPCs and stopped in front of my assigned station. My post was essentially an upside-down *U*-shaped pipe fixed and permanently set into the floor of the tower, about five feet from the edge. Every station had one. These pipes served as anchors for the rappelling ropes that dangled over the sides of the tower and down which the lieutenants would rappel. We SPCs were also fastened to the fixtures by approximately ten feet of safety rope affixed to our Swiss seats. The ropes had sufficient play (and a bit more) to take us to the edge of the tower where we'd launch our lieutenants on rappel (after ensuring they were correctly hooked up to the lines, of course). Should we accidentally slip off the side, we'd only dangle a couple of feet over the edge. After all, falling four or five feet was certainly preferable to plummeting down sixty.

As a safety precaution, two EIs patrolled the tower platform, overseeing the rappels and providing general support if necessary.

As each lieutenant appeared in front of me, I made eye contact and tried not to be too obvious as I scrutinized her for something beyond nervousness. Heck, they were all nervous, but none looked like she was going to panic and bolt back down the ladder.

Until Lieutenant Howard staggered into view.

Twenty officers from my platoon had successfully completed their rappels, and I'd not yet spotted Howard. I wondered if she'd refused to ascend the ladder, but the last five officers finally appeared, and she brought up next to last, prodded along by Lieutenant Lee, who was encouraging her to make it up the last three steps. When all five were standing in front of me, I launched into my speech on how this was going to go down; I'd rope in the lieutenant, double-check my work, and she'd shout her intention to rappel and wait for acknowledgment from her belay. Then she'd step backward off the edge and into the *L*-shaped position and commence her descent down the wall.

The first three lieutenants negotiated their rappels a little clumsily (they were, after all, first attempts) but made it safely to the ground below.

When Lieutenant Howard shuffled in front of me, and before I started to fasten her rappelling rope, I studied her startlingly white face (to be expected) and tried to ascertain what she was muttering under her breath (I think it was the song "Mary Had a Little Lamb," over and over). Okay. That last kind of concerned me, but I had been known to repeat a mantra (in my head, admittedly) when confronted with a stressful situation.

It was Howard's eyes, though, that initially chilled me even more than the thirty-degree temperature. Not as large as saucers (I always wondered about that comparison. Maybe the saucers from a child's tea set?), they were still pretty sizable and fixated somewhere beyond my shoulder.

Notice my comment about "initially." I wasn't buying the zombie act, and neither was Gunny.

"This is horse shit, Captain. Sure she's terrified, but she's not that scared. This is all an act to get you to back off. If you don't want to deal with her, you can send her over to Captain Chavez's station. He'll order her over the side and push her off if she doesn't go." He hadn't appeared to me, true to his promise that he wouldn't materialize unless I was in trouble.

I finished tying off Howard's rope and moved her to the edge of the tower with me. Lieutenant Lee followed us at a discreet distance, offering encouragement to her platoon mate.

"Lieutenant Howard," I said, "yell down to Lieutenant Bruni that you're on rappel." Howard stood, rooted about a foot from the tower's edge. She would have to face me in order to take her step off the tower.

"Come on, Eva. Just do it. The sooner you go down, the sooner you can come back and do your second rappel, and you're done. Easy peasy." Lieutenant Lee was pleasantly relentless.

"I...I...can't."

I head-gestured to Lieutenant Lee to move over a bit and yelled down to Lieutenant Bruni, "Lieutenant Howard on rappel." And I gently positioned Howard for her descent.

"Lieutenant Bruni on belay," floated up to us from below. Bruni was my tallest lieutenant, standing 5'11", and solidly built. She should have been in line to ascend the tower for her second rappel, but I suspect that she had taken the belay in order to reassure Howard.

Surprisingly, Howard complied, but as she turned around and positioned herself to take her step into nothingness, she lunged forward. When she righted herself, I saw that she had gathered a substantial amount of Lee's utility jacket in her left hand and was now holding it in a death grip. Whether by accident or design, she started pulling Lee slowly toward her and the edge. Lee yelped in surprise and desperately clawed at Howard's hands, attempting to release herself from the other's grasp. Instead of relinquishing her hold, however, Howard just clung tighter. As she settled into her L-shaped stance, she was dragging Lee inexorably toward the edge and down the side of the tower. Unfortunately unlike me, Lee wasn't safety roped into the fixed pipe. If she went over the side, there was nothing to arrest her fall.

I didn't immediately process what was happening in front of me and, even today, kick myself that I didn't see it coming and react quicker. It took me about two seconds before I lunged forward, wrapping my hand around both the waist rope of Lee's Swiss seat and her utility belt. I prayed both would hold until I could get her away from Howard.

I was holding onto Lee with both hands at this point but already knew I would need to free up one of them to connect with Howard in a push or, even worse, a punch.

Gunny appeared to my left, hovering inches away from Lee's increasingly prone body.

"You've got this, Abe. You're going to have to hold onto Lee with your left hand and try to push Howard away with your right. If she doesn't back off, you'll have to backhand her." It was like he was reading my mind.

"Leave it!" What was I doing? Lapsing into dog-training language? "Let her go. *Now!*"

Where the hell were the EIs? I thought I was yelling, but my raised voice was probably barely audible over the cacophony of sounds coming from the other four rappelling stations.

Howard's death grip remained firm and fixed as Lee struggled to extricate herself from her grasp. Because she had used her left rappelling hand to connect with Lee, and Lee was still somewhat anchored to the tower by my clutch on her belt and rigging, Howard wasn't going anywhere. Her right hand was occupied where it should be, down by her butt, acting as a brake to stop her descent. I knew that as long as I could hold onto Lee, she wasn't going over, but it was time to break the deadlock. Lee was now on her stomach, half-hanging over the edge, clenching Howard's utility jacket with both hands in the event that if she *did* go over, she'd be attached to Howard.

I freed my right hand and tried pushing Howard away from us, but to no avail.

"Let her *go. Now!*" I roared. Okay. Maybe I barked, but it was loud, even to my ears.

I could barely see Howard's eyes, now level with the edge of the tower. It verified that she must have assumed her *L*-shaped stance (*at least she had gotten that right*).

Howard just glared at me. And then her eyes shifted to over my left shoulder.

She'd spotted the Gunny.

Instead of repeating my command, I took advantage of the diversion and reared back, launching myself forward, delivering a pretty resounding slap to Howard's cheek. It wasn't a glancing blow but rock-solid, landing with a satisfying *whack*. I was gonna have to watch it. I was acquiring a reputation for not being in possession of not only my senses but my actions, but so what?

I have to admit, it felt pretty damn good when my hand connected with Howard's face.

"That did it, Abe," Gunny offered in approval as he disappeared from sight.

"I'm here, ma'am," I heard to my right. One of the EIs (I thought it was Staff Sergeant Jenkins) had noticed the struggle at my end of the tower. "I've got this."

Howard had dropped the hand clutching Lee's jacket, so the latter struggled back onto the safety of the platform. However, when she relinquished Lee, Howard had also relinquished her left hand that should have been wrapped around her rappelling rope. She backflipped against the wall, hanging upside down. Since she was roped in, and Bruni was on diligent belay, she wouldn't fall.

The EI and I dropped to our stomachs and peered over the side to see Howard dangling below us. "If I were you, ma'am, I'd let her hang there for a while as a teaching point," he observed dryly. "But that would mean clogging up the throughput at your station."

Nuts. I so hated being a grown-up sometimes, so I gestured for him to take over as I rose and moved away from the edge, taking Lee with me. He instructed Howard how to regain her stance and encouraged her as she eventually took her first (albeit short) jump down the side. When she reached the ground, Lieutenant Bruni helped her disengage from her rope, and I watched a heated discussion ensue (at least on Howard's part) between the two of them.

Conversation finished, Howard stalked off rather than assume belay, and Bruni glanced up and circled her fingers in an okay.

"I'm sorry I didn't see what was happening sooner, Captain."

"You know, it seemed like an eternity, but I think it all happened in less than a minute. It doesn't help that this station is kind of tucked back here, out of sight. And with all the noise, you probably couldn't hear me screaming." This last I offered with a sheepish grin and a shake of the head.

He turned to Lieutenant Lee, standing along the railing, readjusting her utility jacket. "Are you okay, ma'am?"

"Fine, Staff Sergeant Jenkins. Ready to take this on."

He turned back to me, and I nodded that I could take it from here.

"Okay, ma'am. I'll leave you to it. And just to be sure, I'll keep an eye out for that other lieutenant's next rappel in case she decides to act out again." With this, the Staff Sergeant turned and flagged down the other EI. I assumed he was updating him on what had happened with Lieutenant Howard.

Lee presented herself to me so I could prepare her for rappel. Despite her close call, she was confident and upbeat. Had it been me, I would already have assumed the fetal position well away from the tower's edge.

"Thanks, ma'am. I thought I was a goner there for a while. It just doesn't pay to be a cheerleader, I guess." I detected just a bit of a tremor in her voice despite the confident smile on her face.

"You keep on doing what you're doing, Lieutenant Lee. You didn't do anything wrong. You did everything right. Now announce your rappel, and we'll get you down the wall."

Lee's announcement was answered by Lieutenant Bruni, who remained on belay. I assumed she had stayed in place (rather than relinquishing the position to another lieutenant) to ensure Lee was all right. Once Lee was on the ground, the lieutenants exchanged a few words and a surreptitious hug. Public displays of affection were discouraged, but considering what Lee had been through, I was grateful to Bruni for her support. Reassured that Lee was okay, Bruni headed back to the ladder and her second rappel while Lee assumed belay.

I wondered what had transpired between Howard and Bruni, but my next contingent of lieutenants had arrived for their second rappels. If Howard had been making accusations or babbling about seeing the Gunny, Bruni would most likely have denied witnessing my slug or seeing anyone but Lee and me at the top of the tower. To someone like Bruni, Howard's actions would have been nothing less than cowardice, and she had already chosen to reinforce whatever version of the incident Lee and I might tell.

I was sure word of what had transpired was probably already making its way through the company. By day's end, Howard's stock with her peers, never very high, would have plummeted drastically, never to recover. What she had pulled was bad enough, but Lee was universally popular. Her generosity, competence, and kinky sense of humor had endeared her not only to her platoon but the entire company. Howard would experience the repercussions of her own actions until the company graduated, but I was equally certain it would be subtle and carried out in a manner that offered her no tangible basis for complaint. Jungle justice didn't have to be obvious to be effective.

Almost an hour later, Bob accompanied Howard when she returned for her second rappel. Remarkably, she was no longer in zombie mode, and I wondered what Bob might have said to her to get her up the ladder. Before I could get Howard fitted up, though, he gestured me out of earshot.

"Dickey and I saw most of it, Abe. He's royally pissed. Not at you. At that…lieutenant…if you can call her that. I've seen him pretty mad before—it's usually at me—but this is epic. He's over at TBS headquarters right now, trying to get in to see the CO. Dickey wants her out of the Corps and sent home, but I don't think that's realistic. She could drum up all kinds of excuses, and it's still pretty red where you slapped her. Ouch." As if on cue, we both turned and regarded Howard, unaware of our scrutiny, tucking her utility jacket back in her trousers. Her face was still pretty white, but despite (or maybe because of) her pallor, my handprint glowed, brightly red, on her cheek. "It's a balancing act of punishing her without putting *your* career on the line."

I shook my head. Really? Could it get that bad?

Bob obviously thought it could. "Somebody like her will be sure to make a fuss, and she'll bring you down if she can. She'll call witnesses to make statements about how you 'allegedly' decked Dickey, and he'd be forced to talk about the incident or be proven a liar. And then there's your invisible friend." He paused, trying to ascertain whether I understood the gravity of the situation.

"I've got it," I agreed. "I'll just treat her like any other lieutenant. But Dickey's gotta do something. There were too many witnesses. Worse, Lee could have been seriously hurt."

"I suspect the least she'll get from this is a royal ass-chewing and a counseling entry. I don't think she'll lose her commission." Message delivered, he nodded toward Lieutenant Howard. "So she's the last rappel for your platoon, right?"

I nodded.

"I'll stay here and watch while you get her prepped and down the wall. Then I'll casually check on the other platoons. Once she's down, get your lieutenants together and move them back to the BOQ. Dickey will want to talk to you and me once we're both back. Got it?"

I nodded and moved toward Howard and commenced roping her into her Swiss seat. Bob positioned himself to observe how this rappel developed, and as I suspected, Howard played her role of brave little martyr and went over the side without making a scene. Once she was safely on the ground, Bob tipped his cover at me as a send-off and sauntered over to Dave's platoon.

I heaved a sigh of relief and turned away from the tower's edge. After I untied my safety line and before I headed back down the ladder, I pulled my watch out of my cargo pocket and noted that it was only 1645. Most of the day had dragged, but there were times when it seemed to have gone on at a breakneck pace.

Since Dave and Scott's platoons still had a couple of lieutenants awaiting their second rappels, it would be too late for any of the lieutenants that had wanted to attempt the hellhole to do so. That meant my departing now with my platoon wouldn't deny any of them the opportunity to attempt it.

As I made my way down the ladder, Gunny's disgusted voice observed, "What a twit. She doesn't even deserve to be a supply officer. Too bad the Corps doesn't have horses anymore. She should spend her commitment shoveling shit." *That* made me smile as I navigated the steps for, hopefully, the last time. At least for this company.

As my feet hit terra firma (dirt had never looked so good), I looked for an instructor in order to hand in my tally sheet before I departed the area. All twenty-five of my lieutenants had completed their two rappels, and my roster was a verification that they had completed the requirement.

Gunny Lambert flagged me down and accepted the clipboard. "Thanks, ma'am. Great job today, for the demonstration and what you did up there." He gestured upward at my now-empty station. "I've been teaching this class for three years now and no accidents. You kept my record clean."

"Not a problem, Gunny. I appreciate the compliment, but you can put your money where your mouth is and return the favor by not making me do a demo when I push my next platoon. Deal?"

He smiled and saluted. "It's a deal, ma'am. Have a good evening."

When I approached my gathered lieutenants, Myerson called them to attention and reported all present and accounted for. I acknowledged her and asked her to move the unit back to the BOQ, where she could secure them for the evening, and I stationed myself to the rear of the formation in order to observe behaviors during the walk back. Since this was a movement and not a march or drill, the lieutenants were free to talk, joke, and throw playful insults at one another. Which they did. Howard, however, was obviously not part of the grab-ass, seemingly wrapped in a cocoon of self-inflicted misery and aloofness. Her peers were civil, and Lieutenant Lee made several overtures to her during the mile-long amble. All were politely rebuffed, but I had no doubt the lieutenant was contemplating what lay ahead, either immediately upon our arrival at the BOQ or later when the company (and likely TBS) leadership determined her fate.

Two days later, Lieutenant Howard received a verbal reprimand, delivered by the TBS CO, and a page 11 (counseling entry) in her

OQR (Officer Qualification Record). Of the two punishments she received, the ass-chewing was probably the more memorable.

Most people think that the latter, delivered Marine Corps style, would be a lot of yelling, heavily punctuated by colorful expletives. Not so in this case. Colonel Montoya was a highly decorated Vietnam veteran, recipient of both the Navy Cross and Silver Star, and an acknowledged warrior. He could ream butt with the best of them, or he could play disappointed father so well that hardened SNCOs would sob and beg for a second chance.

Pro forma, Dickey and I were present at the counseling, and neither of us was surprised when the CO assumed the fatherly role as the disillusioned and saddened Ward Cleaver, who had failed not only Howard but an entire generation of Marine officers. Watching her, I knew she was buying it but was still clueless enough to think this was all she was going to receive as punishment for her actions. Well, that is, until the Colonel produced the counseling entry and read its damning contents aloud. Suspecting that Howard fancied herself a veritable barracks lawyer, I had ghostwritten the document, and not only Kelly and the TBS Legal Officer but the base's JAG (Judge Advocate) himself had ensured it was valid, verifiable, and airtight.

With Kelly's (and the JAG's) advice, I'd warned Howard what I would recommend, and that should she receive a page 11 as an officer, it would likely be a career-ender. I think she still harbored expectation of just the oral dressing down until the CO read the entry.

Colonel Montoya concluded the interview with his own call on the situation before dismissing her.

"Lieutenant Howard, we train our lieutenants to the best of our abilities and put them in as many tactical situations as we can. But we can't simulate the fear, the confusion, the peril of actual combat. Rappelling is one of the few training experiences we can provide that actually puts you in danger. True, we have every safety measure imaginable in place, and we've never had a fatality, not even an injury. It's part of the training for all lieutenants because we can go from sitting behind desks to a battlefield in a matter of days. Women as well as men. And even in an administrative environment, we can be presented with physical challenges our friends in the civilian world are never voluntarily confronted with. When you not only freaked but put your fellow lieutenant in jeopardy, you demonstrated that you're maybe not up to the challenge of leading Marines." Here he paused, obviously gathering his thoughts for something he needed to say and not relishing having to do so. "I fear the way you reacted on Tuesday is not an aberration but how you will always react to any stressful situation that personally threatens you. You will always put yourself first, others second. I'm sorry we didn't see that sooner *before* you were commissioned. That said, though, nothing would make me happier than to be proven wrong." He paused and regarded her silently for almost a minute. Howard didn't move a muscle despite the waterworks streaming down her cheeks. "You're dismissed, Lieutenant Howard. Despite your disappointing performance at the rappelling tower, I wish you the best."

Howard crisply about-faced and made for the hatch. I thanked the CO and Dickey for their time and joined her in the passageway. She looked defeated and deflated.

Reality had finally set in: Howard would be lucky if she picked up first lieutenant; she certainly wouldn't be allowed to augment to the regular Marine Corps upon completion of her four-year active Reserve commitment.

In silence, I accompanied her to the classroom where Delta Company was enduring a lecture on rear-area security.

"Ma'am," she said as I prepared to leave her, "when I apologized to Lieutenant Lee, she said if you hadn't grabbed onto her and hit me, she would've gone over the side for sure." She paused and seemed to gather her thoughts. "Thank you. She's good people. You did the right thing. I couldn't forgive myself if she'd gotten seriously hurt because I was"—she gulped—"selfish."

I bit back the response that I didn't care if I had her blessing or not. I suspected her current remorseful attitude was only temporary, and she'd be back to her former egocentric self once the emotion faded.

This acting-like-an-adult thing was really getting old.

"Try to slip in quietly when you take a seat," I responded, ignoring her comment and gesturing to a door that opened into the back of the room.

I didn't look back as I headed back to a Company staff meeting at the BOQ.

That night, I had some pretty weird dreams. I wasn't sure how much was wishful thinking or overactive imagination, but all of them ended with me lying on my stomach, gawking at Howard, who was sprawled on the mulch below me at the base of the rappelling tower. The tower from which I'd pushed her. The weird thing is she's perfectly fine, but in each dream, she looks different. In one, she's dressed as a WWII Marine, sticking her tongue out at me, thumb to nose, and waggling her fingers. You know the gesture. In another, she looks like Elvis (the older fatter Elvis) in a glittery rhinestone-encrusted too-tight onesie. But at least she's smiling and waving. In the last one (that I remember), she's Bucky Beaver. She gets up, waves, and dances around, chattering about toothpaste.

When the alarm went off at 0500 (late start today), I was on my stomach, holding onto a pillow that had slipped off the side of the bed, grasping a corner for dear life. Kind of like I was trying to keep it from falling.

I stumbled downstairs and about tripped over the Gunny, who squatted on the next-to-bottom step.

"You all right, Abe?" he asked, rising and making way for me get to get by. "You were doing a lot of yelling and even more laughing in your sleep last night."

"Yeah. I need tea."

"What was it about? Haven't heard that much noise out of you at night since you did your patrolling thing with the baseball bat months ago." We had arrived at the kitchen. Gunny languidly slid into his usual chair and continued his interrogation. "Was it the scare with Lieutenant Howard?"

I turned from the stove where I had just placed the kettle to boil. "Probably. And the baseball bat thing a couple months ago was because you wouldn't introduce yourself."

"So why the yelling *and* the laughing?"

"My dreams kept going back to the tower and Howard. I guess I subconsciously wanted to push her off, and in my dreams, I did. Each time she got to the bottom, though, she was okay but dressed differently. It was kind of funny, really."

"Don't keep me in suspense. And?"

"In one, she was dressed like you, thumbing her nose at me. In another, she was Elvis. The last one I remember, she was Bucky Beaver, dancing around and singing about toothpaste. All kind of weird but all random thoughts that have run through my brain the past few days."

Gunny roared with laughter. "I particularly like me thumbing my nose at you. That's so Freudian."

"I guess it's funny, but it all comes back to me pushing her off the tower. That concerns me." I poured water into my tea press, moved to the table, and sat down, glumly regarding the leaves and water mingling in the glass pot.

"You psychoanalyze yourself too much. You philosophize too much. You're human. Get over it. If it had been me, I'd have cut the rope. Move on already."

That made me laugh. I *was* too introspective.

"Message received. Time for school," I said, pouring tea into my cup, adding gritty granules, and heading upstairs.

"It's about time," was his laughing retort.

CHAPTER 21

Answered Questions

O N SUNDAY, January 28, Gunny got to view Super Bowl XXIII, the San Francisco 49ers versus the Denver Broncos, at the Louisiana Superdome in New Orleans. Kelly drove down from Woodbridge with beer, chips, other assorted snacks, and jelly donuts (it had gotten to be a running joke between him and the Gunny). The plan was for me to run out during halftime to pick up pizza since both my companions would be riveted to the TV, hoping to see replays of the first half of the game, not to mention flimsily clad dancers during the show.

I'm sure they enjoyed the salute to New Orleans and *Peanuts'* fortieth anniversary. Certainly more than I did as I negotiated the packed Pizza Prince parking lot and, once inside, dodged Super Bowl-charged drunks and waited almost a half hour for pizzas that had been ordered that morning.

Looking back at it all now, I was happy the Gunny got to experience his first Super Bowl in a country that wasn't at war. The next year, 1991, the halftime show would be delayed due to news coverage of Desert Storm.

The 49ers defeated the Broncos by a score of 55–10, winning their second consecutive Super Bowl. I'm told that San Francisco also became the first team to win back-to-back Super Bowls with two different head coaches, but since I was football ignorant, I didn't know if this was significant. San Francisco quarterback Joe Montana was named Super Bowl MVP, his third award (I *did* know what an MVP was.). It was also his fourth Super Bowl victory. That's about the extent of what I can relate on the game. To this day, I still don't understand the twists and turns of first and third downs. Frankly, I watch the Super Bowl for the commercials.

Gunny went to bed happy (if he did go to bed, or maybe just disappeared) that night. I didn't have the heart to tell him that there would be no more live football until the preseason in late August. Maybe ice hockey would provide enough mayhem to keep him interested. Though the Flyers hadn't won the Stanley Cup since 1975, the sport certainly offered enough rough-and-tumble activity, and I didn't think there was enough bullfighting on ESPN to keep him engaged. He'd just root for the bull anyway and be devastated when it made its way later to the concession stand as burgers.

With his growing increasingly out of focus, however, I didn't think the Gunny would be with me long enough to enjoy another professional football season. And believe it or not, that saddened me.

*****

Granna was admitted to Johns Hopkins on January 30 for defibrillator-implant surgery, to be performed on the thirty-first. Despite her forebodings (okay, not so much forebodings as bitchiness tempered by fear), she came through with flying colors. Dr. Proctor didn't plan on releasing Granna from the hospital until Saturday night, and even then, she would have to remain in the greater Baltimore area through Tuesday afternoon for a follow-up appointment. The Quack was onto Granna. He knew if he released her too soon, she'd be back to working ten hours a day within a week, eschewing discomfort and fatigue. Extended hospitalization would likely drive her, my mother, and any staff dealing with her plumb crazy, but Dr. Proctor was taking advantage of having her captive under his care. He'd conspired, ahead of time, with Mother for the extra-long "prison sentence" (Granna's words, not mine) in the hospital and at a local hotel, so she'd booked a suite at the Four Seasons for the duration of her (and eventually Granna's) stay in Baltimore.

Mother called me from her hotel at 2100 on Wednesday night to report that everything had gone fine with the procedure, and Granna had been sound asleep when Mother left the hospital at 2030. Whether it was relief that her irascible parent was out of danger or softening toward me (I detected Granna's influence on that front), Mother actually seemed *pleasant* rather than just polite.

On Thursday morning, I received another call from my mother. This one came to the company office, and the Training Officer arrived, panting, at my door just as I was leaving to relieve Scott as classroom monitor.

"Ma'am, your mother's on the phone. I patched the call through to your office. I think it's an emergency." Message delivered, he high-tailed it back to the company office before Dickey noticed he was gone.

I stumbled across the floor to my phone just as it started ringing, put it on speaker in case the Gunny wanted to hear, and steeled myself for news that Granna had either relapsed or, worse, passed away.

"Mother, is Granna okay? Are you okay?" I struggled to keep my voice neutral.

The woman on the other end of the phone was not the cool, calm, and chatty Mother from Wednesday night. This was a frantic, practically sobbing woman-child, struggling to make herself heard above my Granna's snarling at someone in the background.

"I'm fine, Abigail. Your grandmother is fine. As least as well as that crazed...harpy...can be. When I came in this morning at seven thirty, she'd gotten out her suitcase and was packing, determined to check herself out today, even though Dr. Proctor told her before the procedure that she wouldn't be released until Saturday night at the earliest. She's still attached to IVs, for pity's sake, and looks like death on toast." (Now that was a new one.) "When I refused to help her, she let loose on me with language that would've made *you* blush, and I know you have a high threshold for profanity." I didn't know if I should be flattered or offended by that comment but opted to let it shine on by. Gunny raised an eyebrow and let out a guffaw, which he just as quickly stifled so I could continue my conversation. Mother concluded, "Dr. Proctor just walked in, and they're going toe-to-toe on her release, but my money's on him."

"Okay, Mother. Is there anything I can do to help?"

She sighed with relief. "I know your life is pretty hectic, Abigail, but can you squeeze in a visit up here on Saturday? Just a couple hours. Your Uncle Jeb will be here this afternoon to visit, and your father and JK will come down tomorrow morning. Even with the visits, she'll be like a caged lion by Saturday, and I'll want to wring her scrawny neck. I'm sure she'll want to reciprocate. Anyway if I could tell her you'll be here Saturday morning, she'd be thrilled. And it'd give me a break for a bit. Please say you can. If I tell her you'll be here the day after tomorrow, I'm sure she'll calm down." This was a side of Mother I had never seen. She actually seemed *human* and needy.

"Do you think it's an ambush?" Gunny asked. Whenever Mr. Nebby detected that the caller was Granna or Mother, he positioned himself to listen to both sides of the conversation. Don't ask me why. On some things, he was so nosy and chatty, he made my neighbor look like a Carthusian.

I shook my head. This might not be the mother that had raised me, but I owed her something in her hour of need.

"No problem, Mother. Do you mind if I ask Kelly to come with me? I hate driving up there and a full-size pickup truck is kind of difficult to maneuver in parking garages. He has some kind of sports car that he's always trying to show off, so if he's available, he'll be happy to drive."

"Absolutely fine. If you can give me an idea of the time you'll arrive, I'll make a nail appointment and leave you three alone for a while, but I'll be back before you leave for Stafford to say goodbye. When I get her to the hotel on Saturday night, I'll have no time to myself until we get back to Philadelphia on Wednesday or Thursday." She hesitated and I thought she stifled a sob. "Thank you for coming, Abigail. I truly appreciate it."

We agreed on a time, and I promised her I'd be there with or without Kelly. Though I deeply loved and admired my Granna, I didn't relish a couple of hours of her verbal abuse and abrupt silences, but that's where Kelly came in. Granna adored him, and he reciprocated. I was savvy enough to cash in on that mutual admiration and fervently hoped he was willing and available to accompany me to Baltimore.

Kelly was going to be my bullet sponge.

Gunny decided he'd just be in the way so opted not to accompany Kelly and me to Baltimore on Saturday. He said he'd rather stay back and watch Super Bowl highlights on ESPN, though I suspected he didn't want to deal with a caged Granna, likely on a rampage. I didn't blame him.

*****

We were on the road by 0800, and as we navigated the intermittent spotty and congested traffic on the Baltimore Washington Parkway, Kelly admitted that Jack Keller and Frederick Salton were dead ends (pardon the pun). Keller had been a career Marine and, by the time of his death in 1945, had already served seventeen years in the Corps. Had he not been busted twice, he probably would've been a master gunny or sergeant major due to years in service and accelerated promotions during the conflict. Salton had been in the reserves before the war and activated in 1941. His home of record was Louisiana, and he had only made it to through the eighth grade. Gunny had no accent and obviously had higher education. So that left Calvin Mercer (for now), but since he hadn't reacted to any of the names Kelly had proposed, I wasn't very hopeful that we had the right guy. Kelly hoped to get back into the archives the next week, research Mercer, and confirm if there were any other likely candidates.

The visit with Granna was *interesting*. Mother offered her cheek for a kiss and beat feet almost as soon as we arrived, promising to be back in two hours, tops (and she was). I braved the room first and, as expected, encountered an exceedingly grumpy Granna. However, when she spotted Kelly peeking around the door, she went all smiles. Heck, she would have been thrilled with his just visiting, but he had brought her daisies (her favorite) and a small box of liqueur-filled chocolates concealed in the huge pocket of his duffle coat. He needn't have bothered with the smuggling. He'd smiled and so completely charmed the nurses at their station, he could have led in a donkey, and they'd have asked to pet it while ass droppings plopped to the floor.

It was a good visit. Kelly entertained Granna while I pondered the next steps should Calvin Mercer not work out. When Mother returned, looking more relaxed than when she had left (I suspected a couple glasses of wine while she had her manicure were responsible), Kelly and I prepared to depart.

After a flurry of hugs and kisses, we headed toward the door, with Mother following.

"Thank you, Abigail," she offered again and surprisingly punctuated her words with another hug. "Safe travels home. Hopefully you can come north for the President's Day weekend. Granna...your father...I...would love to see you." With that, she blew me a kiss (*what?*), turned, and disappeared back into Granna's room.

The shocked expression on Kelly's face probably reflected my own.

"Hmm," was all he said as we made our way down the stairs to the parking garage. "Hmm."

"So what do you think the aliens did with my mother?" I quipped.

We were silent the rest of the walk to the car, each occupied with his/her own thoughts. As Kelly opened my car door for me, I said, "How about a drink when we get back to Woodbridge? I'll buy."

"Okay. Yep, you'll buy. I see a very expensive single malt in my future. Probably more than one."

"I'll drive."

"Your truck. Not my car. I deserve to be duty drunk tonight but in your truck. We'll switch when we get back to my place. You drive too crazy."

I knew I drove exuberantly, not badly. However, Kelly had cut me a huss today, and I kept my mouth shut.

By the end of the evening, I was out more than $200, and that was just for booze, Diet Cokes, and a couple of munchies. Do the math. Kelly had obviously enjoyed a lot of single malts.

*****

It was Wednesday, February 7, the day before mess night, our last great formal social event. I had gotten home at noon to prepare for a visit from Granna and Mother, the latter having called the previous night to ask if they could swing south to see me before heading back to Philadelphia. I offered to head up to Baltimore to meet them there, but Mother firmly (albeit nicely) refused. She sounded different. I couldn't put my finger on it. Maybe the week with Granna had been harder on her than I thought.

Gunny and I had just gotten home when a limo pulled up into my driveway and parked behind my truck. The driver hurried over to the side closest to the house to hand Granna out of the car while Mother emerged from the other and quickly made her way to her mother, offering her arm for support. This gesture on Mother's part immediately reinforced two things to me: Granna, while making a show of being fully recovered, was certainly not back to 100 percent yet; and Mother's assistance seemed to be just as much for her as Granna. Something had transpired between the two that had changed their dynamic. And it was more than the shared hospital experience.

Before they had taken more than two slow halting steps up the path, I hurried down the walk and stopped in front of them, delivering a kiss to Mother's, and then Granna's, cheeks. I thanked the driver and told him I could take it from there and assumed his place by Granna's side.

Granna's arm seemed frail, birdlike, in mine, and when I glanced behind her back to my mother, she shook her head, indicating I should *not* comment on her mother's physical state. My grandmother's fragility became even more apparent, however, as we proceeded deliberately toward my house, where we haltingly made our way up the three steps onto the porch and into the foyer. There

Gunny hovered at the entrance to the living room, nervously shifting from foot to foot, uncertain of what he should do.

Mother made an abortive attempt to divest Granna of her coat and gloves, rebuffed with a, "I might be a bit unsteady right now, but I'm neither dead nor a two-year-old." Mother backed off with a barely concealed grin, and Granna flung off her coat (The sable, of course. It was, after all, February.), peeled off her gloves, stuffed them in its pockets, and relinquished the fur to me. As I accepted the coat, I couldn't help but wonder how she could wear such a heavy garment. Heck. The damn thing had to weigh ten pounds but it was probably warm.

"Don't like it, do you, sweetie?" Granna observed, noting my expression of veiled disgust. "Don't worry. When I die, it will go to your mother with the stipulation that it be burned when she's done with it. It's warm, but it smells. Even with that expensive storage place doing all their secret mumbo jumbo with it. The only reason I wear it is because…well, I'm not sure why I wear it. Maybe it's to share the misery with the women who've worn it before me."

"We'll just bury you in it, Mother. Or cremate, if you prefer. Whatever." Mother flashed me a conspiratorial smile—what? Mother actually including me in a subversive act?—and froze in handing me her coat. Her attention was focused on the living room, and she was staring at the Gunny. Not a casual glance. She actually *saw* him.

Had something happened in Baltimore or was Mother acquiring *her* mother's sight to see and chat with the dead?

At the same time, Gunny abruptly abandoned his nervous shifting and locked eyes with Mother's. They just stood there for what seemed an eternity—she studying him, he seemingly amazed that she could actually *see* him. Granna and I simply watched this tableau, part of it but obviously not active participants.

Granna quietly waited for a couple of minutes and, obviously bored with the bipartisan scrutiny, uttered a *harrumph*, brushed past Gunny, and moved haltingly, but determinedly, toward the living room with me in trace. I settled her into a chair with an ottoman and glanced back at the foyer. Mother and Gunny remained rooted in their original places.

As usual, Granna assumed control of the situation. In her typically brusque and businesslike manner, she made introductions. "Prudence, meet Calvin Mather Mercer, a.k.a. Cotton Mercer. He's your father. Cotton, meet your daughter, Prudence Drinker Rush." Introductions made, she turned to me and ordered, "Sit down, child. You look like you've seen a ghost for the first time instead of having lived with one for six months."

She didn't have to tell me twice. The room was spinning crazily around me, and the floor was falling away from my feet, so I collapsed on the sofa and almost immediately got back on my feet.

"*He* isn't my Granpa!" In two steps, I was standing in front of the mantel, grabbing the pewter-framed family portrait that had been taken two months before my maternal grandfather's abrupt passing. I jabbed my finger at the distinguished but jolly-looking older man standing behind Granna and clarified (firmly), "*This* is my grandfather."

"Have a seat, Abe," Granna commanded again. "This is no time for a hissy fit."

I hesitated and threw her what I hoped was my best defiant look but flung myself back onto the sofa, depositing the picture on the coffee table as I did so.

Meanwhile, Granna's words had broken the deadlock, and Gunny/Cotton/Grandfather(?) whirled to face us. He wasn't just mad, he was furious.

"This is ridiculous," he spat out. "Abe said you could be manipulative, but I thought that was just in your business dealings. Why are you doing this? Is this your idea of some kind of sick joke? Or are you saying you knew who—what—I was and kept your mouth shut?" He turned back to confront Mother, who hadn't moved. "Do you buy this fairy tale?"

Mother quirked an eyebrow (how *did* she do that?), sailed regally into the living room (*Really*. How did she do *that*?), and assumed a seat on the sofa next to me. She patted my arm reassuringly, in a totally un-Mother-like gesture, and looked up to regard her father. "Mother told me yesterday. Maybe that's why I can see you now when I couldn't before. But I had had inklings, flashes of you, I suppose, when I was here. Who knows? And yes, I 'buy into this fairy tale.' I think she had good reasons to keep the truth to herself as long as she did."

Gunny (I still couldn't think of him as Grandfather.) assumed his TV-watching seat and perched on the edge, seemingly intent on either strangling my grandmother or hearing her out. Me, I just wanted answers without drama. No matter what the explanation, however, I felt betrayed and confused. I suspected Granna had known who my visitor was for several months and hadn't indicated any recognition, even when she thought she was dying.

I glanced over at my mother as she studied first Granna, and then the Gunny, and back. Maybe she was trying to imagine them when both were young, or maybe she was scrutinizing them for features that might have carried over to her. Whatever her thoughts, she was calm and self-possessed and somehow at ease with the situation.

"I knew the minute I walked into this house who you were, Cotton, and I wanted desperately for you to remember *me*. But you didn't. I truly wrestled with how to break it to you all, but things just got away from me."

Yeah, right. Nothing "got away" from Granna. Not even preoccupation with dying. She turned to me. "And a large part of why I didn't was *you*, sweetie. I intended to tell you when I saw him for the first time that Sunday, but we got caught up in discussing my health, and then Kelly came over to watch football, and I just didn't have the heart to ruin a beautiful day. By Christmas, I think I had figured out why Cotton had stowed away in your baggage, and again there was never the right moment to bring it up. Or maybe I was just too chicken."

Okay. *That* admission, though suspect, was somewhat believable. She sank back in her chair and waved for Mother, who had risen in concern, to retake her seat, then turned back to me. "Sweetie, when we're finished with our discussion, could we have some tea? And I hope you have decaffeinated but not that horrible herbal stuff," she quickly clarified, glancing at Mother. "And some coffee for your mother?"

"Sure, Granna. I have decaf Earl Grey and Irish Breakfast. But you were saying..." Spit it out, woman! True to form, however, Granna would share in her own good time and was probably relishing the suspense.

"I think Cotton's coming here was a target of opportunity, providence, an alignment of the stars—whatever new wave thing they're calling it these days. I think it was intended for him to get closure and for me to share a secret I've held for almost fifty years. But I kept my mouth shut because of the effect his being here was having on *you*, Abe."

"What? Confusion? You enjoyed watching me try to figure out how I got saddled with a bacon-sniffing, jelly-donut-craving pain in the neck?" I glanced over at Gunny, who seemed affronted, and added, "No offense, Gunny."

"None taken, Abe. I guess." Mollified, he flashed me a radiant smile, and I thought how seldom I had seen him smile. Was he remembering? Was he looking at me through different eyes? Was he appraising me now as his granddaughter and not as a Marine captain? I fervently hoped I met his expectations on both fronts.

"Oh, I knew it was driving you crazy, Abe, but ever since your divorce from that Neanderthal, you'd changed. You used to see the funny side of things. You laughed. You socialized. You were so much like *him* when I knew him." Here she pointed at the Gunny. "I had hoped the year in Okinawa would've helped you heal. Even there, though, the Neanderthal's shadow followed you. You were better when you returned, but you still weren't *you*." I thought back to Okinawa and the Douchebag at battalion headquarters. How he had been a constant reminder of the life, and person, I was trying to forget.

I managed a nod, but I was still seething. "I guess you're right. Go on, Granna. Please," I managed through gritted teeth, having decided to emulate my mother (for once) and compose my features, even though I longed to shake Granna until she got to the point.

"I watched the three of you—Cotton, Kelly, and you—and you were more the old Abe. Joking. Sarcastic. Fun. I was even more delighted when you asked for Kelly's help in finding out Cotton's name and background. I'm sure it seemed like I was pushing you two together, and I suppose I was. He loves you so very, very much, Abe. It's written all over his face when he looks at you, but you don't see it."

"Granna, this really isn't the time—" She didn't let me finish.

"You've set boundaries, and he abides by them to be with you. And where you'd been pushing him away, you've started to let him get closer. You trust him. I didn't think I'd ever see that in you again."

She glanced at Mother, who had started quietly weeping. What? Mother, the iron maiden, never let her facade slip in public. "And you've actually started to treat your mother, my daughter, with respect, not just as someone to be tolerated. I thank you for that."

Mother remained silent but grasped my hand in acknowledgment, and I smiled back at her.

It wasn't Mother's fault that Granna had failed to reveal such earth-shattering information. I didn't have an issue with *her*. Granna's role as self-appointed matchmaker and keeper of secrets, however, more than pissed me off.

"I *have* started to think of Kelly as more than a friend. I *do* have feelings for him, Granna. And when I'm ready, I'll let him be more. But that's not your call. It certainly doesn't justify your keeping your mouth shut when Gunny and I have lived this weird life together for almost six months." I glanced Gunny's way. "Help me here, Casper."

"I'm with you, Abe. For me, it's been startling, but also, I guess, fun. And also scary." He paused and shook his head like he was shaking out thoughts that might have crossed his mind but never acknowledged to me, let alone himself. "For me, it's been like being between worlds, and the edges are getting fuzzier. That whoever sent me here has an hourglass that's marking time, and the sands are running out. And we've been powerless to stop it."

"In current jargon, it's been like living in a time warp," I summed up for him and turned toward Mother. "So if my behavior's been a little more…erratic…than usual, at least you know it's not been deliberate or another Mr. Porker escapade."

Mother responded with a very unladylike belly laugh that ended in a very Mr. Porker-like snort.

Whoa! Didn't know she had it in her.

"She can be a real pain in the ass, can't she, Pru?" This was from Gunny, who managed to look sympathetic and delighted at the same time.

"You have no idea." Mother smiled as she grabbed a tissue out of her purse and dabbed at her eyes. How did she manage to keep her eye makeup from running? How could she cry and still look like a mature cover girl? When I cried (which was almost never), I looked like a red-nosed snotty mess. "We can talk about some of the antics she pulled when she was a kid. I raised two boys, and together they weren't half of the handful she was. You'll want to hear about them too."

"You're on." Gunny couldn't seem to take his eyes off my mother. I looked from one to the other, and it hit me—the eyes. Gunny, Mother, and I all had the same blue-green shade of eyes. His were more Aegean and startling, while Mother's and mine were a darker version of the same color. My brother Tad's eyes were the same arresting shade as his grandfather's.

Holy shit! Why hadn't I noticed it before? I had to look at myself in the mirror at least ten times a day, not because I was vain but because part of my job was *looking* the part of a professional Marine officer (even if I wasn't any closer to being one than when I got my orders to TBS). And I'd never considered comparing the unusual color of *my* eyes with those of the dead guy with whom I was currently sharing my life.

Granna noticed my scrutiny and realization. "We'll get to the eyes, sweetie. But first, we need to discuss the matter at hand. What happened in 1942 and how and why did I keep this from all of you?" She sat back, collected her thoughts, and began.

"Jeb—my husband and who you've always thought of as your father, Pru, and your grandfather, Abe—and I were engaged my first year at Bryn Mawr, and we would have been married in June of 1945 when I graduated. Jeb was *supposed* to graduate from Princeton in May 1942 and start working at his family's business. He'd start at the bottom, like all the family men before him, and eventually take the company's reins from his father when he stepped down. Jeb's life was mapped out for him, and it never occurred to him to buck the system. Since the business was struggling, Jeb thought he could bring it back to life. After the war, when he took over, he *did* keep it from failing, but it never became what it had once been.

"He and his best friend, you, Cotton, were inseparable. They grew up together. They went to Princeton together. When they graduated, Cotton was going onto Harvard Law like his father and grandfather before him. He'd clerk at the family's firm and eventually be a partner there. Unlike Jeb, though, Cotton was willing to go to law school but wasn't certain he wanted to spend the rest of his life protecting the legal interests of wealthy clients. He was, what do you say, Abe? A rebel without a clue." Gunny cracked a smile and playfully hung his head.

He was remembering.

"Jeb and I were just engaged when he asked me to a mixer at Princeton. I'd known Cotton since I'd met Jeb, around four years before. We'd double-dated, Cotton always with a different girl, and the three of us had gone fishing and sailing together, but there'd never been a social situation like this one. We'd seldom been alone, and when we were, Cotton treated me like a little sister. At the time of the mixer, he was seeing some twit, a party girl, from the University of Pennsylvania. Anyway, that night, she wound up leaving early with some other guy. Cotton had gotten disgusted with her swilling everything in sight and suggested she slow down. Instead, she drank more and attached herself to another upperclassman. Then left with him."

"She was a sloppy drunk," offered Gunny. "Absolutely disgusting."

So he *was* remembering. And this was certainly getting interesting.

"Jeb was off chatting with a couple of other business majors about a project, and they wanted to find a quiet corner and work out some details. He asked if I minded his being gone for around twenty minutes, and I didn't have a problem with it. I told him I'd stay at the table and keep Cotton company."

Gunny looked up at Granna. "I'd waited for this opportunity for years and wanted to take advantage of being alone, maybe tell you how I really felt. Get you to reconsider marrying Jeb. But Jeb was my best friend, so I decided to just play it cool and keep my mouth shut."

"You should have opened your damn mouth then, you dimwit. I felt the same. I had feelings for you, too, and gave you plenty of opportunity during that conversation for you to say something— anything—that I was more than your best friend's fiancée." Granna abruptly fell silent, maybe collecting her thoughts, but more likely biting back words that were better left unsaid.

"Uh, what happened?" I interjected, breaking the silence that was becoming a little uncomfortable.

"Pearl Harbor is what happened, Abe. Pearl Harbor." It was Gunny, not Granna, who answered my question, and I started at his voice. I turned his way, and he was here, watching me and remembering *with* us. Not like the night when he relived Okinawa.

"It happened the beginning of December 1941. Jeb and I were due to graduate the next May, but I wanted to do something now, not wait. I didn't need to be an officer, a ninety-day wonder. I told Jeb I was going to enlist in the Marines, and he admitted he was thinking the same thing, so we joined up together."

"They enlisted, and *then* they informed us they'd joined up," Granna interrupted, obviously not happy about Jeb's delay in delivering the news. "Can you imagine what it's like, hearing your fiancé on December 25, wishing you Merry Christmas, and oh, by the way, Cotton and I won't be going back to Princeton for second semester. We joined the Marines and ship out at the end of January for boot camp." Granna spat it out, glaring at Gunny, who, at least, had the grace to look embarrassed.

"I offered to go with him to tell you, Fred, but he wanted to deliver the news on his own. He thought you'd wait to get married until he got back from the war or, at least, while he was on leave or after boot camp. And I guess I liked that plan because I thought it'd give me a chance to tell you how I really felt. That you might reconsider the engagement. Neither of you seemed that into each other"—where had he heard *that?*—"It's like you were both doing what was expected of you, and I thought maybe I'd have a chance.

273

When Jeb phoned me Christmas night, your families were already making plans for a wedding in January, before we left. I honestly didn't see that coming."

"The war. Both of you going away to who knew what. Everything was moving so fast, and I needed something to hold onto, something…certain. The wedding became that something to get me through the days until both of you were gone. And I had made a promise." Granna turned to me. "I think you understand, Abe. I think you got halfway to the altar to marry that Neanderthal and seriously considered running away because it wasn't right. Didn't you? I saw it on your face. I so hoped you'd say, 'I don't' and walk away. But you didn't. Because you didn't want to disappoint your parents, and you had made Tom a promise. In my case, I just went with the flow of the hasty wedding. I thought, 'We're already engaged. We might as well get married sooner than later.'"

Guilty as charged. She was right. I *had* considered leaving Idiot at the altar but had convinced myself that a promise was a promise. And I thought he loved me. Boy, had I been a naive twit.

I only nodded in reply.

Mother looked stricken. "You mean you didn't love Daddy?" As sophisticated as my mother was, you'd think she'd have transitioned into calling her father Dad or Pop, especially since my grandfather had died several years ago. Nope. It was always Daddy. Our relationship had come a long way of late, but I was still disdainful of some of her quirks. Heck. I was sure she harbored a lot more about *me*.

"I loved Jeb, Pru. I just didn't love him in the heart-stopping, longing-to-be-with-him way that I thought young love could be. *My* mother insisted that type of love—what we saw in the movies—wasn't real. That I should get on with it. And that's what I did." She stopped, shrugged, and continued, "But we've gotten off topic. I need to explain the what and the why we're here today.

"Four days before the wedding, Jeb announced he was spending the night in Princeton, saying goodbye to classmates and picking up books he'd loaned to friends. He asked Cotton and me to get together and work out some kind of truce since he was Jeb's best man, I was his fiancée, and since the wedding announcement, we'd done nothing but snipe at each other every time we were in the same room. The tension was so thick you could cut it with a knife, but Jeb just blamed it on the war, the wedding, and his and Cotton's shipping out for Parris Island shortly after our four-day honeymoon. He didn't want our wedding weekend to be a continuous battle, and Cotton and I reluctantly—*very* reluctantly—agreed to get together for drinks at some hotel bar in Rittenhouse Square. We spent four hours talking and talking and talking, and it hit me—*this* was the man I should be marrying. Not Jeb. We wound upstairs in a room, and I won't go any further on what went on there, but you can imagine what happened. That night"—she sighed—"it was..."

"Wondrous," Gunny completed her sentence. "But in the light of day, it wasn't a clear-cut we love each other. To hell with convention. We knew we couldn't be together. Jeb was my best friend. All of us were from prominent families. People like us might have flings, but they didn't break engagements to chase 'love.' They gutted it out and did the 'right' thing."

"Three days later, Jeb and I married, and ten days after that, they left for boot camp. When I realized I was pregnant with you, Pru, it never crossed my mind that Cotton could be the father. It was only one night. Jeb and I had had almost two weeks together."

"Did you ever tell Granpa about the one-night stand, Granna?"

Granna turned on me like a cornered alley cat. "It was *not* a one-night stand, young lady. And no, I didn't tell him because it wasn't relevant. And until I saw him"—she gestured toward Gunny—"it never occurred to me that *he*, not Jeb, could be Pru's father."

"That doesn't explain why you didn't say anything earlier," I persisted. "Sure, sure, I understand the Kelly-Gunny-Abe thing. But when did you actually *know*? Kelly's spent a lot of time trying to track down who Gunny was. I have a reputation now for being slightly crazy or at least eccentric, and the Gunny and I have been stuck together for six months, trying to figure out what we'd done to deserve each other. So when did you know for *sure*, Granna?"

"I don't know. You've kind of grown on me, Abe. Has it been that bad?" Gunny quipped.

"Thanksgiving. I knew at Thanksgiving."

The three of us focused incredulously on Granna, now fidgeting uncomfortably in her chair.

"I knew at Thanksgiving," she repeated. She gave herself a shake and was once again the self-assured Granna, regarding each of us separately and then as a group. "Pru and Abe, you two and Tad sitting at the table, and Cotton in the kitchen watching football. It clicked." She turned to me. "You already commented on it, Abe. The eyes."

Gunny was noticeably pissed; I was glad it wasn't at me for a change. "Why the hell did you keep silent, woman? You could have cleared things up then. I'd be...wherever I'm supposed to be. Maybe at rest. I don't know. Abe would already be digging herself out of the crazy category. And Pru—"

"And Pru wouldn't have believed her. Wouldn't have wanted to believe her," Mother quietly stated. "But I'm finally at a place where I'm getting along with my mother and daughter. I'm more...open to what they have to say and what matters to them. And I think they feel the same about me."

Granna nodded and smiled. But I was still with Gunny on this one.

"Why *now*, Granna? Seems to me that you should have shared your secret *before* your surgery. Set things straight with us and maybe *God*, just in case you didn't make it!"

"It's hard for me, my generation, to admit to things like your one-night stand, Abe. And when it happened, it wasn't a fling. We were in love, and the night it happened, we had convinced ourselves that we could make it work. When practicality set in the next day, we knew it wouldn't. So why belabor it? When I woke up from the anesthesia last week though, all I could think about was setting things straight with you, Pru." She gestured toward my mother. "And I told her everything—Cotton and me in 1942, and you, Abe, with your grandfather's ghost as a roommate since last August. But I didn't want to come here today. I wanted to leave it alone..."

"But I insisted we come today, Abe," Mother once again spoke up. "No more secrets. Almost fifty years of secrets. You and my father"—she glanced over at the Gunny—"deserved answers, and

SEMPER FI WITH A SIDE OF DONUTS OR BACON

once I knew what was going on, I wanted to meet my father. I wanted you, and him, to have closure."

She threw Granna a glance, and surprisingly, it was more defiant than angry. "Sure, at first I thought it was a repeat of the Mr. Porker bluff, but then things fell into place—your talking to...nothing... claiming it was just thinking aloud. Your nervousness while I was here or on the phone, and I knew something was up at Thanksgiving but couldn't put my finger on it. I certainly wouldn't have guessed you were unknowingly living with my biological father's ghost. I had no idea what you both were going through, and I know if we had been closer, you would've confided in me."

Granna sniffed and attempted (unsuccessfully, I might add) to look small, feeble, and helpless. "You wouldn't *believe* how hard she came at me to come down here, Abe. As late as this morning, before we left Baltimore, I tried to convince her that this meeting should happen later, that I was still weak and confused." Here, she moaned feebly (*really* bad acting, I thought). "She didn't buy it. Told me to stuff it and suck it up. Pru was determined to meet her father and help solve the puzzle you and Cotton had been trying to solve for six months." She paused, noting her audience was not buying into the vulnerable ole granny act. "Pru obviously gets that stubborn take-no-prisoners streak from *you*, Cotton. Certainly not me."

Even as she made this pronouncement, I erupted into laughter, joined almost immediately by Mother and Gunny. After several minutes of our amusement at her expense, Granna finally joined us, having realized her self-portrayal as a victim was just too far a reach.

"Thank you, thank you, thank you, Pru, for your gift of this meeting. So many questions answered. So much to think about. A daughter. A granddaughter. And a Marine at that! Who's read Clausewitz! Who'd have thought I'd have a granddaughter who's a Marine that's read Clausewitz!" He regarded me with something I could only describe as fondness, an expression far removed from the usual supercilious or amused or calculating looks I had grown accustomed to seeing turned my way since he'd joined me. "And I have grandsons. Grandsons!" he marveled.

And me? I was relieved and satisfied, but also sad. What would happen now? Would Gunny take up residence with my mother? Would he stay with me? Or now that the mystery was solved, would he transition to whatever or wherever? All I knew for sure was that things had changed, and I wasn't as happy as I thought I'd be knowing the Gunny's identity.

"You were the catalyst, Abe," he continued. "I don't think it was chance. I think...no, I *know*...it was predestined. The alignment of all the stars wasn't happenstance."

At this, Granna turned on him what I called the hairy eyeball. Her expression was surprised, maybe a trifle contemptuous. "When did you get religion, Cotton? Why don't you just say *fate?*'"

In a passable imitation of Foghorn Leghorn, Gunny pronounced, "I am stricken to the core, Fred! Stricken, I say! Remember, Calvin is my first name, like John Calvin. I'm called Cotton because my middle name is Mather, like the Puritan. Do you think I might have had a pretty strong religious upbringing? Or maybe you really *are* a witch and, at heart, a nonbeliever?" He just laughed at his little joke, and Granna rolled her eyes in disgust.

"We have fifty years to catch up on, Father," Mother interrupted their exchange. "Where do you want to start?"

After several hours and numerous cups of Earl Grey and Irish Breakfast teas (decaffeinated for Granna, caffeinated for me), pots of French press for Mother, and three rashers of microwaved bacon (for Gunny to sniff), Mother and Granna departed for Baltimore. They'd head for Philly on Thursday.

The live people hugged; Mother and Granna smiled and bid Gunny a fond and tearful farewell that he earnestly returned. They also wrung a promise from me to bring Gunny up for President's Day. And Kelly, too, if I wanted to invite him. I'd have to think about that one, considering all that had transpired today.

After they were safely gone, Gunny and I exchanged sighs of relief. He settled on the couch to enjoy the VHS of *Strange Brew* I had bought him and which he must have watched twenty times. I headed to the stairs and bed and called down, "Good night, you old fart. I love you."

He looked up at me, grinned, and replied, "I love you too, Abe." He paused and collected himself. "I'm very, very proud that you're my granddaughter."

"And I'm proud that you're my grandfather. Aren't you happy now I never let you see me undress?"

His stricken look was enough to give him away.

"Oh, tell me you didn't!"

"Well, only a little peek. Not in the altogether." His sheepish grin was hard to resist.

"I should have known," I responded (with not a little disgust) and continued upstairs to bed.

CHAPTER 22

Mess Night

WOKE UP the next morning longing to linger over a cup of tea and discuss the previous day's revelations with Gunny but realized that would have to wait until we had a lull in the day's activities or tomorrow morning, after the mess night. I was facing an exceedingly long day between preparations for and actual event that would start at 1800 with cocktails on the Quarterdeck. Mess night really wouldn't conclude until Friday morning, however, when we mustered at 0700 for a five-mile run. Ostensibly the run was to sober up those lieutenants (or staff) still drunk from the night before, but it was really the tradition of shared misery—a long, long night of partying followed by an early-morning PT session, frequently punctuated by lieutenants pulling out of the formation to blow cookies. Some wouldn't quite make it, and those in front of him or her might get splashed, or those behind the hurler would be running through barf.

Lovely.

Next to the Marine Corps' birthday, mess night is one of the Corps' most celebrated traditions. It is at once a festive and somber occasion where Marines, attired in their dress blues or evening dress, gather to share the Corps' customs and courtesies as well as to build camaraderie and esprit de corps. Spouses or significant others are not present. A mess night is exclusively the Marines assigned to the unit and their invited—usually military—guests.

A Marine is assigned to be president of the mess, and at TBS, it is almost always one of the company's lieutenants. However, in our case, Dickey had appointed himself to that role, likely in a vain attempt to curry favor with the TBS CO and/or the guest of honor (in our case, a medal of honor recipient). Dickey had been slow on the uptake when the CO asked him on three separate occasions if it was true that he (not a lieutenant) was going to be mess president. Dickey was so clueless, he thought the CO was confirming this great monumental idea and wanted to be reassured that Dandy Dickey would, indeed, have the helm.

Even this far into the company's tenure, I was still dumbfounded by how dense Dickey could be.

The mess president is in charge of the occasion and controls the flow of events for the evening. He or she plays straight man to the mess's vice president, Mr. Vice, as the title has come to be known. Mr. Vice acts as the enforcer of the president's decisions and also regulates who may speak to the president. At a TBS mess night, Mr. Vice is always a second lieutenant who has demonstrated he can think on his feet and indulge in lighthearted repartee. He or she sits alone at a table facing the VIPs and is literally at the base of the mess.

The vice president is a coveted assignment, and Bob had convinced Dickey to let the lieutenants choose their own Mr. Vice since they would have a better idea of who had the inventiveness to keep things rolling. I think Dickey agreed because it was dawning on him that his usurping the president's position had not earned him any brownie points with Colonel Montoya. Worse, he likely detected (though he couldn't actually pinpoint) disapproval from Bob and the SPCs. He'd ceased preening himself on his role as president at mess night meetings, his self-satisfaction consistently met with silence (really, silent disapproval) from us.

Delta's Mr. Vice was Lieutenant Emerson from—surprise!— Doug's platoon. The staff captains had only recently learned that Emerson was the instigator of and brains behind Fourth Platoon's antics. We knew him as a cutup who did a credible Rodney

Dangerfield, though we'd had no idea he'd conceived of and orchestrated the platoon's reign of terror since the company formed in August. Obviously, the lieutenants had. Emerson's was the only name presented as a potential Mr. Vice candidate. He was elected unanimously, chosen by not only the lieutenants but the captains as well.

There are many mess-night traditions: parading the beef, charges and fines, port and cigars to name a few. After a brief intermission upon completion of the meal, the mess reconvenes and offers toasts in a prescribed order.

Before the commencement of toasts, however, the mess's attention is brought to a table situated at the entrance to the banquet hall. It is the Table for Fallen Comrades or Table for Absent Friends.

The table is often draped in black, with one empty chair, and placed near the entrance so everyone who walks past it is reminded of all the fallen comrades who are not present, having given the full measure of devotion to country and Corps. A candle atop the table signifies the flame of eternal life. A Purple Heart is displayed to reflect the shedding of blood and the ebb of life in battle. Identification tags, which are blank, could bear the name of any Marine and are usually to the right of the upended wine glass. The dinner setting, china and cutlery, are inverted as the fallen comrades break bread in spirit only. Depending on the mess, the table may contain a dress white cover lying atop a sword and white gloves.

As each element of the table is explained, the mess grows increasingly sober with the knowledge that the occupants of this table contributed to the battles won and Corps' continued reputation for courage, honor, and sacrifice. These fallen comrades are celebrating with the mess, but they are celebrating from the grave. They have earned the remembrance and respect of their living comrades at arms.

After a respectful silence, the toasts begin, and the mood again becomes festive, even raucous. Toasts are made with port, but the toast to the Marine Corps is made with grog or rum punch.

Once the honored guests depart, lieutenants adjourn to their rooms, change into PT gear, and conduct carrier quals down the BOQ passageways.

Traditionally, carrier quals are conducted while the wearer is still in his/her dress blues. Booze or water is sprayed across a long table, and the participant launches himself, on his stomach, at the wet slippery surface and wildly slides forward until his/her feet catch the edge. This practice has gradually transitioned into two tables, head to toe, and the object not to catch one's feet but to see how far a slide can be achieved. To see carrier quals as originally practiced, check out the opening scenes of the movie, *The Great Santini*.

At TBS, the quals are conducted in the company's BOQ passageways, in PT gear because dress blues are expensive and saturation in alcohol and oil-laden water (to enhance the length of slide, of course) can pretty much destroy the wearers' uniforms. Lieutenants don't have a lot of money, and most are still paying for their uniforms, even after graduation.

"Shy this morning?" I addressed the quiet house as I prepared to depart at 0600. "Or are you getting your dress blues spiffed up for tonight?" My questions were met with silence, but as I drove to base, the familiar buzzing in the back of my head indicated that I wasn't alone.

By the time I opened the door to my office, Gunny still hadn't appeared. "Before I get sidetracked, let me remind you. Just because I know you're my grandfather doesn't give you special privileges. No visits to my lieutenants' rooms. Got it?"

Crickets from Gunny, but Neil, who had stopped to unlock the door to his office (his was next to mine), glanced my way and laughingly responded, "Aye, aye, ma'am. Thank you for the reminder! I promise I will *not* creep into your lieutenants' rooms tonight, whether I'm drunk or sober." And he disappeared into his office.

Ho, boy. I was just thankful it had been Neil and not Dickey.

The day flew by with last-minute uniform inspections and adjustments and a two-hour rehearsal (totally unnecessary, but the practice pacified Dickey). Before I knew it, it was time to change for the cocktail hour to be held—of course!—on the Quarterdeck.

As I meandered around the room during cocktail hour, a Diet Coke in my hand (there would be enough inebriated lieutenants tonight that SPCs were, again, sober and watchful), I noted how sharp and polished these very junior officers were. I was on the alert for Lieutenant Elvises but breathed a sigh of relief when I didn't detect any. Neil must have made some pretty dire threats, or maybe his guys had just matured. Graduation was just three weeks away, and many of these lieutenants would be assigned to the Fleet (Marine operating forces) while awaiting orders to their MOS schools. They'd be expected to behave as adults and junior leaders, not frat boys and sorority girls on spring break. At least not in front of the troops.

First call sounded, and I knew we had five minutes before the bagpiper piped us into the banquet room. For unmilitary types, first call is also called "Assembly of the Buglers," an historical military tune adapted to horse racing. Historically, this bugle call was the first of each day, used to alert and gather other camp buglers.

As we lined up behind the VIPs, now stationed behind the piper, I scanned the room one last time, to no avail. Then it hit me—the buzzing in my ears had stopped. I couldn't recall when, but it was definitely gone. And so was the Gunny.

We moved into the banquet room and took our seats. For this occasion, we were not seated by platoon but were an integrated population, and I could spot my lieutenants, uniforms different from their male counterparts, sprinkled around the mess tables. I had been a popular commodity; both Doug's and Neil's lieutenants wanted me to sit with their platoons. I didn't flatter myself, though. I suspected they wanted a glimpse of my ghostly companion, and the best chance of getting a glimpse was wherever I was, but SPCs were obviously part of the sprinkle, with one seated per table.

The chef paraded the beef, preceded, of course, by the piper, and the president pronounced it unfit for human consumption. After the expected laughter and hoots to his feeble attempt at humor, Dickey reversed his verdict, pronounced it consumable, and dinner service began.

Salads were already on our chargers, and a variety of dressings in those frustrating little packets provided in bowls placed the length of the table. I hate those damn things. You can seldom open them with anything less than your teeth or a pair of scissors. Most of the lieutenants around me were equally frustrated, eyes focused on how

I was going to slay my salad-dressing monster. Obviously, my fellow SPCs had instructed their platoons as I had mine—watch the SPC sitting with you. Whatever he or she does, do it. When I tried, for the *third* time, to rip the creamy ranch dressing packet open, I resorted to starting to rip with my teeth. There was an audible exhalation of breath around me, and my audience followed suit.

Salad dressing now atop the anemic lettuce posing as a salad on my plate, I looked up and noticed several lieutenants had not yet started their salads. Then it hit me—not everyone was raised with a table set with a myriad of forks, knives, and spoons. So I picked up my salad fork, making a show of selecting the one furthest left on the table. I was happy there wouldn't be multiple courses that required the seafood fork, soup spoon, fruit knife and fork, fish knife and fork, or dessert knife. I'd been to several hoity-toity dinners that had enough cutlery at the place setting that you had to sit five feet from the person next to you and needed a key to determine what flatware to employ for what course. This meal would be straightforward, with salad, main course, and dessert (usually some kind of cheesecake or tart). Dessert would arrive with its own fork or spoon.

There was only one wine glass. The diner chose red or white from carafes already placed on the table. Port carafes would appear later for toasts; rum punch would be served in individual glasses to salute the Marine Corps.

We got safely through the salad, the plates were whisked away, and the main course—*always* some kind of beef (usually prime rib), baked or mashed potato, and green beans—was placed in front of us. This was the next dilemma facing my mess mates: how do you cut your meat?

Though I invited the lieutenants served before me to start eating, many refrained until I was served. Most were merely being polite, but many genuinely didn't know how to "acceptably" cut their serving of meat, so I nonchalantly took my dinner fork into my left hand, knife in my right, and cut one bite of beef. Though I'd been raised to proceed with fork in left hand, I'd adopted the American practice of transferring my fork to my right to actually get the food to my mouth. When we were younger, JK, Tad, and I were all teased at school for eating with our left hands, and all three of us had adopted the American style rather than spend interminable lunch periods enduring snarky comments from our dining companions. More like fellow hogs at the trough, as I remember high school.

I thoroughly enjoyed my dinner companions and the periodic back and forth between Mr. Vice and members of the mess. The lieutenants started in on each other first, likely assessing the climate of the room, before taking on larger targets like the TBS or company staff. A typical exchange went something like this:

Lieutenant Ahern rises, stands at attention, and announces, "Mr. Vice. Lieutenant Ahern requests permission to address the mess."

Mr. Vice looks to Dickey, as president, who approves Ahern's request and responds, "Lieutenant Ahern, please enlighten us." Had Dickey disapproved, Lieutenant Ahern would've been told to sit down and shut up (or similar shutdown).

LIEUTENANT AHERN. Sir, it has come to my attention that Lieutenant Shaw had already heavily imbibed before reporting to cocktail hour. He is now extremely intoxicated, and those officers sitting on either side of and across from him are concerned that he might hurl on them. This could endanger not only their dress blues but likely cause sympathetic vomiting from them and maybe even the rest of the table.

MR. VICE. Lieutenant Shaw, please rise.

Lieutenant Shaw rises and identifies himself, "Lieutenant Shaw, sir." He's obviously not the worse for drink and appears stone-cold sober. "I am shocked and deny Lieutenant Ahern's accusation. I have never been more sober and will do whatever I need to do in order to prove my innocence and maintain my reputation as an officer and a gentleman."

MR. VICE (AFTER CONSIDERATION). Very well, Lieutenant Shaw. You can jog around the room until I order you to stop. If you are, indeed, drunk, you'll pass out after a couple of laps. If you're sober, as you claim, you'll be able to keep it up for a while.

Lieutenant Shaw, the company's superathlete, smiles, nods, and commences his jog around the tables.

LIEUTENANT AHERN (STILL STANDING AT ATTENTION). Mr. Vice, request permission to be seated.

MR. VICE. Uh, no. You can join Lieutenant Shaw. I'll let you know when you can stop.

Lieutenant Emerson was obviously enjoying the heady taste of power.

The lieutenants had planned their strategy wisely. Interspersed among their charges against one another, they poked at the company staff. Those seated at the VIP table were not subject to charges, but SPCs, Bob, and the Training Officer were. Doug's platoon had two dozen tacos delivered to him during dinner, and he was fined $5 for insulting the quality of the food by ordering out. Dave Kesselring's lieutenants charged him with being a closet Junker and produced photoshopped pictures of him in Bismarck-era uniforms and pastimes. Scott, never particularly erudite, took a hit for being the academics officer. Of course, Neil was charged with willfully molding his platoon into wannabe Elvises. Bob was presented a black hood and whip, acknowledging his role as the company enforcer. I didn't escape comment either, taken to task for being a ghost whisperer. My defense was pretty lame, and as punishment, I was presented a chain and required to spend the rest of the dinner hour making audible groaning sounds and shaking my prop when cued by Mr. Vice.

SPCs had interspersed *their* retaliation charges throughout the dinner hour. My target was Lieutenant Myerson, who was presented a huge mock lensatic compass that was used for classroom instruction and at least two feet in diameter. On cue from Mr. Vice, she had to stand, turn ninety degrees, and announce an azimuth—any azimuth—whenever requested by the mess.

The best and most persistent charge of the evening was levied at Lieutenant Emerson, Mr. Vice. Technically he really wasn't supposed to be a target, but the six captains pulled rank and conspired to pay him back for his role as Fourth Platoon's prank mastermind. After all, we couldn't stand by and not avenge Doug's ongoing leadership challenges. Oh, and when the tacos had arrived and before Mr. Vice could order Doug to consume all of them, Doug had passed out four to each of the other captains, leaving himself only four to personally ingest. They weren't particularly palatable by the time they arrived, but each member of the CPA downed his/her tacos, relishing the payback that was about to occur.

Mr. Vice had just issued his second judgment when one of the messmen appeared with a single shot glass perched on a silver tray.

"Compliments of the CPA, Mr. Vice," he solemnly intoned, placed the shot glass on the table in front of Mr. Vice, and departed.

Before Lieutenant Emerson could respond, Doug rose and requested to address the president of the mess. We had actually drawn Dickey into the conspiracy, and he immediately granted the request.

"Mr. President, on behalf of the Captain's Protective Association, I would like to acknowledge Mr. Vice's role in making Fourth Platoon's TBS experience so memorable." We, the other five captains, rose, water glasses in hand as Doug raised his to Mr. Vice and toasted, "To Mr. Vice."

Lieutenant Emerson was cornered, so he had to acknowledge the toast and down the shot glass's contents—151-proof white rum. Lieutenant Emerson sputtered a bit but got it down.

Yes, Doug had introduced a toast before the official toasts had commenced and not with port but water.

This tableau was repeated five more times: messman depositing a shot glass, one of us rising and making a toast to Mr. Vice and his downing the drink. We didn't want to kill him, so three of the glasses contained plain tap water, but Lieutenant Emerson didn't know that and regarded each delivery with dread. Abbreviated shots of white rum, one of tequila, and one of vodka weren't excessive (particularly as they were spaced out over an hour and a half), but we had made our point—we *knew* the architect of the pranks that had impacted not only Doug, but all of us.

Before we commenced toasts, Mr. Vice announced we had fifteen minutes to "shed a tear for Lord Nelson," and there was a mad scramble as the mess's participants made for the head (bathroom). The term refers to the fact that Lord Nelson's body was preserved in a barrel of brandy after his death at Trafalgar. Legend has it that en route back to England, sailors would request to "shed a tear for the

Admiral," drawing brandy from the keg and urinating in it to replace the fluid. True or not, I found it a novel way to announce a bio break.

Upon our return (much refreshed, I might add), Dickey, as president, drew our attention to the Table for Fallen Comrades. As one, we stood and turned to respectfully, even reverently, regard the table, and I froze.

Gunny was seated there, resplendent in enlisted dress blues. His long-sleeved midnight-blue coat had a standing collar, seven gilt buttons, and, unlike the male officers, red trim rimmed the collar, front edge of the jacket, and epaulettes. Full-sized medals were positioned over his left pocket, and ribbon-only awards were displayed over the right. The sleeves of his jacket glittered with gold, red-bordered gunnery sergeant chevrons.

I was aware of my surroundings, but not. The room, my messmates, Dickey's droning fell away around me. All I saw was my grandfather's eyes, so much like my own, directed at me. He was smiling proudly and nodding in approval. And it finally hit me like I had been punched in the gut.

My companion of six months—my grandfather—was dead.

I'd become so accustomed to his being a huge part of my life—sometimes unwelcome, often frustrating, but always interesting—and realized I felt more alive than I had in two years. All because of this dead guy who had invaded my life. At some level, I always knew he was a ghost, which meant that he was dead, but he was so vibrant, so involved, I guess I had tucked away from the reality of the situation.

A tug on my sleeve by the lieutenant on my right brought me back to the present, and I realized I was still standing while the rest of the mess had resumed their seats. I hastily retook mine.

For the next half hour, I went through the motions of rising, toasting, resuming my seat, repeating as necessary, while my eyes remained fixed on the fallen comrades' table and its single occupant.

Dickey finally invited us to join him at the bar, and my attention returned to my place setting as I gathered up my program and favor (a camouflaged bandana) before I quit the room with the rest of the company. When I looked up again, the table was empty.

As I passed by the fallen comrades' table on my way out of the dining room, I lingered beside it, at first casually, but then focused on what had changed. It was subtle; the Purple Heart was no longer lying at the top of the inverted place setting. It was now lying on the dinner plate.

I managed to get through the rest of the evening, smiling and laughing when expected, exchanging playful insults when provoked, sliding down the passageways alone and in tandem as part of carrier quals.

I gratefully changed into dry sweatpants and shirt and headed for home a 0015.

When I opened my front door, I was greeted with nothing but the tick of the clock in the living room. No buzzing. No TV tuned to *Alf* or a John Wayne movie. No grumbling roar about donuts or bacon.

Silence.

I went to bed in silence, and the same greeted me at 0500 when I dragged myself out of bed. I'd slept little, thinking about the night's events, keeping an ear open for any Gunny-type sounds. There were none.

When I staggered into the kitchen to brew my tea, my eyes were immediately drawn to the table. Though I had not placed them there, my Sam Browne belt, sword, and scabbard were there once again, arranged separately, one above the other. The sword's blade and scabbard gleamed in the light of the overhead lamp, polished by ghostly—and I knew—loving hands. The belt was buffed to high gloss, without the myriad fingerprints I always seemed to leave there, despite much careful handling.

I left off filling the kettle and collapsed into the Gunny's usual seat, crying like a baby at his absence but still hopeful that this wasn't goodbye.

When I arrived at my office at 0630, there was a note from Bob on my door. It stated that formation would be delayed until 0730, student billet holders had been advised of the time change, and all SPCs should report to the conference room at 0645. I threw my gear into my office and was just heading out the door when Neil appeared, with a quizzical look on his face and holding a like-note in his hand.

"What now?" he asked. "Who pooped in his mess kit this time? SPCs or lieutenants?" I assumed the reference to "he" was directed at Dickey.

"It's always something, isn't it?" I was dreading a Dickey lecture and had no patience this morning for posturing.

The other captains were already seated in the conference room when we arrived, and I glanced around as Neil closed the door behind him and sat down next to me at the table. We all looked pretty good considering we hadn't gotten more than four hours' sleep the night before, and none of us had had more than one drink, in addition to the wine and port at dinner.

Bob got right to the point. "I apologize for not getting in contact with you earlier about the delayed formation time. Would've given you a chance to get a little more sleep. However, I was already here at 0615 when I got a call." This was met by a collective groan from the rest of us.

"Holy shit on a shingle, Bob," Scott grumbled, banging his coffee mug down on the table so violently, a good portion of its contents splashed onto Dave's T-shirt. "What did his highness decide to do to us now? We all change into utilities, flaks, and packs and take a twenty-mile stroll through the boonies?"

That one drew a few half-hearted laughs. Absurd as a hike sounded, it wasn't entirely improbable. Not with Dickey at the company's helm.

"Nah. I actually have good news, guys. Were any of you there when Dickey took that nosedive into the wall during carrier quals last night?"

We'd all heard about the rather spectacular header Dickey'd taken the night before. Apparently Fourth Platoon had added copious amounts of baby oil to the water and beer lubricating the floor of their carrier runway. Dickey must have hit a particularly slippery patch, accelerated (rather than slowed), and hit the bulkhead with a resounding crack. Lieutenants got him to his feet, with a bit of slipping and sliding as they did so. And despite blood streaming from his nose and looking not all there, Dickey'd shaken off any further offers of assistance. He did accept a clean wadded-up T-shirt from Doug and pressed it to his nose before he bade his good nights and wandered off to his office.

"That's *good* news?" exclaimed Doug. "How's that good news? He's probably going to have Fourth Platoon's balls on a platter. Mine included."

Bob grinned and waved his hands to the contrary. "It's good because he's gone until Monday. His wife called this morning. She was his duty driver last night, took one look at him when he got in her car, and drove him straight to the clinic. His nose is broken, and his eyes are pretty much-swollen shut. He's on bed rest until Monday. And she's got both sets of his truck keys, so he's not going anywhere."

Doug wasn't reassured. "That just delays the pain until Monday. *Then* he'll have our balls on a platter."

"Relax, Doug. You're off the hook. He *knew* about the baby oil. I distinctly heard Lieutenant Emerson tell him about it and warn him to not take too much of a windup, but Dickey just laughed it off and played macho. It would all come out if he tried to do anything to you or your lieutenants. So relax and enjoy a Dickey-free morning."

Doug almost deflated in relief, and Dave slapped him on the back with a, "Buck up, buddy! You're free and clear. And so are *we* until Monday!"

"The 0730 formation is just a safety brief," Bob continued. "The usual don't drink and drive, and then I'm turning the company over to you guys. Tell them when you want to see them on Monday and secure them." He moved to the door. "And you're welcome," he finished, flashing us a grin and was gone.

And that's what we did.

*****

I pulled into my driveway around 1200 and marveled that I was home this early on a weekday and had no military obligations until Monday. I'd stopped on my way home to pick up groceries and dry cleaning (as well as running other assorted errands). Since I hoped to be sharing a TV with Gunny later that afternoon, watching an old John Wayne movie or some kind of sports rerun on ESPN, I was also armed with a dozen jelly donuts and two pounds of bacon.

Before I even set foot out of my truck, however, I heard NB trilling from the end of the driveway, and my heart sank. Interestingly enough, in her arms was an enormous bouquet of yellow roses. It was so large that I could barely make out her eyes over the jungle of greenery and blooms, but I knew it was her despite the size of the arrangement. Nobody wore those hideous housedresses anymore, and nobody else I knew (or with whom I'd willingly associate) would dance from foot to foot like a three-year-old in need of the potty.

"Oh, Abe! Hello! I have something for you!" *Please* let them not be silk flowers. Or plastic. I prepared myself to say something complimentary about her bouquet, but I hated artificial flowers. I didn't particularly like fresh ones either. I could tolerate dried, though I did appreciate recently cut unassuming long-lasting daisies.

As she drew closer, I saw that the bouquet was neither silk nor plastic, but at least two dozen beautiful, barely opened, hopefully fragrant yellow roses interspersed with ferns and delicate white baby's breath. Okay. This was really nice.

I jumped out of my truck and hightailed it down the driveway before she got any closer to my front door. And I admit, I wanted to confirm that the roses smelled as good as they looked.

They did.

"What's up, Mrs. Nolan? What a lovely bouquet. Secret admirer?"

"Oh no, Abe. I wish. But these are for *you*. Delivered a half hour ago by a florist's van from Philadelphia. *Philadelphia!* Not a local florist. Your grandmother, maybe?" With that, she reluctantly relinquished her fragrant burden.

"Probably. Thank you, Mrs. Nolan. I appreciate your taking the delivery for me." I stepped back and made for my door. Surprisingly NB didn't follow.

"You take care now, Abe," she called. "Since you're home early, maybe share a cocktail with me tonight? That is, if you don't have a date." Typical NB. Random acts of kindness followed by consistent acts of nebbiness. I gave a noncommittal wave and maneuvered myself and the flowers through the front door. Damn, those flowers smelled heavenly!

I removed the sealed envelope tucked in the bouquet, and the bold fountain-penned "Abe" confirmed that the flowers were from my grandmother. Inside, the card simply read, "Call me when you get this. Love, Granna."

I hastened to the phone and dialed Granna's house. I knew she wasn't returning to work for another two months, and then only for meetings that absolutely required her attendance.

She answered on the second ring.

"Hi, Granna," I started. "It's Abe. Thank you for the flowers. They're absolutely stunning."

"You're very welcome, sweetie. I know roses aren't your particular favorite, but gladiolas aren't in season right now. That would have been my first choice." Roses? Gladiolas? Huh?

"I'm not following you, Granna."

"Gladiolas represent remembrance, but in my day, yellow roses did as well." She inhaled deeply and continued, "I had a visitor last night."

"I'm still not tracking, Granna. Who visited you last night? What's that got to do with the flowers?"

"Cotton. Your grandfather. He came to say goodbye."

I didn't know how to respond, so I didn't. I just sank down in Gunny's TV-watching chair.

"Abe? Are you still there?" Granna sounded concerned.

"Yes, Granna. I am. He came to say goodbye? What does that mean?"

"It means he's gone on, sweetie. He said he couldn't tell you in person, that you'd try to persuade him to stay, and he'd be too tempted to. But he knew that it was time that you *both* moved on."

"But he said goodbye to you..."

"Yes. He did. But saying goodbye to me was more to thank me for introducing him to you and Pru. He said goodbye to you in the best way he knew how—attending your mess night."

There was a question in her voice, and I answered, "Yes, I saw him. At the Table for Fallen Comrades. He was in dress blues, and he looked…splendid."

There was a sharp intake of breath and then a prolonged sigh on Granna's end. "He was such a good-looking devil. And in Marine dress blues, he must have been magnificent."

"Yup," was all I could manage.

"He said something about a belt and the sword scabbard. That you should take better care of them and to stop leaving your grubby fingerprints all over them. Does that mean anything to you?"

Through tears, I smiled and glanced into the kitchen where my sword, scabbard, and Sam Browne still lay where Gunny had left them. "Yes. It does."

"The flowers are from him via me. He said it was time you remembered you were a woman as well as a Marine, but he stipulated he wanted flowers that signified remembrance. To remember him. Hence, yellow roses."

"Thanks, Granna. I get it. I really do. But I miss him."

"It's time to move on, sweetie, just as Cotton has. Do you understand?"

"Yes. Thank you. I'll call you Sunday as usual."

"Talk to you then, sweetie. I love you."

"I love you too, Granna. Bye for now."

CHAPTER 23

An End and a Beginning

I SPENT THE remainder of Friday puttering around the house and studiously ignoring the silent TV set. When I unpacked my groceries, I threw the donuts and bacon into the garbage can, gathered up the bag, and threw it in the communal dumpster. Maybe I half-hoped that flagrant disposal of Gunny's beloved foods would lure him back. It didn't.

I made a brief call to Kelly. He wasn't home, so I left a message on his answering machine that I knew the Gunny's identity and would fill him in later. I asked that he not call back. I'd call him.

I knew he'd respect my request.

There were so many roses, I had to divide them up into three vases, placing one in my bedroom, one in the dining room, and the third on the kitchen table. The flowers' sweet scent followed me wherever I went in the house, and instead of saddening me, they made me smile a little.

I spent a good portion of Saturday sleeping and thinking. By Sunday morning, I had more or less reconciled myself to the Gunny's permanent absence.

I told myself it was all for the good, that he could rest now, knowing he had left a daughter and three grandchildren. It seemed to be a family trait to turn one's back on the past and expectations for the future to join the Marines. He had loved his platoon but nevertheless led them into seemingly hopeless assaults on a lump of earth called Sugar Loaf. I had joined the Marines out of desperation to keep a marriage together but stayed for love of the Corps, its people, traditions, and well-earned reputation for valor. I wasn't sure if both of us had succumbed to the siren song of the Marine Corps, or we were just wired the same. Either way, I was proud of my grandfather, just as I knew he had been proud of me.

I hoped that if the country were ever drawn again into war on my watch, that I would live up to my grandfather's standards. I knew I could—and would—perform as ordered. However, to this day, I still look at things differently, I come at problems differently than my peers, and I know my value lays not in blind acceptance but respectfully challenging the system.

"This is the way we've always done it" didn't resonate with my grandfather, and it certainly doesn't with me if it doesn't make sense. Saving lives, if at all possible, while accomplishing the mission, does.

*****

It was time to close a chapter and start a new one in my life. On Sunday evening, I phoned Kelly before placing my weekly call to Granna.

"Hey," I said. "Are you busy Tuesday night?"

"Nothing that can't wait until Wednesday. Why, what's up?"

"Would you like to go out? Like go out on a date with me? Someplace nice where we can dress up, and I can put on makeup? But not China Garden," I hastily added, remembering our last meal there. I didn't relish going to the trouble to dress up and having a waitress sniffing my breath all evening.

There was an audible intake of breath on Kelly's end, and my heart sank.

"That's if you want to," I hastily added. "If you don't, that's okay too. No harm, no foul."

Kelly chuckled. "I would love to, Abe. And it won't be China Garden. I promise. Pick you up at 1900 on Tuesday evening?"

"Great. See you—"

He cut me off before I could finish. "You don't know how long I've waited to do this. Thank you. And since this is a date, even though you're asking *me* out, I'm paying for dinner."

"No, thank *you*. For being there. For helping with the Gunny. For being so patient. And yes, you're paying for dinner. See you Tuesday night."

I hung up to his laughter in my ear and headed upstairs to my bedroom to survey my closet.

I wasn't sure I still owned anything classier than slacks and blouses, let alone a dress. Or makeup. But somehow, I'd manage. Even if it meant calling in reinforcements from Philadelphia to help.

A NOTE TO *the reader*: This novel is largely a work of fiction. However, it does contain military terms and acronyms that might be confusing to the casual reader. There isn't consistent use of military terms—you'll see "door" used as well as "hatch;" "hallway" as well as "passageway." It wasn't intentional. Sometimes, I just got on a roll and went with it.

The following reference is provided for clarification and is *not* confined to military jargon (as will become evident). Also, the acronyms and definitions herein might well have changed or evolved since 1989–1990, the time period of this book, so a quick check with Wiki might yield a totally different meaning! Also thanks to Wiki and military manuals for definitions.

MISCELLANEOUS TERMS AND ACRONYMS

azimuth. According to Army manuals, it is a horizontal angle measured clockwise from a north baseline. The azimuth is the most common military method to express direction.

battalion staff sections. At the time of this novel, the following battalion staff section designators were in use:

S-1: Manpower and personnel

S-2: Intelligence and security

S-3: Operations

S-4: Logistics

S-5: Plans

S-6: Communications and IT

CG. Commanding General

company. A TBS company was comprised of four to five platoons. Delta company, in this book, included five platoons.

cover. Hat

CPA. Captains Protective Association

deck. Floor

DIRLAUTH. Direct liaison authorized

DSN. Defense Switched Network

five-paragraph field order. A means of organizing information about a military operation in the field. It provides a structured format to a unit that makes it easy to find each specific requirement. The five paragraphs can be remembered with the acronym SMEAC (situation, mission, execution, administration/logistics, command/signal).

HQMC. Headquarters Marine Corps

jody. A traditional cadence call-and-response sung by military personnel while running or marching.

ladder. Stairs

lensatic compass. A compass comprised of a cover, base, and reading lens. The cover is used to protect the compass and also incorporates the sighting wire, which helps determine direction. The base also contains the movable bezel ring which surrounds the compass itself and is usually marked in degrees (0–359) or compass points. It is luminous, which aids in night navigation.

MCRDAC. Marine Corps Research, Development, and Acquisition Command

military time. A time format using a twenty-four-hour time system that eliminates the need for the designations a.m. or p.m. This novel uses military time.

monitor. The individual at HQMC who draws up (cuts) a Marine's orders.

MOS. Military occupational specialty

MPS. Maritime Prepositioning Shipping. The Marine Corps now refers to this is as the Maritime Prepositioning FORCE.

MSgt. Master sergeant; often referred to as a Top.

MTO. Motor transport officer

NB. Nebby bitch

NROTC. Naval Reserve Officer Training Corps

obstacle course. Consists of fourteen obstacles: seven low jumps; up-and-over bar; combination; log wall; medium rollover log; vault logs (four in series); double pullover bar; and rope climb.

OCS. Officer Candidate School

OD. Officer of the Day

PFT. Physical fitness test

platoon. A platoon at TBS during this time was anywhere from twenty to seventy lieutenants. In 1989, women were assigned to their own platoon, therefore, smaller numbers. Since then, platoons have become coed.

PLC. Platoon Leader's Course

Quarterdeck. The general meaning is "the part of a ship's upper deck near the stern, traditionally reserved for officers." The Marine

SEMPER FI WITH A SIDE OF DONUTS OR BACON

Corps traditionally refers to an indoor area reserved for ceremonies and formal events as a Quarterdeck.

rappel. To descend a rock face or other near-vertical surface by using a doubled rope coiled around the body and fixed at a higher point. Swiss seats are employed in this book rather than a rope wrapped around the body.

Sam Browne belt. Named for Sir Samuel James Browne, VC, it is a wide belt, usually leather or patent leather, supported by a narrower strap, passing diagonally over the right shoulder. It can be worn alone or, for ceremonies, with a sword.

SPC. Staff platoon commander

TBS. The Basic School

TECOM. Training and Education Command

terrain association. The process of matching the topography on a map to the terrain around you. It should not be confused with *terrain appreciation*, which is the process of assessing terrain and how it will affect an operation.

the Idiot. The main character's ex-husband is Tom Maxwell, also referred to as "the Neanderthal."

topographic map. A map that shows the physical features of the land. Besides just showing landforms such as mountains and rivers, etc., it also shows the elevation changes of the land. The closer the contour lines are to each other, the steeper the slope of the land.

ABOUT THE AUTHOR

CLAIR LEARNER is a retired Marine whose military service included assignment to a variety of challenging and unfailingly interesting jobs. Despite an impressive repertoire of experiences, however, she considers her time as a staff platoon commander training second lieutenants at TBS in Quantico to be one of the more notable.

Upon retirement from the Corps, Clair joined a Fortune 500 company where she worked as a management consultant until fully "retiring" two years ago.

Clair is already at work on a sequel to *Semper Fi with Donuts...* She hopes you are anxiously anticipating its publication.